The NEBADOR series:

Book One: The Test

Book Two: Journey

Book Three: Selection

Book Four: Flight Training

Book Five: Back to the Stars

Book Six: Star Station

Book Seven: The Local Universe

Book Eight: Witness

Book Nine: A Cry for Help

Book Ten: Stories from Sonmatia
2016

Also by J. Z. Colby:

Standing on Your Own Two Feet:
Young Adults Surviving 2012 and Beyond

an epic young-adult science fiction adventure

by

J. Z. Colby

for Meghan

**Nebador Archives**

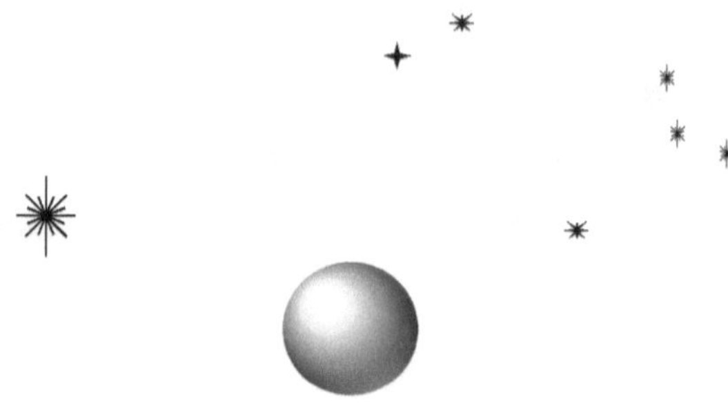

Copyright © 2015 by J. Z. Colby
All rights reserved

Illustrations by J. Z. Colby and Anne Marie Beltzer

The back cover image is the Pinwheel Galaxy, M101, courtesy of NASA.

The four main tactics of debunking, listed in chapter 37, are from the writings of Stanton Friedman, used with permission.

For other print editions, ebooks, dramatic audiobooks, previews, samples, biographies, comments, questions, artwork, writing contests, Ask Kibi advice, deep learning notes, Nebador citizens, and more, please see:

**www.nebador.com**

**Nebador Archives**
**Kelso, Washington, USA**

Library of Congress Control Number: 2015943764
Manufactured in the USA

ISBN: 978-1-936253-82-1
**NEBADOR9PBG**: paperback, 6" x 9", 377 pages,
   global edition (10-point Georgia type)

**Greetings, young people of planet Earth,**

The Muses, or whatever you would like to call those mysterious sources of inspiration, don't always just inspire.  Sometimes they issue orders.

For a long time, Calliope (epic poetry) was my main inspiration, as she probably is for most novelists.  Thalia (comedy), Melpomene (tragedy), Erato (love), and Polyhymnia (sacred poetry) also had things to say, of course.

Then, as I was finishing *NEBADOR Book Six* and beginning *Book Seven*, another presence began to be felt, almost like a shadow lurking in the corners of my mind.  It took a while, and many long walks and meditations, to figure out who it was.

Clio, the Muse of History, started speaking more and more clearly and . . . almost forcefully . . . as *Book Eight* passed and *Book Nine*, the epic conclusion of the NEBADOR saga, began to be drafted.  But even as the other Muses stepped aside and Clio's voice became dominant, I became aware that writing and polishing *Book Nine* wasn't all she expected of me.

She also instructed me to GIVE *Book Nine* to anyone who is led to discover it by the mysterious workings of the universe.  I don't expect anyone to understand this who lives their life solely by the rules of human society.  Those of you who can understand, will understand.

This story is for those who are young and would like the Earth to still be livable when you grow up.  A few older people, with their eyes and ears open, might also enjoy it.

I'm sorry, but the ultimate fate of the planet in the story was not revealed to me, and I chose not to just "make something up."  Perhaps that will encourage people to continue pondering the themes of the story long after reading it.  That would be good, and very timely.

J. Z. Colby
2015

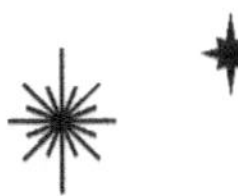

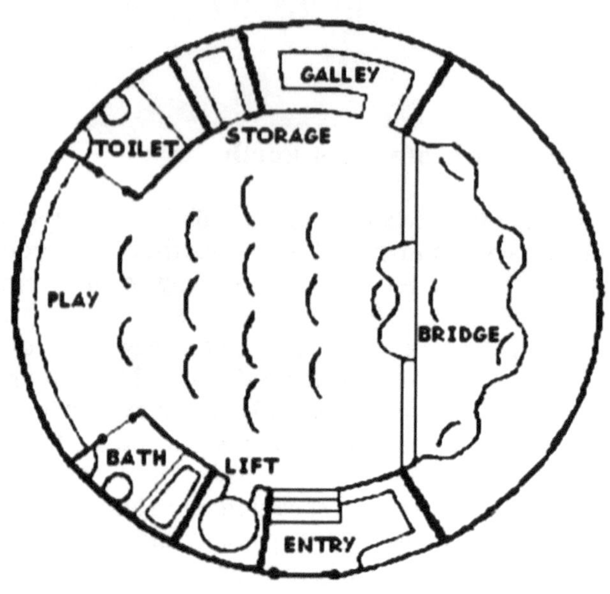


## Acknowledgements


Wonderful people throughout the author's life provided unique and irreplaceable lessons and inspirations:

Juniper Russell

Vicky Ball

Linda Dezzutti

Jennifer Carolyn Gates

Rachael Bleich

Paula Wells

Sarah Satterthwaite

Ashley Riddle

Antonya Pickard

Esther Smith

Dottie Frisbie

Martha Higgins

Susanne Koller

Charleen Cox

Meredith Herzog

Patricia Sharp

Peter James

Valuable readers gave the author feedback after digging through early drafts of the book:

Karen Oster

Cecelia Harper

Excellent critiquers commented on thousands of passages, then provided reactions during in-depth interviews:

Sidney Oster, 14

Dylan Oster, 15

Catherine "Cat" Harper, 16

Alex Chalcraft

Careful publishing assistants, proofreaders, and technical helpers brought the final manuscript as close to perfection as possible:

Cecelia Harper

# Contents

**Part 1   Ko-tera Three, 3662**

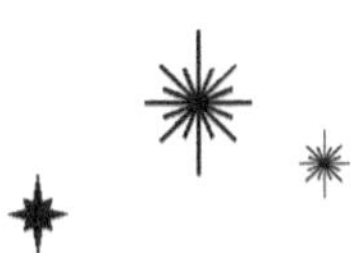

"... the earth belongs to the living ... no man may, by natural right, oblige the land he owns or occupies to debts greater than those that may be paid during his own lifetime.  If he could, then the world would belong to the dead, and not to the living ..."

— Thomas Jefferson, paraphrased

## Part 1: Ko-tera Three, 3662

### Chapter 1: Misunderstanding

The knock on the front door of the little house was assertive, almost commanding.  The middle-aged woman, sitting at her dresser, quickly put down her hair brush and hurried to answer.

When she opened the door, two men and a stern woman in military uniforms faced her, causing her mind to go blank with respect and fear.

"Jan Ko-korna?" the man with the most stripes inquired, holding open his military I.D. for her to see.

"No . . . I'm Syble."

"Did you, or did you not, write this letter and send it to the local air base?" He thrust out a photocopy of a hand-written letter.

The woman looked at it, but didn't have time to read it before the man pulled it back.  "That's my daughter's writing."

"How old is your daughter?" he inquired forcefully.

"Seven."

"Seven-year-olds can't write cursive script!" the military woman, of much lesser rank, asserted.

"This one can," Syble Ko-korna replied with a hint of pride.

"Where is she now?" the man demanded.

At that moment, the front door was pulled open wider to reveal a slender seven-year-old girl, tall enough to be mistaken for eight or nine, with a bulging shoulder bag at her side.  "I'm the one who wrote the letter and mailed it."

The mother, with tears of worry gathering in her eyes, knelt down and caressed her daughter.  "Why, Honey?"

"It's time for me to start my work, Mother."

"But you're only seven . . ."

"It would have been better if I'd started when I was five, but I stayed to make sure you were okay after Dad died.  Now look at you — finishing your diploma, two or three hobbies in your spare time, and you even have a boyfriend!"

"I don't understand when you talk like this," Syble said, crying openly now. "I'm supposed to be the one taking care of *you*."

The military man was speaking. ". . . in possession of classified information, without proper clearance, is a federal crime . . ." Neither mother nor daughter were listening.

"Mother, you know better than anyone else that I don't need any taking-care-of."

". . . so we're going to have to take Jan Ko-korna into custody . . ."

The military woman stepped behind the seven-year-old and opened a pair of handcuffs.

"Don't be mad at them, Mother," Jan said, putting her hands behind her back to receive the handcuffs. "It's a phase they have to go through. In a little while, a month or two I think, I'll be doing my work and we'll be able to visit, prowl the Open Air Market like always, look for goodies and stuff."

The military woman, with a firm hand, guided young Jan Ko-korna out the door and toward a gray van parked in front of the house.

Her mother stood in the open doorway and cried.

✳

A solid wall divided the front two seats of the van from the passenger area in back. Gray metal covered all the side and rear windows. The girl tried to strike up casual conversation with the military woman, but got no response as the woman buckled Jan's seat belt, then her own.

One of the men slid the passenger door closed, and Jan heard the engine start and felt the vehicle begin to move down the street, away from her childhood home.

*Good-bye, Mother. I'll see you again soon, I promise.*

Jan closed her eyes, let a slight smile appear on her face, and focused her mind on imagining a map of the city, and the van's location from minute to minute, during the long drive.

✳

Jan Ko-korna knew when they arrived at the air base north of the city. She heard a motorized garage door open, then close behind them as the driver shut off the van's engine.

When the vehicle's side door was opened, the girl beheld hard benches, metal lockers, and equipment racks — everything necessary for receiving busloads of new recruits.

The stern military woman told Jan where to sit or stand at each point in the process, and watched her like a hawk as forms were filled out, her picture taken from all sides, and her shoulder bag searched.

The ugly gray corridor seemed to go on forever. As she walked alongside the stern woman, Jan glimpsed military people of all ranks going about their business, but taking a moment to stare at the little girl in handcuffs.

She remembered war movies she'd watched, and figured out each person's rank from the stripes on their shoulders. Her escort was a mere sergeant, but the man who had done the talking at her house was a colonel. She saw more of those, and most other ranks, but didn't notice any generals.

Without a word, they stopped in front of a gray metal door. The sergeant unlocked it, removed the handcuffs, and motioned for the girl to enter.

After the metal door was closed behind her, Jan felt relief that the first leg of her journey was complete. A sigh escaped her as she looked around. The room was as ugly as the corridor outside, but contained a small couch with a stack of sheets and blankets, a table and two chairs, and a bookshelf. A door on the back wall led to a little toilet room.

Then she spotted the large one-way mirror on the wall, and mentally frowned, but didn't let it show on her face.

*

Jan Ko-korna began her stay at the air base by making sure none of her vinyl records had been scratched. Then she searched the room for a record player. Finding none, she shrugged, not really wanting to dance for the goons behind the mirror, anyway.

She made her bed on the little couch, washed up at the sink in the toilet room, and settled onto the floor to look over the books in the bookshelf. The trashy adult novels hardly received a glance, and she wasn't quite desperate enough for the automotive repair manuals. She had no idea how a book on philosophy had made its way into the air base, but picked it up and got comfortable on her make-shift bed.

Without appearing to look, she glimpsed figures in the control room behind the one-way mirror. Two or three were present at a time, and they would sometimes speak loudly enough for Jan to catch a few words. She soon gathered that the colonel from her house was in charge, and a psychologist was taking notes. The stern female sergeant came and went.

With no clock or window, the arrival of a meal tray, through the slot at the base of the door, was Jan's only clue that evening was at hand. The macaroni and cheese was way too salty, the broccoli had been cooked to death, and the carton of milk was slightly sour.

She picked at her food for several hours, read a page or two between bites, and eventually crawled into bed.

Half an hour later, someone in the control room was kind enough to switch off most of the observation room lights.

*

On Jan Ko-korna's second day at the air base, the colonel came in about mid-morning and sat down in one of the chairs at the table.

Jan seated herself across from him in the other chair.

The colonel glared at her for a moment, then said, "Being in possession of classified information about military assets, without proper clearance, is a federal crime."

Jan let a few seconds pass before speaking. "That's probably true in most cases. In my case, it is not, because I was the source of the information. It is a well-established legal principle that the source of any information is entitled to it.  If any of *you* had known the rocket was going to blow up, you would have fixed it . . . I *hope*."

The colonel blinked and tried to hide his confusion and frustration, without complete success.  After a long moment, he managed to collect himself.  "So . . . what else do you know about . . . things that might blow up?"

"I can't tell you, because I believe that information would be highly classified."

"Why don't you let me be the judge of that?" he responded with his anger barely hidden.

Jan took a slow breath.  "Because, since I believe that, I would be breaking the law if I told you."

"But I have top-secret clearance."

"I believe the things I might tell you would be classified *higher* than top secret.  And by the way, since I've told you that much, you also would be breaking the law if you continued to pressure me."

Jan had seen pictures of erupting volcanoes that looked calmer than the colonel.  She made herself breathe slowly and evenly as he struggled with himself, eventually rose, and finally left the room without saying another word.

✳

She figured there would be a price to pay.  It started that very afternoon.  Whatever book she was reading would disappear while she was in the toilet room.  She thought about keeping the next book with her, but decided to let them play their little game.  She always took her shoulder bag, but resisted the temptation to form an attachment with anything else.

By late afternoon, she was quite bored.  At the bookshelf, she looked back and forth between *Lady Ta-horna's Secret Lover* and *Fuel Injection Diagnosis and Repair*, but couldn't decide which book would have the most interesting plot or richest characters.

Macaroni and cheese, broccoli, and black tea filled her evening.  Someone must have noticed that the milk was sour.

While in the toilet room to wash up before bed, the couch disappeared.

With tears close, Jan looked inside herself for the strength to continue down the path she had chosen.  Somewhat to her surprise, she found it, made her bed on the concrete floor of the observation room, and curled up to sleep.

✳

"What the HELL is going on?" Jan clearly heard an old but stern male voice demanding in the control room the next morning as she nibbled cold pancakes and sipped orange juice.

"But, Sir . . ."

"We were just . . ."

"I thought you meant . . ."

Jan smiled, guessing what was taking place.

The commotion moved to the corridor just outside the observation room.

A key, held by nervous fingers, fumbled in the lock.  The door swung open.

"Now get out of my sight, all of you!" the general ordered.  "Find something useful to do for the rest of the day, if you can, and be in my office at zero-seven hundred tomorrow for re-assignment!"

"Zero-seven hundred?" the colonel questioned.

"No, make it zero-six hundred, and if I'm late, wait for me ... AT ATTENTION!"

"Yes, Sir!" the colonel, the sergeant, and a couple of others Jan couldn't see, all said as they saluted and scurried away.

The general, with steel eyes, watched them go for a moment, then softened his gaze as he turned and looked into the observation room.

Jan stood just inside the door with her bag on her shoulder and a smile on her face.

"I am *so* sorry," the general said in a kindly tone.  "I told them to *invite* you to the air base, and then *learn* everything they could *from* you.  I didn't tell them to *dissect* you!"

Jan chuckled for the first time in two days as she stepped into the corridor and walked with the general toward his office.

"I had to go to the capital," he continued, "and explain to Congress why we received a letter telling us exactly what system on the rocket was going to fail, and yet we did nothing.  As I'm sure you know, the system did fail, as you predicted, and the rocket did explode, as you predicted."

"I saw it in the newspaper the morning they came to get me.  That's how I knew to be ready."

They entered the general's plush office and he gestured for Jan to take the comfortable chair across from his desk.

"I hope they didn't treat you *too* badly.  I'm not sure I want to know why the couch and most of the books were out in the hallway."

Jan smiled while reading the name plate on the general's desk.  "I think they were trying to see what I was made of.  It was kinda fun.  I'd never been in handcuffs before, nor slept on a concrete floor."

Two-star General Malcolm Ko-fenral huffed and frowned with anger again.  "By God, there just *aren't* enough toilets in the entire air base for that colonel to clean!  Maybe I can find some weeds that need pulling."

Jan laughed just as a young sergeant poked his head in the door.  "Can I get you anything, Sir?"

The general took a deep breath to relax.  "What would you like, Jan?  After what we put you through, you name it, and it's yours."

"I know it's a strange time of day for it, but I could use a salad, maybe a little blue cheese dressing ..."

"Hey, that sounds good!  Two of them, Sergeant, with olives, sunflower seeds, you know, and blue cheese on the side.  Hot tea for me."

"Fruit juice," Jan requested.

The sergeant saluted and headed for the kitchen.

"I only still have my job," General Ko-fenral explained, "because the rules that made it impossible for us to respond quickly to a tip from an outside source were *written* by Congress.  Pointing that out, without making them angry, was the *trickiest* thing I've ever done, but I seem to have pulled it off."

"Congratulations," Jan said with a smile.  "Actually, I was pretty sure that would be the case, and that's why I used this opportunity to reveal myself, knowing the timeline would probably remain intact, even though the poor rocket is in pieces."

The two-star general, sixty-something, stared at the seven-year-old girl.  "I'm not going to pretend to understand what you just said, but I want to share with you what I realized on the flight back.  We just do *not* have the right people here at the air base to work with you properly."

With wide eyes, Jan nodded agreement.

The general smiled back at her.  "Luckily, we have them not far away.  A kindly old general, good friend of mine, runs the safe-house program for this area.  He and his executive, a sweet lady, are very good with people, even children — they have to be for that program — but it's very under-utilized these days . . ."

The sergeant entered with their salads and beverages, and made sure the general and his guest had everything they wanted.

General Ko-fenral and Jan Ko-korna continued to talk as they ate salads, later got sandwiches in the cafeteria, and eventually enjoyed slices of apple pie together.  He made some telephone calls, and as the afternoon was passing, Jan started feeling hopeful about the people who ran the safe-house program.

As dinner time approached, the call came in that the transport had arrived.

Jan swallowed, remembering the handcuffs and the ugly gray van.

## Chapter 2: A New Home

The passenger area of the safe-house transport contained six comfortable seats. Jan's swiveled when she pushed with her feet.

After switching on a dome light and closing the side door, Major Lisa Ka-markla took another seat. Unseen, a lieutenant started the engine and departed the air base.

Jan placed her shoulder bag on the floor, then looked at the female officer. "You're not very old for the rank you have."

The major smiled. "Twenty-seven. I joined quite young, got a college degree, set goals for myself, and took extra courses whenever I could. I've been working for L-Six — the safe-house program — for more than a year now, but just a few weeks ago I earned the security clearance necessary to work in programs like . . . yours."

"Top Secret Umbra," Jan mumbled, gazing at the pretty wood-grain paneling on the walls.

Major Ka-markla's eyes opened wide with surprise. "Um . . . when we get to the facility, the security sergeant will need to search your bag . . ."

Jan locked eyes with the woman. "As long as he's just looking for dangerous stuff, and doesn't scratch my records!"

The major swallowed. "Yes, he's just concerned with weapons, explosives, things like that, and will be very careful. I guarantee it. What kind of music do you like?"

The girl relaxed. "Good dance music. My collection is from all over the world, and took every penny of allowance my mother could give me."

"Do you dance?"

"All the time.  It's one of the things that keeps me from . . . going crazy."

They continued the long drive in the unmarked military vehicle that did not allow its passengers to glimpse the passing city or countryside.  As Major Lisa Ka-markla slowly got to know young Jan Ko-korna, she became aware that all her military training had not completely prepared her for this assignment.

✳

". . . and he was *soooo* handsome, but when I kissed him, he wiped it off and said something about germs."

"I'm sorry," the major said with sympathy.  "Just too young, I guess."

Jan nodded, then let a long moment of silence pass before speaking again.

"Lisa," she finally said, gazing up at the dome light, "have *you* ever been in love?"

The major's mind raced, remembering that her personal and military lives were supposed to remain completely separate.  But it *was* her assignment to be this little girl's body guard, and that would mean being her companion and confidant.

"Yes.  When I was sixteen.  But staying with him would have forced me to give up all my goals.  It was the hardest thing I've ever done, much harder than any military training.  After a long mental and emotional struggle, my goals won."

Jan nodded.  "I think I understand.  That's kind of like . . . me and my mother."

As Major Ka-markla pondered the girl's words, she overheard the driver talking to the facility by radio.  "Any idea where we are?" she asked, assuming the girl would be clueless.

"Um . . . Appala Hills, about five miles past the big shopping center, then south on a back road, but not quite to the crest of the hills.  So that would put us on 125th or 127th Road.  But 125th doesn't go far enough, so it would have to be 127th . . ."

Jan saw Lisa's mouth hanging open, so she smiled.  "You didn't think they were starting a new top-secret-umbra program because I was *slow*, did you?"

The major swallowed several times to find her voice.  "Nothing . . . slow about *you*."

The girl smiled again.

✳

Jan heard an electric gate slowly open, and she easily noticed the echo of the concrete parking garage.  The lieutenant shut down the van's engine, and Major Lisa Ka-markla looked at her young passenger.  "Ready?"

Jan nodded and shouldered her bag.

A military man saluted as the major stepped out of the van with the girl close behind.

"At ease, Sergeant.  This is Jan, our new resident."

"Welcome, young lady.  I'm Sergeant Ben Ta-nibon.  I . . . um . . . have to search your bag."

"I know.  You *will* handle my records as if they were fine art treasures."
"Yes, Ma'am!" he said with a smile.
The sergeant led the way inside through a steel door.
"He's cute!" Jan whispered to Lisa.
Lisa frowned back.

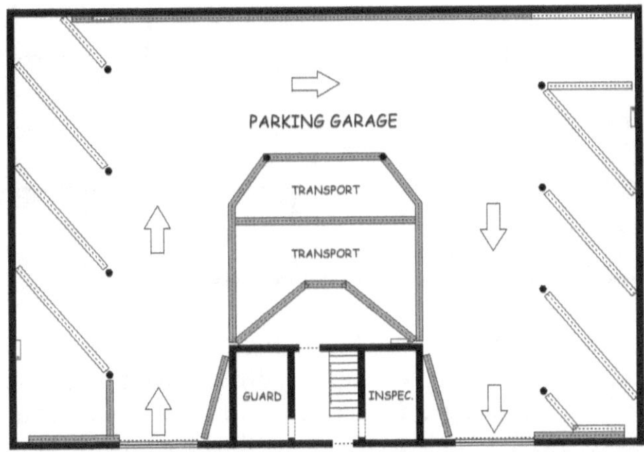


At the same level as the parking garage, on one side of a staircase, the girl glimpsed a little guard room with desk and radio.  The three of them entered the room on the other side, with shelves and cabinets behind a table.  Jan glanced at the poster of things not allowed upstairs, from knives to nuclear weapons.

"Even if you had something you couldn't bring in," the sergeant explained, "we'd just keep it for you in a locked cabinet."

"Even a nuclear bomb?" Jan asked with teasing eyes.

"Well . . . we might have to find a better place for one of *those!*"

Major Ka-markla, standing in the background, chuckled.

"So this must be your music collection," the sergeant declared, lifting the record holder out of the girl's bag.

Jan held her breath.

He pulled off the cover, saw forty of more vinyl discs stacked up, looked for any hidden compartments, and replaced the cover.  "Looks safe."

He set it aside and Jan breathed again.

Everything else in the bag passed inspection, until the sergeant came to the girl's tiger-striped dance leotard.  He held it up and cleared his throat. "Now *that* looks dangerous.  What do you think, Major?"

The female officer grinned and laughed.  "You could keep it down here if you want, Sergeant."

"No," he said, barely holding in a smile, "I'm not sure that would look good.  I guess . . . with some reservations . . . I'll have to let it in."

"Thank you!" Jan said, grinning.

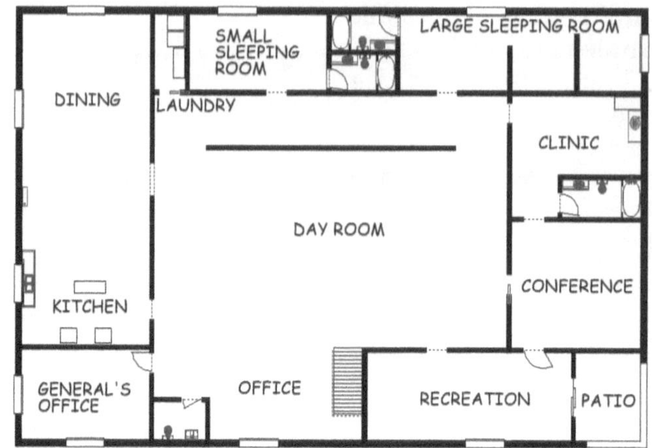


Major Ka-markla led the way up the stairs.

Jan frowned.  The upper level, supposedly for use by human beings, was uglier than the parking garage.  Concrete floors, gray walls, and a suspended ceiling with flickering lights gave the place all the charm of a prison.  A few old couches and floor lamps were shoved together on one side of the large open area.  For a moment, Jan remembered with fondness the observation room at the air base.

Major Ka-markla guided Jan toward a conference room on the right side of the building.  "General Bo-seklin is anxious to meet you.  He's the commanding officer of this facility, originally built as a high-security safe house, but it hasn't seen much use in recent years.  This is still the program office, but we have two other locations, smaller and nicer.  The general's excited about a top-secret-umbra program under his watch."

They stepped into the conference room.  More gray walls and buzzing fluorescent lights . . . a dark gray table . . . folding metal chairs.  Three aging military officers looked at Jan, two male and one female.  The general *had* to be close to retirement age, if not his own funeral.  The colonel, a stern man with rough features, and the major, wearing a motherly expression, were not quite as old.

Lisa sat down and gestured for the girl to take the chair beside her.

Jan didn't move.

"We just know what General Ko-fenral told us on the telephone," the general said with a kindly old voice.  "I realize it's almost dinner time, but we'd like you to give us a brief description of your skills and abilities so we'll know how to proceed.  Please, sit.  We don't bite."

Jan immediately liked the general, but still didn't sit.  Instead, she began to speak slowly and firmly.  "I will tell you everything you could *ever* want to know, and probably many things you *don't* want to know, but I do not live, or work, in rooms that look like jail cells."

"Now listen here, young lady . . ." the stern colonel started to say, but General Bo-seklin raised his hand for silence.

After a slow breath while looking directly at Jan, the general spoke. "What do you suggest?"

Jan looked around the conference room a bit more, then wandered back out to the large main room, her bag still on her shoulder. Everyone followed.

"This place needs *serious* work, but I think we can cobble something together for tonight. No, I can't tell you anything useful in five minutes while everyone's getting hungry. If you want to know what I can do, then we need three or four pizzas and plenty of drinks. You have someone who can accomplish that?" she asked, turning and making eye contact with the general.

The security sergeant standing beside the stairs, with hands behind his back, had heard everything. The general pointed to him. He saluted and descended the stairs.

"The rest of you are on duty until twenty-one hundred," the general informed.

"While Ben's on the pizza run," Jan resumed her instructions, "we need to arrange these couches in a circle, find some little tables for food and drink, and sprinkle the floor lamps around. Then we need to turn off these *ugly* lights before my *brain* starts flickering, too."

Major Ka-markla failed to suppress a chuckle. "Sorry, Sir. I'll move couches."

The colonel stepped up to help her.

"Us old folks can do *something*," the general asserted. "Sarah, help me with those little coffee tables stacked in the dining room."

Jan smiled, and began arranging floor lamps.

✳

An orange glow began to take form in the conference area of the life-monitor ship Tirilana Kril in high orbit. The glow soon became a large, golden bird.

"Greetings, Shemultavia!" a smaller white bird said as she waddled up from the bridge where a lanky reptile and a huge spider remained at their control consoles. "It appears that the Temporandek Teacher has installed herself in a situation like you described, bok."

The golden bird nodded. "I am well-pleased, Captain Drinn-tala, and it is not at all too soon."

"How long do you think it will take her to prepare her people?"

"Several years, I would think, at the least."

"Bok. Isn't that dangerously close to the first tipping point?"

"It is, but that's what we have to work with. Melorania thinks we will have a human response-ship crew by then."

"That would be very good, bok, since the monkey mammals of this planet are its biggest problem."

"You may now return to Satamia Star Station for some well-deserved rest and less-stressful assignments, Captain."

The white bird nodded thoughtfully as Shemultavia faded from sight. Eventually she took a deep breath, shuddered slightly from the fatigue of a long mission, and returned to the bridge. "Navigator, flight plan for home, please."

The spider went to work at his console.

*

Within an hour, a half-way comfortable meeting area had been created in the top-secret military facility, and the pizzas had arrived.

Getting the ceiling lights off was more difficult, as they didn't seem to have a switch.

Jan sighed and headed down the stairs. The sergeant looked at the general, he nodded, and together Jan and Ben located the circuit-breaker box in the parking garage. While the sergeant wondered what the proper security protocol might be, Jan flicked off every breaker that said *lights*.

When they returned to the upper level, everyone was standing around in amazement. The flickering and buzzing had stopped, and the floor lamps cast a soft glow around the circle of couches and coffee tables.

"*Now* we can hear ourselves *think*," Jan declared.

*

While everyone else milled about, the youngest person grabbed a paper plate, slice of pizza, and can of juice. She quickly claimed a small couch against the back wall, allowing her to see anyone who ascended the stairs. After taking a few bites, she looked around.

"There should be a record made of our sessions. We'll often want to go back and listen to them again, and I *hate* repeating myself. Tape recorder?"

The general, selecting a slice of pizza, nodded. "Excellent idea! Major?"

She was already in motion toward her gray metal desk next to the stairs. From a nearby shelf she pulled an old reel-to-reel unit and tried to blow the dust off, then located a blank tape in her desk. "Can you operate this, Sergeant?"

"Yes, Ma'am."

During the next few minutes, everyone took the edge off their hunger while the security sergeant set up the tape recorder and a chair for himself just outside the circle of couches.

The executive officer passed out note pads and pencils.

Eventually, everyone and everything was ready that could be, given the circumstances. The little girl at the head of the circle of military officers set aside her paper plate, drew her legs up under her, and took a deep breath.

*   *   *

**Chapter 3: Session One**

"General, does this program have a name or number yet?" Jan asked.

"What did Malcolm say, Sarah?"

The executive officer looked at her note pad. "P-Seventeen."

"Sergeant," the girl began, "would you open the session by starting your tape and announcing the program number, session number, date and time, please?"

The sergeant looked at the general.

He raised his eyebrows and nodded.

After pressing the *record* button, the sergeant cleared his throat. "Um . . . Program P-Seventeen, Session . . . One?" He paused to glance around. "Thirteen October 3662, nineteen hundred hours, seven minutes."

The girl smiled and nodded, then looked slowly around the room. "My name is *Heather*. Some of you know a different name, but that name, first and last, must be left behind and forgotten."

For the first time that evening, the colonel nodded his approval.

"Also present at this meeting are . . ." She gestured to the person on her right.

The young female officer glanced at the general before speaking. "Major Lisa Ka-markla, security."

"Colonel George Ba-kerga, security chief."

"General Samuel Bo-seklin, commander."

"Major Sarah Ma-soran, executive."

The major turned and looked at the sergeant behind the tape recorder.

"Me?"

"You're in the building during a highly-classified meeting, Sergeant," Colonel Ba-kerga asserted, "so you're technically in the meeting."

"Um . . . Sergeant Ben Ta-nibon, security."

The colonel turned to the general. "No one else in the building, Sir. I did a walk-through just before . . . *Heather* . . . arrived.  The lieutenant who was driving the blind transport went home.”

“Thank you, everyone,” Heather said softly and closed her eyes.

“I’d like to start with a question . . .” Colonel Ba-kerga tried to say.

“Please don’t,” Heather snapped, eyes flashing and pinning the colonel.  “I have a *thousand* thoughts swirling around in my head, and to be any use to you, I have to figure out which ones are important right now, and how to organize them.  If I try to answer questions at this point, my mind will be going in twenty different directions.  I *promise* I’ll take questions just as soon as I’ve said what I need to say.”

The colonel frowned deeply, but noticed a slight smile on the general’s face, so he said no more.

“We’ll give that format a try tonight,” the general announced.

Heather closed her eyes again.

Everyone waited as the reels of tape slowly turned.

✳

“I am not a savant.  A savant has some kind of extraordinary mental ability, like memorization or calculation.”

She saw several slight nods.

“Neither am I a voyant, although my letter about the rocket might make you think so.  A voyant can see things that most people can’t — things far away, like clairvoyance or remote viewing — things in the past not otherwise recorded, sometimes called psychometry — or things in the future, pre-cognition.”

She saw discomfort on every face in the room.

“The fact is . . . I was *born* with an entire *lifetime* of memories, knowledge, education, experience — and if a seven-year-old may dare to use the word — wisdom.”

Major Ka-markla’s mouth opened, but no sound came out.

Heather smiled briefly.  “I could read as soon as I could focus my eyes — the newspaper, the encyclopedia, anything.  Drove my mother crazy for a while, but luckily she’s not the kind of person who desperately *needs* to be a mother to someone, so she got used to it and eventually realized how lucky she was.”

Major Ma-soran frowned with sadness.

Heather made comforting eye contact with the woman, then went on.  “I realize there’s nothing very useful about a lifetime of memories and wisdom.  You can find *that* in any old-folks’ home.”

The executive officer’s frown changed to a chuckle.

“The unique thing about *my* memories is that the person I got them from is living in the same time-frame that I am.  In other words, she’s seven right now, and will die at age eighty in 3735.”

The general twisted his face with disbelief.  The colonel frowned.

Heather ignored both.  “The important thing to realize is that I cannot *see* the future.  I cannot sit here in the present and reach into the future with some ability.  I *remember* the future.  If a future event is in my memory, great!  If not, there's nothing I can do about it.  I have the memories of only one person, not some kind of all-knowing omniscience."

Only soft breathing could be heard in the silence that followed.

*

"I do not know who gave me these memories, but it must have been someone with powers far beyond us mere mortals.  I call it *God.*  If that offends you, you can use any word you want.  I don't care."

She noticed frowns on several faces.

"He hasn't spoken to me directly, telling me why He did it, or what He wants me to do with it.  But He did leave me a clue."

The discomfort in the room turned to curiosity.

"My memories are not complete.  There are things I *cannot* remember that anyone should, like the source person's name, where she lived and went to school, the names of her husband and children, things like that.  When I try to find those things, it's like someone spray-painted over them with black.  Believe me, I've been trying for seven years — I'd like nothing more than to know who's in my head.

"I know it's not *me* in the future, because I remember a fairly normal childhood, without any unusual knowledge, and that child had two left feet and couldn't dance if her life depended on it."

Both female officers, young and old, laughed.

Heather smiled.  "I don't understand why all that *biographical information* would be missing — I hope you can get a scientist on the team who might know something — but I realized it was a gift from God.  If my memories have been pre-censored, that means I'm free to share the rest with ... whomever I think should have them!  And I can't think of anyone who would make better use of my future memories than our own Department of Defense."

Several voices started to speak, but fell silent when they noticed Heather glaring at them.

"Even though my memories are not complete, I've learned a lot from what *is* there, and you can help me figure out even more."

She saw their happiness at being included in the process.

"Our source person lived all her life, except for vacations, in this city, as I have many memories of local events, and few from any other city or town."

The general nodded agreement with her logic.

"She was a clinical psychologist, a mental-health therapist at the doctoral level.  I figured this out after I ran into some college students in the library about a year ago.  Some of them were graduate-level psych students, and I knew a *lot* more than them."

Major Ma-soran raised her eyebrows.

"Also it fits with glimpses I have of college classes she's teaching, seminars she's leading, lectures she's giving, stuff like that."

Colonel Ba-kerga nodded.

"She was not a government agent of any kind, did not serve in the military, was never a political leader on any level, never worked in industry, and was not a scientist."

Heather saw some disappointment in the room, as she had expected.

"But she was a highly-intelligent, well-educated citizen who kept up with the news, read in-depth articles on anything of substance, and had a broad understanding of most topics, including the hard sciences.  She was successful, highly-respected, and middle-of-the-road politically."

Colonel Ba-kerga took a deep breath and smiled slightly.

"If anyone could bring you the judgment of the future, about events in the world through 3730 or so, she could, and therefore, I can."

Heather could see the magnitude of the project beginning to dawn on several of her listeners.

"If that sounds useful, I would be happy to work for the Department of Defense, given appropriate living and working conditions, and a good package of salary and benefits."

Suddenly the frown returned to the colonel's face.  "What makes you think you can dictate terms to us, considering we have you in our custody?"

General Bo-seklin cleared his throat.  "You don't have to answer that, Heather."

After a moment of tense silence, she spoke.  "I'd like to.  It needs to be said."

The general slowly nodded.

"The memories I have *cannot* be taken from me by force, intimidation, drugs, or brain surgery."  After a pause, she went on.  "I have, at least mentally, lived an entire lifetime . . . and died.  I am the *last* person in the world you can scare."

She glanced at the colonel.  He kept his eyes on his note pad.

"There is no way my memories of the future," she went on more softly, "could be shared with you quickly even if I wanted to.  It will take years to get at them.  It can only be done in a safe, respectful, teamwork environment. That team will need to include several scientists.  A philosopher and a psychologist, also, to help keep us sane.  The things that team will have to learn, to deal with knowledge of the future without making a complete *mess* of it, will make college look like kindergarten."

She paused to let her last statement soak in, then slowly turned to the colonel.  "There *is* a place on that team for a hard-nosed, skeptical security chief."

Colonel Ba-kerga glanced up from his note pad.

Heather looked around the circle.  "I gather that this facility has become nearly useless to the military and is in danger of being torn down.  I also sense that most of you have been passed over for promotions and more interesting assignments, and are just looking forward to retirement."

She knew the truth of her words when all her listeners smiled and looked at their notes.

"Instead, with a little hard work remodeling and lots of hard work team-building, which I will help with at every step, this program will become *the* most important thing happening in the military, in *any* military, indeed in any government anywhere in the world."

They were all looking at her now.

"I cannot prove this to you in the short term.  I can only show you in the long term.  Are you up to it?"

Their faces told her they were going to try, if for no other reason than because they had little else to do.

Even Colonel Ba-kerga.

* * *

# Chapter 4: Getting Comfortable

When Heather announced that she was finished with her presentation, the four officers discovered, after looking at their notes, that almost all their questions had been answered.

Before anyone else could speak, the general asserted that the discussion of Heather's salary and benefits would take place between the two of them in his office.

The colonel remained silent.

Major Ka-markla's hand came up slowly.

Heather pointed to her.

"You have offered to work for the Department of Defense.  Do you realize that by doing so, you will be able to share your . . . um . . . future knowledge *only* with the Department of Defense, and that the secrecy rules for a program like this are *very* strict?"

"I do," Heather said without hesitation.  "I know you will need to supervise all my activities to make sure I don't, you know, stop in for a chat at some foreign embassy . . ."

Everyone chuckled.  Heather could see the sergeant smiling behind his tape recorder.

". . . and I know you'll need to monitor my mail and telephone calls.  You'll get no security problems from me.  If any other government or corporation learned of my memories, I'd be worth *millions* to anyone who could snag me. I don't want to live my life hiding under bridges.  I want a home and a family. I'll still visit my mother, but she can't protect me now that I'm starting my work, so in a sense, you guys will have to be my family."

She let a long moment pass so they could ponder her words.

"But I won't live in a cage," she went on softly.  "My future memories stay here, but my dancing and skating and hiking and other fun things happen out there in the world.  You need to monitor and protect me.  Fine.  I need a

facilitator to drive, help me do business, and just be someone I can talk to."
She looked at Major Ka-markla.

The young female officer nodded.

⁂

With nine o'clock approaching and full darkness cloaking the hills around the little facility, the executive officer made note of several more topics that needed to be discussed at future sessions, and the general closed the meeting.

At Heather's direction, the sergeant announced the time before stopping his tape.

Colonel Ba-kerga nodded with approval and growing respect. "Remember, everyone, your note pads do not leave the building.  Sergeant, you'll have to do a double shift."

"Yes, Sir."

"I'll get more security personnel in here as soon as I can, but top-secret-umbra clearances don't grow on trees."

"No, Sir."

"Major Ka-markla," the executive officer began, "you'll have to stay with Heather tonight.  It will take a few days to get this place up and running."

"I'm prepared, Ma'am — always keep an overnight bag in my car."

"Good.  I'll get food and drink in here by morning, but it may take another day or two to find a cook."

"We've got left-over pizza!" Heather proclaimed with a grin.

The general laughed.  "I'll try to get in about ten so you and I can meet, Heather, and I want everyone here by thirteen hundred."

⁂

The three older officers departed, leaving Major Ka-markla in command. "Sergeant, double-check all the gates and doors, including the one in the bomb shelter."

"That's a hundred-foot crawl!" he said with wide eyes.  "I think there's some knee pads down there."

"Oh, cool!  Can I come?" Heather asked excitedly, bouncing up and down.

"Not tonight, young lady," the major asserted.  "You and I have work to do up here.  This place hasn't been used in weeks.  Hopefully all the bedding is still here."

Following Lisa to the sleeping rooms at the back of the building, Heather frowned at the gray walls and thin, lumpy mattresses on squeaky bed strings. "I'll sleep on a couch, thank you."

"I understand.  Grab some sheets and blankets."

Returning to the large main room, they quickly had two couches near each other for them, and another near the stairs for the sergeant.

"Girls' side and boys' side!" Heather noted with a grin.

Lisa laughed.  "In the military, we don't always get the luxury of separate quarters."

A few minutes later, the sergeant returned.  "All secure."

"We're both armed," the major said, "and no one can get in without a bomb or a bull dozer, so you can sleep, Sergeant."

"I guess . . . a bomb or a bull dozer would wake us."

Heather giggled.  "I don't suppose there's a record player anywhere . . ."

Both adults shook their heads.

"We'll have to do some shopping tomorrow!"

* * *

## Chapter 5: Sketches

When Major Ka-markla awoke, about a quarter hour before sunrise, Heather was already up, stretching and doing some simple dance steps in an open area of the concrete floor. Sergeant Ta-nibon continued his adventures in dreamland.

"Hi, Lisa."

"Hi, kid. You'll do just fine in a military facility if you're used to getting up before the sun."

"I don't *always* get up this early, but I want to peek at every inch of this place before Sam gets here."

The major raised her eyebrows. "You mean General Bo-seklin? I'm not sure he'll let you use his first name."

"Then he can't call me *Heather*, can he?"

The major chuckled, and a moment later the sergeant began stirring.

"Good morning, Ben!" Heather said, still prancing about.

"Did I miss the bombs and bull dozers?"

"Yeah. They were very quiet bombs and bull dozers. Lisa and I are gonna creep around. There's cold pizza."

"No coffee?"

"Major Ma-soran promised to have something brought in," Lisa remembered, combing her hair, "but no idea when."

"I think she'll be up early, making arrangements and stuff," Ben speculated while tucking in his shirt. "I saw a sparkle in her eyes last night that I've never seen before."

Lisa, opening a can of juice, nodded. "You might be right. I think Heather touched their hearts with all her talk about this place becoming important."

"That wasn't just talk, you know," the girl said while stretching her calf muscles.

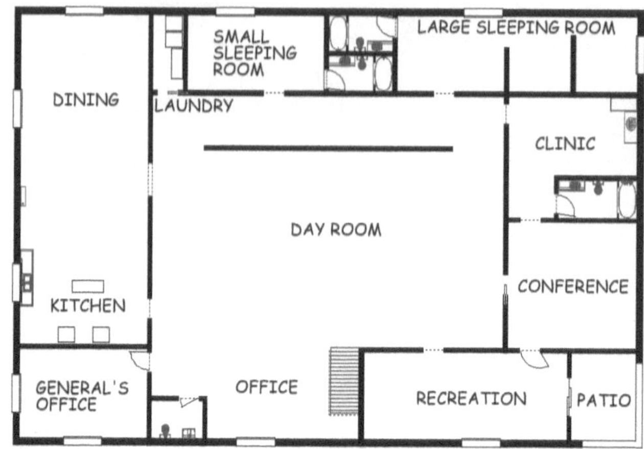


Heather grabbed a note pad and pencil.  The two females started at the stairs and went clockwise around the building.  Ben wanted to stay near the radio, especially since the first arrival would probably bring coffee.

"This area beside the stairs is *supposed* to be the office," Lisa explained.  "Major Ma-soran's desk . . . Colonel Ba-kerga's desk.  But it's so ill-defined that it's almost impossible to keep safe-house guests out."

Heather started sketching.  "How about a counter across here, in line with the wall on the other side of the stairs?  Some nice, varnished wood."

Lisa looked at the sketch.  "I like that.  The fax machine and the mailbox could go on it."

"Yeah.  What's this?"

"Staff toilet room, and here in the corner is the general's office."

"Hmm . . . he just needs some nicer furniture," Heather said while standing in the doorway, sketching.  "I have a hunch he likes to entertain visitors."

"He might, if the place wasn't so ugly."

Heather snickered and Lisa smiled.

"This door?"

"Kitchen, but let's go in through the dining room."

After stepping through the wide doorway, Heather frowned at the dingy little stove, apartment-size refrigerator, and wobbly metal shelving with nothing but a few spice canisters.  She sketched as she wandered.  "Roomy, but it needs professional equipment if *any* cook is gonna be happy here."

"Military people work wherever they're assigned."

"When we get done with this place," Heather boasted, turning her attention to the dining room, "people will be *begging* to work here!"

"Except . . . few of them will have the necessary clearance."

"Oh yeah, that.  Hopefully there's a cook somewhere with top-secret-umbra who can make a decent pizza."

Lisa laughed and followed Heather out.

✳

"World's smallest laundry room," the girl mumbled after poking her head in and making a quick sketch. "I like how this wall separates the big room from this corridor — makes it more private back here." She quickly paced off the width. "Eight feet. Enough for some comfy chairs and little tables for people who don't wanna schmooze in the dining room."

The major smiled.

"And these are the sleeping rooms," Heather said in recognition.

"This small one holds two single roommates or one couple," the major explained

Heather sketched.

"It's so strange watching you work. I have a niece who's seven, and she's very bright, but just barely beginning to write a few simple words, and can only draw stick figures."

Heather raised her eyebrows. "There's a clinical term for it, you know."

Lisa shook her head slightly.

"Age-inappropriate behavior."

Both females burst into laughter as they entered the other sleeping room.

"When we get a family, we put them in here."

"So . . . they eat in the dining room . . . hang out in the big room . . . and just sleep in here?"

"Mostly. Also, there's a recreation room in the southwest corner, with a little open-air patio."

"Cool," Heather mumbled, finishing her sketch. "We could put a couch and a little desk in here if we move the bedding cabinet into the corridor. And I'm beginning to see dusty green walls and light blue tie-back curtains."

"Wow. I hope you can talk the general into spending all that money."

"I know I can."

✳

"This is our little clinic. Doc comes over from the air base when we get safe-house people. Has it's own toilet room."

Heather peeked around and sketched. "Mmm, nice big bath tub."

"And we can go straight though this door into your favorite room . . ."

"Eeew. The dreaded conference room."

Lisa laughed. "Let's hurry straight across."

Although the recreation room was currently jail-cell gray like everything else, and contained only an old tumbling mat and a couple of dead potted plants on the patio, Heather's eyes lit up when she stepped in.

"You see something, don't you?" Lisa asked.

"Yep," the girl said, concentrating on her sketch.

✳

When they returned to the outer office where the sergeant was pacing, Major Ka-markla declared she was having cold pizza for breakfast, and asked Sergeant Ta-nibon to show Heather the lower levels.

"You're not worried about me being alone with the little girl in the bomb shelter?" the sergeant inquired with a half-smile.

The major looked at them both. "I think you're tough enough for the job, Sergeant. Let me know if she's too hard on you."

Heather snickered as the pair headed for the stairs and the major started opening pizza boxes.

✳

"Lisa already told me I can't flirt with the staff," Heather shared when they got to the garage level.

Ben laughed. "You've seen the inspection room . . ."

"Let me make a quick sketch. So you put dangerous stuff like guns in the locked cabinet, and other junk on the shelves."

"Yeah. Sometimes safe-house people arrive with all their family heirlooms . . . dishes . . . you wouldn't *believe* what else."

"I've known for a while that I had to be ready to go, so I kept my little bag packed, and when the gray van pulled up, I just popped in my music."

"I'm sorry you had to leave your home," he said as they crossed the corridor and stepped into the other small room. "Guard room. Radio. Munitions cabinet. Boring."

"It needs a nice couch, soft lighting, books and magazines . . ."

"I'm not holding my breath!"

"You'll see."

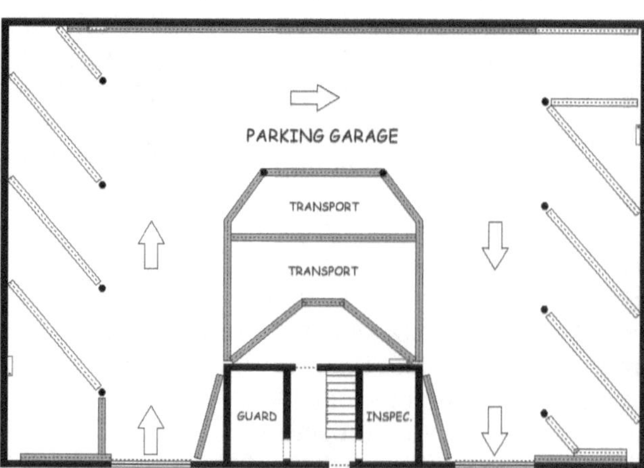


They stepped into the echoey garage. Ben explained the yellow and red lines on the floor, and that parking beside any red line would get your car towed away and crushed into a little cube *before* they yelled at you.

Heather laughed as she strolled and sketched. "Except the blind transports."

"Yeah. Only those can park in the middle."

"Plenty of fire hoses. We need to take this ladder upstairs so I can peek in the ceiling."

"That'll be up to Major Ma-soran."
"It's only an eight-foot ladder.  I could *dance* on the top of it!"
Ben laughed, but said no more on the subject as they went back inside.

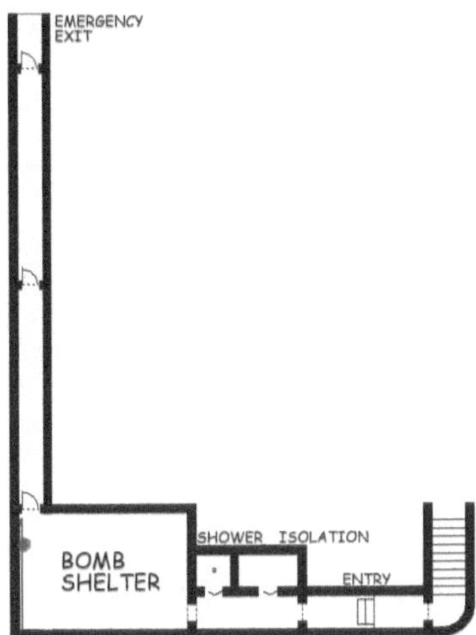


Heather lurked down the next stairway like a pirate entering her treasure cave. "Har, har, matie!"

Concrete changed to smooth stone.  They turned a corner, crept through a steel door, and smooth stone changed to rough stone.  As they descended more steps, the ceiling became lower, forcing the sergeant to hunch over.

Another steel door creaked as it was opened.  "Multiple doors in case of bombs or fallout," Ben explained.

"Way cool, a little tiny bunk room."

"It's an isolation room in case someone's sick."

"Porta-potty room . . ." Heather identified as she began her sketch.

"Drain in the floor, so it's also the shower, *if* there's water to spare."

They wandered into the largest room of the bomb shelter, the same size as the general's office but crammed with ten bunk beds, a table where six could eat if they sat close, a bench stacked with boxes of supplies, and two water barrels.

"I guess ugly is okay down here."

"Yeah.  I hope we never have to use it.  You know, don't you?"

"Yes, I know."

She said no more on the subject.

*

Ben got knee pads, they strapped them on and crawled, side by side, about a hundred feet along the emergency escape and ventilation tunnel, passing three doors.

"The doors are like air locks for when there's fallout," Ben explained, "but we normally leave them open to keep the place fresh and dry.  Here's the end.

It's a weedy ditch behind the building."

Heather examined the window screen, tight-fitting to keep bugs out, and the grill of thick steel bars.  "Fallout is just dust, right?  Pure air can't become radioactive."

"Right.  If you have enough dirt or rock between you and the outside, and can keep the dust out, you're good."

They crawled back to the bomb shelter, Heather sketched a little more, and they ascended to the garage level just as the first radio call came in.

*　*　*

## Chapter 6: Just a Warm-Up

"Major Ma-soran coming in!" Lisa yelled down.  "E.T.A. two minutes!"

"Upstairs, young lady," Ben asserted.  "Only military personnel, and those in transit, are allowed down here when any of the doors or gates are open."

Heather pretended to pout, just for a second, then smiled and dashed up the stairs.

Lisa was starting to see when the seven-year-old child was in control, and when the eighty-year-old psychologist was speaking.  As Heather waited at the very top of the stairs, nearly bouncing up and down with excitement, the seven-year-old was clearly present.

As Major Ma-soran climbed the stairs slowly with a box in her arms, she was greeted by the smiling girl, but also thought she glimpsed the wise old eyes of the psychologist who had already experienced a future — if she was telling the truth — that she and her fellow officers couldn't imagine.

Finally arriving at her desk, she brought out sweet rolls, a thermos of coffee, and a carton of milk.

Heather wasn't paying attention.  She was looking at the box Ben was bringing up the stairs.

"I believe this is for you, young lady."

She received the box with a grin and sat down on the floor to carefully unpack the brand new record player.

"Coffee, Sergeant?" the executive offered.

✳

Clutching hot coffee and sweet rolls, the three military people gathered on couches to chat about the upcoming day's tasks, and for a few minutes didn't think about their new resident.  The radio came to life again, and two minutes later Sergeant Ta-nibon stood at attention as General Bo-seklin drove into the parking garage.  The sergeant secured the gate, then helped the general carry boxes upstairs.

The four were deep into coffee and sweet rolls when a faint throbbing sound began.  They looked at each other.  A moment later, other instruments joined the drums, soon building to a full orchestra.  All four slowly rose and looked around.

"Recreation room," Major Ka-markla suggested.

Indeed, the music became louder as they approached the door, pulsing with a vibrant dance tune that easily stirred the blood.  The general carefully turned the doorknob.

Heather, now in pink leotard and leather dance shoes, moved skillfully on the old tumbling mat to the rhythmic music coming from the record player.

The four slipped in and leaned against the wall.

Heather smiled at them but didn't stop dancing.

The music became fuller and the beat faster as the minutes passed, and the girl's movements became stronger to match, her feet in perfect time to the song, her arms tracing elegant shapes in the air, her hands adding flare to the rhythm.

As the song built to its final climax, she began to leap with graceful legs while her arms reached for the sky, then slowly returned to lower and smaller movements as the music faded and she held a final pose.

The four military people clapped vigorously.

Heather stretched up to her full height.  "That was just a warm-up exercise."

"My God," was all the general could think to say.

✳

With cold pizza, sweet roll, and milk in hand, Heather settled onto a couch.  "Thank you *so* much for the record player, Sarah!  I'll pay you back as soon as I get my first check."

The general smiled.  "That *is* what we need to talk about this morning, isn't it?"

"I just wanna look above the stupid suspended ceiling first.  I've seen everything else.  Ben wants approval before bringing up the ladder."

The general looked at his executive.  "Your call, Major, but I can't imagine she could dance like that and not handle herself on a ladder."

Major Ma-soran twisted her mouth back and forth for a moment.  "Two strong spotters around the ladder."

Lisa and Ben looked at each other and nodded.

✳

A few minutes later, the ladder was in place.  Heather climbed without fear or effort, then quickly removed ceiling panels and handed them down, reaching six from the ladder's position.  Finally enough light penetrated, revealing the older ceiling above.

"Wow!  Can you see this?  It's beautiful up here!  Varnished log trusses, and the original ceiling is finished with stained tongue-and-groove boards!  This is amazing!"

Both the executive, at her deck, and the general, in his office, felt compelled to take a look.

"Can you see it, Sam?  Isn't it pretty, Sarah?  Why would *anyone* want to cover up such beautiful wood?"

"I really don't know," Major Ma-soran admitted.  "That suspended ceiling has been there ever since I've worked in this building, which has been a long time!"

General Bo-seklin didn't say anything, but he was smiling.

✳   ✳   ✳

## Chapter 7: Negotiations

Heather frowned at the folding metal chair in the general's office. "George won't be in 'til one, right?"

"At the earliest.  He's looking for enough security staff with the proper clearance, and is coming up short.  He just might have to qualify some new ones."

"Be right back."  She dashed out, and returned a moment later pushing Colonel Ba-kerga's plush rolling chair.  After moving the folding metal thing out of the way, she installed herself across the desk from the general.

He looked at her.  "Something tells me you're going to get your way in this negotiation."

"Yes, but I have to be reasonable because without you, I'd spend the rest of my life . . . you know . . . hiding under bridges."

He nodded.  "So we need each other.  Where do we start?"

"I've decided this place is usable, but it needs *lots* of work.  Paint, carpets, hardwood floors, tile, curtains, light fixtures ... and that *ridiculous* suspended ceiling has to go.  All new equipment in the kitchen, lots of comfortable furniture, and a whole bunch of plants.  Some artwork, pillows, a few other details.  I'll have complete lists, organized by phase, in a day or two."

"We can get most of that done by enlisted craftsmen, but the equipment and furniture will be expensive."

"I'll be blunt.  God is trusting us to do a little bit of the work He usually has angels do.  We can't hope to do that if our environment makes us feel like we're in prison."

The general rubbed his chin.  "Interesting way of looking at it.  You don't want to tear out any walls or stairs?"

"No, the building is great.  It's just had all its beauty covered up for a long time."

"Good.  Which sleeping room do you want?"

"Neither.  In fact, it's okay with me if you continue to have safe-house people once in a while.  My digs will be the recreation room and patio, my dance floor will be in the old conference room, and I'll use the toilet room in the clinic."

He cleared his throat.  "I wasn't expecting *that*.  But I can see how they all form a suite . . . except when the clinic's in use."

"That'll be rare, and when it is, I'll use the staff toilet."

The general made some notes.  "Keeping it available as a safe house will help justify the expense . . . we'll need a protocol for announcing when someone's in the building without umbra clearance.  Okay, what's next?"

"Food."

"Lunch is being brought in."

She smiled.  "No, I mean I want most of the food here to be several notches better than the usual military . . . um . . . stuff.  Lots of vegetables, fresh fruits, whole grains, organic whenever possible, you know.  So that means we need an open-minded cook willing to work with me."

"Okay . . . Major Ma-soran is looking for the cook, so talk to her.  Staffing a safe house was *easy* compared to this umbra level.  Next?"

"I get any medical care I need *or want*, paid for by the military."

"No problem.  You can get almost anything done at the air base."

Heather shriveled her nose for a second, but the general didn't notice.

"Next?"

"I get Lisa or some other young, open-minded lady as a facilitator to drive, help me do banking and other business, go skating, whatever, during my free time.  Priscilla Ka-mentha."

"What?"

"My new, public name.  Made it up last night at about three in the morning.  I'll need I.D."

The general made notes.  "Next?"

"Sixty thousand."

"I only make sixty-five!"

"Yeah, I wanted to be . . . reasonable."

He wrote, but wore a wrinkled brow.

"And I have complete freedom to spend it, save it, invest it, give it away, burn it, anything I want."

He looked at her for a moment, then continued writing.  "Next?"

"Only to share what I think a good work schedule would look like."

"I was *hoping* we'd get to your part in all this."

She smiled.  "Like I said last night, this won't be quick and easy.  *Knowing* the future is only part of the job, the part I can do.  Figuring out what to do with that knowledge, *if anything*, will almost be harder.  That's where the team comes in."

"I sense that, and I'm already looking into some highly-respected people from the University."

"Good. So here's my idea. You give me a topic in the morning. I take the rest of the day planning my presentation, maybe reading some background material. Then I sleep on it. The following morning, the team meets from nine to noon, the time most people are thinking best, and I share what I've got. Discussions will often continue through lunch and into the afternoon, and finally I'll unwind, probably by going skating or dancing or something. The next morning I get another topic. It's a two day cycle, so three topics a week."

The general looked at the seven-year-old girl and rubbed his chin. "I like it. It's relaxed, but contains some discipline. You get topics Sunday, Tuesday, and Thursday, the teams meets Monday, Wednesday, and Friday."

"That's what I was thinking. Saturday, I'm completely free. I do this three weeks on, one week off, during which I usually get out of town with my facilitator, go camping, sightseeing, whatever."

"That's nine, almost ten topics a month. So each look into the future will cost us about five hundred, plus benefits."

"Reasonable?"

He was silent for a long moment. "Reasonable."

✳   ✳   ✳

## Chapter 8: More Proof

When Heather pushed the comfortable chair back out, Colonel Ba-kerga was sitting behind his desk in a folding metal chair while interviewing a young woman in uniform.

"Sorry, George. Thought you wouldn't be in so early."

He flashed her a slight frown as he stood up and received his chair. "Neither did I, but I stumbled upon a good security candidate. You can help me with something, Heather. Have a seat."

Heather took the folding chair and seated herself beside the desk, facing the candidate.

"Let's pretend, Corporal Do-forva, just for a moment," the colonel began, "that you come to work in a top-secret-umbra program, and on your very first day there's a serious, high-level meeting taking place — a general or two, colonels, majors, and perhaps several well-known civilian scientists. You quickly hear that the topic is the possible outcome of some highly-classified weapon system or tactical initiative. A records specialist sits behind a tape recorder. No one is laughing or smiling. Can you picture all that?"

"Yes, Sir."

"Then a little girl — how old are you, Heather?"

"Seven and a half."

"A seven-year-old girl stands up, and begins leading the meeting. She's not only leading the meeting, she's the main speaker. And *no one* is interrupting her. Can you picture *that?*"

"Um . . . barely, Sir."

Heather could see the suppressed smile on the corporal's face.

"I know, it's way out there. Now we jump ahead. At the end of the day, you go home. You occasionally go to a tavern, drink a beer . . ."

"Yes, Sir."

"Okay, you go to the tavern, all your buddies are there, and they're swapping stories about funny things that happened to them that day.  What do you do?"

"I . . . um . . . think of something to share that has *nothing* to do with any classified program I work in, Sir, like perhaps something I did the previous weekend."

Heather clapped.  "You found a good one!"

✳

Not much later, a lieutenant arrived with a box of sandwiches and drinks, and the security sergeant came up the stairs carrying a small television.  They both entered the dining room.

Heather found a couch and worked on her remodeling plans for a few minutes, until she heard Lisa call her name.

"Heather!  You'd better get a sandwich before they're all gone!"

"I guess I should," Heather said, hopping up.

They entered the dining room together.

"There's the president!" someone said, looking at the television.

Heather froze.  Her mind was suddenly filled with recognition of the scene on the television — the banquet table, the podium, the other guests all in suits and elegant dresses — it was all so familiar.  She looked up at Lisa.

The major was just standing, casually watching the events a thousand miles away.

Heather heard the master of ceremonies announce the president.  The president rose and people started clapping.  Heather knew she didn't have much time.

She urgently tapped Lisa on the shoulder.

Without quite taking her eyes from the television, the major bent down slightly.  "Hmm?"

Heather cupped her hands and whispered something in Lisa's ear.

Major Ka-markla's mouth dropped open and her eyes bulged with horror.  Before she could think of anything to do, everyone in the room, and millions more all over the country, heard the rifle shot that ended the president's life.

✳

In the chaos that followed, Heather managed to get a sandwich and can of juice, then returned to her remodeling plans.  She knew they would come looking for her soon.  In the meantime, she worked on the furniture list.

When she sensed, about ten minutes later, their eyes upon her, she looked up to see Sam, George, Sarah, and Lisa all looking down at her.  Everyone else in the building, including the new security corporal, was there too, a little farther back.

The general cleared his throat.  "I don't know how to put this delicately.  If you knew the president was about to be assassinated, why *in God's name* didn't you tell us?"

Heather looked at all the people looming over her.  Some almost had smoke coming from their ears.  Ben looked ready to give her a spanking.  George appeared to be considering handcuffs.

She took one more slow breath.  "I'd be happy to tell you, tomorrow morning at nine o'clock, after everyone's had a chance to cool off, get a good night's sleep, and eat a hearty breakfast."

She turned her attention back to the remodeling plans.

Without asking any more questions, they slowly filtered away, and no one spoke to her for the entire rest of the day.

The eighty-year-old psychologist in her steeled herself for what she had to endure.

The seven-year-old girl wanted to cry.

But after dragging herself through several dance exercises, she was finally, for the first time in two days, able to get some sleep.

✳   ✳   ✳

## Chapter 9: Session Two

"Program P-Seventeen, Session Two, fifteen October 3662, zero-nine hundred hours, three minutes."

Heather looked around and saw everyone looking back with a little less hostility than the day before, but not much. "Present at this session are myself, Heather . . ."

"Major Lisa Ka-markla."

"Colonel George Ba-kerga."

"General Samuel Bo-seklin."

"Major Sarah Ma-soran."

"Two-star General Malcolm Ko-fenral."

"Sergeant Ben Ta-nibon."

"Corporal Ginny Do-forva."

"No one else in the building, Sir," Colonel Ba-kerga stated, "and everyone present has proper clearance."

They all looked at Heather.

Part of her wanted to run and hide. "Good morning, everyone. Yesterday our president was assassinated. We should first hear Major Ka-markla's experience of the event."

Lisa frowned, and didn't like doing what she had to do, but couldn't think of any way to avoid it. "Yesterday, approximately ten seconds before the shot was fired, Heather whispered in my ear, I quote, *He's about to be assassinated.*"

The major waited for the rumble of voices to die down, then continued. "I froze, and had no idea what to do. Upon reflection, I can't think of any meaningful action I could have taken in so short a time, but I'm open to feedback."

"Perhaps some other time, Lisa," Heather jumped in, "but today we should focus on the topic, which is, if I may take the liberty of paraphrasing the general, *Why didn't I tell anyone sooner?* Is that close enough, Sam?"

He nodded slowly.

"In the future, I'll get the topics in writing, and they will be much less emotionally-charged. Today we're winging it. I apologize."

Several people nodded slightly, but most still had their arms folded.

"There are *three* reasons I didn't tell you sooner that this president was going to be assassinated, and I will share them in order of importance. The least important is . . . you simply didn't ask . . ."

The grumbling cut her off, so she waited patiently.

"You had been here nearly a *day* before the assassination!" General Ko-fenral burst out. "Why *the Hell* didn't you say something?"

"Malcolm," General Bo-seklin stepped in, "we've decided on a format in which we don't jump in with questions until the main presentation is complete."

"Okay, Sam, it's your show, but this had better be good!"

Everyone looked at Heather again.

She forced herself to breathe slowly and deeply. "I'd like you all to try to imagine how this process would go — how this team would function — if I was constantly trying to remember every bad thing that will happen in the future, and you were running around trying to stop them. I would be in a constant frenzy, struggling to remember enough details to allow you to pin down the time and place, and you would be hounding me for more information. You, and everyone in your chain of command, would be under constant suspicion of causing, or at least conspiring about, every event. None of us would have time to *think*. My mental health would go down the drain, this program would become the target of everyone's anger and resentment, and *no one* would be critically analyzing whether the events even *should* be stopped."

Heather looked around the circle and saw some of her listeners relax a little.

"The truth is, I certainly *did* know of the assassination of this president, as I remember seeing it on television — the original broadcast and dozens of replays. But I did not have the date and time memorized. Please recall that the person whose memories I have is a child right now, a normal child. I had no idea the event was at hand until I stepped into the dining room with Lisa and recognized the scene."

Most of those in the circle now appeared much more relaxed, almost forgiving.

"I wish I could stop now, but unfortunately that's the *least* of the three reasons."

She let a long moment pass.

"What I am going to do next is what I *hope* this team will be helping me do in the future. You're all familiar with the Beklan Empire?"

"Of course," General Ko-fenral answered with a slight laugh. "Half our budget goes to keeping them contained!"

"After the end of this century, the Beklan Empire will become one of the most peaceful, respected, and reliable nations in the world.  They will never again give anyone any trouble, and will be a constant ally and partner in military, scientific, and cultural projects."

"Hard to believe," Colonel Ba-kerga mumbled.

"I agree," Heather admitted.  "It happens because they go through a deep economic depression later this century.  That causes their leadership — and their attitude — to change completely.  As the saying goes, *cooler heads prevail.*"

Several listeners nodded with interest.

"That economic depression was at least partly caused by the arms race and the two proxy wars we will fight with them in coming decades."

She could see several people in the circle putting the pieces together.

"Our president, recently deceased, was opposed to that arms race and the first of those two proxy wars, which, as you know, is on our doorstep."

Both generals and several others had their mouths open, becoming aware of the complexity of what Heather was doing.

"I am certainly *not* fond of assassins," Heather continued, "but knowing the good outcome of that entire chain of events, which happens to include the death of our president, makes me skeptical about any desire to change that future."

A long silence followed, during which the mouths that were open slowly closed.

"Wow . . ." General Ko-fenral began, "I didn't realize what we were dealing with here.  My . . . apologies for my judgmental words earlier."

Heather nodded.  "Just so you know, the assassin had none of this in mind.  His beef was some social policy, I don't remember which."

"And," General Bo-seklin began tentatively, "there's an even *more* important reason you didn't tell us?"

"There is.  What I am about to tell you cannot be verified now or at any later time, but it will be the judgment of most people in the future, including many highly-respected historians and forensic researchers.  The opportunity and weapon appear to have been made available to the lone gunman by persons high up in the Department of Defense — *our* Department of Defense."

The rumble threatened to overwhelm the meeting, so Heather raised both hands for silence.

"It is one thing for this team to find fault with the actions of other governments, other departments of this government, or even mistakes made by the Department of Defense itself.  It is quite another to get into direct conflicts with the possibly-illegal actions of your superiors.  This program would be cancelled, your careers would be ruined, and my life would be in danger.  It's just not worth it.  I hope you understand."

✳

For the next hour, the officers huddled in General Bo-seklin's office, and during that time, no one was allowed in or out of the building.

Heather accepted a neck massage from the new corporal.

"By the way, I'm Ginny."

"I've got lots of names."

Ginny chuckled. "So that little situation the colonel — I forget his name, the security chief — was making up, that was all true?"

"George, Colonel Ba-kerga. Yep, all true, exactly as he said it. That's why it was so easy to play along!"

Both females laughed heartily.

"You're . . . twenty?"

"Nineteen."

"Are you okay talking about things? You know, boys and stuff."

"Sure. At the right times and places."

"I'll tell Lisa — Major Ka-markla. She's my body guard and facilitator, but probably can't do it all the time."

"Thanks. It would be pretty boring just sitting in the guard room."

Heather looked at her papers again.

"What're you working on?"

"Plans for remodeling this place. I want to have them in good shape by tomorrow. Sarah — Major Ma-soran — might have a cook by then, too."

At that moment, the five officers emerged from their conference. The sergeant and the corporal stood and saluted.

"At ease," General Bo-seklin said. "Start your tape recorder, Sergeant."

Everyone returned to their places in the meeting circle.

"We have agreed," General Ko-fenral began, "that this program is no longer probationary. That must be some kind of speed record for a program of this type."

Heather smiled.

"Colonel Ba-kerga?" the visiting general prompted.

The security chief cleared his throat. "What I have to say, my security people have heard, but it's worth repeating, and good for everyone to hear, especially after what happened yesterday and today."

He let a long moment pass.

"We have all just seen an example of how complex — and sensitive — the material in this program is going to be at times." He saw several heads nod. "Fact is, if you break secrecy in a normal top-secret program, you'll get a year or two in federal prison. But if you break secrecy in *this* program, I'll *make sure* they throw away the key. That applies to everyone — officers, enlisted personnel, little girls, *and* whomever you might have told."

Heather and George shared a moment of eye contact, and the girl nodded her acceptance of the warning.

"We have also developed a protocol," General Bo-seklin announced, "and will probably come up with more as time passes. This one, we all agree, is of supreme importance, and I think Heather will be able to join us in that opinion."

He looked all around the room before continuing.

"There will be NO actions taken, of *any* kind, based on *anything* that comes to light in this program, unless we have at least *three* votes to do so. There are four, and only four, possible votes — myself, General Ko-fenral who will not be here at every session but has clearance for all program records, the team as a whole, and Heather."

The girl's eyes widened slightly. "Yes, I can join you in that opinion."

"And one final thing," General Bo-seklin added. "We get all the money we need for remodeling."

"Whoopee!" the youngest person in the room cheered.

⁕ ⁕ ⁕

## Chapter 10: Getting Organized

"Good morning, Sarah," General Bo-seklin greeted cheerfully after arriving the following day. "For a while, those stairs seemed to be getting steeper all the time. Now they're easy again."

His executive officer smiled from her desk.

"What does our day look like?" he asked, going through the mail she handed him.

"Heather has completed the remodeling plans, and would like to meet with you at your leisure. She's out shopping with Major Ka-markla right now, back by thirteen hundred."

"Good. I want to spend the morning at the University. There's a physics professor who knows something about time travel and all that."

"Spooky stuff. I've started the paperwork on Heather's new legal name and I.D., which you'll have to sign."

"George is okay with that name?"

"Yes. He checked several databases, and didn't find any problems. Let me see . . . I'm interviewing a cook at fourteen hundred . . . Sergeant Ta-nibon is training the new security corporal . . . and George has a couple more coming in for interviews."

"Okay. Tell Heather fifteen hundred with me, as I want plenty of time to rattle doors at the University. What about lunch?"

"Lisa and Heather are bringing."

"Good. I'm gonna make some phone calls, then head out."

The general went into his office, closed the door, and imagined what it would look like with carpets and drapes, maybe even a little art on the walls.

*

". . . five years at the City Skyline Hotel as a sous-chef while I was in the reserves," the stout lady was explaining to Major Ma-soran when Heather grabbed a folding chair and sat down nearby, "then I decided to take some of those free classes at the air base, and got all kinds of security clearances. I didn't think anything would come of it, but suddenly I was offered a job in the P-Fourteen program. The new management at the Skyline was way too full of itself, so I accepted, and was there for two years, until the program shut down."

"Can you tell me a little about that program?" the major asked with a straight face.

The woman frowned. "No. I have no knowledge that you have P-Fourteen clearance."

Heather and Sarah exchanged smiles.

"Just testing," Major Ma-soran admitted.

"I figured that would come at some point."

"Heather, this is Maria Ta-benro. As far as I'm concerned, you're hired, Maria, but Heather has a test for you, something she got from a television show."

"*Chef versus Chef*," the girl revealed.

The woman grinned. "One of my favorites!"

Heather hopped up. "I'll go get your box ready!"

When the girl had disappeared into the dining room, the applicant looked at the major. "And Heather is?"

"Your supervisor, assuming you pass her test and the two of you get along."

The candidate raised her eyebrows.

✳

When Maria stepped into the dining room and saw the kitchen, her face fell.

Heather knew it would happen, and was ready with catalogs open at one of the dining tables.

Maria nearly drooled when she saw pictures of the stainless-steel professional equipment. "Six burners, grill, salamander, and convection oven. Sweet. And *two* big refrigerators!"

"The one with glass doors will go over here for stuff you want people to just serve themselves," Heather explained, indicating a place by the door, "and the other will be back there for your supplies."

"Okay, so we're just putting up with this old junk for a little while . . ."

"Right. We're also getting three big pantry cabinets, all new tables and counters, and serving line warmers."

"Excellent. Floor?"

Heather pointed to another catalog. "This beautiful tile, with as many rubber mats as you want."

Maria smiled. "And you would be my supervisor?"

Heather blushed. "I guess so. I just want lots of good, healthy food. Junk food is okay once in a while, but I really want to avoid the usual over-cooked military . . . stuff."

"Okay, I see that in my test box — vegetables, real cheese, organic eggs, whole-grain macaroni, fruit and yogurt.  Looks like I get to be a chef again!  How many am I cooking for?"

"Dinner time . . . I bet the officers will hang around to try it . . . seven or eight, counting you."

Maria fell silent and began seeing what she had to work with, quickly locating knives, cutting boards, pans, and spices.

Heather watched for a while, and was quite amazed when Maria started slicing vegetables and sautéing them in a hot frying pan with a little butter and garlic.  But the girl soon heard Major Ma-soran's voice announcing it was time for her meeting with the general.

*

"The physicist with time-travel theories is a little wacky," General Bo-seklin admitted once the two of them were together in his office with the door closed.

"Isn't that almost necessary for working in a program like this?"

He glanced at her.  "I see your point.  Thing is, the military's been looking for people with abilities like yours for *years*.  The Beklan Empire seems to find them, but we just kept coming up with kooks and wannabes . . . until you.  So we never really got around to assembling any real, working teams.  From this point on, we're in uncharted territory.  As a result, we don't know who to grab from the universities.  I think the physicist will be okay, but the psych people were *terrible*, babbling stuff about mandatory reporting to the police when they hear of any kid not attending school . . ."

Heather started laughing.  "I should take the Graduate Entrance Exam — no, make it the Doctoral Entrance Exam — so we'll be safe!"

"Good idea.  I'll have Sarah arrange that.  But I did finally locate a shrink that will qualify for the clearance, I believe.  She'll have to sit through George's lectures, of course."

"You mean the *throw away the key* lecture and the *little girl running the meeting* scenario?"

Sam smiled and nodded.  "Okay, let's go through your plans, phase by phase."

She set a sheet of paper with lists and sketches in front of the general.  "Phase One is removing everything we don't absolutely need that is being scrapped or replaced — suspended ceiling in the big room, most of the old furniture . . ."

*

Maria lightly coated each serving of tasty casserole with hollandaise sauce, then topped each with a little shredded cheese.  The leafy lettuce salad included several other finely-sliced vegetables and was finished with a tangy dressing.  Finally, the frozen yogurt parfait was soft and spoonable, she explained, because she had blended in fresh fruit before freezing.

General Bo-seklin stayed to try everything, even though he and his wife were going out that evening.  He looked at his executive.

Major Ma-soran looked around the dining room and saw thumbs up from all the security people.  Finally, she looked at Heather.

"When can you start?" the girl asked Maria Ta-benro.

*

Heather immediately became Maria's favorite supervisor of all time by doing the dinner dishes.  The security people pitched in, and with Maria handling the left-overs, the kitchen and dining room were quickly rendered spotless.

After sponging out the sink, Heather grabbed a towel to help Lisa with the drying.  "I know it's short notice, but . . . anyone want to go skating?  Or at least, take me?"

"I'm supposed to be off duty, but I must admit, I don't have anything planned — don't *dare* plan anything until the colonel gets more people.  Corporal Do-forva is staying here tonight, but I do want to train her on outing protocols.  We don't have to skate, right?"

"Nope.  I've never been to this rink, but you can usually watch everything from the snack bar."

"Okay, let's do it.  Corporal Do-forva!  We're going skating!"

*

The security ladies changed into civilian clothes, and both had shoulder purses that held the usual things in one compartment and their side arms in the other.

Corporal Do-forva and the two security men-in-training witnessed the exit procedure for the first time, with Sergeant Ta-nibon operating the electric gate only after checking the road outside for anything of concern.

"Girls' night out!" Heather declared from the front passenger seat of Lisa's car.

"Why didn't we use the blind transport?" the corporal asked from the back seat.  "I thought safe-house guests weren't supposed to know where this place is."

Lisa and Heather both laughed.

"Heather technically isn't a safe-house guest," Lisa explained.  "She's an independent contractor, and has full program clearance."

"Oh."

"But even with all that, she *should* still use the blind transport."  Lisa glanced in the rear-view mirror and saw Ginny's confusion.  "The deciding factor is that Heather already figured out *exactly* where we are!"

The corporal laughed.

*

The two security guards, officer and enlisted, appearing to be the skater's mother and sister, nonchalantly strolled the entire skating rink while Heather waited in line for rental skates.  They didn't see anything that bothered them in the layout or the people.  The few other non-skaters were hiding in the snack bar, so the pair eventually headed that way.

With ice-cold drinks in hand, they found a couple of seats that overlooked the rink and noticed Heather stretching in a carpeted corner.

"Our primary strategy is to maintain the impression that she's just a normal kid," Lisa began, "athletic and sociable, but otherwise unremarkable."

Ginny nodded.  "That would almost be assumed about any athletic person."

"Yeah, Colonel Ba-kerga says it'll make our task a breeze as long as Heather plays along."

"Does she show any signs of . . . bragging?"

"Not yet.  Remember, there's an eighty-seven-year-old mind in that little head."

"She's on the floor now," Ginny observed, "just getting used to the skates, I think."

"Remember, her name is Priscilla Ka-mentha out here.  She'll have I.D. soon, and we'll have guardianship documents, but the colonel wants us to avoid flashing those, or our military I.D., unless necessary."

"Makes sense."

"She worked with the colonel to highlight a map you need to study that shows all the places she used to frequent.  Those are off-limits for a year or two, and he's gonna meet with her mother before they start visiting so she doesn't create any security problems."

Ginny nodded.  "Being tall for her age, she'll be attracting boys in a few years, and already has an eye for *them*."

"I know.  I had to make a rule about Ben, and it will apply to all the new security guys."

Ginny chuckled.  "She's getting comfortable out there and has joined the good skaters in the middle."

"I'm sure she'll have the place wrapped around her little finger in a few weeks."

"What're our rules of engagement?"

"Handle everything as discretely as possible, but in a pinch, no limits.  The colonel switched to that level after . . . the thing with the president.  He may be an ornery old grump, but he knows his job."

The corporal laughed.  "I'll keep your exact words to myself."

"Thanks."

"Clear the floor!" the D.J. announced.  "Art and dance skaters only!"

They watched as Heather began to skillfully move her feet to the music while going forward or backward.

"I thought so," Lisa said less than a minute into the song.  "Her skating's up there with her dancing. And look, she's got admirers already."

"Should we be worried?"

"Not as long as it's on the social level. This, and other places she goes with one of us, is her entire life outside the facility.  Look how she's using her arms to go with the music, but not the large ballet-like movements that would be out of place here, and not for balance like most of the others."

"I can get around the rink, but not *that* gracefully!" the corporal admitted.

✳

After several songs for all skaters, the D.J. switched on his microphone again.  "Speed skaters only!"

"Look, she's doing that too!" Lisa noticed with surprise.

"And is keeping up with the best of them!" Ginny declared, "except that tall guy about my age."

"He's noticed her, and look, is inviting her to take the lead!"

"We'll have to keep an eye on him," the corporal said with slight worry.

"I've already spotted him being friendly but respectful with all the girls.  I think he's okay.  But *you* might want to catch his eye."

"I might be able to impress him with my target shooting, but not my skating!" Ginny declared.

✳

Once the session ended, the two security people found Heather, already in street shoes, gazing longingly into the glass case where all the items for sale were displayed.

"Hi Lisa, Ginny.  Guess what I'm getting with my first check!"

They followed her gaze to a pair of glittery purple dance skates, and both ladies whistled when they saw the price tag.

✳   ✳   ✳

## Chapter 11: Remodeling

The following morning at zero-nine hundred hours, four craftsmen arrived from the air base. Heather was ready with plans and checklists spread out on a table near the stairway, but knew she had to wait.

"Good morning, specialists," Major Ma-soran said, rising from her desk and striding into the main room.

They saluted.

"At ease. You fellows are cleared to work around classified programs, are you not?"

"Yes, Ma'am!"

"And you have greater rank and make more money because of that, do you not?"

"Yes, Ma'am!"

"So the fact that I have brown eyes is . . ."

"Top secret, Ma'am!"

She noticed the general observing from his doorway. "And the fact that General Bo-seklin has gray hair is . . ."

"Top secret, Ma'am!" they said through smiles.

"And the fact that the person in charge of this remodeling project is seven years old, is . . ."

"Top secret, Ma'am!" they said with wide eyes, glancing at the little girl in old jeans and a T-shirt.

"Good. She knows this place, she knows the plans, and she's fun to work with, but neither she, nor I, will put up with any disrespect."

The major strode away as quickly as she had come, disappearing into the general's office and closing the door.

With four young men looking at her, Heather giggled and blushed. "Um . . . gosh . . . let me see . . ." She found the sheet of paper she wanted, and tried to recover. "This is a classified program that meets in the morning, so after today, you can't arrive before noon.  You can eat lunch here if you want, even dinner.  I want you to be happy, well-fed, and proud of your work."

They nodded with appreciation.

"I'll be working right with you, but I can't do heavy stuff . . ."

Two of them dramatically flexed their arm muscles.

Heather smiled and grabbed another sheet.  "Phase One is getting rid of some old stuff.  See that suspended ceiling?  It goes."

They wandered around the room and looked it over.  "No problem," one said.  "In the side rooms, too?"

"No, they have hard ceilings.  But I want you to remember, every minute you're working, that the log trusses and boards up there are going to remain visible when you're done, so you have to *carefully* remove every screw so you do as little damage as possible.  Can do?"

"It'll be slower that way."

"Not a problem."

"Okay, sure.  The base loves it when we salvage stuff."

"Let's start over here with the outer office, so we have to move the major's and colonel's desks into the big room . . ."

✳

They cleared the office of furniture while Heather got the little stuff, then brought in ladders.  The electrician was up in the ceiling first, disconnecting the old light fixtures.  Heather received ceiling panels as they were handed down, stacking them near the stairs.

By noon, with the desks replaced, Major Ma-soran could look up and see varnished logs and stained boards instead of dingy white panels.  She smiled at the general, who watched the process from his office door.

✳

The four men and Heather were working their way across the big room in the middle of the afternoon when the test proctor arrived from the air base, a squirrelly little man with glasses.

"I am supposed to administer . . . let me see . . . this is quite unusual . . . a Doctoral Entrance Exam."

Major Ma-soran welcomed him.  "Sorry about the construction work.  There's a conference room over here you can use."

They walked that way.

As soon as he sat down, he wasted no time.  "Name and rank of the applicant?"

"No name, no rank, this is an unofficial, unrecorded test."

"I *cannot* proctor a test without filling in all the blanks on the form!" he asserted.

The major sighed.  "Jane Doe, cadet."

"The Doctoral Entrance Exam can *only* be taken by commissioned officers who have documentation of a master's degree."

She let a long moment pass and took a deep breath.  "You haven't worked around classified programs before, have you, Lieutenant?"

"No."

"Don't worry, you won't be working around them in the future, either."

He was clearly flustered as she led him back out to the stairway. "Sergeant, exit procedure for the lieutenant."

Heather, carrying an armload of old ceiling panels, exchanged smiles with Sarah.

The lieutenant wore a frown of worry as he descended the stairs.

When he was gone, the general stepped out of his office. "I think I might have a solution."

By the end of the week, the suspended ceiling was gone. At dinner on Friday, Heather sat with the craftsmen to talk about Phase Two, walls and light fixtures. They took the color swatches and model numbers, planning to get all the materials on Monday before arriving.

That evening, to celebrate, Heather dragged the tumbling mat into the big room under the newly-liberated log trusses. She danced for the security people until she was exhausted, curled up on a couch at about nine o'clock, and was instantly asleep.

## Chapter 12: The First Envelope

After a Saturday spent with Ginny hiking along forest trails, eating pizza, and window-shopping, Heather was thinking of sleeping half the day on Sunday.

To her surprise, the entire P-Seventeen team began arriving shortly after ten o'clock, including Maria the new cook.  They pretended to ignore Heather, still in pajamas, as they carried bags and boxes to the dining room, but she noticed barely-suppressed grins.  She slipped away and quickly dressed, wondering what was up.

When she returned to the main room, everyone was lounging around on couches, but she noticed something new.  The little four-drawer mailbox that used to perch on the corner of Sarah's desk had been replaced by a huge new one with at least a dozen drawers.

With a smile, Major Ma-soran dangled a shinny new key.

Heather came near. "Mine?"

Sarah nodded.

With slightly-nervous fingers, the girl took the key, then approached the new mailbox with some hesitation.

The officers all had drawers, and Maria even had one.  But none of them said *Heather* or *Priscilla*.  Part of her — the seven-year-old part — wanted to pout.

Then she noticed a tiny label on the bottom drawer that bore the single letter *H*, and realized the possible danger of displaying her name — any of her names — when people without clearance were in the building.

She put her key in the bottom lock, and it opened.

Then she nearly jumped through the ceiling as party horns and poppers started going off behind her.  She turned to see Maria entering the room with a platter bearing a small cake, upon which danced three little candles.  Lisa, Ben, and Ginny came behind with bowls of ice cream.

"Wow!  Every kid's dream — cake and ice cream for breakfast!"

"Not *every* kid," the general began, "gets the things in their mail drawer that *you* just got."

Heather turned back, and indeed there were two envelopes in her drawer. The first said *Priscilla Ka-mentha*.  She opened it to find a check for half her first month's pay, and an I.D. card.

When she looked at them again, her eyes were no longer dry.  "You . . . really do . . . believe in me."

The ladies in the room were grinning and nodding, but the general cleared his throat.  "Of course, there is another side to getting a check for more than two grand."

Heather blinked to clear her eyes, then looked at the second envelope, labeled *P-17 — Topic 3 — 22 October 3662*.  "That's tomorrow."  She opened it, read the type-written sentence, and noticed Sam's and Sarah's initials underneath.  "Oh, that'll be interesting, and not too deep, but slightly challenging for the team.  Good choice."

"Now I'm absolutely *sure* you're the real deal," Major Ma-soran declared, "as no seven-year-old, and few adults, would have the *slightest* idea what that topic was about."

Heather smiled, slipped the sheet back into its envelope, and went to blow out her three candles, then eat cake and ice cream for breakfast.

❋

After the party wound down, Maria made Heather and the security guards some scrambled eggs and toast.  Even as the girl nibbled on her eggs, she became distant and thoughtful.

The officers and cook departed, except Major Ka-markla, on duty that day. She noticed Heather get a note pad and wander into the back of the building.

About an hour later, the new man on the security team found Heather sitting on the table in the inspection room, several sheets of notes spread out in front of her.

"Hi, Matthew."

"Is this a good thinking room?"

"Yeah.  Very quiet, cooler than upstairs."

He left her to her work.

Two hours after that, Lisa finally discovered Heather in the bomb shelter, on a bunk, scribbling away, with seven or eight sheets scattered on the floor.

"Hi, kid."

"Hi, Lisa," she said while continuing to make notes.

"I didn't realize your preparation time would be so intense."

"Neither did I.  I think it'll get easier as we go, but there's so much the team doesn't know yet."

The major swallowed.  "Um . . . we have a request.  We want you to tell someone when you're coming downstairs.  I know you want the run of the place, and I can understand that, but we're supposed to be protecting you, and that could be hard if we don't know where you are."

"Yeah, sorry.  That's reasonable.  I will."

"Thanks."

Heather suddenly tossed the note pad aside.  "I think I'm about as ready as I can be, except, you know, lots of dancing to clear my head.  What's for dinner?"

*

The next morning, after several dances in the recreation room while the security people arranged the couches for the meeting, Heather pranced into the dining room to find Maria serving a hearty breakfast.  She filled her plate, then noticed the general sitting with two people she didn't recognize.

"Good morning, Sam.  May I sit with you guys?"

The young woman of about twenty-five on the general's right looked a little timid, almost mousy, but made friendly eye contact.  The man on the general's left, maybe forty, had an angular face and didn't look directly at anyone.

"Sure, Heather!  I heard music coming from the rec room.  Was that you?"

She smiled.  "Who else?"

He laughed.  "Heather, this is Susan Bo-kamla, psychologist, and Richard Tu-feltin, historian."

"And you must be . . ." the man began, not quite looking at her, ". . . let me guess . . . the general's daughter."

Sam laughed again.  "Thanks, Richard, but I have *grandchildren* older than Heather!"

"I'm not related to Sam," she revealed, "but he'd be a wonderful father or grandfather to have."

"Why, thank you, Heather!"

Between bites, Heather experimented by silently stretching her arms over her head.  She noticed Sam and Susan glance up, but not Richard.

"So . . ." the historian continued the guessing game, ". . . you must be the daughter of one of the other officers."

Heather chuckled.  "Mmm!  These hash browns are delicious!"

*

At the end of breakfast, the general had to confer with his executive about something, and the new psychologist busied herself collecting all the dirty dishes on the table, so Heather stepped beside the historian and offered her arm.  "May I guide you to the meeting circle?"

"You're very observant, young lady," he said, taking her arm lightly, "but I don't understand how a little girl could be in the building during a top-secret meeting.  They practically went to the cemetery to interview my dead parents before letting *me* come!"

Heather chuckled again.

*　*　*

## Chapter 13: Session Three

"Program P-Seventeen, Session Three, twenty-two October 3662, zero-nine hundred hours, twelve minutes," Ben announced for the tape.

"Good morning, everyone," Heather began.  "This session should be a little more relaxed than the last one."

Nervous laughs came from most people in the room as they remembered the assassination of the president, and their feelings and attitudes immediately following.

After all the military people had stated their names, the security chief added, "Also in the building is Maria Ta-benro, the new cook.  Everyone has proper clearance, including the two who have not yet been introduced."

"Susan, would you tell us about yourself?" Heather requested.

The woman had been looking at Heather with confusion, but managed to find her voice when asked to speak.  "I . . . just completed my doctorate in psychology.  My . . . um . . . dissertation was on mental states found in extremely stressful environments, like . . . um . . . refugee camps, and how counseling services can be provided to those persons."

"Thank you.  Richard?"

He smiled at Heather without quite looking at her.  "Doctor of History, specializing in recent and current events.  Co-chair of the History Department at the University.  Married, two children."

"Thank you, and welcome to the team.  You are both very brave for agreeing to the terms of umbra clearance."

They, and others in the room, chuckled.

"I've already explained to them," the general mentioned, "that our format does not allow interruptions during the main presentation."

Heather nodded and closed her eyes.

*

"Two years ago, the Trilbourne Accord was signed by the confederation of island nations in the Southern Ocean that had, until then, remained completely neutral and open to trade and tourism by anyone in the world. It was drafted behind closed doors, and its signing was barely noticed by the media. Within a week, everyone had forgotten about it, except those directly involved."

Heather found the type-written sheet in her stack of notes. "Specifically, today's topic is *Will the Trilbourne Accord be effective in achieving its goals?* This topic has several purposes. First, it's a test of me. Hardly anyone knows about the Accord, and it's too new to be in that dusty encyclopedia in the conference room."

Both General Bo-seklin and Major Ma-soran smiled.

Heather noticed a concerned look on Lisa's face. "Don't worry," Heather began, "I don't mind being tested. The quicker I can establish a track record, the better this team will function."

Lisa nodded.

"Second, it's a small topic, easy to talk about, and fairly non-controversial. That's good for the team right now, as we still have many things to learn . . . about what we're trying to do here."

Colonel Ba-kerga, somewhat to Heather's surprise, nodded agreement.

"Third, it will introduce a few concepts that will be . . . um . . . challenging to some of you. People in the future often know things that are hidden in the present."

She could clearly see uncomfortable looks on several faces. The new psychologist, however, was listening intently. Heather took a deep breath.

"The Trilbourne Accord never fulfills it's *stated* purpose because it was not designed nor intended to. It does, however, fulfill its *real* purpose for a few decades, and is then tossed into history's dustbin, along with many other such trade agreements."

The rumble in the room was almost a growl. Heather waited patiently with a calm, neutral expression. Eventually, everyone fell silent.

"Do you know what a *wealth pump* is?" she asked the entire room.

Most faces showed complete ignorance. The historian wore a thoughtful expression.

"Okay, basic structure of empires." She looked around. "Um . . . um . . . portable blackboard from the conference room. Sorry I didn't think of it sooner."

Two security guards hopped up to fetch it.

While they were gone, Colonel Ba-kerga strode to his desk, returned with a camera, and handed it to Sergeant Ta-nibon at the tape recorder. "No erasing until it's photographed."

Heather nodded as the blackboard was brought in and placed against the wall.

"Every empire has a heartland or core, which receives the primary benefits of being an empire. Outside that, usually close geographically, but not always, is the inner circle of allies. They are fairly powerful themselves, so the imperial core can't extract much from them — usually one to five percent of their wealth. Finally, farther away, are the external tributaries, also called subject nations. They get sucked dry, in the ten to fifty-percent range."

She stopped drawing and turned to face the circle. "I know exactly what you're all thinking right now. Sarah, would you give voice to the thought in the room, please?"

"But even as I think it," the executive officer admitted, "I know in the pit of my stomach that it's probably wrong."

"Good, but please say it anyway."

"Um . . . we're not an empire."

"Did she capture everyone's reaction?" Heather asked, looking at the entire team.

Most heads nodded.

"Okay, let's review a few facts," the girl said, turning to the blackboard and drawing a funnel shape. "We currently have about six percent of the world's population, and consume about twenty-five percent of the world's wealth. By the end of the century, our population will be four percent, and our wealth consumption thirty percent."

The room was filled with a tense silence.

"General, how many military bases do we have on foreign soil?"

He swallowed to moisten his dry throat. "About a hundred."

"By the end of the century, there will be more than two hundred. That, ladies and gentlemen, is the basic structure, and the essential definition, of *empire*."

She looked at the historian, and saw intense fascination on his face.

✳

"Just so you know, the Beklan Empire also does not call itself an empire, so its common people have no idea they live in one."

The historian nodded.

"The Trilbourne Accord is simply *not* a free-trade agreement. Those island nations had free trade for *centuries* before the Accord. They chose, of their own free will, to produce a small number of high-quality works of art and craft, and charge high prices for them. We and our allies didn't like that. It made *them* money, not us. Three years ago, we sent a battleship to visit them, even though that was illegal in their waters under their laws. But they had no way to respond militarily. They had, and still have, little more than canoes and spears."

She could see most of her listeners trying to understand, but struggling against past assumptions.

"The Trilbourne Accord is a *wealth pump*. Under implied threat of military force, in the thin disguise of so-called free trade, it transfers as much as possible of the wealth of those islands to our imperial core. The quality of the arts and crafts produced there has begun to fall and will continue to do so, as well as the standard of living of the people.  In a decade, the growing poverty will hurt the tourist trade, and in three decades, few people will visit and the arts and crafts will be forgotten."

Several faces in the room wore frowns.

"Eventually, we will write them off, cancel the treaty, and they will be rid of us.  But they will be a broken people, pushed back to stone-age grinding poverty."

She let a long moment of silence pass.

"That's how empires work.  I am not advocating *for* those island nations, nor *against* us.  If those craftsmen and fishermen someday managed to create an empire, they would do the same thing to others.

"The important thing, for this team to begin to learn, is how to step back and view events from a perspective not much different from God's.  Only then will you be able to handle, without catastrophic results, knowledge of the future."

*

"Are we *always* going to feel this small after your presentations?" General Bo-seklin asked when Heather opened the session to questions.

She smiled with sympathy.  "For a while, then you'll get the hang of it and help me analyze things."

The doctor of history raised his hand.

"Richard?"

"I've studied the Trilbourne Accord in depth, and don't remember anything about a battleship."

"Probably top secret," Sarah suggested.

"I . . . think I know someone who can find out," the general pondered with a frown.

"That would be a nice verification of my memories," Heather said, "but please be careful."

"I will.  Actually, you can't send a battleship somewhere without lots of people knowing."

"And I'd just like to say," Richard went on, "that even without the battleship, the thing stank of back-room arm twisting, so I wouldn't be surprised if Heather's analysis turns out to be completely accurate."

Everyone absorbed the historian's words in thoughtful silence.  The psychologist's hand crept up timidly.

"Susan?"

"So . . . you're not in favor of helping the people who . . . got the raw end of . . . that treaty?"

"No.  I love people, but I, and this team, can only learn how to handle the gift we've been given — knowledge of the future — if we step way, way back. No one can see a process clearly from the inside — in other words, while being involved with it.  You and Richard are going to listen to Sessions One and Two tomorrow morning, right?"

They both nodded.

"In Session Two, you'll learn why I didn't say anything about the assassination of the president before it happened.  Please make sure you understand those reasons well . . ."

*   *   *

# Chapter 14: Walls

"Session Three ends at eleven hundred hours, fifty-seven minutes.  This record includes one blackboard photograph."

"Mobile Construction Unit Five to facility," the radio in the outer office suddenly squawked, "we are three minutes away, and decided to accept that offer of lunch."

Corporal Do-forva hopped up to respond.

"Now Heather has to go to *work*, believe it or not," the general announced with a grin.

Everyone laughed and headed for the dining room, toward the aromas that had been making their mouths water for the last half hour.

Heather returned the general's grin.  "The construction guys are fun, and I can stop to dance or do other things any time I want."

"How about a Doctoral Entrance Exam?" he asked, still smiling.  "I had Doctor Bo-kamla bring one."

Susan, listening to the exchange, blushed at one of the first uses of her new title.  "But . . . that test requires a month or more of study . . ."

"Do you really think so," the general asked with raised eyebrows, "after seeing Heather lead that meeting?"

"Um ... maybe not ..." the psychologist replied, looking at the seven-year-old who appeared quite willing to take a Doctoral Entrance Exam cold.

"People without program clearance entering the building!" Corporal Do-forva yelled before heading downstairs.

*

In the dining room, the historian was frustrated by not being able to continue discussing the morning's topic.

"Even if the construction guys weren't here," Colonel Ba-kerga explained, "we need to get any serious discussions onto the taped record."

"In academia, ideas evolve at the water cooler, on the phone, in notes stuck in each other's mailboxes, even on the tennis court . . ."

"If we were just working with ideas," Major Ma-soran said, "that might be possible.  But in *this* program, we're playing with fire."

The historian frowned, but a moment later he nodded agreement.

✳

Heather and the four craftsmen ate quickly while they conferred, then left the dining room.

After General Bo-seklin finished a leisurely lunch, he discovered his desk, chair, and filing cabinet in the middle of the big room.  Stepping to his office door, he beheld the craftsmen laying down drop cloths, removing the old fluorescent lights, chipping at rough spots on the walls, and sanding. Heather received a light fixture after it was removed by the electrician on a ladder.

She spotted the general.  "I decided today would be fine for that test, since tomorrow will be a prep day.  These guys know what they're doing, and are gonna go room by room."

"I'll see if I can tear Doctor Bo-kamla away from Maria's apple pie."

Heather laughed and carried the old fixture to the pile by the stairs.

✳

"This is an informal test," Susan began after they settled into folding metal chairs in the conference room, "and will not be recorded anywhere, as that would mean putting your name into several databases, from where it would get into countless more."

"Not okay," Heather said flatly.

"That's what I understand.  So I will just be verbally giving General Bo-seklin the results, and he will attest to your . . . um . . . *educational equivalency* . . . for anyone who needs to know, but there will be no other record or evidence."

"That sounds like the best we can do."

"This test has four parts, each of which has a one-hour time limit."

Heather received the first test booklet, scratch paper and pencil, and went to work.

Less than half an hour later, a knock was heard.  "I need to ask Heather a question," came the voice of one of the craftsmen.

Susan opened the door a crack.  "She's taking a test."

"I'm in charge of the remodeling," Heather asserted from the table, "so I'll have to multi-task a little."

The psychologist thought about it.  "You can speak to her briefly in my presence, but you cannot show her any written materials."

The craftsman quickly put the papers he was carrying behind his back. "Um . . . we're about to put up the new lights, and the installation diagram says they point down, but I remember you saying something about that."

"Yeah, we're using them as indirect lighting, to bounce off the ceiling, so they point up."

"Thanks," he said, and wandered away, looking thoughtfully at the diagram.

When Heather took a stretch break between tests, she noticed that the general's office had been put back together. People were wandering by to admire the dusty green walls and blue trim, and the craftsmen were busy moving the outer office furniture.

At her next break, the office was done and the dining room tables were in the big room where Heather knew they would remain for several days.

Doctor Bo-kamla handed the general a hand-written sheet of paper without any names or signatures. "It would be hard to believe these scores if I hadn't proctored the test myself."

"I don't plan to ever use the actual scores. These are all passing, I presume . . ."

"Oh, sorry. Normally, it's up to the college. Most draw the line at six hundred, a few elite schools at seven hundred."

The general looked over the four numbers, all in the upper seven-hundreds. "So . . . a person might get scores like this if they already *had* a doctoral degree?"

The psychologist nodded slowly.

The general took several slow breaths to help him adsorb the evidence in his hands, then sighed. "How do you like being on the team?"

"I feel like a fish out of water."

"We all do, believe me, Doctor Bo-kamla. We all do."

By dinner time, the senior officers had gone home. The four craftsmen finished the dining room walls, then moved the old kitchen equipment to that end of the room. Heather made sure it was all arranged so Maria could function for two days while the kitchen itself was refinished.

When the workers were finally gone, Heather plopped onto a couch. "Why do I feel exhausted?"

Lisa chuckled as she wandered over from the office. "You had a big day."

"That test was a very strange experience. Many times I was about to pick one answer, then had to remind myself what year this is."

"So . . . knowledge is relative to the time period?"

"In some ways, yes. The basic math and science stays the same, but stuff on the edge of knowledge, like how the universe formed and how genetics works — that stuff is changing rapidly. I happen to know that we share most of our D.N.A. base pair sequences with all other animals, even insects. No one would believe that in 3662."

"What's D.N.A.?"

"Deoxyribonucleic acid, the molecule that encodes genetic information."

"Oh."

"And *of course* the social sciences swing every which way over time, and then swing back again! But Sam said I passed, so I'm happy."

"This was supposed to be your unwinding time.  Wanna get out of here?"

"Yeah!  I have a vision of the future, about half an hour from now, and in my vision I see a banana split."

"I know just the place!"

* * *

## Chapter 15: Knowledge

With the large central room now serving as both meeting room and dining room, Heather's couch was in the corner near the old conference room. She knew she had worn herself out the previous day when she didn't wake up until both Sarah and George were busy at their desks. She wandered over in pajamas. "Is it really morning?"

Sarah smiled at the seven-year-old. "Did someone burn the candle at both ends yesterday?"

Heather nodded.

George cleared his throat. "Got some new rules for you, young lady."

She sat down in front of his desk.

"Today, for the first time, you'll be preparing for a session while non-program people are in the building."

"Yeah. I was wondering about that."

"Here's what we came up with. While you're working with a note pad, non-program people can't be in the same room with you. If you need to confer with them, even work with them, hand your note pad to a security person, or lock it in your mail drawer."

Heather nodded. "Doable."

"I'll tell the workers," Colonel Ba-kerga concluded, then turned his attention to something on his desk.

"I'm constantly amazed," Sarah began, "how grown-up you think and talk, Heather."

"I never really had a childhood. I could observe and analyze all my own developmental stages when I was a baby. Now, I can watch other children play, and join in for very short periods without them getting suspicious, but all the while I'm aware of the psychological functions of play, so I'm never really *playing*, with my whole heart and mind, like they are."

"Do you regret that . . . trade-off?"

Heather was silent for a moment. "On reflection . . . no. But it's a long way from here to . . . creating a team that can join me in the work I must do."

"You'll be patient with us, I hope."

Heather smiled and sighed. "I'll try."

"Got your envelope?"

Sarah saw the mind and heart of the seven-year-old in full control for a moment as Heather's eyes sparkled with curiosity and she dashed back to her corner to get her shiny new key.

Maria was walking on air all day long as she cooked in her make-shift kitchen and watched the craftsmen transform the other end of the room, first with paint, then light fixtures, and finally the most beautiful floor tiles.

Only two more days, she reminded herself, until the new equipment and tables arrived.

"Good morning, everyone," Heather said from her couch on Wednesday morning. "There are now *three* of you sharing a ride here in a blind transport. Please tell us about yourself, Doctor Po-selem."

"Please, call me *Chris*," begged the only person in the room with wild hair. "Physics is my game, has been all my life. I'm *thrilled* to be part of something that needs to know about time travel. I'm also fascinated by *you*, young lady. At breakfast, I spotted from a mile away that you are *not* seven years old, even though you look the part."

She grinned. "Actually, most people guess eight, sometimes nine."

He laughed deeply.

"The main presentation today will be short," Heather began, "as we want plenty of time for discussion. The topic was especially chosen to get Doctor Po-selem — Chris — sharing his thoughts and theories with us."

She relaxed and closed her eyes for a minute.

"*How do you know your knowledge of the future is accurate?*" she read. "*Might it be of some other reality, such as a parallel universe? Could any actions by you in the past, or any of us in the future, cause your knowledge to become inaccurate?*"

Heather looked around the circle and saw discomfort with the questions on several faces, especially the women, but the physicist appeared ready to do handsprings.

"I had an easy day prepping yesterday," she admitted, "and got to lay tile in the kitchen with the guys."

The mood in the room lightened.

"I must admit, I look forward to getting a philosopher on the team . . ."

"Working on it," General Bo-seklin slipped in.

"I know someone!" Doctor Po-selem volunteered. "I'll talk to him as soon as . . . oops, I forgot. No, I won't talk to him. Not one word. Ever."

Heather grinned and Colonel Ba-kerga gave the physicist a stern look.

"Thanks, Sam," she said. "Maybe you could get that name from Chris."

The general nodded.

"So . . . playing philosopher temporarily . . . the word *knowledge* has a very strict definition, which I'm going to use today. To be *knowledge*, we have to *believe* it, we have to have *good reasons* for believing it, and it has to be *true* to the best of our ability to discern.

"Using that definition of *knowledge*, my so-called *knowledge of the future* may, or may not, be accurate."

She saw everyone paying close attention, especially Doctor Po-selem.

"Criterion One — yes, I do *believe* my knowledge is accurate, and is of *our* universe."

Several people nodded slightly.

"Criterion Two — are my reasons for so believing good enough? I guess that's up to the military, since they're paying the bills."

Doctor Po-selem threw back his wild hair and howled with laughter. Susan was leaning forward and paying close attention.

Heather smiled at the psychologist before continuing. "Here are some of my reasons. First, everything I remember about the future *fits* with the world I'm living in now. The places all have the right names, and the famous people are all the same. The social and political processes seem to be the same, and at the right places in their evolutions. Even though the person whose memories I have is a child at this point in time — a normal child without any knowledge of the future — she will read about events of this time period, and earlier, in high school and college later on. Her education is supplemented, of course, by some direct memories, like seeing the president assassinated on television."

A moment of sadness came over the team.

"Those are my reasons for *believing* that my memories are accurate. They seem good to me. I cannot think of any more tests I can apply, other than the third criterion itself. If you think of any, please share them at the appropriate time."

She saw two or three pencils go to work.

"Criterion Three — are they *true* to the best of our ability to discern? This is where my track record comes in. I imagine having a score board, like at a ball game, on the wall somewhere in here." She looked around, as if to pick a wall, but noticed Colonel Ba-kerga shaking his head sternly, so she flashed him a cheesy grin.

"One point for the battleship," General Bo-seklin interjected.

Heather licked her finger and drew a *one* in the air, but then stopped and frowned. "Maybe half a point, since that wasn't technically knowledge of the future, even though it only becomes publicly *known* in the future.

"But back to our questions. In the seven years before I came into this program, about a dozen major events happened that I knew beforehand were going to happen. My mother thought it was pretty weird that I was looking at the newspaper every day, while still in diapers . . ."

Chuckles came from all around the circle.

"Unfortunately, none of those predictions were documented, so they don't count for anyone but me. In the twelve days I've been here, we've had one event that I was able to document, about ten seconds before it happened." She made another mark in the air. "You'll hear about that on the Session Two tape, Chris."

"I'm doing that this afternoon."

Heather nodded. "I might be able to develop a good score more quickly by working in Crisis Mode and trying to predict every little thing, but we've already discussed why that's not going to happen, and wouldn't, in the long run, do our country or our world any good."

She was glad to see understanding nods from the general and executive officer.

"That leaves one more question." She grabbed the type-written sheet again. *"Could any actions by you in the past, or any of us in the future, cause your knowledge to become inaccurate?"*

Doctor Po-selem was almost off his couch with anticipation.

"This brings up the thorny question of how much effort it would take to change the future. In the previous seven years of my life, I tried very hard to conceal my . . . weirdness . . . but a few people did notice. My mother and I got very good at hurrying off to some appointment we didn't really have."

Several people chuckled.

"Did that change anyone's life, anyone's important *decisions*, enough to effect future events in any substantial way? I don't know. That's where I hope Chris can help us."

He looked ready to explode with thoughts and theories.

Heather continued speaking. "I never actually *told* anyone, including my mother, anything of substance about the future. Thinking about national and world events is not my mother's strong point. She's very good at putting on make-up."

Major Ma-soran smiled.

"I only shared with her my knowledge of a few minor, local things, like the fact that Pier Twelve Amusement Park was closing last year, so could we *please* go on the rides one more time before it suddenly, without warning, shut its gates. Those little predictions impressed my mother, but having a daughter who is weird, in any way, is sufficiently embarrassing that she was quite willing to keep it between the two of us."

Doctor Po-selem's hand was in the air like an excited schoolboy.

"Patience, my dear physicist," the seven-year-old scolded.

He slumped onto his couch and almost pouted.

Heather smiled at him. "And so, assuming I didn't do anything earlier to mess things up, that brings us to the questions that will probably keep this team awake at night. What will it take to change the future? Is it even possible? Do we need to guard against the slightest slip, or will it take a major effort? And, most importantly I think, how do we figure out *what* to do if we decide some future event needs changing?  Would it be the most obvious, direct action, or would something more subtle be better?"

She could hear deep breathing all around the circle.

"My presentation is over, but I want Chris to just listen while everyone else gets a chance to throw out questions and comments."

Heather could see Sarah trying hard to hold in a smile.

✳

General Bo-seklin began the discussion by asserting that until an explicit decision to the contrary was made, even the *slightest slip* was a violation of top-secret-umbra security.

Colonel Ba-kerga nodded.

Several people complimented Heather on her analysis of the topic, but couldn't think of questions.

Major Ma-soran raised her hand.  "Has anything NOT happened that you believe should have?"

"No.  I've been able to find every major event in newspapers or news magazines, although my memory of *when* things should happen, has not always been perfect.  Gosh, we've been so busy, I forgot to ask if we could get newspapers in here . . ."

"Already sent in subscriptions to several," Sarah assured.

The room fell silent until Heather noticed that Susan the psychologist had anguish written all over her face.  The girl leaned forward and looked at the woman.  "I know you feel completely lost here, but believe me, we need you. You've listened to Session One, so you know what we have in common."

Susan dabbed at the tears that had gathered in her eyes.  "I thought I was going to counsel refugees, or something like that.  I know how to do that . . . at least, I think.  I don't know how to do this."

"Welcome to the club," the general said.

Many others echoed the same thought.

"I'd like to spend some time with you every week," Heather said.  "This program is as much about us, as people, as it is about the abstract work of studying the future."

After a few moments to collect herself, Doctor Bo-kamla agreed.  After all, she admitted, there weren't any refugees who needed her services at this time.

✳

Eventually Heather looked at Doctor Po-selem.  "Thank you for being patient, Chris."

"Thanks for making me be patient.  I know now that the team-building process going on here is as important as the technical stuff . . . maybe more important."

Heather and several others nodded.

"And I'm honored to be part of it.  I'll try to keep the human aspect in mind as I talk, but if I get lost in my theories, please throw something at me."

"I will," Heather promised with a straight face.

He smiled.  "I think I should start by explaining the Time Traveler's Paradox."

"But I don't see how she fits the definition of a time traveler," Colonel Ba-kerga challenged.

"She fits it because when *anything* goes back in time, even just information, the paradox is operative.  That's the main reason, television shows notwithstanding, that scientists believe time travel into the past is impossible.  Travel into the future does not create the paradox, just as long as . . . you never come back."

He saw that he had their undivided attention.

"Okay, imagine that you go back in time, even just one minute, and stop yourself from going back in time.  In a more extreme case, you could kill the earlier *you*, or if you go back far enough, one of your ancestors.  In any case, if you stop *you* from going back in time, then you wouldn't be going back in time to stop *you* from going back in time!  Paradox!"

He could see them squinting and twisting their faces in thought.  Only Heather nodded with understanding.

"In Heather's case, her memories could allow her to find the source person, and somehow influence that girl's life so she doesn't *get* those memories.  How could Heather possibly have those memories in that case, the memories that allowed her to find the source person?  Hence, the Time Traveler's Paradox.  Scientists debate what would happen — Heather might lose her memories and become a normal seven-year-old girl . . . the universe might explode . . . no one knows."

He glanced at Heather and saw her mouth hanging open.  "I presume," he continued, "you haven't made any attempt to find the . . ."

"No, I haven't, and it would be nearly impossible because . . ."  Since he hadn't yet listened to Session One, she gave a brief summary of the memories she should have, but didn't.

"Fascinating!" the physicist blurted out, his eyes big and round.  "No biographical information.  Surgically removed.  That *would* be a fairly good protection against triggering the Paradox.  Not perfect, but good."

"So that would mean," Heather jumped in excitedly, "that God *knew* the Time Traveler's Paradox was a danger, so He censored my memories to remove that temptation!"

"But always remember," Doctor Po-selem added with a worried frown, "that if *anyone* ever went to the trouble of analyzing your memories enough to find the source person, the *least* that could happen would be that your memories would be changed, and very possibly erased."

"That . . . won't . . . happen," General Bo-seklin asserted more firmly than he had ever spoken about anything before.

⁎　⁎　⁎

## Chapter 16: Banking

The craftsmen checked the kitchen floor tiles, then got lunch and wandered out to the tables in the large room.  As soon as no one was watching, Maria danced around her make-shift kitchen with happiness for a moment.

Heather chatted with the men about the laundry room and sleeping rooms, which they expected to finish that day, easily.  Then she apologized, but absolutely *had* to get some other things done.

The foreman ruffled her hair.  "I *think* we can do our jobs without you . . . but you have to be here tomorrow to carry that new stove up the stairs for us!"

Heather grinned.  "I wouldn't miss it!"

Lisa wasn't surprised when the girl slipped into the seat beside her.  "I had a hunch we'd be going somewhere today."

"I need to open a bank account."

"Only if you want to do something with your paychecks."

"I do.  Lots of things."

The adults at the table laughed.

Sarah caught Lisa's eye.  "I have the guardianship documents — all the program officers and Corporal Do-forva."

Lisa nodded, then looked at Heather.  "Right after lunch?"

"Sure.  I just want to talk to Susan for a little while.  I think . . . we're going to need each other."

✳

The bank was happy to open a savings account for the little girl with her mother signing everything and making all the real banking decisions.

When Priscilla Ka-mentha presented her I.D. card and stated, in no uncertain terms, that only a checking account would be useful, and they'd be happy to go elsewhere if necessary, the account officer looked at Major

Ka-markla, in uniform.

The major nodded agreement with Priscilla, and the account officer quickly got her supervisor.

The account supervisor emphasized that *every* check would have to have her mother's signature.

When Major Ka-markla brought out the guardianship documents and revealed that there were actually *five* people who could each function as a guardian, the account supervisor didn't know what to do, so she got the branch manager.

The branch manager prepared five signature cards, but then stopped and explained that the account could not be opened until the signature cards were complete.

Major Ka-markla whistled.

General Bo-seklin, Colonel Ba-kerga, Major Ma-soran, and Corporal Do-forva, all in uniform, emerged from the waiting room and crowded around the account desk.

The branch manager looked up and swallowed.

Priscilla turned and looked at them with grateful eyes. "You guys are so sweet!"

"We were on our way to the air base," Sam explained as military I.D. cards were shown and signatures given, "and had a hunch one of our own would need a little back-up."

Sarah looked at Priscilla with smiling eyes. "In recent days, we've seen how dedicated you are to your work, even when that means juggling two or three projects at once."

"And it's a pleasure," George added, "to arrange security for someone who actually *cooperates* with us."

Ginny grinned. "And besides, you're an awesome skater!"

Everyone chuckled until the branch manager cleared her throat. "The minimum deposit to open an account is one hundred."

Priscilla pulled her first check from her shoulder purse. "What will the hold time be for this check?"

The woman raised her eyebrows at the size of the check, then remembered that a general and several other military people were still looking at her. "Well . . . um . . . it's a local check from the base, so . . . um . . . no hold time."

"Great! In that case, after you deposit it, I'll need a counter check to make a withdrawal!"

∗

With enough money in her purse to do a great deal of damage in any store, Heather scribbled a list as Lisa drove.

"There's a shopping center just down the road," the major offered.

"Not today, thanks. Mostly I want to work with the guys on the sleeping rooms. Tomorrow the new kitchen stuff's coming, so we won't get *anything* else done, and I'll have to prep for a session at the same time."

Lisa pointed the car back toward the facility.

Heather continued scribbling.  "Let me see, I owe Sarah for the record player, you for a bunch of stuff — I kept a list — and Ginny a little . . ."

❋

Lisa said good-night shortly after delivering Heather back to the facility.

The craftsmen, with help from their young supervisor, finished the safe-house sleeping rooms and departed.

Only Corporal Do-forva remained on duty.

Doctor Susan Bo-kamla, the psychologist on the team, arrived just as Heather was finishing dinner.  The three of them got slices of apple pie from the make-shift kitchen and sat down in the temporary dining room.

"Susan's agreed to be my therapist," Heather explained.  "I'm really glad I can talk to all of you — well, I have to be a little careful with George . . ."

Ginny smiled with understanding.

". . . but I need someone who really knows how to spot mental ruts I might be getting into.  I hope you understand," she said, looking at Ginny.

"Completely!" the corporal assured the seven-year-old.  "And I promise you, the others do too.  We're all *amazed* at what you're doing.  Everyone — even the general — thought you'd just be making little predictions, you know, *next week someone's gonna highjack flight 123*, and we could do something about it, or not.  I've overheard the officers saying their heads are *spinning* with the new perspectives you're giving them."

"Well . . . they'll have to get their *own* therapists!"

Ginny and Susan both laughed.

"We'll probably meet in the bomb shelter — I promised Lisa I'd tell someone when going downstairs."

"Okay.  That's probably the best place for privacy."

Heather nodded.  "Mmmm, I love Maria's apple pie.  She's gonna be a very happy cook tomorrow!"

❋

Susan had never been fond of creepy basements, but as they descended the steep stone steps, she took Heather's word that it was completely bug-free and rodent-proof.

Heather gave a tour and explained all the supplies, but didn't ask the psychologist to crawl to the end of the long tunnel.

Susan looked askance at the porta-potty.  "Um . . . if it's okay with you . . . I'll use the one upstairs."

Heather snickered.  "As long as there's no radio-active fallout up there!"

They got comfortable at the table in the middle of the room.

"I'm going to need a friend who's not in the military," Heather began.

Susan nodded.  "That's what I'm here for."

"I do need a therapist, but I also need much more than that.  I need someone who will stick with me through thick and thin, help me at certain times when no one else will, and keep *everything* we talk about between you and me."

Susan smiled.  "That's what confidentiality is all about!"

"Before you make the final decision about being my therapist and ... friend ... I need to tell you two things.  All other details will be filled in as they become known."

"O . . . kay."

"There will come a time when the survival of our civilization will depend on my memories."

Susan's mouth suddenly became so dry, she couldn't have spoken even if she knew what to say.

"And at that time, I'm fairly sure the military will turn against me, and I will have to leave here, and do what needs to be done, by myself . . ."

✳   ✳   ✳

## Chapter 17: A New Kitchen

Heather's envelope on Thursday morning requested an overview of the country's relationship, over the next decade or two, with a small nation that had nuclear weapons.

She expected lots of topics like this.  They would allow her to impress the team with knowledge of things they thought were top secret, build a track record by predicting events in the near future, and slowly introduce more concepts they needed to know.  And such topics focused on the remainder of that century, which was naturally more interesting to the military than the distant future.

By noon, she was completely prepared for the following day's session.

*

The craftsmen ate lunch as if nothing special was happening, but everyone could see the big truck parked in front of the facility.  Maria could hardly stop grinning as she tended the make-shift serving line.

After lunch, the four men, with barely-hidden smiles, sauntered around the newly-tiled kitchen, rubbing their chins and exchanging opinions.

Heather finally called their bluff.  "Okay, guys, are we putting in kitchen equipment, or redoing more walls?"

They grinned.

Maria let out the breath she had been holding.

They brought up a powerful electric winch, then covered the stairs with a thick sheet of steel.  Ben and Matthew changed into work clothes, all six men put on leather gloves, and the first refrigerator was carried into position at the bottom of the stairs.

Wide cargo straps were carefully placed by the craftsmen and attached to the winch cable.  Everything was checked and double-checked.

"Gosh," the foreman said when all appeared to be ready, "we need one more helper, someone smart enough to press the green button when I say *go*, and red button when I say *stop*. No delays, no back-talk. I wonder who could handle that critical task . . ."

Heather grinned as she stepped to the winch. "Would you explain that again, Sergeant? It sounded pretty complicated."

The room erupted with laughter.

Once everyone got serious, the foreman checked the straps again, made sure all observers were safely out of the way, and said, "Go."

＊

As the huge refrigerator seemed determined to twist sideways, the process had to be stopped half a dozen times before the thing was finally upright on the second level. After the straps were removed, the six men made quick work of moving it to its new home in the kitchen. The foreman took measurements, the refrigerator was nudged into position, and Maria took over to prepare it for operation.

The second refrigerator, with glass doors, took even longer, and Heather was forced to put the winch into reverse a couple of times.

Finally, they brought the big stove to the base of the stairs. Heavier than the refrigerators, the winch moaned and groaned, but the big appliance stayed on course.

＊

All six men collapsed onto chairs or couches, extracted their sore hands from leather gloves, and gladly received the cold drinks Maria brought out.

"That was the worst of it," the foreman said. "The rest will be child's play." They all grinned at Heather.

She blushed.

Once everyone was refreshed, they brought up the three tall pantry cabinets, bulky but light, and the counters and work tables. Padding was placed on the stairs so the round dining tables could be rolled. Real wooden chairs with soft upholstery came next, followed by several wheeled kitchen carts.

Maria was so excited by the new furniture and appliances that she almost forgot to take the dinner casserole out of the oven. After everyone ate and most of them departed, she stayed for hours more, moving food into the new refrigerators and making sure everything was working perfectly.

When the cook finally went through the exit procedure at nearly midnight, the security guard made sure the electric gate was secure, then dashed upstairs to make himself a snack in the brand-new kitchen.

＊

Heather presented her memories of the future on Friday morning. The new philosopher, Doctor Larry Bo-leden, explained why one event that always followed another was not necessarily *caused* by the first event. They could just as easily both be caused by something else, with one coming to pass more quickly than the other by its nature.

Heather and Lisa did the lunch dishes as the craftsmen prepared to lay tile in the dining room. It went so quickly, with Heather's help, that by mid-afternoon the five had moved on to refinishing the little clinic tucked away in the far corner of the building.  The girl was visibly excited, as this was the first of three rooms that would soon become her private suite.

* * *

## Chapter 18: Good as Gold

"I've paid all my debts," Heather said, half to herself as she contemplated her to-do list while Lisa drove. "I can get purchase orders from Sarah for most of the little stuff the facility needs."

"We should set the date for the open house."

"Yeah ... the dance studio, my room ... carpet almost everywhere ... wood floors, furniture ... how about Friday in two weeks?"

Lisa nodded. "In the afternoon after the session?"

"Yeah."

"By the way, *where* am I going?"

"Oh, sorry. Stamp and coin place up here on the right."

*

"We have some nice sets of pretty stamps, young lady," the woman said in a sweet voice.

"Mom, didn't you say you were getting bullion precious-metal coins, things without numismatic value?"

Major Ka-markla tried to sound sure of herself. "That's right. Which ones would *you* buy, honey, if you had enough money?"

The clerk chuckled. "You'll have to save up your allowance for a *long* time to afford those, young lady!"

"I *know*. Oh, look, mom! One ounce gold coins! Those are the prettiest!"

Major Ka-markla figured out how many she could get with the thick wad of cash Heather had entrusted to her. She had to breathe for a moment to steady her nerves before making such a huge purchase, but wore a nonchalant expression as she spoke to the clerk.

The woman nodded and counted out the shiny yellow coins. "I wonder if one of these might be yours someday, young lady, maybe after mom sees a report card with straight A's."

Lisa hoped her maternal tone of voice was convincing. "She'd have to be very, very good before *that* happened!"

*

"Now, I know you don't have to tell me," Lisa said as she drove, "and I know your contract says you can do anything you want with your money, but gold is about the *last* thing I'd guess a seven-year-old would buy, so ... I presume its value is going to go up ... maybe, way up?"

Heather just smiled. "Girl knows future. Girl buys gold. Girl's friends *might* want to pay attention."

"I'll have to see what I have in my saving account!" Major Ka-markla declared as she turned a corner.

*

As soon as they stepped into the skating rink, Heather spotted the owner, a graying but athletic man of about fifty. "Hey Simon, are my skates in yet?"

"Not yet, Priscilla. They make each pair to order, so maybe next week. Will you judge the art skate again?"

"Sure!" she said, handing him a vinyl record in a protective case.

Major Ka-markla, in civilian clothes, wandered the entire rink, then got comfortable in the snack bar.

Although Colonel Ba-kerga was skeptical, Lisa was convinced that Heather's public life as Priscilla Ka-mentha actually lowered the chances of anyone taking an unhealthy interest in her. She was so confident, outgoing, and well-liked that any potential abductor would realize, if he had half a brain, that he would immediately have the entire civilian *world* coming after him.

Lisa smiled to herself. He'd also have the entire *military* coming after him.

And since the skating rink drew kids from several schools, no one would ever guess that Priscilla Ka-mentha didn't attend any of them, especially since her public personality did nothing to hide her general intelligence.

The only things hidden were her knowledge of the future, her contract with the Department of Defense, and her other names. Both Lisa and Corporal Do-forva had watched and listened carefully on many occasions, and they knew others had been planted to do the same. No one had ever observed the slighted slip.

The only way Lisa could imagine keeping Heather safer was to lock her in the bomb shelter, or the equivalent somewhere else. And doing so, Lisa knew and Colonel Ba-kerga grudgingly admitted, would cause her value to them to immediately cease.

"Clear the floor! All skaters off the floor!" the D.J. bellowed.

Priscilla coasted over to the music booth. "Side A," she said softly as the D.J. handed her a microphone.

"Hi, everybody, I'm Priscilla Ka-mentha!" she said while skating out a little way so she could be seen. "It's time for all you art and dance skaters to find your courage, come out and skate to the music! This song is another from my private collection, and I have *four* coupons to the snack bar for those who can feel the soul in this wonderful piece from the other side of the world."

She returned the microphone and the music started.  About a dozen skaters came out, most somewhat timidly, as *skating* by itself was hard enough, but doing it on one foot at a time, as Priscilla and a few others did, *while* moving to the music, seemed a nearly-impossible goal.

The two older dance-skating couples, and the young man of about twenty, knew they wouldn't get snack bar coupons as Priscilla was looking for kids who were struggling against shyness or clumsiness.

Priscilla was skating backwards, enjoying the music and going slowly so she didn't have to look behind her, when the young man skated near.

"Hi, Mark."

"Hi, P.K.  That freckled red-head about eleven found her courage, just came out."

Priscilla looked as Mark floated away.  She remembered the freckled girl watching the art skaters during previous sessions, and saw now that she had the music in her, but just needed to get off two feet, neither of which yet dared to come off the floor very far.

For the remainder of the song, Priscilla picked out the coupon winners and kept an eye on the red-head without staring.  As the music faded, she asked for the microphone again.

"Good art skating, everyone!  The winner who gets a *folded* snack bar coupon also gets a free private lesson with me over by the lockers."

She handed out coupons to three young skaters who dashed toward the snack bar, and one redhead who stood grinning with embarrassment and happiness.

✳

After twenty minutes of exercises on the carpeted floor, all on one foot at a time, Mandy was beginning to think she might be able to skate with a little grace and beauty someday.

"Thanks, Priscilla.  I've never had a . . . popular girl . . . be friendly with me."

"Why do you think I'm popular?  I don't have any friends my age."

"Why not?"

Priscilla shrugged.  "Just not into the same stuff, I guess."

"I'll be your friend!"

"How old do you think I am?"

"Um . . . ten, maybe nine."

"Seven and a half."

"Really?"

Priscilla nodded slowly.  "Still want to be my friend?"

Mandy took a deep breath.  "Yes!"

✳

Priscilla went by the snack bar to tell Lisa about her new friend, and they agreed that a chat with George would be necessary to work out the limits of the situation.

The skating session was almost over, but Priscilla had one more thing she wanted to do.  She spotted Mark practicing figures in the middle of the floor, and glided over.

"Hi, P.K."

"You know that nineteen-year-old I sometimes come here with?"

"The cute one with short hair?"

Priscilla smiled.  "I was hoping you might have noticed her."

"Your big sister?"

"Just a friend.  I don't know for sure, but I have a hunch she might like it if you asked her out . . . as long as she doesn't have to be a great skater."

He took on a dreamy expression.  "No ... as long as she's good at *something*, you know, not just sitting on the couch and watching television."

"She's good at lots of things!"

✳   ✳   ✳

## Chapter 19: Cognitive Dissonance

Sunday dawned quiet and still.

Heather danced to a couple of songs in the recreation room to wake up, then wandered out to see who was around.

Ginny was sipping tea and looking at a magazine. "Good morning, kid."

Heather smelled the corporal's tea. "Mmm. I think I'll get some of that. You know, I love people, but need a break now and then. I think Sundays will be my quiet days."

"You're different from me. If I had my choice, I'd have *six* quiet days a week."

Heather laughed. "Susan's like that." She hopped up, got a mug of tea from the new kitchen, and returned. "You know that good skater about twenty?"

"Yeah."

"His name's Mark and he thinks you're cute."

Ginny blushed. "I saw some boys looking at *you*, you know."

Heather sipped her tea and looked far away. "I made a friend, eleven-year-old girl, and me and Lisa are gonna talk to George about it, but I bet he'd hit the ceiling if I wanted to bring a boy home."

Ginny chuckled. "The boy's parents would hit the ceiling, too."

Heather sighed.

The envelope in Heather's mail drawer contained another easy near-future question that she felt prepared to tackle after refreshing her memory with some background information from the encyclopedia.

She got the remodeling plans and spent an hour wandering around the building, checking things off her list and making sure all the new furniture had been ordered.

Ben arrived, and they all ate sandwiches together.

The afternoon passed slowly as Heather pondered the following day's topic, danced, read part of Ginny's magazine, and counted her gold coins.

*

"Good morning, everyone.  Today's topic may be about a small country with large strategic importance because of it's location on one of the world's most important shipping lanes, but it's also an excellent case study of a human mental process that touches every level of our civilization, from family life to geo-politics.  Doctor Bo-kamla, would you begin by describing *cognitive dissonance* from the psychologist's perspective, please?"

Susan, much less comfortable speaking to groups of people than Heather, took a deep breath as she stood.  "It's very difficult to hold two conflicting beliefs in our minds at the same time.  We get very uncomfortable, and usually push one of them away by denying it.  The most *deeply held* notion usually wins, often the one we learned in childhood.

"For most people, the process of denial during cognitive dissonance seems to be necessary to avoid ... a violent reaction of some kind ... or insanity itself."

Heather then asked Doctor Bo-leden, the team philosopher, to take over. He described how the rational tests of logic and utility, that people used when thinking clearly, were usually forgotten during conflicts of belief.  The winning idea could easily be the worst for everyone.

Heather then described two possible futures.  One was based solely on the country's culture and religion, the other on external pressures from international politics.  The two futures were as different as night and day.

By the end of the session, the team was starting to get a good sense of why the little nation was so hard to understand, and would continue to be in the actual future that Heather described, which bounced back and forth between what *they* wanted to be, and what the rest of the world wanted, without ever really deciding.

She knew it would take many more sessions before the team could see the same process at work in their own country.

*

All that afternoon and the next, Heather worked with the craftsmen on the new dance studio in the old conference room, and her own private bedroom in the old recreation room.  She wasn't bothered that the patio had steel bars keeping out, or in, anything larger than a sparrow, and smiled as she painted the gray bars blue.

The session on Wednesday caused all the officers to squirm when they learned how many of the military's false-flag operations, in which they pretended to be the enemy to sway public opinion, would leak out in years to come.

On Friday, while talking about the future of some little alliance, Doctor Bo-leden explained the *Ad Ignorantiam* fallacy, the belief that if an idea is not proven false, then it *must* be true, or if not proven true, then it *must* be false.  With that bit of wisdom under their belts, most team members suddenly realized that the alliance was based on completely incorrect assumptions, and was therefore destined to fail.

Heather smiled, and was very happy that others, for the first time, could help her explain the forces at work in the present that would shape the future.

Also by Friday, all the walls and trim had been painted, new light fixtures installed, and every floor tiled that wasn't destined to have carpet or hardwood.

As soon as the craftsmen ate lunch in their favorite dining room, they started hauling roll after roll of new carpet up the stairs.

"Interesting color," General Bo-seklin commented. "About halfway between the green walls and the blue trim. What's it called?"

"It's a slightly de-saturated cyan," Heather informed him.

He cocked his head and squinted. "Oh."

Heather couldn't do any of the carpeting herself, but was right there to sweep floors or move stuff. Again they started with the outer office, then the general's office.

When the workday drew to a close, the men sat down at a dining table with Heather to look over the plans and checklists. They estimated another day of carpeting, two for wood flooring, and one for furniture and clean-up.

"Perfect! Just in time for the open house on Friday! You guys have to be there — I could have the general make it an order . . ."

"Not necessary. We're ahead of schedule, so no one will question it when I say the job goes through Friday."

Heather grinned. "Just wear nice clothes!"

"Let's look at this from their point of view," Colonel Ba-kerga proposed, late Friday afternoon, after Major Ka-markla and Heather described the situation.

The two females nodded, glad he was willing to give it any consideration at all.

"One of the first things she, or her mother, is going to want to know, is where you go to school."

"Since I'm not at my grade level, I have a private tutor," Heather replied.

"Good so far. And where do you live, and when can she come over to . . . play? . . . hang out? Whatever."

Heather grinned. "In a top-secret military facility."

"See the problem?"

"Sir," Lisa began, "I realize it's a problem, but we need some kind of solution. We can't expect Heather to go her entire life without friends."

The colonel set his jaw. "You're right. I just don't see it yet, and neither do you. But the public *Priscilla Ka-mentha* has to stay separate from the military, or anything top-secret, or we might as well just sell tickets to her sessions. So . . . do what you can out in the world with your friend, fudge on the questions about school and home, and put on your thinking caps.”

“We will,” Heather promised.

When they had gone, Colonel Ba-kerga mumbled to himself, “Safe-house security was *so* much easier.”

Major Ma-soran, at her desk, chuckled.  “But not nearly as much fun.”

✳

After everyone but the guards had gone home for the week, Susan came in.  She and Heather got desserts and headed for the bomb shelter.

Heather talked for more than an hour about a deep sense of loneliness, and the frustration she felt at not being able to have casual friends.

Doctor Bo-kamla had an insight, and shared it with Heather when the seven-year-old was done talking.

Heather thought about it for a few minutes while playing with the crumbs on her dessert plate, then nodded.  Her loneliness was not just from her current life as a child, but partly, perhaps mostly, from the last ten or fifteen years of the life she remembered of a now-nameless retired psychologist.

✳   ✳   ✳

## Chapter 20: A Little Solution

Heather knew there were a hundred things the facility needed before the open house, so she showed Ginny her shopping list at breakfast.

"Hmm . . . my car is pretty small, you know . . ."

"We could take the blind transport!"

"True.  Why don't you wait for a purchase order for all the big plants, and arrange for a truck from the air base?"

"Okay!  And we can get all this little stuff today, and go skating!"

By the time they got to the skating rink, the passenger area of the large van was filled with Priscilla's purchases — a few things she knew Maria wanted, accessories for the offices, a sound system for the dance studio, lots of floor pillows, and a bird feeder for her patio.

Priscilla completely enjoyed the skating session, handed out snack-bar coupons after the art skate, and spent lots of time chatting with Mandy.  But she was most happy when she saw Mark and Ginny laughing and talking, side by side, in the snack bar while the corporal continued to keep a sharp eye on all security concerns.

After the skate, Priscilla and Ginny found themselves going through the exit doors just behind Mandy and her mother.

"Mom, this is my new friend Priscilla.  She's that really good skater I told you about, and she's giving me lessons!"

Everyone exchanged greetings.

Ginny knew enough about the situation to spot an opportunity.  "We were about to get some dinner somewhere.  Would you folks like to join us?  It would give these two chatter boxes more time to, you know, chatter."

"Could we, mom, please?" Mandy begged.

"I'm buying," Priscilla announced with a grin.

"Well, okay, but you don't have to pay for us, sweetheart.  Your allowance can't be *that* much yet."

"Oh, yes it can," Priscilla said for only Mandy to hear.

The eleven-year-old snickered.

✳

They got comfortable around a large table at the nearest pizza parlor, and selected a pizza that everyone would enjoy.

The two girls chatted about happenings at the skating rink, including Mark's interest in Ginny.

Ginny tried to ignore the young ones as she juggled answers to the mother's questions.  "I'm just the baby-sitter," she explained.

Suddenly Priscilla looked at her new friend with big eyes and a serious expression.  "Can you keep a secret, a very important secret?"

Corporal Do-forva stopped breathing.

"Sure!" Mandy declared.

Priscilla looked at Mandy's mother.  "Can *you* keep it, too?"

The corporal wondered if her heart was still beating.

"Well, sweetheart, as long as it's nothing that could hurt anyone."

"I'm from another planet, I live in a space ship, and that's why I can't invite you to my house.  But there's gold everywhere on my planet, just like dirt, so I have gold coins out my ears.  Here's one for you!"  She pulled a gold coin from her pocket and spun it on the table in front of Mandy.

"Wow, thank you!" the older girl said and hugged her friend.

Ginny breathed again, just as the pizza arrived.

✳

Mandy's mother wasn't sure if Priscilla was actually very poor, and that's why she didn't want to reveal her address, or if some mental-health problem was causing her to live in a fantasy world.  The gold coin would tell which, she decided.  If fake, then embarrassing poverty was probably the explanation.  If real, then Priscilla was most likely a rich kid who had to see a shrink every day, and would never really grow up.

In either case, she was charitable enough to allow her daughter the friendship . . . as long as it was limited to public places.

✳

Heather was puttering around the facility on Sunday, doing what she could to get ready for the open house, while at the same time pondering Monday's topic, when Corporal Do-forva arrived.

"I thought what happened was important enough to report to Colonel Ba-kerga immediately, so I called him last night."

"How'd he take it?"

"Well ... I told him in the same order it happened, statement by statement, and I think he stopped breathing for a little while, just like I did.  But when I got to the end, he laughed!  Have you ever heard Colonel Ba-kerga laugh?"

Heather snickered.  "No.  A slight smile or two, but never laughter."

"He sends his compliments on your creative solution to the problem."

Heather chuckled, remembering the look on Mandy's mother's face.

"Do me a favor, okay?" Ginny asked.

"Sure, what?"

"I'm supposed to get off at eighteen hundred, and me and Mark are going out, so don't do anything to make me have to stay longer."

The girl grinned. "I promise!"

✳　✳　✳

## Chapter 21: Count-Down

"I am constantly amazed at what excellent examples we are getting of how our delusions and fallacies affect culture, politics, and history," Heather began.

She could see the wheels turning in several of the faces around her. They sensed something was wrong with the recently-enacted law they were discussing, but couldn't quite put their fingers on it. Most of them didn't have enough background in philosophy yet. The philosopher was smiling, but didn't know the future.

"Yes, as some of you have guessed, the law will fail miserably. The seeds of its destruction could be seen, even now, if someone was brave enough to look in the right places."

"But not by seven-year-olds," the general dared to slip in, just for comic relief.

Heather laughed. "The problem lies in the process that was used to model the law's effects when it was written. A very common habit called the *Hasty Generalization* was at play all during the drafting process, and *that* team didn't have the good sense to get a philosopher. Doctor Bo-leden, you have the floor."

Still smiling about her comment, he stood and came up to the blackboard. "Hasty Generalizations come in two flavors, both essentially statistical problems. The committee that drafted the law did, as I remember, get the opinions of a few people. Unfortunately, that sample was very small compared to the number of people the law would effect. When the sample size is extremely small, the validity of the survey drops very low, approaching zero."

He paused in his chalk scribbling to make sure they were following.

"The other problem occurred because the legislative process is political. The party in power only asked the opinions of its *own* people. Therefore, the sample was not representative of the people the law would affect. You combine both of those, and the committee actually had no idea what would happen."

Heather stood back up. "We could debate whether the committee even *wanted* to know the real outcome. The law will obviously succeed in transferring a fair amount of wealth from one class of people to another. But knowledge of the committee's intentions will never become public, so I have no knowledge of them. Anyone who wants to explore *that* can of worms will have to do it another time."

The entire circle of listeners grinned at her as they began raising their hands with questions.

*

With part of the facility completely remodeled, and the rest of the carpet expected to go in that day, excitement was high at lunch as nearly everyone worked on lists of things they needed to get or do before Friday.

The university professors were each tempted to bring five or ten of their fellows, since the facility would not be operating in any classified mode during the open house.

But since the place was only so big, and Major Ma-soran could only scrape up four blind transports for the occasion, she set a limit of three guests each. She knew she had to save room for a few generals and colonels.

*

All Monday afternoon, Heather floated between the three craftsmen busy installing carpets, and the electrician putting in the security lamp that would glow green when, and only when, an officer or guard used a special key.

The two safe-house sleeping rooms were quickly carpeted, followed by the clinic.

The men had to scratch their heads a little in the new dance studio as they prepared to install padding all over, but carpet only along the outside edges. They looked at Heather askance. She pointed to the general's signature on the plans, and smiled.

The excited seven-year-old almost got in the way as they carpeted her new room, but managed to humble herself when they gave her dirty looks. She sighed, knowing she'd have all evening to inspect it.

Finally, as dinnertime approached, the center of the large room, where the P-Seventeen team met, was covered with the same beautiful blue-green carpeting. With their last burst of energy, the craftsmen put all the furniture back, knowing the following two days would be long enough without any extra work.

*

Once the building was silent, with only Lisa drying the dinner dishes, Heather crept about the facility. In each newly-carpeted room, she stretched out on the soft floor and rolled over a few times, just to get the feel of it. Sitting up on her knees, she imagined all the new furniture in place, furniture already waiting at the air base.

Eventually, she entered the old recreation room, now *her* room, and examined every inch.  When she found a loose carpet thread, she ran to Sarah's desk for scissors.

Finally, she lay on her back in the middle of the big room and gazed up at the log trusses.  They let her thoughts soar, unlike the old suspended ceiling, and she knew her thoughts would need to soar in the coming years, in that very room, to avoid a disaster from which her world would never recover.

"Hi, kid," Lisa said, towering over her suddenly.  "Want a scoop of orange sherbet with me?"

"Yeah!"

*

Lisa and Heather got Maria's first few pancakes on Tuesday morning, then departed before anyone else arrived.  An hour later, they stepped into the nursery as soon as it opened.

"Are you mommy's little helper today?" the woman asked with a sweet smile.

"Yep!  I love little plantsies!"

"In that case, you can pick out one of these that need homes."

Heather gazed at the tray of two-inch pots with tiny dying plants in them, took a slow breath, and selected a small cactus that *might* survive if given some well-drained soil.  "Thank you!  Can I leave it here until we go?"

"You sure can, Honey!"

The woman's eyes grew wide when both early shoppers grabbed the largest flat-bed carts and headed down the first aisle.

*

"Plantsies?" Lisa inquired with a smile.

"I can act the part when necessary."

"Does it ever bother you when people talk down to you?  I mean . . . you could easily *run* this entire business."

Heather chuckled.  "Sometimes I get tired of it.  There's also a part of me that likes it a little.  Okay, here's the indoor potted plants.  One list for you, one for me . . ."

Over the next hour, the pair assembled seven flat-bed carts near the cash register — plants ranging from two to six feet tall, big ceramic pots, wheeled planter dollies, a bird bath, and bags of potting soil, sand, and gravel.

While the woman verified the purchase order, Lisa backed the truck into the loading zone.

Heather made sure she remembered her sickly little cactus.  Somehow, she could relate to it.

*

After getting Wednesday's topic, Heather turned her mind to the trickiest part of the remodeling job.  The craftsmen had never before laid a dance floor.  They were putting complete trust in a sketch drawn by a little girl.

"Okay . . ." the foreman began after polishing off a quarter of his sandwich.  "Since it's floating on a carpet pad, we can't use nails, so we'll glue the plywood sheets together today, and do the hardwood tomorrow, but you can't take the weights off until . . . Friday morning." He looked at his little supervisor.

"That's close, but I can get the guards to help me. I don't need to dance on it at the open house, it just has to look nice."

The foreman and one helper made the plywood base, two layers with all the seams offset, strong glue between. The other two craftsmen tossed gloves to Ben and they brought up a hundred concrete blocks. Heather tried to lift one, waddled a few feet, then gave up.

By mid-afternoon, the workers were happy to turn their attention to the normal hardwood flooring, eight feet wide, that would completely surround the big meeting room. It went quickly, and by dinner they had the back half completely finished.

That evening, with Ginny's help, Heather re-potted a dozen large plants while pondering what the team needed to hear about the proxy wars the country was about to fight.

✳

"I must admit," General Bo-seklin began as soon as Heather opened the session to questions, "when you first said *proxy wars* weeks ago, we weren't quite sure what you meant."

"My apologies. I've tried to adjust my terminology back to this period, but its half a century, sometimes three-quarters, and I don't always know the right terms."

"We figured it out, and several others you've used, but it's often a bit humbling, as the terms you use tend to be more . . . um, honest . . . than those used today."

"I think that's natural, and you'd find the same thing in any time period."

"So . . . it's public knowledge in the future that we're actually going to be indirectly fighting the Beklan Empire?"

"It is, and it's also public knowledge that in any proxy war, most of the people who die are not ours or theirs, but the local people instead. That part of the world will never forgive us, *or* the Beklan Empire. But the whole point of a proxy war is that the people who are hurt and killed don't vote in our elections. The voters here don't care enough about our differences with the Beklans to support a war in which millions of our own people die. But they *will* support a war in which millions of people with different-color skin, and funny names, die in some far-away land, if for no other reason than the television sport of it."

Colonel Ba-kerga narrowed his eyes. "Are you opposed to this war?"

Heather closed her eyes for a moment. When she opened then, the team knew that the person looking back was very far from seven years old.

"I am not afraid to voice my opinion that anyone who truly loves war is insane. But that does not change the fact that if war happens, then something in human nature is making it happen. I am not here to change human nature, nor do I believe anyone would succeed in trying to do so.

Given all that, no, I cannot say that I am opposed to this war."

*

The hardwood strips covered the dance floor quickly with one man spreading glue, two fitting the pieces, and one placing weights. The rest of the flooring in the large room took hours more, but the craftsmen stayed after dinner to get it all done.

"I'm beginning to see the overall design and color harmony," Lisa declared after letting the men out, "and I like it. Is it shaping up like you imagined?"

Heather nodded with a far-away look in her eyes. "It has moods, and they'll affect my work sometimes, but it's happiest in the morning when the team meets. I'll often want to get away in the late afternoon when the place is feeling a bit grumpy."

The major looked askance at the girl, wondering what she sensed that the rest of them couldn't.

Heather shook her head slightly and focused on Lisa again. "Help me hang some curtains?"

Lisa smiled and nodded.

*

On Thursday morning, after seeing the barely-hidden smile on Sarah's face, then opening her mail drawer, Heather glanced up to see if the new security lamp was glowing green. It was, so she read the topic sheet aloud for Ginny and Lisa to hear. "*No topic for you for Session 11 on Friday. Doctor Po-selem will be giving a special presentation.*"

"How do you feel about that?" Sarah asked from her desk.

"Great! Chris is always fun, and hasn't had much he could say about recent topics. I had a hunch he was doing some thinking, maybe some research. And that means I can play with furniture and plants all day today!"

*

Heather danced several songs on the new hardwood floor around the big room, keeping the music very low. Then she whispered farewell to the old gray couch that had been her bed for nearly a month, and placed a masking-tape X on it for removal.

As noon approached, the radio came to life. "Mobile Construction Unit Five to facility, we have *three*, count them, *three* trucks full of furniture, so we'll just be parking in front, E.T.A. two minutes."

Heather could feel butterflies in her stomach as Sarah chatted on the radio and Ben went downstairs to oversee the parking.

As they ate homemade pizza, Heather showed the craftsmen sketches of where all the furniture should go. They laid a sheet of plywood over the new hardwood floor, then hauled down all the old couches.

That made plenty of room to move the three officers' gray metal desks into the big room. Brand new varnished wooden ones were set in place, with plush chairs on wheels behind each. All three enjoyed moving their files and desk tools into the beautiful new furniture.

While the officers organized their pencils, the men carried beds, end tables, small desks, and chairs to the sleeping rooms, then a new desk and examining table to the clinic.  The safe-house corridor got linen cabinets and stuffed chairs, and the dance studio received shelves for the sound system.

Heather was right there as each item was placed, sketches in hand, usually quite happy with the placement, occasionally requesting an adjustment.

When they came to her room, she danced outside the door while they brought in a large bed, wardrobe, cedar chest, roll-top desk, bookcase, and wing-back chair.  "Just make it look nice," she begged.  "It will take me *weeks* to figure out where everything goes, and the open house is tomorrow!"

✳

Finally, the four men and one girl looked at the carpeted area in the middle of the big room.

"This is the heart of the place," Heather explained.  "The new blackboard mounts on the back wall, right in the middle.  Couches go on the sides.  Bookcase over there.  Then just stick ten of those comfy rolling chairs in the middle, and we'll arrange them later."

"That leaves two extra rolling chairs," the foreman pointed out.

"General's office, for his guests."

The man nodded.  "He'll like that."

Getting the old metal desks down the stairs was the worst part, after which the new meeting area was quickly furnished.

Over dinner, the four craftsmen and Heather took one last look at the plans and checklists, then slapped hands for a job well done.

"Want to supervise our next assignment?" the foreman asked.  "You're better than . . ."  He stopped and looked around.  ". . . most of the grouchy ol' officers we get!"

Heather smiled, but knew she would be quite busy in the coming weeks, months, and years.

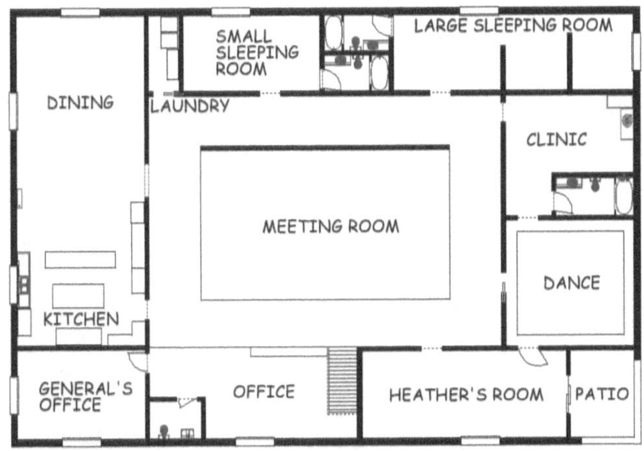


At about twenty-two hundred hours, Maria finally decided her kitchen, and the many trays of food stacked in her refrigerators, were ready.  Ben let her out.

Lisa left at twenty-three hundred, promising to be back by six in the morning.

Ginny stayed up with Heather as she went from room to room, making sure everything looked its best.  They both fell onto couches at about one in the morning.

Ben finally got some sleep at two, on the soft new couch in the guard room.

*   *   *

## Chapter 22: A Warning

Everyone was on duty.

Heather had plenty of helpers to get the concrete blocks from the dance floor onto the patio, where all the extra plant stuff was already crammed. She swept and vacuumed, but resisted the temptation to try the new floor. The team was already arriving for breakfast, including General Ko-fenral from the air base, and Maria needed all the help she could get.

The dining room buzzed with excitement over the newly-remodeled facility and the unusual topic of the session. General Bo-seklin was in his element, presiding over a vibrant and promising new military intelligence program, and assuring the visiting general that the information they were receiving, although they hadn't acted on any of it, was *already* justifying the expenses.

"When do we start acting on this new information?" General Ko-fenral asked.

General Bo-seklin cleared his throat. "I think Doctor Po-selem will be shedding some light on that issue today."

"Program P-Seventeen, Session Eleven, nine November 3662, zero-nine hundred hours, seven minutes."

"Good morning everyone. Present are myself, Heather, and . . ."

Everyone with program clearance in the entire world was there — all five officers, six enlisted personnel, four professors, one cook, and one little girl.

"This is a very special day, as the remodeling of the facility was just completed . . . let me see . . . about an hour ago."

The entire room erupted with laughter. Even the guards by the stairs had trouble keeping straight faces.

"It's also special because I get to relax, listen, and ask questions for the first time!"

Both General Bo-seklin, in his most impressive dress uniform, and the physics professor, with his wild hair, flashed her cheesy grins.

"I hope everyone likes the comfy new seats. Sam has *three* in his office!"

Murmurs of delight came from all round the circle.

"The blackboard is also brand new," Heather continued, "and I trust everyone remembers that no erasing is allowed until Ben photographs it. So with that, I give the floor to Doctor Po-selem."

He stood, faced the blackboard for a moment, then turned around and looked at the circle of military people, psychologist, historian, and philosopher. "Wow. This isn't as easy as giving a standard lecture to wide-eyed undergrads. How do you do it, Heather?"

She just smiled.

"Um . . . I've been meeting with General Bo-seklin and Colonel Ba-kerga, and we worked up some hypothetical questions I could put to my physics colleagues all over the world, with the pretense that I was just working on a very speculative article, almost science fiction . . ."

Neither Heather, nor anyone else, could remember the convoluted theories the physicist presented over the next hour, but as best they could tell, his logic and math were sound. He and his colleagues were in agreement that very tiny influences by someone with knowledge of the future would probably not change it, but there could be exceptions. He advised Heather, and all team members, to stay away from world leaders of any kind.

But when he started talking about large, purposeful changes to the future, everyone was on the edges of their seats. He assumed that none had been attempted, and both generals verified.

"And yet," the physicist went on, "there wouldn't be much purpose for the military to study the material that Heather is giving us, unless . . . the possibility existed that *someday*, after hearing of *something* in the future that was just *too* terrible to swallow, the Department of Defense decided to act."

As Doctor Po-selem looked around at his listeners, no one denied the possibility.

"And I think it's safe to assume that the bigger the problem, the bigger the intervention that will be needed."

"Naturally," General Ko-fenral admitted.

"So, applying these theoretical equations," the physicist continued, pointing at the blackboard, "the greater you find the necessity of changing the future, the greater the possibility that doing so will cause our timeline to diverge from the one with Heather's memories . . ." He looked around to see if they were still with him. ". . . and the greater the possibility that the time traveler will vanish — in other words, that Heather's memories will disappear, and she'll suddenly become just a seven-year-old girl wondering where her mommy is."

Heather frowned at the notion.

"Are you counseling us to *never* act on the foreknowledge we're getting?" Colonel Ba-kerga asked with suspicion and disapproval written all over his face.

Doctor Po-selem stared at the floor for a moment before looking up and speaking. "No. I can't say I had a religious bone in my body before joining this team, but it's painfully obvious that this . . . gift . . . was arranged by . . . someone, someone very powerful. As I've said several times, backwards time travel, even by mere information, just *isn't* natural, in any sense of the word. I can't imagine any reason for going to all this trouble unless it was intended to be used at some point."

He noticed the colonel's slight nod of agreement.

"But . . . I just hope everyone will keep in mind that we *might* — no, it's more accurate to say that we will *probably* get only one shot at something big, and we will *probably* lose Heather in the process."

After a long silence, General Ko-fenral took a deep breath. "By *lose Heather*, you mean her memories would disappear."

The scientist looked up toward the ceiling for a moment. "At least. And I wouldn't be surprised if her other predictions — those that had not yet come to pass — suddenly became inaccurate."

Heather still wore a slight frown, but didn't show any signs of surprise.

※

The questions came at Doctor Po-selem for nearly an hour, and he was hard pressed to explain his theories in language they could understand, but he tried.

Finally, at a slight gap in the discussion five minutes before noon, Heather stood up, and the physicist used the silence that followed to quickly retreat to his chair.

"I'm sure these questions will continue to . . . um . . . *haunt* us, probably for the entire future of this team. The green security lamp is about to be switched off, and your note pads must be locked in your mail drawers. Every imaginable goodie is waiting in the dining room, there will be tours, all the *non-classified* schmoozing you desire, and I will dance for you at one o'clock — I mean thirteen hundred."

They smiled or chuckled.

"And don't forget — the team is on vacation next week!"

Several people pulled appointment calendars from their pockets.

Thinking of nothing else that needed saying, and seeing no one with urgent announcements, Heather nodded at Sergeant Ta-nibon behind the tape recorder.

"Session Eleven ends at eleven hundred hours, fifty-eight minutes."

※　※　※

## Chapter 23: Celebration

The radio was soon squawking with entry requests for the blind transports, all of which were making two trips.  They were followed closely by cars of military people with enough clearance to know where the facility was, including the four craftsmen who had just remodeled the place.

Colonel Ba-kerga made sure the tape, blackboard photos, and note pads were locked away before anyone opened the door.

Lisa switched off the security lamp.

Heather re-arranged the meeting space for people eating and chatting in small groups.

Generals, colonels, majors, and professors began pouring up the stairs after the security people checked I.D. cards.

As she carried trays of appetizers and drinks to the office counter, Heather felt a moment of sadness that her friend Mandy, her skating buddy Mark, and her mother, whom she hadn't seen in a month, could not be among them.

✳

Heather stayed in the background, just playing the part of someone's daughter or granddaughter helping out for the day.  She knew there were several different levels of knowledge present in the open-house guests, and had a hunch the interactions between them would be fun to watch.

The team members, with top-secret-umbra and P-Seventeen clearances, all knew who she was and what the newly-remodeled facility was for.  Even within the team there was a division, as the military people knew where the facility was located, but the university professors did not.  Heather sensed no concern over that small issue.

All the military officers not on the team knew that General Bo-seklin had scored something big, and would love to know what it was, but had no intention of risking years in federal prison to find out.  They were, however, certainly not going to close their ears if someone let something slip.

The visiting professors were completely in the dark, knowing only that their colleagues advised the military on something top-secret in this newly-remodeled facility. They were very open about their curiosity, and the team professors equally blunt about their inability to answer.

The enlisted craftsmen from the air base were in a class by themselves, knowing Heather was much more than someone's daughter or granddaughter, but not really knowing what.

Heather listened as Sam and Sarah gave tours, Lisa mingled but stayed near her, and George kept an eye on everything. She hadn't realized it at the time, weeks before, but her offer to co-exist with safe-house guests had provided the perfect excuse when a social situation required an answer about the purpose of this or that room, but secrecy did not allow an honest one. She overheard Sam use it several times, and Sarah twice.

At five minutes before one o'clock, she finished pouring another tray of punch cups, grabbed her shoulder bag from a corner of the kitchen, and slipped into the clinic's toilet room.

✳

The music began quietly, a classical piece hardly interrupting anyone's conversation, the sound softened by coming from the dance studio, through its open door.

The dancer, in a flowing white dress, emerged slowly from the back corridor, almost shyly, dancing just enough to catch the eye, then disappearing again.

The song picked up tempo slightly, and the dancer finally stayed in view, tracing slow, graceful shapes in the air with her slender body and arms, gliding back and forth on the golden hardwood floor along the right side of the large room.

Suddenly the music became bright and urgent, and the dancer leapt onto the long section of floor, her feet moving to the faster rhythm, her arms reaching for the ceiling, her hands playing melodies on unseen instruments.

All conversation ceased, food and drinks were set down, and people emerged from the dining room to watch.

Four times the dancer moved gracefully along the golden floor, then leapt and twirled as the music reached its climax.

Mouths hung open, and many eyes sparkled with delight. If asked, they would have sworn the dancer was six feet tall.

She pranced along the floor five more times as the music softened, each time becoming slightly smaller and more delicate.

As the song approached its final notes, the dancer slowly spun herself into a little ball that carefully settled onto the floor, small enough to walk right by and not even notice.

Complete silence filled the room for several long seconds, until someone brought their hands together, and a heartbeat later everyone was clapping with all their might.

✳

Heather had eaten little before the dance, but now, still in her white dress, she filled her plate with enough food to raise eyebrows.  Everyone, especially the visiting professors, wanted to sit at the same table with her, but only a lucky few could.

Colonel Ba-kerga had been uncomfortable with the situation, and Heather understood why.  In this facility, she shared her memories of the future.  Out in the civilian world, she was a dancer and a skater.  By dancing in the facility for people not on the team, she risked someone connecting the two.

She had agreed on a compromise with her hard-nosed security chief.  If she was Heather on the team, and Priscilla out in the world, she would have no name on this occasion.

It had been easy before the dance — carrying food and drink trays, she had blended right in with the low-ranking security guards.  Now, as people pelted her with questions about where she had learned to dance, and had she applied to this or that ballet company, she kept her mouth as full as possible, smiled when she could, and gave vague answers to some of their questions between bites.

When the first guests began filtering away shortly after two o'clock, Heather used the distraction to get back into casual clothes and start helping Ginny with the dirty dishes.

Soon Corporal Do-forva was called away to drive a blind transport, so Heather got the entire dishwashing station to herself.  Maria, busy keeping the serving line and appetizer trays fresh and presentable, gave the seven-year-old a smile and nod of thanks.

About three o'clock, General Bo-seklin graciously bid farewell to the remaining guests, and half an hour later, all the guards were back from transport runs.

*

"Security de-briefing!" Colonel Ba-kerga called.

Heather had a hunch this was coming.  The large meeting room was quickly made usable again.

"First, I want to know if *anyone* was more interested in *anything* than they should have been."

"No problems with the military people," Major Ka-markla began, making eye contact with the lower-ranking guards to make sure.  "The only thing I spotted was the visiting professors trying to find out what the program was about."

Several others, including General Bo-seklin, nodded agreement.

"Heather?" the security chief prompted.

"Some of them tried to get my name while I was eating, but they failed.  Their curiosity was just because of my dance, so nothing to worry about from my point of view."

"I was at the next table over," Major Ka-markla added, "and she made good use of mouthfuls of food to change the subject a number of times."

"I really *was* hungry!"

Everyone chuckled.

"Maria!" the colonel yelled. "The next topic affects you!"

She hurried out of the kitchen, wiping her hands.

"No team meetings next week, so the guard schedule is very light, usually just one.  Bring things to read, take classes at the air base to work on your ranks and ratings, clean your cat boxes . . ."

Several people smiled.

"The officers will be in and out," he went on, "and Major Ka-markla will call in twice a day any time she and Heather are traveling."

The major nodded.

"Maria will leave plenty of sandwich makings and left-overs, but won't be serving regular meals, unless we get a large safe-house group."

"I had almost forgotten about *that* possibility," Major Ma-soran admitted.

An hour later, most of the guards had gone home.  The three senior officers finished some necessary paperwork, then wandered into the large meeting room.  They could hear Heather and Major Ka-markla chatting with Maria in the kitchen.

"Next week may *seem* like we're returning to the old days," the general began, "when this facility was being forgotten and put out to pasture, but it's just temporary."

Major Ma-soran smiled.  "The fresh paint and new-carpets will remind us."

"After today, I think we finally know the score," the colonel said, "about what we can and cannot do with Heather's . . . gift."

The general nodded.  "We'll use these breaks to step back and get a fresh perspective.  Let's have lunch together on Monday, Wednesday, and Friday, but also remember to use Heather's weeks off for your own vacations or training."

The three, infused with a new sense of purpose and excitement for their jobs, warmly shook hands, got their coats and briefcases, and headed downstairs to go through the exit procedure.

"Okay kids," Maria said, surveying her brand new, and again spotless kitchen, "there's enough left-overs from the party for most of next week, considering hardly anyone will be here.  I'll be in Monday or Tuesday to begin re-stocking."

Heather hugged the stout lady.  "Thank you, Maria.  Today wouldn't have been possible without you."

"Thank *you* for such a beautiful place to work!  Money alone could not have brought this place back to life.  Remember, I saw it before the remodeling — old and gray, and ready to crawl in a hole and stay there.  It took a spark from you!"

Major Ka-markla chuckled and nodded.

Maria got her coat, and the corporal on duty descended the stairs with her.

*

Heather wandered into the middle of the meeting circle, lay down on her back, and gazed up at the log trusses. "We did it, Lisa."

Major Ka-markla relaxed into a plush chair. "Was it really only a month ago we started?"

"Yeah, just a month. I guess it couldn't have happened so quickly without ... you know ... the president."

"Yeah."

The silence lingered, and they could hear the guard come back in from the parking garage.

"So," the major began, "any idea what you want to do with your week off?"

"Sleep in my own bed tonight, for the first time, and get up about noon tomorrow."

Lisa chuckled. "Knowing you, that new dance floor will be calling to you at about zero-five hundred."

Heather laughed, still on her back.

"How was it, dancing on the floor out here today?"

"It was okay, but I could tell it was laid on solid concrete. I avoided some jumps I could have done on a better floor."

"You really impressed them."

"It's nice to have something I can do in public. My contract doesn't allow me to tell fortunes at the Psychic Fair."

Lisa laughed. "And after you sleep in tomorrow?"

"First visit with my mother tomorrow afternoon. George has met with her twice, but she'll *still* try to learn more than I can tell her."

"I'm sure you can handle it."

Heather nodded. "But I want you right there to temper her ... parental authority."

"Okay. And for the rest of the week?"

"Hmm ... it's November ... how about some sand dunes, ghost towns, hot springs, things like that?"

"Perfect this time of year!"

*　　*　　*

## Part 2: Ko-tera Three, 3667

## Chapter 24: Friday

"... and as we've studied before, all people, all groups of people, indeed all organisms everywhere, are always seeking to privatize their profits and socialize their costs. No one likes paying taxes on their income, or sharing it with anyone they don't have to. Everyone likes to pull resources out of the environment, dump wastes into it, and have society as a whole take care of injuries and accidents. Which session was that, Lieutenant Do-forva?"

Seated on a couch with Ben behind his tape recorder, and the other records specialist with camera, she already had a binder open on her lap and was flipping pages quickly. "Um ... three sixty-two."

The tall twelve-year-old standing near the blackboard looked around the large meeting room at the generals and scientists in the inner circle of plush chairs, more generals, colonels, majors, and professors filling the couches that ringed the carpeted area, and another dozen majors, lieutenants, and professors in comfortable folding chairs on the surrounding hardwood floor. Several people made a note of the earlier session number. "You should probably schedule a replay of that session, Sarah," Heather said.

Colonel Ma-soran, the executive officer, nodded.

"So, as we've touched upon more than once before, one of the proper functions of government is to protect the *Commons*, all things that are part of the *Public Trust* — parks, clean water, fresh air, you know the list — from those who would abuse them for private, short-term gain. One of the quickest ways for a government to lose its legitimacy is to cease protecting the Public Trust, and I believe Doctor Tu-feltin can give us some examples a little later ..."

The historian in the front row nodded vigorously.

"... but the issue in question is the recent court interpretation that gives groups — corporations, unions, whatever — all the rights of citizens. Opponents anticipated that it would result in major abuses of the Public

Trust, and even in a few short years, it's now crystal clear that they were right, as I'm sure you are all aware."

Three-star General Ko-fenral, seated in the inner circle, and beside him Two-star General Bo-seklin, both nodded.

"So now Heather gets out her crystal ball ..." the twelve-year-old announced with dramatic hand motions.

The room filled with chuckles.

Heather smiled and made eye contact with her dear friend and therapist Doctor Bo-kamla.

Susan knew what Heather was doing. A moment of comic relief could help the listeners relax and absorb an otherwise-difficult concept.

"As I'm sure you can imagine, opponents of the interpretation, from both the environmental and social justice camps, will fight against it, tooth and claw, for years, even decades to come. Their efforts will fail. As much as we like justice, we love our groups, of all kinds, even more. The *tribe* is in our blood, and always will be. *Justice* is a newcomer."

Heather scanned the room and saw intense curiosity in most of the professors' faces.

The military people looked steeled for the moment they would find out if this was something they should act upon, or not, knowing well they might get to change the future only once.

"The solution to the problem, that brings our government back to its legitimate role of protecting the Public Trust for *everyone*, is, unfortunately, about twenty years away, and will come from some little court case in a rural county, I don't remember where. It will work its way up through the courts, and eventually the entire country will suddenly realize that we gave corporations and unions the *rights* of citizens, without ever giving them the essential *responsibilities* of citizens."

About half the room was nodding. The other half looked confused.

"Of course, we all know that corporations and unions have some responsibilities now — they pay their taxes, blah, blah, blah. But they are missing the one that every flesh-and-blood citizen has, and is constantly aware of. Individual citizens have a responsibility to obey the law *or else be put in jail*. Groups of all kinds *do not* have that fear. They have no risk of their actual *persons* being arrested, jailed, imprisoned, or even, in extreme cases, put to death."

No one in the room appeared to be breathing.

"Therefore, their responsibility to obey the law is paper-thin, and can be brushed aside with money, while none of the actual *people* who control the groups even break a fingernail. That omission in the recent court interpretation will cause *trillions* in damage to our economy and our environment. It will cause *massive* damage to the legitimacy of our government. But it will eventually be corrected, and we, as a nation, will learn many hard lessons in the process."

They all breathed again.

*

Questions centered on how the justice system could jail an entity that had no single, identifiable, body.

It was a complex question, Heather admitted, and would take another decade, after the basic mistake was corrected, to work out the details. But she assured them that in the future, people would not agree to sit on boards of directors, or be officers of corporations, without very careful consideration and serious background research.

Eyes were wide and many heads nodded agreement before Heather closed the session.

"The security lamp will stay on during lunch today, so we can chat about this thorny subject, but please remember to make a note if you think of something the team should hear. Alpha Study Group meets at one o'clock to go over logical fallacies with Doctor Bo-leden, and anyone's welcome to sit in who wants a refresher on that stuff. Any other announcements?"

"Generals and colonels," General Ko-fenral began, "in General Bo-seklin's office at twelve hundred thirty. Should be a short meeting."

Heather waited another moment, then nodded at Ben behind the tape recorder.

"Session Five Forty-Five ends at eleven hundred hours, thirty-seven minutes. Seven blackboard photographs."

*   *   *

## Chapter 25: Saturday

By seven in the morning, music was pulsing from the dance studio, causing both Colonel Ka-markla in the dining room, and the garage-level security sergeant, to tap their feet.

Lisa emerged from the dining room sipping a steaming mug, and ambled toward the source of the music.  She paused at the top of the stairs, yelled, "Coffee's ready, Sergeant!" then continued toward the dance studio and looked in.

Heather was stretching and warming up to the music.

"Good morning, kid."

"Hi, Lisa.  Do I get to be with you today?"

"Yep.  I only took the promotion with the understanding that I *wasn't* being kicked upstairs to do paperwork all the time."

Heather chuckled.  "I'd hate that too.  But . . . do you know how packed my schedule is today?"

Lisa rolled her eyes.  "Where do you find the energy?"

"Not from coffee!  It's very bad for your kidneys."

If that had come from anyone else, Colonel Ka-markla would have brushed it off.  Considering who had just spoken, she stepped to the nearest table and set down her mug.

The song ended and a moment later the reel-to-reel tape player stopped and began to rewind itself.  Heather leapt through the door.  "Wanna eat whole-grain banana pancakes with me?"

※

The little store, nestled in a quiet corner of the old downtown area, was about half antiques, one-third rare books, and the remainder hard-to-find music.  The owner, a short man with thin hair and bright eyes, had barely unlocked the door when Priscilla and Colonel Ka-markla entered.

Priscilla took a deep breath.  "I love old things!  Good, quality, enduring old things.  Good morning, Mister Ta-sorel!"

Lisa, in civilian clothes, began to browse while also checking to see if anyone else was in the shop.

"Good morning!" the owner called.  "I had a hunch I'd be seeing you today, Priscilla.  That tape compilation you ordered is done, and I have *two* new things you might like."

She grinned.  "Let me listen, please, please, please!"

He handed headphones over the counter and carefully placed the needle on a rotating vinyl disc.

Half a dozen bars into the song, the girl was moving her feet, then her arms, and finally her whole body, limited only by the headphone cord and the narrow aisle.  She flashed him a thumbs-up before she was halfway through the song.

"They *really* know how to use full orchestra to make good dance music overseas!" she declared as she set the headphones down.  "Why can't *our* country do that?"

He shrugged.

"Can you get it on tape?"

"I knew you'd like it, so I went ahead," he replied, setting the thin box on the counter.  "I *think* you'll like this one, but I'm not sure . . ."  He placed the needle on another record.

Priscilla took up the headphones, and was soon swaying to the erotic drums and wind instruments.

"Almost . . . primitive.  It's a new genre for me, but I like it.  Tape?"

"No, sorry, and considering where it's from, I doubt that'll ever be available."

"Okay, make me one, use all your noise-reduction tricks, you know."

The bright-eyed little man nodded and began to ring up Priscilla's purchases.

✳

Three well-known ballet teachers, all with trophies in glass cases from their performing days, watched intently as Priscilla danced to a piece of music *they* would not have chosen.

The twelve-year-old wore only tights, leotard, and leather dance slippers, allowing her critiquers to see the slightest mistake or weakness.

Colonel Ka-markla sat off to one side, feeling quite amazed that such a talented young dancer was willing to continue working for the Department of Defense when doing so put such strict limitations on her public accomplishments.

The song ended, Priscilla bowed to her judges, then seated herself on the floor in front of them.

"Nice," one began, "but every so often I see a hint of sloppiness where you could have perfect precision if you studied in a regular ballet program.  Your *port de bras* breaks the rules constantly, your turnout is irregular, and your fourth and fifth foot positions are weak.  I'll admit, it's nothing the audience is going to notice, only your teachers and advanced fellow performers."

Priscilla nodded. "I'm aware of some points when I want to tighten up my fourth and fifth, but my *port de bras* will probably always be . . . unusual."

"Your *relevés* are lower than they could be," the second teacher began, "and your *frappés* and *dégagés* could be much crisper, but I have to say that your over-all interpretation of the music is . . . amazing."

"Thank you. *Frappés* have always given me trouble."

"You could work out all those little issues," the third teacher declared, "and a few more that I see, if you would just accept our invitation to join the Metropolitan Ballet Company. I know that going professional can be a scary step, but you really are ready for it. You would immediately be in the middle ranks, working directly under world-class dancers."

"But you know I think most of the music you play is . . . boring."

The second teacher sighed. "Most great dancers humble themselves for the honor and fame, then discover that the music grows on them when they dance to it every day."

Priscilla smiled, then continued to listen as they critiqued her dancing for the next quarter hour. Finally she handed each teacher the agreed-upon amount of money and slipped into the dressing room to change.

✳

"Do you get your money's worth from those critiques?" Colonel Ka-markla asked as they sipped drinks and waited for their sandwiches to be made.

Priscilla shrugged. "Sometimes. I really do try for better fourth and fifth foot positions, but they're almost not . . . humanly possible."

Lisa chuckled. "You should have seen their faces when you told them their music was boring."

"They've heard it from me before. Mostly what I get from those critiques is reminders, every time, that dancing might be something I love to do, and I guess I'm pretty good at it, but it's not my real purpose. It's not what I *am*."

"Are you sure?"

Priscilla's sandwich was placed before her, so she took a bite while she thought about the question.

"Yeah. I try it on, so to speak, every time, for a few minutes, an hour, maybe a day. I roll it around in my head, imagine living and working in a world-class company. That might be ten steps up for a little girl dreaming of being a ballerina. I was once that little girl, five, six years old. For me, now, it would be ten steps down."

Lisa finished chewing a bite. "I see what you mean. It would be hard to top what you do three times a week. And the Department appreciates your continued commitment to your work. We have many independent contractors who make much more than you, and are worth much less."

Priscilla laughed and took another bite.

✳

When they arrived for the afternoon session at the skating rink, Priscilla immediately spotted the tall boy waiting for her in their usual spot. They wrapped arms around each other and shared a deep kiss before she turned her attention to putting on skates.

The large woman from the orphanage struggled into the seat beside Colonel Ka-markla in the snack bar. "If they made these any smaller, I'd have to use two."

Lisa smiled. "I think they designed everything for the kids."

"You fit in them okay. How do you stay so trim?"

"Join the military. You'll find out," the colonel said with a friendly smile.

The woman laughed. "I don't think they'd take me."

Lisa held her tongue.

"Do you think this relationship is good for them?" the woman asked, gesturing toward the skating floor where Priscilla and the boy were skating together slowly, holding hands.

The colonel didn't immediately answer, remembering the three or four other times they had had this exact same conversation. "For Priscilla, it's very important. Her therapist practically ordered it."

"Oh, yes. That's pretty unusual, isn't it?"

"Not for someone who does the kind of work Priscilla does."

"Which you can't tell me about."

The colonel smiled slightly. "How are you feeling about its effect on Brian?"

"Have to admit, all his bad habits seem to be gone, almost like they were never there. He hasn't had an incident since you sat down in my office two years ago, I called him in, and you showed him pictures of Priscilla . . ."

✳

The young couple huddled close at a little table in the dark restaurant dining room. A candle flickered in its holder between them. Sparkling cider bubbled in stemware.

"Your body guard's giving us more space tonight," Brian observed.

Priscilla glanced, and could barely see Lisa at a table in the lounge. "Remember, it's not *you* she's protecting me from."

"I know, but it's nice that she's farther away."

Priscilla smiled, leaned forward, and they kissed until the candle started burning their chins. They both chuckled and leaned back.

"Partly it's because I just passed all my tests," she explained, "and I'm packing now, too."

His eyes opened wide. "Your own piece?"

Priscilla opened a side compartment of her shoulder purse and handed the purse to him. "Look, but do not touch."

"It's a cannon!"

"It's only a thirty-eight," she said, taking her purse back. "I've fired a forty-five. *That's* a cannon!"

Warm bread and garlic butter arrived. Brian spread, then handed her the first slice. "*How* did you get a concealed-carry permit at twelve?"

"The military can make just about anything happen. When I asked to take the classes and tests, they smiled and said okay.  When I got better scores than most of their *security* people, they started thinking and talking, and realized it would make their jobs easier.  Of course, they had to emancipate me — minors can't get carry permits — but that was easy considering my educational level and income."

Brian chuckled.  "I get the feeling you could do anything you set your mind to."

"I hear *you're* getting some pretty good grades, too!" she declared with gleaming eyes.

He squirmed.  "Yeah, well, every time I'm tempted to get into trouble, I think of you, and I *know* I'd lose you if I screwed up . . ."

She nodded.  "It wouldn't be my choice, it would be the orphanage."

"I know.  And I just *don't* want to lose the only good thing I've ever had, so I have lots of time for homework."

Baked salmon with asparagus tips appeared in front of Priscilla, and a sirloin steak with baked potato in front of Brian.

"Anyone . . . interested in adopting you?" she asked between bites.

He laughed, not quite between bites.  "You asked me that last year.  People don't adopt thirteen-year-old boys with criminal records, and they don't adopt fourteen-year-old boys with criminal records."

Priscilla smiled.  "Just checking.  From my point of view, being completely selfish, if anyone *did* get interested, I'd have to do something to ruin it."

He grinned and shook his head.  "I don't think it'll be a problem."

"How long do I get to keep you tonight?" she asked.

"The usual — in by ten."

"I really look forward to the day I can keep you all night."

He looked into her dreamy eyes for a long moment.  "Me too."

✳   ✳   ✳

## Chapter 26: Sunday

Lieutenant Do-forva, eating breakfast and reading the newspaper in the dining room, glimpsed Heather emerge from her room, yawning and stretching, at about nine o'clock.  She knew the girl would get the next topic from her mail drawer, stop by the kitchen to get juice and say hello, then put on some music in the dance studio.

When a quarter hour had gone by, and Heather had neither gotten juice nor put on music, the lieutenant became a little concerned.  The twelve-year-old could be spontaneous, but her Sunday-morning routine was very predictable.

A minute later, a soft whimpering sound began, so Ginny rose to investigate.

She found Heather in a fetal position on the floor, right in front of the mail drawers, crumpled sheet of paper in hand, eyes red and cheeks wet.

"What's wrong?" Ginny asked, kneeling down.

Having a listener, the girl began crying loudly and clutching at the lieutenant desperately, but spoke no words.

The garage-level security sergeant was quickly up the stairs.  "What can I do?"

"Get Doctor Bo-kamla in here."

He strode into the office and grabbed a telephone.

"Come on, girl, sit up and tell me what's the matter," Ginny coaxed.

Heather sat up so she could clutch onto her listener more tightly, but continued crying like a baby who had just learned about hot stoves.

"We're getting Susan.  Do you need a medical doctor?"

"...no..." the lieutenant heard among the crying and whimpering.

"Doctor Bo-kamla's on the way," the sergeant informed.  "Can I get anyone anything?"

"I bet your blood sugar's low," Ginny said to the crying girl.  "Will you drink some juice?"

Without waiting for an answer, the sergeant headed for the kitchen. A minute later, he lined up six different cans for Heather to choose from.

"Hey girl," Ginny asserted, "peek out of those feelings for a moment and pick one, or I *will* get a medic, and he'll feed you *intravenously*."

Heather made some effort to collect herself, and grabbed a can of juice randomly. Her shaking fingers weren't ready to open it, so Ginny helped.

Over the next quarter hour, Heather slowly relaxed as she sipped her juice, but still didn't attempt any words. Lieutenant Do-forva noticed that she continued to clutch the sheet of paper that contained Monday's topic, so guessed that Heather's distress had something to do with it. Doctor Bo-kamla arrived and the sergeant let her in.

Susan joined Heather and Ginny on the floor. Heather continued to whimper and gaze around like a lost child.

"She hasn't spoken a clear word yet," Ginny reported, "but had enough presence of mind to start drinking juice when I threatened intravenous feeding."

"And the paper in her hand is . . ." the psychologist questioned.

"Tomorrow's topic, I think, but she hasn't let anyone see it."

"I . . ." Heather started to say, but then lapsed into deep sobs again.

"You can take all the time you need," Susan said, joining Ginny in comforting the girl. "Anything stressful happen yesterday?" the psychologist asked, looking at the lieutenant.

"Nothing in the security log, and Lisa didn't mention anything before she went home last night."

"I've been . . ."

Everyone waited as Heather struggled to get her feelings under control.

"I've been pretending all this time . . ." she managed to gasp out before breaking into howls and tears again.

Another quarter hour passed before Heather could explain her statement. By then, the sergeant had managed to cook up scrambled eggs and bacon, a combination nearly guaranteed to put a smile on Heather's face.

Still seated in the same spot on the floor, the twelve-year-old ate in silence as the lieutenant and the psychologist sat near, and the sergeant hovered within earshot.

"You know," Ginny began, "with a score of eighty-seven to one, and that *one* a matter of subtle word definitions, you're the very best pretender *any* program about the future has ever had!"

"I didn't mean that," Heather said, then took another bite of eggs. After chewing thoughtfully for a long moment, she pulled another tissue from the box, wiped her eyes again, and added it to the large pile.

"I didn't think so," Ginny assured.

"I've been . . . pretending to myself . . . that the wonderful life I have . . .

could just go on and on."

"Are you sure it can't?" Susan asked.

"Yeah.  The end starts tomorrow at . . . you know . . . zero-nine hundred."

Heather refused to show them the crumpled piece of paper, saying they would find out soon enough.  She asked them to not tell anyone else that she was stressed out about it, and they agreed to only log that Doctor Bo-kamla came in for support.

Susan stayed the entire day, and sometimes Heather talked, but never about the next day's topic.  At other times, the girl would just find an environment that seemed to fit her mood, claiming she needed to spend some time preparing.

While washing dishes in the kitchen, she gazed out the window at the green hills.  Curled up on her favorite bunk in the bomb shelter, she closed her eyes and imagined what she would say the next morning.  Lying on her back on the cold concrete of the parking garage, she let her mind go blank and listened to what she called *the music of the spheres*.

Susan was always near in case Heather wanted to talk, but was painfully aware that the mental and emotional needs of this twelve-year-old were unlike any of her regular clients, and unlike anything she had studied in school.

At nearly midnight, Heather got ready for bed so Susan would go home and get some sleep herself.

As soon as the psychologist was gone, Heather changed back into casual clothes.  She could think of plants that needed watering, some windows that could use a wash, and a floor or two that needed scrubbing — just enough stuff to keep her busy until the day shift started arriving in the morning.

## Chapter 27: Monday

Doctor Bo-kamla arrived at seven o'clock, worry written on her face. Heather was already dancing.

"You didn't sleep, did you?" Susan asked from the dance studio doorway.

Heather flashed her a grin. "But I did remember to keep my blood sugar up. And I *promise* you, I'll be in bed right after lunch today."

"I guess . . . you know your rhythms better than anyone else."

"I must admit, I surprised myself yesterday. After five hundred and forty-five sessions, I didn't think *any* topic could bother me."

"You were wrong."

Heather nodded as the song ended. "What's Maria cooking?"

Nine o'clock approached, and with Ben on vacation, Ginny was behind the tape recorder. As she chatted with the new records specialist, a young sergeant just learning the procedures, she spotted Heather coming out of the dining room laughing about something with General Bo-seklin. More officers and professors were coming up the stairs and finding seats, so Ginny turned her attention back to the binder the sergeant had open on his lap.

A few minutes later, General Ba-kerga stopped by the couch. "You comfortable with that machine, Lieutenant?"

"Yes, Sir. Lieutenant Ta-nibon and I have been switching off for several sessions now."

"Good. I'm going to start a walk-through."

After the general was gone, the sergeant took on a puzzled expression. "Walk-through?"

"Someone has to make sure no one's in the building without proper clearance. Any security person could do it, but George must have noticed we're all busy. He's mellowed a lot since making general and becoming security chief of the whole air base."

The sergeant nodded and looked at the binder again.  "So the tape goes in this slot after the session?"

"And the blackboard photos in this plastic sleeve after we number them with the black marker . . ."

Once the tape was going and the formalities were out of the way, Heather stood silently and looked over the assembled team.  As was always the case, few of them had any idea what the topic would be.  Part of their commitment was regular attendance, except for occasional vacations, as no one could predict when certain expertise would be needed.  Even the generals and colonels who planned the topics were often surprised by who was most involved in the discussions.

"Today . . . is going to be . . . a little different," Heather began solemnly.  "For the first time, we're going to look deep into the next century — at least, as deep as I can take us — and . . . that will be far enough."

Heather noticed General Ko-fenral frowning.

"We'll be looking at conditions in a much broader sense, and not discussing any specific laws, treaties, or events.  A thorough exploration of this topic will require *at least* three sessions, easily six, and to be frank, I can't predict when we'll get back to regular topics."

Now most of the officers and about half the professors were frowning.  Heather felt a fleeting desire for a hole to crawl into.

"I hope all of you will try very hard to be present at all three sessions this week.  Is anyone missing, Sergeant?"

The new records specialist, who had just completed the team attendance checklist for the first time, fumbled with his binder for a moment.  "Um . . . only Lieutenant Ta-nibon is absent."

"That's right, Ben's on vacation, sipping tropical mangosteen cocktails somewhere . . ."

Chuckles coursed through the room, lightening the mood.

Heather added her own smile.  "Also, I'm not sure when we'll have time for questions, possibly not today.  I've warned Maria that we definitely won't get out early, and might be late.  She promised to keep everything hot."

More smiles and nods helped with the mood.

Doctor Bo-kamla was, as usual, quite amazed at Heather's ability to manage the emotional tone of the meeting, and knew very few of her fellow psychologists could do as well.

Heather drew in a slow breath as she took some random steps in the middle of the meeting circle and gazed at the floor.  Eventually she looked up.  "I will begin the topic with a very personal story.  I will, as you have heard me do many times, use first-person pronouns when I really mean *the person whose memories I have.*  You'll have to forgive me.  The accurate term is just too clumsy."

They all nodded their forgiveness in advance.

"You probably remember me saying that I died at age eighty in the year

3735.  I don't know if you ever noticed, but I never said I died *of* old age.  I was very careful to always say I died *in* old age.  It is certainly true that my body was failing in some ways, but none of those were fatal.  My eyesight was almost gone, down to just unfocused light and dark, with almost no color.  My hands were weak, but nothing unusual for that age.  I walked with a cane, but rarely fell, and luckily never injured myself doing so."

Heather saw that her listeners had settled into the story, their earlier discomfort replaced by a tender sadness.

"The truth is, I did not die of any of the ailments usually associated with old age.  I died of starvation."

After giving them a few moments to recover, Heather began to chat about the circumstances of the last few years of the life she remembered.  It wasn't long before she focused the story on the relevant events.

"... and I clearly recall the young man, about fifteen, who carried my groceries home the last time I was able to get any.  I remember him so well because he was the last human being I ever spoke to.  I could not see him clearly, of course, but knew he had dark hair.  His voice was soft and musical, and I remember thinking he could have been a talented singer.  I gave him a small gold coin as a tip, and he was tongue-tied with gratitude."

Heather glanced at her audience, and judged she was holding their interest.

"Two weeks later, I journeyed to the little grocery store again.  A block and a half south, three short blocks west.  When you're nearly blind, counting blocks is important!"

Several people smiled, and Doctor Tu-feltin grinned without quite looking at Heather.

"Sea gulls squawked, as usual, but no human voices came from any direction.  I arrived at the store, but found it locked and silent.  I called and knocked, but got no answer.  Feeling with my cane, I discovered that the stuff they usually had out on the sidewalk — bundles of firewood, buckets, sometimes pumpkins and squash — were all gone.  I worked my way completely around the outside of the store, calling out for anyone who might hear, but found nothing and no one."

Heather could sense they shared her frustration.

"The one thing I could not do, and wished with all my heart that someone would help me with, just for a minute, was to read any sign that explained why the store closed, or where it might have moved to."

General Ba-kerga nodded with sympathy.

"I went back to the store several more times, in case I had just gone on a bad day, and I walked as far as I could in every direction, always planning my route beforehand, and carefully counting blocks.  I called and listened.  Only the sea gulls called back."

Several team members sniffled.

"Although it was dangerously far — eleven blocks each way — twice I undertook the long journey to the nearest busy street.  Or I should say, the nearest street that had *once* been busy.  Both times I sat on a bench for hours, and never heard a human voice or a vehicle."

"Wow . . ." someone said softly.

"My mind was still sharp — I realized I had created my own trap.  Because the city water system had failed about eight years earlier, I had been careful to get a house that had a roof-top rainwater catching system.  I actually *bought* the house.  By that time, not many people bothered with such formalities."

Several team members chuckled nervously.

"But I didn't realize what would happen if the neighborhood ceased to have a store.  I must explain that by 3730 or so, the store was little more than a trading post.  Few factory-made goods were for sale anywhere.  Mostly it handled vegetables from people's gardens, some fresh fish, a little home-canned food, firewood, and second-hand stuff.  Even so, it had provided me with the basics."

She saw nods of understanding.

"So at some point in the middle of April 3735, the little store was gone without a trace, all other people seem to have left the neighborhood, and I was completely without the ability to relocate myself to . . . anywhere the necessities of life might be available.  I was angry for a while that no one, not even the fifteen-year-old young man, had cared enough to come tell me.  But I eventually let go of my anger, counted my blessings, and started searching my cupboards."

After a moment of silence, Heather began laughing and crying at the same time.  Most people in the room were unsure how to respond.

"The most memorable experience . . . of the last month of my life . . . was spending an entire day . . . working with barely-seen kitchen tools and weak hands . . . to get a jar open . . . only to discover that it was very hot mustard!"

They laughed with her, but many eyes were far from dry.

✳

"I could go on for days sharing memories from the last few weeks of our old psychologist's life, as they are much closer in time for me than most of the topics we've covered.  But that would give the team little additional insight.  Suffice to say that she died in her own bed, dealing bravely with the pain but not letting it make her crazy.  I guess that's about the best anyone could hope for under the circumstances."

Most people nodded with long faces, while Colonel Ma-soran dabbed at tears.

"Susan, however, as my therapist, might get to sit through a more detailed account."

Many of those long faces chuckled, and Doctor Bo-kamla smiled back at Heather.

"If you do that, please record it," General Bo-seklin requested.

Heather nodded.  "So . . . why was a respected, successful, retired psychologist, with plenty of money and other assets, who owned and lived in a nice little house in a middle-class suburb of *this* great city, unable to get utilities, groceries, or any kind of help with anything?"

"That's what we're all wondering," General Ko-fenral said as everyone else nodded.

Heather turned to the blackboard and marked off every ten years from 3650 to 3750 along the bottom, and the numbers one through eight along the left side. "Doctor Tu-feltin, what was the population of the world in 3660?"

"Almost exactly three billion."

"Thank you. As you know, I remember few precise dates from the future, but sometimes one was so memorable that it stuck in my mind. On the thirty-first of October, 3712, as close as these things can be estimated, the population of the world will pass seven billion . . ."

Several people whistled.

Heather glanced at them with an understanding smile, then turned back to the blackboard. "I don't remember exactly when the other whole billions will be passed, but it's a smooth exponential curve that looks something like this." She finished sketching a curving line that went up more and more steeply as it moved from left to right. "As you know, it will be a fairly peaceful and very prosperous half century. Deaths from wars and natural disasters — thousands or at most tens of thousands — don't show up on this scale."

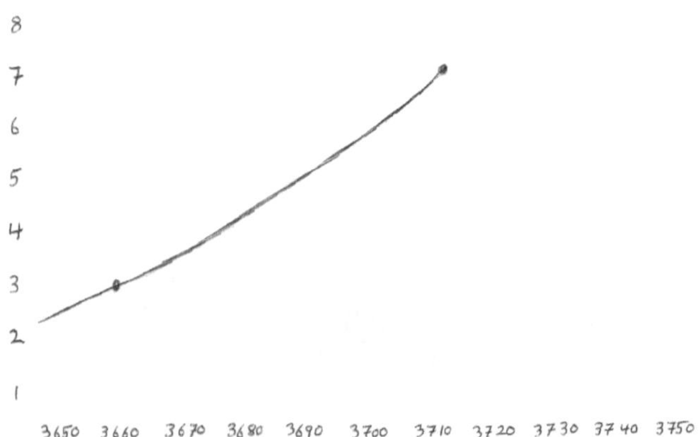


"I'm confused," Doctor Po-selem said. "This seems to contradict the story you just told."

Heather put a finger to her lips.

The physicist glanced around and saw several people glaring at him. "Oops, sorry, I forgot."

"As Chris just experienced, incomplete stories will often be confusing. One of the reasons this date is so memorable is that it's the *last* time the human race will pass a whole billion."

Heather was quite sure no one was breathing. She couldn't think of anything she could do to help them at that moment, so she returned to the blackboard.

"We just barely reach an estimated seven and a half billion in 3717." She continued the population curve up a little, then sketched a hump at about the right date and level. "After that, things start happening very quickly. The last official estimate I could get was *two* and a half billion in 3730." She sketched a line sloping down steeply to that point. "I had radios and batteries. Too bad I couldn't eat them."

Except for a few nervous chuckles, the entire room sat in stunned silence.

Heather knew she dared not pause for long. "I do not know what happened to world population after that, as all official news broadcasts failed later that same year. It could have recovered quickly, leveled out, continued to drop more slowly ..." She sketched several alternate curves with arrowheads. "... or continued to follow this trend right down to the bottom. In that case, our old psychologist didn't miss much."

Several mouths were hanging open.

"Judging by local conditions, and what I could learn from amateur radio operators, it was most likely one of these bottom two situations."

Some cheeks were wet. A few people looked like they wanted to run and hide.

Heather knew how they felt. She had experienced the same range of emotions just the day before.

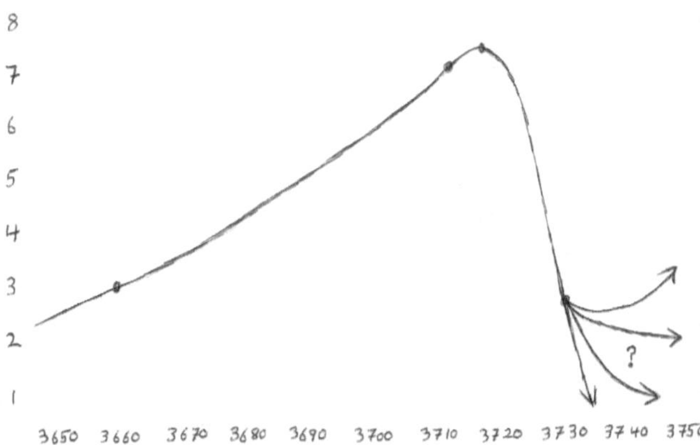



"It's almost eleven o'clock. Yes, I know why this population crash happens, and I promise not to leave you in suspense. But I believe many of us have needs, so I'm going to declare a fifteen-minute break. However, I want everyone to hold their discussions until we've taken one more step together."

Several people dashed for the toilet rooms.

Heather collapsed into her plush chair.

General Ko-fenral made a thumbs-up sign. "Good call on the break."

Susan came over. "What can I bring you?"

"Tropical mangosteen cocktail, double shot of rum, crushed ice, lemon twist."

The therapist chuckled. "I'll see what I can find."

About twenty minutes later, the team members slowly, reluctantly, dragged themselves back to the meeting circle.

"I'm going to tell you what caused the population to crash," Heather began when she stood up after everyone got settled, "but I'm not going to give you, at this time, any details. I think you need to hear it from one of your own scientists. Unfortunately, the kind of scientist we need is not yet on the team . . ."

"We'll get one!" General Bo-seklin declared.

Heather nodded. "Once the proper scientist has spoken on what I'm about to describe, then we can all discuss it much more fruitfully, and I can fill in actual events."

She turned and looked at the blackboard silently for a moment. "There is nothing unusual about this population curve. Any undergrad biology student would recognize it. Any organism . . . I repeat, *any* organism . . . will always strive to maximize its population. Then it will reach some kind of limit, usually the food supply, and the population will fall. Yeast in a vat of wine . . . deer on a wooded island . . . people in the world . . . no real difference."

A few of her listeners looked a bit offended by the comparison. Heather couldn't bring herself to care.

"Many different kinds of limits could have done this to us, but the one that will get us is not even on our radar yet. Maybe someday we'll talk about why that is, and I'm sure Susan will have some insights to contribute, but we aren't ready to do that today."

They looked relieved. Heather saw Colonel Ma-soran make a note.

"What crushes us is . . . we gain one of the powers of God, without also gaining the wisdom of God."

She saw that she had their undivided attention.

"We began, in about the year 3500, to change the climate of our planet. It started very, very slowly and has not been noticeable, is *still* not noticeable, and will not *BECOME* noticeable until after the year 3700. But the change is happening, slowly, every year, accumulating more and more, compounding and reinforcing itself."

Several people were trying to take notes. Others just stared with wide eyes.

"By the time it's clear what's happening, it will be irreversible. Scientists from that point on, for as long as there *are* scientists, will argue about *when* we could have done something. Most will agree that we could have stopped it if we had acted in 3650 or 3660. Almost none will suggest we could do anything after 3680."

She took a moment to bracket those years on the blackboard, then turned around and saw realization dawning on a few faces.

"Yes, isn't it interesting that I have brought you these memories, and you have grown to trust me, just as we are passing the middle of the time period in which *maybe*, if scientists of the future are correct, something can be done to avoid a collapse of our population, and therefore our civilization, in the near future?"

Several heads nodded slowly.

"It's almost noon.  I want to end by giving you some hard numbers.  These are the numbers we need a scientist, a *climatologist*, to talk to us about as soon as possible."

She turned to the blackboard and drew a simple graph as she spoke.  "Plus one degree Celsius in 3715, plus two degrees in 3721, plus four degrees in 3729."

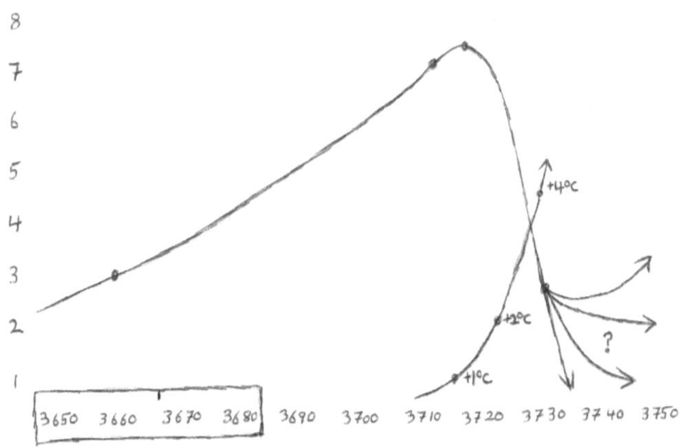


She turned back to the team.  "What I have shared with you today is too big to understand completely in any short timeframe.  Many of you will have emotional reactions, and believe me, I've had them too.  In the coming days and weeks, we will take this apart, piece by piece, and get any expert advice we don't have among us.  We'll digest it together, until we understand it and no longer feel overwhelmed by it.  Then, and only then, will we have the knowledge and wisdom to begin contemplating what, if anything, can or should be done."

"Well said," Three-star General Ko-fenral declared.

"Ginny, please close the session," Heather requested.

"Program P-Seventeen, Session Five Forty-Six ends at twelve hundred hours, seven minutes.  Two blackboard photographs."

*

At lunch, Heather tried to sit with others and listen to the conversation, but her eyes were soon closing against her will.  She barely managed to finish her salad and enchiladas before dragging herself to bed.

While she began her fifteen-hour nap, the generals and colonels met in General Bo-seklin's office.

For the first minute, they just looked at each other.

Colonel Ma-soran, as the program's executive officer, decided to break the ice.  "This is the *one*, isn't it?"

Every face held a mixture of excitement and dread — excitement that all their time, efforts, and expenses would finally be vindicated — dread about the nature of the prediction itself.

General Bo-seklin took a deep breath.  "It looks that way, but we need to know a lot more, and as Heather said, there's no way to do that in one day, even one week."

"And yet," General Ko-fenral stepped in, "there is some urgency about this.  If the scientists she quoted were correct . . . will be correct . . . you know what I mean . . . then we act *now*, or very soon, or forget it."

"Forgetting it . . . doesn't sound like a good plan," Colonel Ma-soran strongly suggested.

After a long moment, General Bo-seklin nodded.  "I'll have a climatologist in here on Wednesday, even if it's without clearance just to study the hypothetical situation.  And I want all those civilian professors in my office in five minutes.  Lisa, George, help me put the fear of God into them about doing anything prematurely . . ."

✳  ✳  ✳

## Chapter 28: Wednesday

By Wednesday morning, Heather was back to her normal routine of getting at least some sleep each night, and dancing each morning to wake up her mind and body.  She wandered out to the office when she smelled breakfast cooking.

"Good morning, Heather," Colonel Ma-soran greeted from her desk.

"Hi, Sarah.  It was really nice to have an empty mail drawer yesterday.  I hope it still is."

"Actually, it's not."

Heather frowned as she unlocked it, then burst out laughing when she discovered only her paycheck.

"Don't worry," Sarah assured, "you won't be getting regular topics for a while.  My guess would be a long while.  We have that non-cleared scientist today."

"Yeah, I met with Sam yesterday to figure out how to handle that.  We agreed someone had to lead the meeting that he'd respect."

"I'm sorry it has to be that way, but I also know *everyone's* going to be watching him to see how he handles you even *being* on the team.  If we see the slightest disrespect, then he won't be invited back.  By the way, Maria made bacon and eggs."

"That's the *real* reason I got up!"

*

"Good morning, everyone," the short little lady, who usually sat in the back row, said from Heather's place.  "For the benefit of our guest, I'm Betty Ko-silma, doctor of chemistry.  Anyone missing, Corporal?"

"Just the lieutenant on vacation."

"Good.  Please notice that the security lamp is off, as we have a guest speaker today.  Welcome, Doctor To-marin.  We are grateful that you were able to come on short notice, and we are all looking forward to whatever light you can shed on the hypothetical scenario we are studying.  Please take a moment to tell us about yourself."

The tall, nearly-bald man acted quite uncomfortable with the person leading the meeting.  "I'm ... surprised that a military program would have ..." He glanced around, but didn't see anyone who shared his discomfort, so he tried to collect himself.  "I'm ... um ... a doctor of meteorology and climatology, and I teach at East Valley College.  But I must point out that I haven't had a chance to prepare anything ..."  As he spoke, he tried to address his comments to someone other than Doctor Ko-silma, but the layout, with the generals beside or behind him, made it difficult.

Betty noticed and ignored it.  "No preparation was necessary, or even desirable, as we want a completely fresh opinion on our study scenario."  She stood and picked up the chalk.  "And even though we've already discussed some other aspects of it, today we're just going to work with the most essential element, the hypothetical temperature data, so we can get a very objective analysis from you."

She started drawing on the blackboard.  "We have a reference year, at which point the average annual temperature has been completely stable and unremarkable for decades.  Our data points are year forty-eight with plus one degree, year fifty-four with plus two degrees, and finally, year sixty-two with plus four degrees.  You have the floor, Doctor To-marin."

The chemist sat down in the chair next to the blackboard.

The climatologist appeared reluctant to respond to her invitation, but couldn't see any other option.  "Um ... okay ... these data points must be anomalies, exceptions in an otherwise stable climate ..."  He looked at the generals.

"No," Doctor Ko-silma began, "these are representative points along a smooth curve."

He pretended not to hear for a moment, but when he saw all the officers nod toward the chemist, he breathed a sigh and turned back to the blackboard.

"Then something's wrong here, as nothing like this has ever happened before.  This is not a climate scenario that could take place on our planet.  You must be modeling conditions on another planet ..."

Again he looked at the generals, but cast his gaze wider, also glancing at the male officers in uniform, and the male scientists he recognized.

They all looked at Betty.

She took a slow breath.  "Although it's hypothetical, we're interested in knowing the effects such a change would have on *our* planet."

He stared at the blackboard, careful not to look at the woman scientist.  "Then there must be a mistake.  These must be tenths of a degree."

"Nope.  Whole degrees."

"Fahrenheit?"

"Celsius."

A long moment passed as he continued to stare at the blackboard.  "Oh my God . . ."

*

Without much further difficulty, they managed to get the climatologist to describe the severe droughts, massive forest and grassland fires, powerful tropical storms, and devastating floods that would come as the scenario approached plus one degree.

Between plus one and plus two degrees, the ice caps would melt, he was sure, causing the oceans to rise inches per year, then feet per year, too fast for anything in their path to be saved that wasn't on wheels. But the greatest damage would actually come from the jet stream, steady winds high in the atmosphere, that would become chaotic, or stall completely, as the poles became ice-free. Severe weather systems, hot or cold, would stay in one place for weeks, or be funneled into regions that had never before experienced such weather.

His nerve failed him as he attempted to imagine conditions approaching plus four degrees. He begged for a break in the presentation.

Doctor Ko-silma stood up. "Fifteen minutes. Remember, the security lamp is off."

*

"Can you explain, Doctor, why these effects are so extreme," General Ba-kerga requested, "when the temperature changes we're talking about seem so small to us non-scientists. Even four degrees Celsius is less than typical night-to-day variation."

"Because these are yearly global *averages*. They usually vary only hundredths of a degree, at most a few tenths, even across a decade. What we're talking about here is like going in and out of *ice ages*, but that happens over thousands of years. To see whole degree changes over mere decades is more like a climate *explosion* than a climate *change*."

General Bo-seklin squirmed in his chair. "I know it won't be easy, and I realize the science is probably fuzzy on this, but please give us some idea of what the world would be like four degrees hotter than today."

The scientist breathed to steady his nerves. "It might come close to an extinction event for the human race, even though a few people live in such climates today. Very few. But nothing we call civilization would be possible. People could survive only in tiny tribal groups in scattered climate niches, like caves. The equatorial latitudes would become completely uninhabitable. Humanity would be pushed as far north and south as they could get, and therefore divided into six or seven regions that would have little chance of contact with each other."

"What is a rapid climate change like this called?" General Ko-fenral asked.

The climatologist was silent for a long time. "It has no name. It's never happened to the human race, and it's never been studied, even hypothetically. The only word that comes to mind is . . . Hell."

The entire team sat staring at the blackboard in silence.

*  *  *

## Chapter 29: Friday

"Wasn't *he* fun?" Heather asked the entire team from her seat.

The room erupted with nervous laughter.

"Sorry about his attitude," General Bo-seklin said, turning to look at Doctor Ko-silma. "Considering his disrespect of women, there's no way he could be on the team."

"Thanks for subbing for me, Betty," Heather said with a grin. "I owe you one . . . or maybe two or three."

"Any time. After twenty years in academia, my skin's pretty thick."

"He seemed to know his stuff," Heather admitted, "and what he described, in general, matches my memories. I can, and will as time allows, give you details about multi-year snow droughts, super-storms, blocking anti-cyclones, fire storms, land hurricanes, major cities abandoned as sea-level rises, including our capital, and all the other gory details, but that's not as important as today's topic."

She stood up and looked around. "*Why* is the climate changing? *Why* will the average annual temperature go up so quickly? *Why*, if we trust my memories, will the population of the world crash within the lifetime of . . . anyone about my age or younger?"

Doctor Po-selem raised his hand timidly.

"Chris?"

"I know we're not supposed to interrupt, but you *did* phrase it as a question, so I thought I'd offer a possibility . . . if you want."

Heather grinned sheepishly. "I did phrase it as a question, didn't I?"

Everyone chuckled or smiled at her.

"Sure, let's brainstorm, see if you, or anyone else, can come close. You have the floor, Chris."

He stood and rubbed his chin for a moment. "Some scientists have become concerned about the heat energy we're releasing in the modern age.

Ships, trains, cars, trucks, airplanes, electrical generation, building furnaces, industry ... it all comes to quite a bit.  Most physicists think the planet's ability to radiate heat away into space, at least at night, is sufficient to compensate, but that notion is untested."

"Interesting.  Anyone else?  Richard."

Doctor Tu-feltin the historian stood, but stayed by his chair.  "As I understand it, we don't really *know* where we are in the ice-age cycle.  Perhaps this inter-glacial period is just destined to be much warmer than the world currently is, and so it's a natural continuation of what began eight or nine thousand years ago."

"Also interesting.  Anyone else?  Sarah."

"I've read that our use of antibiotics might lead to highly drug-resistant diseases.  Could that cause such a population crash?"

"Thank you, Sarah.  Anyone else?"

With facial expressions, they surrendered.

"I appreciate your thoughts, and many people in the future will look in those same places, because the real cause is so ... surprising.

"Chris, you get half a point for proposing an *anthropogenic* cause — a *man-made* cause.  Every school kid after 3715 will be able to say *anthropogenic climate change*, even if they don't know what it means.  But no, the extra heat we generate is not the problem, although it certainly *adds* to the problem.

"Richard, half a point, as you are completely correct about that possibility, but the *speed* of the heating trend in question has another cause.

"Sarah, half a point, as you also mentioned an anthropogenic cause, and diseases, especially drug-resistant ones, will play a large part in bringing the population down.  But that is a *proximal* cause, not a *primal* cause."

Colonel Ma-soran nodded.

"Remember on Monday I said it's not even on our radar yet?  Everyone take a deep breath, hold it for five seconds, then let it out."

They did, a little self-consciously.

"There.  That's the problem."

After a few seconds, Doctor Ko-silma's mouth dropped opened.  "Oh my God.  Carbon dioxide."

Heather drew the offending molecule on the blackboard, along with its formula, $CO_2$.   "This little beastie is not on any scientist's or environmentalist's radar because it's as natural as apples and daisies.  Every animal, and even plants at night, release Carbon dioxide.  Also any fire, all decomposition, and many other chemical changes.

"It's a *greenhouse gas*, acting just like the glass on a greenhouse by letting in light but trapping heat.  Every school kid will know that term before the end, too.

"Since it's completely natural, the ecosystem has ways of pulling it back out of the atmosphere, and has been doing so since the beginning.  Plants in sunlight do most of the work, but water and soil help, too.

"So it's not the *presence* of Carbon dioxide in the air that's causing the heating trend, it's the presence of *too much*. Like I said on Monday, it started very slowly in about 3500. Today there are more than three billion breathing people in the world. About a third of those are driving cars, trucks, airplanes, and such. Most are heating their homes, and cooking, with fire. There will eventually be seven and a half billion. All of them *want* to breathe, drive cars, and heat their homes.

"By the time the world recognizes the problem, in about 3710, here's what the situation will look like."

She turned to the blackboard and drew four boxes. "This is rough and simple, but it's the single most important thing I can give you from the scientific thinking of the future.

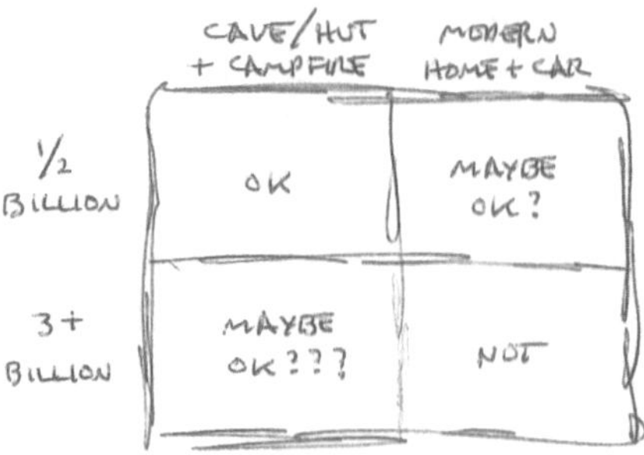


"We know the ecosystem of the planet can handle half a billion people living in caves or huts, and cooking on little campfires. Scientists of the future *think* that about the same number could have a small modern home and a little car. As another option, *maybe* a larger number could have the caveman life-style, but that's very debatable. What's *not* debatable is billions of people having a modern life-style. The Carbon Cycle of the planetary ecosystem can't handle it. Hard, cold reality. Death trap. End of story. I'm very, very sorry."

Heather sat down.

The silence, as they gazed at the blackboard, stretched for several minutes. Heather hoped Doctor Tu-feltin, the blind historian, could visualize it.

"I open the session to questions."

Still the silence lingered for another minute or two.

"So ..." Doctor Tu-feltin finally said, "this is the scientific consensus of 3730?"

"Society was in shambles by then, Richard. Most scientific thinking and writing on the subject will be done in the teens and early twenties."

"And the population right now is ..." Doctor Bo-leden inquired.

"Three and a half billion," the historian informed.

General Ba-kerga wore a suspicious frown. "How did they arrive at half a billion as a workable population?"

Heather spoke from her seat.  "Primarily by looking at world population before Carbon-based energy sources — coal, oil, and natural gas — began to make our modern lives possible.  They correlated that with Carbon dioxide data from bubbles trapped in the ice caps.  The planetary ecosystem does not seem to be bothered by half a billion cavemen or peasants, and their typical activities.  The belief — or at least hope — that half a billion could have modern, comfortable lives is based on the very *best* in efficient housing and transportation — tiny, well-insulated apartments, and itty-bitty cars or scooters like used overseas.  *Forget* big luxury cars, airplanes, and most modern industries."

Another minute of silence passed.

"What, exactly, will be the direct cause of two-thirds of the people dying?" Colonel Ma-soran asked with a long, sad face.

"The collapse of commercial agriculture as we pass the plus-one-degree point.  It's completely dependent on a stable climate, modern transportation, electricity, hybrid seeds, chemical fertilizers and pesticides — all produced far away from the farms.  When any one of those becomes a problem, it can usually be fixed.  When *all* of them become problems . . ."

After a moment of thought, Sarah nodded.

"There will be warning signs.  When the honey bees die off on land, and the little sardines in the sea, you'll know that human civilization is doomed. That will happen in the teens."

Several people cringed.

"Growing food will still be possible, even in the 3730's, as long as you have a source of water, such as a stream coming from a mountain canyon. Gardens and small fields, worked by hand, sent food to the little store near my house, and probably continued to produce and sell food *somewhere* after I was gone.  But we don't, and indeed can't, feed billions of people from a few little gardens and fields worked by hand."

The silence lengthened as noon approached.

"Heather, in your opinion," Two-star General Bo-seklin asked, "is this the future event we should be most concerned about, and maybe ... do something about?"

Heather looked at him and took a deep breath.  After blinking several times, she slowly nodded, just once.

✳  ✳  ✳

# Chapter 30: Friday Afternoon and Evening

Few team members had much appetite.  Those who ate lunch barely tasted their food.  Maria wondered if she had accidentally left out all the spices.

The generals and colonels gathered in General Bo-seklin's office again, but for a long minute, no one knew where to start.

"I am amazed," Sarah said after a while, just for something to say, "at Heather's ability to give us a highly-condensed version, without any extraneous detail.  She's like — what's that new kind of focused light?"

"Laser beam," George replied.

Lisa nodded.  "She's had twelve years to think about how to tell us."

The silence returned.

"We are obviously not ready to talk about what we're going to *do*," General Ko-fenral began.  "I think we should take a few weeks just to ask questions — Heather, the scientists, especially the chemist.  Please make sure she's coming on Monday."

Sarah nodded and made a note.

"There's a part of me," George admitted, "that wishes Heather didn't have such a damn good track record."

Lisa laughed.  "I don't think she would have told us about this, even if we asked directly, until she had that track record."

Sam nodded agreement.  "Let's go tell everyone that we'll be in Learning Mode for a while, and invite them all to bring in questions, answers, articles, suggestions for experts to listen to, and anything else that might help us understand this stuff."

They all rose and headed for the door.

✳

The scientists seemed reluctant to leave, as if they were in a place of safety, and the world outside might eat them alive. Many had articles in their files they planned to bring. Doctor Betty Ko-silma assured Colonel Ma-soran she wouldn't miss a session.

Eventually the professors made their way downstairs and into the blind transports. Most received gentle reminders about security from Colonel Ka-markla. A few got stern looks from General Ba-kerga, who had somewhat reverted to his old ways, considering the topic now under discussion.

Doctor Bo-kamla sensed her young client might want to spend some time talking that evening, so she stayed.

✳

Once most of the visitors were gone, General Bo-seklin stepped out of his office with Colonel Ma-soran close behind. He saw who was hanging around the meeting room, and heard Maria in the kitchen. "Good. Just the right people. Short meeting, everyone! You too, Maria!"

They all found seats.

"Sarah had an intuition, and I'm going to follow it. The temptation will be great for someone to leak something at this point. Things could happen fast. You people, who are all based here, and Doctor Bo-kamla, who might as well set up her office in the bomb shelter . . ."

Susan looked embarrassed. Lisa smiled and Ginny chuckled.

". . . effectively form an Inner Support Team. I'm not sure if you're primarily supporting Heather, or each other . . ."

"I feel light as a feather!" the twelve-year-old declared. "A great weight was lifted from my shoulders this week . . . or at least . . . you guys get to help me carry it, now."

Sarah and Maria both looked at the girl like proud mothers.

"Fact remains," Sam went on, "we don't know what's ahead. Although I'm not asking you to take on a greater share of the load concerning the topic, you are here more often than the others. That may force you to make decisions, or take actions, concerning Heather or each other, without perfect information or regular leadership."

After a moment of silence, Susan spoke softly. "Do you have any idea how unusual it is to hear something like that from a military officer?"

Sam took a deep breath. "I think I've learned a thing or two from . . . *someone* . . . in the last five years." He smiled at Heather, and she grinned back.

"I can't define this idea any better right now, but we'll meet on Fridays when we can. Bring questions and thoughts."

He looked around at his people, but didn't sense any concerns that had easy answers. "Everything in good shape for the weekend?"

"Guard schedule is all set," Lisa reported. "Heather will be out most of tomorrow with Lieutenant Do-forva."

"Kitchen's well-stocked," Maria announced. "I'm finishing a couple of things, but I'll be out in an hour or two."

General Bo-seklin nodded and said good-night.

※

"You said you wanted to counsel refugees," Heather began after she and her therapist got comfortable in the lowest level of the facility, "so having your office in a bomb shelter sort of makes sense!"

Susan laughed. "That means I'd have to put the address in the telephone book . . ."

"No, never mind, forget I said anything!"

Susan smiled, but her smile quickly faded. "In a sense, we're both psychologists, right?"

Heather blinked a few times. "In a sense."

"So you'll know what I'm talking about when I express my worries about your . . . little matrix."

"If I don't, I'll ask."

"Good." She pulled a paper sketch of it out of her purse and unfolded it flat on the table.

|  | Cave/Hut & Campfire | modern Home + Car |
|---|---|---|
| ½ Billion | OK | maybe OK? |
| 3+ Billion | maybe OK??? | Not |

"I know politics is not a strong point for either of us."

Heather nodded.

"But I know enough to realize that this is not a *problem* that can be solved by the normal political process. Our leaders like to make little adjustments to the existing rules and declare problems solved. Anything more drastic is . . . unthinkable."

The girl frowned slightly.

"There's a word for this kind of problem, took me a while to remember. This is a *predicament*. I'm sure you know, as well as I, that human beings are not very good at handling predicaments — problems that are unsolvable within the current structure of society."

"I think . . . I agree."

"So you and I need to put our heads together, because the rest of the team is NOT going to want to hear this. When we get to talking about what we should *do* about this . . . climate change and population crash . . . the rest of the team is going to be looking for simple *solutions*. I'm not saying they shouldn't try, but someone has to be ready to explain the insanity that's going to show up everywhere — from the grocery store to the president's office — when this gets out."

Heather stared at the copy of her little matrix with big, round eyes.

"That will have to be you and me."

Heather nodded slowly as she continued to stare at the sheet of paper.

* * *

## Chapter 31: Learning Mode

Lieutenant Do-forva noticed an unusual intensity about Heather all day Saturday.

At her dance class, she put so much energy and heart into each movement, even at the barre, that the teacher repeatedly looked on with amazement.

For lunch, Heather ordered several things she had never tasted before, and savored every bite.

During the skating session, she seemed torn between kissing Brian in the game room, and using her best art-skating techniques for every song.

Finally, Heather insisted on paying for all three of them at the finest restaurant in the area, where every meal came in seven courses, with lots of time between each for sipping drinks and sharing intimate conversation.

Ginny, sitting alone at a corner table, wished *she* could have brought a date, too.

✳

With no topic to prepare on Sunday, Heather slept in, then she and Lisa spent the entire afternoon at Doctor Bo-kamla's house.

They took turns reading articles and case histories aloud, all shedding light on the human ability — or more often, inability — to handle problems with no solutions.  The most troublesome were those where the person or group was under pressure to solve it anyway, and could not just walk away.  The result was usually some form of violence, and sometimes temporary insanity.

At first Lisa felt completely inadequate, like a child among intellectual giants.  But as the afternoon progressed, she began to understand what they were so concerned about.  And, she realized, a military command structure was about the *worst* environment to be in when unsolvable problems — predicaments — were staring you in the face.

Monday morning was abuzz with thoughts and opinions. Most of the team members arrived early, anxious to chat about the issues that were weighing so heavily on their minds and souls. Maria had a dining room full of people at breakfast.

Heather was in a light but quiet mood, enjoying her reduced responsibilities. She didn't have to be the main speaker at most meetings now, maybe ever again. A little voice, that only spoke at very quiet moments late at night, told her she still had an important part to play, but that voice didn't yet give any details.

"Today we're going to get much more comfortable with the science underlying anthropogenic climate change. Doctor Ko-silma, you have the floor."

The little lady came forward from the back row of folding chairs. Her keen eyes took in the blackboard and chalk, tape recorder reels turning slowly, and assembled generals, colonels, majors, and professors. "When I agreed to advise this program, two years ago, I thought it would be an easy bit of supplemental income. And it was . . . until we discovered that the *Big One* would be all about chemistry."

The room filled with sympathetic laughter that released some of the tension. Susan and Heather made eye contact and exchanged smiles.

Doctor Ko-silma cleared her throat. "I realize I have to keep this on the non-scientist's level. If you were even first-year chem students, I'd tell you all about the hydroxyl radical and how it's involved in chemical reactions that can both increase and decrease radiative forcing in the atmosphere, and I'd expect you to get it . . . or switch your majors."

She saw several smiles.

"Today, I'll try to restrain myself. Heather already gave you a good sketch of the balancing act that is always going on between sources and sinks of . . . what did she call them? Oh yes, *greenhouse gasses*. Interesting term, never heard it before, but it fits. There are a number of gasses that help the planet hold in heat. We'd be locked in a permanent ice age, with average global temperature about minus twenty degrees Celsius, otherwise. I'd be giving this talk wearing *lots* of animal skins and writing on a cave wall."

Several people chuckled.

"Our most powerful greenhouse gas is water vapor, but it only stays in the air a few days, and is not greatly affected by human activities, so it's not our concern. On the other end of the scale are a number of rare chemicals that contribute little to the planet's overall heat-trapping ability. The only ones we need to worry about are Carbon dioxide, $CO_2$, Methane, $CH_4$, Ozone, $O_3$, and Nitrous oxide, $N_2O$." She wrote the formula for each on the blackboard as she spoke. "Of these four, $CO_2$ is by far the most important. In terms of human sources, the other three come from the same activities — heating, electrical generation, industry, transportation, and agriculture — so they can be ignored in the sense that if we solved the $CO_2$ problem, the other three would also cease to be problems . . ."

After a break, Doctor Tu-feltin the historian stood and spoke from beside his chair.  Heather stayed at the blackboard with chalk in hand.

"The conventional wisdom is that civilizations primarily rise and fall based on political and military events.  There are always historians who propose alternate theories, but they are generally ignored.  While the primary political forces are certainly powerful, in the last week I have come to believe that we would be foolish to ignore other factors."

The blind historian smiled without looking directly at anyone, and several people chuckled.

"I found five articles that analyze the correlation between human fortune and climate, and brought the best two for you to read.  Were you able to make copies, Colonel?"  He turned this way and that, but didn't know where the executive officer was seated.

"Lieutenant Do-forva is at the air base doing that,"  Colonel Ma-soran assured, "and will be back by lunch."

"Thank you.  The correlations are strong, although human efforts sometimes result in successful adaptations to minor climate changes, such as the aqueduct system built almost two thousand years ago.  But in the long run, climate cannot be ignored.  We, in the modern age, might *think* we have disconnected ourselves from weather and climate with our heating and air conditioning, but that, I now see, is an illusion."

A rumble of concern coursed through the room.  Doctor Tu-feltin waited.

"But the most interesting article was a study that looked at anthropogenic climate change in the *past*.  Three times in recorded history, the human population has been greatly reduced in a short span of time — once by plague, once by genocide, and once by a combination of the two.  In all three cases, after examining ice cores, tree rings, and lake sediments, the researchers concluded that with many fewer people around, large areas of forest were able to grow back, the Carbon dioxide level dropped, and the climate cooled . . ."

A few minutes remained before noon when Doctor Tu-feltin sat down. Ginny was behind the office counter, quietly collating papers.  Heather stood to take questions or announcements.

"It seems," General Ba-kerga began with his suspicious frown, "that we have been told, several times now directly or indirectly, that people are bad and trees are good."

Heather tried very hard not to smile.  "Only in the current context.  With a heating trend about to make our beautiful planet into a desert, anything that breathes or burns is bad, anything that absorbs $CO_2$ and keeps it out of the atmosphere, like trees, is good.  If an ice age was looming, the roles would be reversed."

George reluctantly nodded.

After a long silence, General Bo-seklin cleared his throat and stood up. "It goes without saying that the notes from Doctor Ko-silma, and the articles from Doctor Tu-feltin, are required reading. Enjoy your lunch."

Heather tried very hard to keep to her usual activities between sessions, but it felt forced. However, she wasn't yet ready to give in to the temptation to curl up on a bunk in the bomb shelter and never come out.

Both the chemist and the historian had to answer many questions on Wednesday morning after everyone had a chance to ponder their talks and read the handouts. Eventually, Doctor Bo-leden the philosopher stood.

"Both Heather and I have talked about the nature of *knowledge* on several occasions. It's useful to keep in mind what the word means in the strict, philosophical sense. But since we have finally come face to face with something we might want to do something about, we need to remember . . . that's *not* how most people think."

Heather smiled to herself.

"We almost need a political scientist," Doctor Bo-leden continued, "but I'm not sure one of those could *ever* get umbra clearance . . ."

Several people chuckled.

". . . and we've also realized how incredibly hard it would be to get new team members caught up with our process at this point. They might have to listen to five hundred and . . . how many?"

"Fifty," Lieutenant Ta-nibon, sporting a new tan, answered.

"That's a lot of tapes! So I'm going to do my best to play political scientist today. I want you all to think back to the early days, in the fall of 3662, when Heather had little or no track record. Until the president was assassinated, everyone, except General Ko-fenral who knew about the rocket, thought this was a big joke. The only reason we put up with this brash little girl . . ." He winked at her. ". . . was because Congress had mandated that the Department of Defense close the . . . um . . . *psychic gap* we had with the Beklans.

"That's what it would feel like for *everyone* not on the team if we went public with this, or any, warning about the future. Heather's track record would mean nothing to them, and it wouldn't matter how many generals or professors vouched for it. Human beings, in large groups, simply do *not* see that as *knowledge*. A few individuals would, and maybe a few small groups, but not society as a whole, and certainly not the government as a whole."

Heather could see Susan nodding.

"So what I'm getting at is . . . whatever we decide to *do* about Heather's warning of anthropogenic climate change and population crash, we're going to have to do, in a very real sense, without Heather, *regardless* of whether she loses her memories or not . . ."

When Doctor Bo-leden concluded his talk and answered some questions, it was close to lunchtime. Heather stood.

"Although I think Larry is right about where my track record counts and where it doesn't, I want you to know that I'll help in any way I can, at every step. Bringing you this . . . warning . . . is not just some little thing I do on the side. It's my life purpose, and I have the feeling in my bones that it's my *only* life purpose." She glanced at the clock. "Chris, can I bump you to Friday?"

"I'll be here!" Doctor Po-selem promised.

"Thanks. I know we all feel a sense of urgency, and if my memories are correct, there is *great* urgency, but that doesn't mean we'd do a good job if we tried to rush."

She glanced at her note pad. "There's a handout from Larry on the office counter. Also, many team members are starting to get here for breakfast to have more discussion time, and you're all welcome. Transports are available from the air base starting at seven o'clock. Sam?"

"Generals and colonels in my office . . ."

*

The dining room was packed with people Friday morning, with eight at each table instead of the usual six. Heather helped Maria constantly, then perched on the counter by the sink to eat her eggs and sausage.

The twelve-year-old could feel an air of expectation in the room as she stood to open the session. Everyone fell silent.

"I'm nervous too."

Several people grinned back at her.

"The pieces of the puzzle are starting to fall into place. Please remember that even though I know what's coming, I do *not* know what we should do about it. If I knew of a solution that worked, I wouldn't have these memories, and we wouldn't be here."

Doctor Po-selem the physicist threw back his head and laughed. Doctor Bo-leden the philosopher grinned.

Heather smiled. "Chris, you have the floor."

The physicist stood and ruffled his already-wild hair. "I'm sorry to have to announce that my *favorite* topic, the whole time-travel question, is at the same place it's been for a year or more. I put a hypothetical question to another physicist once in a while, but nothing new has come to light. Everyone is convinced that if some kind of information came back in time, and we did something to change it, it would, at very least, disappear. Opinions differ on how much we'd have to do — some say that *anyone* in the present just *knowing* the information would cancel it — but most think some definite action would be necessary. The problem is, it's almost impossible to do any sort of experiment. The only possible experiment is right here in this room, and that has already disproven the first possibility I mentioned."

He saw understanding nods, even from the military people, so he moved on.

"When Heather dropped the *Big Bomb* on us two weeks ago . . ."

Everyone in the room chuckled nervously or smiled.

". . . I decided I should do what a physicist is supposed to do. I should crunch some numbers. I picked a willing grad student and we set up a modeling system that can juggle a hundred variables and give us a plot over a period of time. He set it up so I can put in my own data cards for the starting values, and my own program cards with formulas, and no one but me will ever know what the variables mean, or even what the time scale is . . ."

Doctor Po-selem took a few minutes to convince General Ba-kerga that his modeling system would not create any security risks, then went on to explain the very simple model he tried on his own. With only four variables for animals, plants, Carbon dioxide, and temperature, and some starting values he pulled from a biology textbook, his plot had the planet heating slightly after about a thousand years.

He sensed his model was too simple, so all during the previous weekend, he worked with Doctor Ko-silma to improve the formulas.

"Even though she promised not to drag the rest of you through it, she did make *me* include the hydroxyl radical, Methane breakdown, and Ozone concentration. We were soon up to thirty variables!"

The team chuckled in sympathy. The chemist, in the back row, grinned.

"I'm afraid the results might hurt someone's feelings, but as a scientist, I have to share them anyway." He glanced at Heather, then grabbed a large roll of paper from beside his chair and held it up for everyone to see. "Our model reaches the plus-two-degree point in about three hundred years."

The room erupted in a rumble of confusion and frustration. Heather stayed in her seat with a relaxed smile on her face. Lieutenant Do-forva stepped into the circle to get a photograph of the sheet the physicist was holding.

Eventually Doctor Po-selem rolled his paper back up and the room fell silent. "And as scientists, we have to be open to improvements in our models. I give the floor back to Heather."

The twelve-year-old saw everyone looking at her, and could see tender concern in both Susan's and Sarah's eyes.

"My feelings are not hurt at all, Chris. I would *love it* if someone could convince me this thing wasn't going to happen in my lifetime. But I remember it too clearly, and I also remember many computer models that said the same thing as yours."

"Can you help us improve the model?" he asked from his chair.

"Only with concepts. You'll have to dig up the numbers and figure out the formulas."

The physicist and the chemist both nodded.

Heather stepped to the blackboard. "Let's start with deforestation." She began to write on the board. "It goes on constantly, especially in the tropics, until 3720 when it becomes illegal to cut down *any* living tree."

She turned and saw many eyes open wide.

"Ocean acidification. As the pH goes down, the oceans can absorb less $CO_2$. That will reverse someday in the far future, once the oceans have dissolved all the calcium deposits and killed all the shellfish, but that's much too late for us."

Both the chemist and the physicist wore frowns as they took notes.

"Next, a huge volume of Carbon and Methane is trapped in the permafrost of our vast arctic tundra.   It starts thawing about 3710, and is a positive-feedback loop with a tipping point about 3715."

Both scientists furiously scribbled.

"Just a little farther south, after the heating climate allows insect pests to move in, the boreal forests will start burning, and their peat bogs will release massive amounts of stored Carbon."

Chris moaned, but kept writing.

Heather waited a moment for the two scientists to catch up, then went on. "Out-gassing of Methane hydrates on the ocean floor . . ."

"Oh my God, I didn't think of that either," the chemist muttered while writing.

"Another tipping point."

General Ko-fenral cleared his throat.  "Would you explain that term, please?"

Heather turned to her listeners. "A *positive-feedback loop* is any situation in which the movement of a variable causes the system to move the variable even further in the same direction.  A wobbling wheel on a car is a good example.  The wobble only gets worse the further it progresses.  A *tipping point* is when a positive-feedback loop becomes self-perpetuating and can't be stopped, like when the wheel falls apart even though the driver may be slowing down."

Several people looked at Doctor Po-selem for verification.

"Perfect," he said, "although in that example, the car will eventually come to a stop, even without one of its wheels.  A tipping point could also send a system into some kind of critical mass that goes *BOOM*."

Heather laughed, then went on to mention several more factors the two scientists might want to include in their model.  Eventually she gave the floor back to the physicist.

He stood and looked at the chemist.  "What are you doing this weekend, Betty?"

She chuckled.  "I think I'll be in the computer room at the University with you!"

✳

Heather was very quiet all weekend, spending as much time as possible with Brian on Saturday, and with Susan on Sunday.  Both her boyfriend and her therapist came to the same conclusion — Heather was steeling herself for some dire fate.  They just didn't know what it was, and when they asked, Heather claimed not to know, either.

She seemed to be her cheerful self again on Monday, dancing for a solid hour before anyone arrived, chatting with people at breakfast, and opening the session as if they were about to discuss some minor treaty.

"I see that Chris has another big roll of paper."

The physicist was grinning from ear to ear.

"You have the floor."

Doctor Po-selem stood.  "Come on up, Betty.  You deserve more credit than me, and you can help me hold this thing."

The chemist reluctantly came up from the back row.  "It took us about twenty hours to set up all the formulas, and about ten minutes to get the results."

Chris nodded.  "When you've got ninety-three variables, the interactions are quite complex!"

Several people moaned in sympathy.

"We kept everything very conservative and by-the-book," Betty explained.  "But even so, using different estimates of some items that came from different scientific studies, we could get a temperature curve heading for the moon anywhere from the year 3700 to 3780."

A rumble of voices filled the room.  The two professors waited for it to die down.

"You guessed it," Chris confirmed.  "Heather's warning is smack in the middle."

Betty nodded.  "We printed the one that almost exactly matches what Heather says is coming, and the numbers and formulas we used to get it were all very reasonable.  You can't get any closer with a mathematical model.  What this tells us is simply that Heather's memories are solidly within the realm of reality."

Chris unrolled the large printout, Betty took the opposite corners, they held it up for everyone to see, and Lieutenant Ta-nibon took a picture.

"Damn . . ." Heather grumbled with a frown.

✳  ✳  ✳

## **Chapter 32: Predicament**

For the remainder of that week, several other scientists spoke, and many questions were asked and sometimes answered.  Some clarity was added to the team's understanding of the situation facing them, but no great breakthroughs occurred.

Heather knew she was supposed to be on vacation that week, but didn't say anything, and no one else seemed to remember.  She was enjoying the new routine in which others had to prepare for the sessions, instead of her.  She wasn't sure when it would feel right to take another vacation — perhaps never again.

✳

"Program P-Seventeen, Session Five Fifty-Five, twenty-six June 3667," Ginny said for the tape.

"All team members are present," Ben announced.

"I didn't think anyone would miss *this* one," Heather said, standing up.

Many smiles greeted her from the three layers of the circle.

"Learning Mode will never end, but the generals and I agree it's time to start talking about . . . you know . . . possible actions."

The three generals in the room all nodded.

"I want to start with some warnings, some of which our beloved generals may *not* like."

"When did that stop you before?" General Ko-fenral asked with a grin.

Heather just smiled back and a number of people chuckled.

"My first warning is that we *dare not* limit our thinking in *any* way at this point in the process.  We are going to truly *brainstorm*, and anyone who censors themselves, or anyone else, is washing dishes after lunch, with me inspecting each one."

Doctor Po-selem made funny haunting noises.

Heather smiled.  "If Susan thinks we should *nuke* all sources of pollution,

I want to hear it."

The timid psychologist cringed.

"And if George thinks we should paint peace symbols on every military vehicle, that goes on the list too."

General Ba-kerga almost cracked a smile.

Heather turned to the blackboard and wrote both ideas while her audience chuckled.  When she turned back around, Doctor Ko-silma had her hand in the air.

"You mentioned that there came a time when all deforestation stopped, and even the cutting of a single living tree was illegal.  But that came far too late.  I know from the models Chris and I did that this wouldn't be a complete solution, but if it could be made to happen *now*, it might be *part* of a solution."

Heather was writing as the chemist spoke.

"The human population has to start falling in a controlled manner," Doctor Tu-feltin the historian began, "but I have no idea how that could be accomplished.  If we don't, nature will do it for us starting in about 3717, if your memories are correct."

"Fossil fuels could be heavily taxed," Colonel Ma-soran suggested, "at least beyond a certain small amount so poor people don't freeze in the dark."

Heather continued getting the gist of each idea onto the blackboard, and every time she turned back to the team, another hand was in the air, ready to speak.

The ideas continued to flow for the rest of the morning, and more came up during lunch.  Heather made sure the security guards, and Maria, knew that their suggestions could just as easily save the world.

✳

When the team returned on Wednesday morning, they were greeted by large sheets of paper pinned to the walls wherever there was space, each displaying their ideas in Colonel Ma-soran's neat lettering.

On Friday, the flood of ideas was starting to slow, most just slight variations on previous suggestions.  As eleven o'clock was passing and the room had become very quiet, Lieutenant Ta-nibon's hand crept up.

"Ben?" Heather called.

He was silent for a long moment as his tape recorder reels continued to turn.  Finally, he spoke just one word.  "Pray."

If the room had been quiet before, they could now hear a pin drop.

✳

Eventually, General Bo-seklin cleared his throat and stood.

Heather took her seat.

"Although new ideas will continue to be welcome, we certainly have something to work with.  Heather and the team were supposed to be on vacation *last* week, but we were ... how do I say this? ... in the middle of something."

Smiles filled the room.

"I appreciate all of you sticking with the process, as it may have been *the* most important time for this team . . . maybe for much more than this team."

He could see several people nodding.

"I've been on the phone all week, and I learned that the Department has five political scientists, highly educated and experienced, and they actually *do* have top-secret-umbra clearance."

"Cool!" Heather said softly.

"They were busy this week, but they'll be here all next week, and during that week, the building will be closed to non-military personnel while the staff gets some hard, cold opinions on our situation and our many ideas. It will all be hypothetical to them, although they'll know from the program number that it has something to do with a psychic ability. That's a good thing, I think, as it will keep them from taking it too seriously and therefore feeling inhibited about chatting with us openly."

He noticed Heather nodding agreement.

"We're not trying to get them caught up with the team, intellectually or socially, nor will they have any decision-making power."

Several people looked relieved.

"So . . . the team and Heather are on a belated vacation next week, and you *will* need to go somewhere," he asserted, looking at Heather, "even though I'm sure you'll be dying of curiosity."

"I can die of curiosity in the mountains or on the beach."

Many people chuckled.

"Maria!" the general called.

She stepped out of the kitchen, oven mitts on her hands.

"You will *not* be on vacation next week, as we'll have ten to fifteen at every meal, every day."

She nodded.

"We'll come back for one week to process what the political scientists had to say, then take our regular vacation, which you *will* get, Maria."

She nodded again, then begged, with body language, to tend her oven. The general nodded and she dashed away.

✳

As Friday afternoon passed, Heather slowly wound down from the most intense month of her life.

During lunch, she overheard some professors expressing a preference for one sort of action to change the future, over another. At the Inner Support Team meeting later in the afternoon, some officers began speculating about which actions the military could best pursue. As the three generals chatted, while getting ready to go home, they clearly wanted to emphasize certain options to the political scientists.

What Heather never heard was what she knew her friend Susan already believed — that none of the options would, in reality, be acceptable to the world.

✳

"Good morning, sleepy!" Ginny said from a couch when Heather staggered out of her room the next morning.

The twelve-year-old stood on the hardwood floor in bare feet and pajamas. A moment later, a huge yawn escaped her. "Do *you* get to come with me?"

"Yep. Lisa's jealous, but she's a colonel now."

"I figured Sam would make her stay next week. Part of me would *love* to be a fly on the wall. Another part of me doesn't even want to *know* . . ."

Both females burst out chuckling and Ginny nodded agreement.

While Heather stretched, got breakfast, and packed, Lieutenant Do-forva called lodges and resorts to make reservations. With summer at hand, only the less-popular had openings, which Heather preferred anyway. By noon, they were on the road.

⁕

"It feels funny driving a car," Ginny said after a lull in other conversation about a hundred miles along, "when I work for a top-secret team that *knows* we are destroying our future with Carbon dioxide."

"Yeah, I know. Makes me feel a little . . . dirty . . . too. But individual action would have no effect."

"Not even a tiny bit that would add up if lots of people drove less?"

"Nope. It's built into the market system. If you and your friends don't buy fuel, that causes the price to drop a little because of less demand. The lower price motivates others to use more."

"Oh. Makes the situation sound pretty hopeless."

Heather was silent and thoughtful as they motored their way into the mountains.

⁕

After hiking around a small alpine lake, the pair collapsed into soft meadow grass beneath towering pine trees. Squirrels scampered from branch to branch, and a deep-blue sky over-arched the entire idyllic scene.

"There they are, Ginny, doing their best to pull Carbon dioxide out of the air, keep the Carbon, and give us the Oxygen to breathe . . . and burn."

Lieutenant Do-forva frowned. "And . . . they can't keep up."

Heather nodded.

Ginny continued frowning. "I felt a little sick as we were driving through those logging areas on the way here."

"Me too. We're creating the problem on both ends. Too much $CO_2$, not enough trees."

After a long and thoughtful silence, Ginny sighed. "So . . . correct me if I'm wrong . . . the only way to avoid . . . you know . . . would be to fix it on *all* sides — less people, less burning, and more trees."

Heather didn't say anything, but she smiled.

⁕

The huge orange fireball of the sun was setting over the ocean as the pair sat on a sand dune partly covered with wiry grass. A pleasantly-cool sea breeze blew their hair back toward the green hills behind them.  Gulls wheeled overhead, eyeing the humans for possible handouts.

"As I remember," Ginny began, gazing at the waves, "the ocean is soaking up some of the $CO_2$, but is slowly loosing that ability."

"Right, as it gets more acidic.  In the process, most sea creatures will die, leaving almost nothing but jellyfish.  Scientists think it will become alkaline again someday, and then be able to absorb much more Carbon dioxide."

"In time to help?"

Heather took a moment to think about how to respond.  "Help the planet, and whatever remnants of life are still hiding in deep, slightly-cooler places, maybe."

Ginny frowned as she realized what Heather hadn't said.

✳

They returned to the city in time for Heather to spend most of Saturday with Brian.  They arrived at the top-secret facility to find the security lamp off and one of the sleeping rooms occupied.

Heather glimpsed the man on Sunday at breakfast, tall and dark-haired, about forty, sporting a colonel's stripes.  He spent most of the day in General Bo-seklin's office with various members of the command and security staff.

Since the security lamp remained off, and no one was volunteering any explanation to her, Heather guessed she should stay inconspicuous.  She danced to soft music with the studio door closed, watered plants, filled the bird feeder, and met with Susan in the bomb shelter.

She wasn't sure if the need to remain inconspicuous would extend to the important team meeting the following morning, and hoped someone would tell her.

✳   ✳   ✳

## Chapter 33: The Bottom Line

On Monday morning, after Heather filled her plate with scrambled eggs, bacon, and melon slices, she noticed a free space at the table with Sam, George, and the new colonel. With only slight hesitation, she slipped into it.

"Good morning, Heather!" General Bo-seklin greeted. "How was your vacation?"

"Wonderful! I'm not sure who got the most sunburn, Ginny or me."

The general laughed.

Heather noticed the new colonel paying close attention to the interactions. "Where's Malcolm today?" she asked.

"General Ko-fenral," Sam said for the newcomer's benefit, "had to take care of some business at the air base, so he grabbed breakfast there, but he wouldn't miss this meeting for anything."

"I was wondering . . ." Heather began as she broke a strip of crispy bacon in half, ". . . if you'd like me to help Maria during the meeting . . ."

"No, Heather, Colonel Bo-torin is joining the team, so you can stand up as its rightful leader."

The colonel's eyes opened wider. "You must be the voyant."

Heather tried to suppress a smile of embarrassment, without complete success. "Not technically, but it's close enough for now."

"Almost time to start," General Ba-kerga mentioned.

They all concentrated on their food, knowing more complete introductions would come soon enough.

*

"Good morning everyone. I hope the vacation last week, for those of you who got one, was relaxing and refreshing."

Most of the professors nodded.

"Our poor military staff worked their tails off."

A few of them verified with smiles.

"We stand at an important moment in history," Heather continued. "We have identified a bit of a . . . situation."

Nervous chuckles coursed through the room.

"We have brainstormed up many possible solutions."

Several people glanced around at the big sheets still pinned to the walls.

"The next step we should take is . . . unknown to me." She paused and took a deep breath. "Sam, you have the floor."

General Bo-seklin stood. "The security lamp has been off this morning so we could make proper introductions before our conversations went too many places. Corporal, you may switch it on now."

The young security guard standing beside the stairs stepped into the outer office while pulling a key from his belt, and a moment later the green light came on.

"The political science team was here all last week, and it was *no* vacation for any of us in the building."

Several people chuckled in sympathy.

"One of them sensed that this was *not* a hypothetical scenario, and asked to be on the team. We've been grilling the poor guy for two days . . ."

The new colonel smiled.

". . . and he's now gotten three or four tapes under his belt."

"Four," the colonel announced.

"Good," General Bo-seklin said. "He has a list of six more, and I want Heather to look at that list this afternoon and add to it, while keeping the number reasonable."

She nodded from her chair.

The general turned back to the team. "Colonel John Bo-torin, please tell us about yourself."

He stood and looked around, carrying himself and filling his colonel's uniform with confidence. "This is an honor. Usually the P-series programs are just the butt of jokes, and the S-Nine team I was on assumed the same thing . . . until we got here. We were greeted by a two and a three-star general, and fly-by-night P-series programs just do NOT get that kind of leadership. We were never told who was on your team, of course, but we assumed a couple of wacky wannabe professors with mail-order degrees. Now, standing before you, I *recognize* most of you from televised debates, documentaries, and testimony before Congress. I don't know if you realize it, but this is truly an elite team."

Everyone in the room breathed in the compliment.

"I have a doctoral degree in political science, and as you can see, I am career military. I have a wife and three children, almost grown, and being on this team will not keep me away from them any more than my last assignment."

He took a moment to make eye contact with most people in his audience. "I have a reputation for being very blunt, and I think you need that right now. I have promised Generals Ko-fenral, Bo-seklin, and Ba-kerga that I will not sugar-coat anything.  I have all the reports from the S-Nine team that just assessed the political dimensions of your alleged problem and possible solutions, and the generals have asked me to present those to you this week. It will be my honor to do so, but don't expect to arrive at the end of the week feeling good about your suggestions."

A rumble ran through the team as Colonel Bo-torin sat back down.

Heather stayed in her seat with a slight smile on her face as the rumble slowly died down.  Finally she stood.

"Although every member of this team has hopes for one or more of the ideas on our lists ..."  With sweeps of her arms, she indicated all the sheets on the walls.  "... we are ready to listen to any and all criticisms."

Most members of the team nodded, some more quickly than others.

"I'd like you to start, Colonel, by telling the entire team the assumptions you were working under."  She returned to her seat.

He stood again.  "The situation given was that in recent centuries, people began to burn fossil fuels — coal, oil, and natural gas — and by so doing raised living standards and life expectancy, and thus the population grew. Nothing surprising about that, except that most people, even most scientists, are not aware of the direct connection between energy and population.  It made sense the moment I heard it.

"Because of the increased burning, breathing, and deforestation, the $CO_2$ level in the air began to creep up.  In about the year 3700, signs of a heating trend in the global climate will be obvious.  By 3710, the ice caps will be melting, and severe droughts, massive floods, and other unusual weather events will become quite common.  Even before 3720, commercial agriculture will be collapsing and famine will follow.  By 3730, the average global temperature will be four degrees Celsius above normal, with no end in sight, and the human population will be down to one-third its peak, and rapidly falling.  At that point, our information fades.  Did I leave out anything of substance?"

A long silence followed.  Doctor Ko-silma's hand came up slowly.

"Betty?" Heather called.

"Also by 3720, we're looking at sea-level rise wiping out coastal cities, which only makes matters worse as refugees move toward inland agricultural areas."

"Oh, yes, that was in there, too," Colonel Bo-torin admitted.

The room remained silent as both the colonel and Heather looked around. Eventually she said, "With the sea-level bit added, that's a good summary."

"Okay," he went on.  "The other four political scientists believed it was all hypothetical, and will probably go to their graves thinking that.  My intuition told me otherwise.  That's why I'm here."

"In a very real sense, none of that is a problem, and you need to understand why.  Human beings are very adaptable, and all throughout pre-history and history, have shown the ability to adapt to major changes in their environments, including climate changes.

"But they can only do so once the change manifests clearly enough for them to *see*. The saying *Monkey See* . . . the rest is unimportant . . . contains the word *see* for a reason. We humans only accept certain *kinds* of data as valid information. If we can see it, touch it, taste it, it's real, we accept it and do something about it. To a human society, an intuition, which brought me to this team, is NOT valid information. The pronouncements of a voyant, which warned this team of the coming climate change, is about as *far* from valid information, to a human society, as you can get."

Heather could see Susan nodding.

"The *situation* may be climate change and population crash. The *problem* is the time lag in the situation because of the planetary scale of it. I'll go through your suggestions one by one in more detail, but in general, there is no way to get the world to concern itself, in 3670 or 3680, with a disaster that won't manifest clearly until 3710 or later."

✳

For the rest of the morning, Colonel Bo-torin proceeded to shred their precious lists of ideas.

All those suggestions that required the passage of laws were completely impossible, politically, because of the powerful web of special-interest groups that always held a tight grip on Congress. Laws only got passed that benefited at least one large and powerful group, or a coalition of smaller ones, and offended no one.

Ideas that required the president to adjust the rules concerning pollution, even if a sympathetic president was in office, would barely get written down before that president was out, and the new president would immediately undo those same rules.

The colonel tried not to laugh, but couldn't suppress a smile at those suggestions that relied on people, individually or in groups, to take voluntary action.

As noon approached, Heather knew Colonel Bo-torin wasn't finished, but could see that the team was emotionally exhausted. She stood up, and the colonel deferred.

"We'll continue on Wednesday. It's time to drown our sorrows — I mean nourish ourselves — with Maria's good cooking."

About half the room smiled, and a few even chuckled. Under the circumstances, that was about all Susan could hope for. Even before rising from her chair, she knew she would need to hang around for several hours and listen to team members express their frustrations.

✳

Wednesday was no different.

Proposed treaties and international agreements were studied to death, Colonel Bo-torin explained, and ratified so slowly, even when they were ratified, that the deadline, 3680, would be far in the past before anything was done.

Geo-engineering projects, like seeding the atmosphere with sulfur compounds to create a cooling effect, would involve such a huge risk of unintended side-effects, that international conflicts could easily spring up if anyone felt wronged.

Eventually, as eleven o'clock was passing, Colonel Bo-torin looked at the team with a steady gaze. "There *was* one suggestion that we couldn't find any reason to fault, although it may not be a *complete* solution."

A hopeful sparkle returned to many eyes in the room.

With a straight face, he continued. "It had something to do with peace symbols on military vehicles . . ."

Doctor Po-selem the physicist burst out laughing.

Many others shared in the moment of lightness as Colonel Bo-torin stood by the blackboard smiling.

Heather and Susan looked at each other while grinning, both thankful for any help they could get with team morale.

✳

After a short break, the political scientist cleared his throat.

Everyone found their seats and fell silent.

"I have finished summarizing the reports of the S-Nine team. I want to leave you with something useful, instead of the complete negativity I've had to dump on you so far."

Some faces in the room became slightly less dejected.

"One useful way of looking at the world is that it's composed for four kinds of people. Unfortunately, only two of them are represented on this team.

"Military people are good at dealing with hard, cold reality, and that's why this program has been, in one sense, successful under the Department of Defense. Military people are smart enough to understand the warning that Heather brought us, and they are used to applying command and control systems to effectively solve problems. If the military had a free hand, I believe we could lick this thing. Many people would not *like* the actions we would have to take, but they would, someday, appreciate that human civilization wasn't wiped out in the 3720's and 30's."

"But since this is a democracy with civilian leadership," General Ko-fenral interjected, "we do not have a free hand."

"Right," Colonel Bo-torin admitted. "The second group represented here is academia. They are motivated by noble and honorable ideals — truth, efficiency . . ."

"Elegance, tradition, clarity," Doctor Bo-leden the philosopher added.

"Right. But, alas, neither of these groups runs our civilization. Two other groups do. The common people have control of a democracy by their votes. They mostly want to be left alone to pursue their economic, social, and religious lives. They are not fond of being taxed or told what they can and can't do, unless it clearly benefits them.

"The other controlling group is the big money and power people.  Their biggest concern is positioning themselves to profit, money or power-wise, from any event.  Disasters are no exception, and the bigger the disaster, the bigger the opportunity for profit.  It has not entered their darkest dreams that there could *ever* be an event so dangerous, that they should help solve it, instead.

"The values and thinking habits of both controlling groups are going to cause them to fight, tooth and claw, against any effort that we, the military and academia, might propose for dealing with the coming climate change and population crash.  That, ladies and gentlemen, is the bottom line."

The room remained very quiet as Colonel Bo-torin returned to his seat.

* * *

## Chapter 34: The Vote

"We have been humbled," Heather said on Friday morning to the somber group. "I believe it was good for us to go through the brainstorming process we did, and maybe something we thought of will still be important in some way. I don't know. Remember, at this point in the process, I'm in the same boat with you. The only future I know anything about . . . is the one we don't want."

The team agreed with nods and weak smiles.

"One of us was insightful enough to realize, weeks ago, that we were looking at an unsolvable problem, at least politically — in other words, a predicament. I know my dear friend and therapist Doctor Bo-kamla is going to hate me for this, but I want her to speak to you today about what she saw back then."

Heather took her seat and Susan came up.

"*Hate* is probably too strong a word," the psychologist said with a smile.

Many people chuckled, knowing how close they were.

"And I knew Heather wanted me to do this. I just wasn't sure what I was going to say . . . until I listened to Colonel Bo-torin's final summary on Wednesday."

The colonel nodded respectfully.

"It started, of course, with Heather's little matrix that I'm sure you all remember."

Ginny, handling the records binder that day, found the paper copy and handed it to the psychologist.

Susan unfolded it and clipped it to the top of the blackboard. "Even after all our thinking and talking, it's still a completely-valid picture of the situation."

|  | Cave/Hut<br>& Campfire | modern<br>Home & Car |
|---|---|---|
| ½ Billion | OK | maybe OK? |
| 3+ Billion | maybe OK??? | Not |

"There's no humane way to get rid of three billion people, and there's no political way to lower our living standards to the peasant level. And, as we know from both Heather and our scientists, we cannot feed our current population without today's complex system of commercial agriculture."

Several professors nodded agreement.

"I could accept, in my own mind, that this was a nasty predicament, but for weeks I didn't know what to do with it, where to take it. Now I do."

She looked around at the tired but hopeful faces.

"I believe this team created a trap for itself by assuming that *we* had to find a solution, that *we* had to lead the world out of this situation. That assumption was reinforced by the fact that it had to be done *now*, long before most other people could see and understand the problem for themselves.

"I believe that assumption is wrong, illustrated by Colonel Bo-torin's . . . um . . . *shredding* of our ideas . . ."

Muffled chuckles came from several places in the room.

Susan smiled slightly. "So, I realized what we need to do, and now, with my heart in my throat, I place the idea on the table for this team to consider. I believe we must find the courage to let go of our assumed leadership concerning this . . . predicament . . . tell the world everything we know, and let them . . . um . . . work it out . . . using whatever knowledge and wisdom the human race possesses. Maybe they will, and maybe they won't. I don't know."

The psychologist quickly returned to the safety of her seat.

Heather closed her eyes and let a long moment pass, half-hoping that someone else would suddenly volunteer to lead the meeting. Eventually she opened her eyes, didn't see anyone volunteering, and reluctantly stood.

"Thank you, Susan. You surprised me. I was expecting you to go over cognitive dissonance and all that. But it's certainly true this team has studied that stuff to death, so no harm done.

"Unfortunately, I have to announce that your suggestion would not work

. . . because . . . in the future I know, not far from today, with plenty of time to do something about it, the world *will know* the essence of what we know, from another source, and will choose to do nothing about it."

※

Doctor Bo-kamla, in her seat, briefly reconsidered the strong word Heather had proposed earlier.

But unlike the psychologist, the team leader did not get to sit down before all three generals demanded she elaborate.

Heather took a deep breath. "Starting sometime about . . . now . . . a few scientists will become concerned about pollution, resource depletion, population growth, and other related issues. They'll start constructing models, and using computers to run those models, just like Betty and Chris did.

"But they won't have *me* to nudge them in the right directions, so they won't pinpoint the problem — the one that will actually get us — for quite a while. They *will* realize the next century isn't going to be pretty. They'll write articles and try to get them published. The first book for non-scientists will come out . . . let me think . . . just two years from now."

"And what will happen to those articles and that book?" General Ko-fenral asked urgently.

"Most of the articles will never see the light of day. Science, as most of you know, has a system in which nothing gets published unless it is acceptable to established scientists. Predictions of doom and gloom make people uncomfortable. Scientists are people too."

Doctor Po-selem sighed, then nodded.

"As for the book, the newspapers and other voices for both liberals and conservatives will go into high gear to demonize and vilify it. The money and power people will attack it ruthlessly. The common people will never know about it. Most of academia won't touch it with a ten-foot pole. Even a world war hardly unites people as much as the effort that will go into silencing that book. As a result, few copies will sell, until about 3705, when it will be dusted off, updated, and become a best-seller . . . much too late. Other books like it, sprinkled through the years, will have a similar fate."

"Where is the military in all this?" General Bo-seklin asked.

Heather looked at him. "As far as I know, the issue never comes to their attention, pro or con. They're busy with the Beklan Empire, the proxy wars, and all the other things they must do. That's why, five years ago, I offered my services to the Department of Defense. I already knew, from living through it the first time, that no other sector of society was up to the task. Each sector — politics, religion, and all the rest — had a wise voice or two, but not enough to change the course of civilization."

※

At General Bo-seklin's request, Doctor Bo-leden the philosopher stood to give the team a better understanding of how any controversial scientific article was excluded from publication, and, often enough, the scientist's reputation ruined in the process.

Then Colonel Bo-torin the political scientist verified Heather's analysis of the groups that would battle against the book she mentioned. Liberals and conservatives might have a different approach to handling problems, he explained, but the suggestion that any problem needed more than slight adjustments to existing policies was completely unthinkable.

Susan nodded agreement.

Finally, General Ko-fenral himself stood and spoke. The military rarely looked more than four years into the future, as any effort to do so could be, and usually was, made worthless by a new president coming into office. The only such efforts were the P-series programs, and they were probably all failures in the future Heather knew. It was, therefore, quite believable that in that future, the military played no decisive role, one way or the other.

With eleven o'clock approaching, Heather declared a short break. She immediately dashed to Susan, just rising from her seat, and stood before her, head bowed. "I'm sorry."

The psychologist smiled down at her young charge. "You are only allowed to reveal things about the future that do not offend anyone."

Heather looked up, saw the barely-suppressed grin on Susan's face, and they both burst out laughing at the same moment.

"In that case . . . I wouldn't be able to say *anything!*"

The psychologist continued laughing and wrapped her arms around her young friend. "Your task in life does not allow you to pander. That's why you need a team of good people around you. Otherwise, you'd just be a carnival freak or a street-corner preacher."

They separated and Heather twisted her face. "Eeew."

Susan laughed again, then slipped away to find a free toilet room.

※

As the team returned to their seats, Heather felt that either the room and all its furnishing were coming to life around her, or Maria had slipped something into the scrambled eggs. She looked at Susan, and the psychologist looked back with a mischievous smile and sparkling eyes, not at all her usual facial expressions.

As soon as everyone got settled, Doctor Po-selem raised his hand.

"Chris?"

"I'd like to propose a vote."

A rumble immediately arose throughout the large room.

The P-Seventeen team, a program of the Department of Defense, was not a democratic body that took votes on every little issue, indeed on *any* little issue. Only one program action would call for a vote — a substantial effort to change the future they were studying.

In the entire five years of the program's existence, no such vote had ever been taken, nor even proposed. Whether they remembered the early sessions personally, or had listened to those tapes later, every team member knew that any effort to change the future would probably result in Heather losing her memories and becoming just another twelve-year-old girl.

Only the security corporal standing by the stairs was unaware of the implications.

"Now wait a . . ." Three-star General Ko-fenral tried to say.

"You'll get your vote!" Heather asserted so forcefully, and made eye contact so sternly, that the general fell silent.

"Doctor Po-selem," she continued more softly. "You have the floor."

He stood, ran his fingers through his wild hair, and took a deep breath. "I do not make this proposal lightly. I, perhaps more than anyone else, am painfully aware of what it could do to . . . our beloved Heather."

She smiled from her seat.

"But we need to find *something* we can do, since everything else we've thought of has been eliminated. The one thing I am *absolutely* certain is that *no one* on this team wants to just sit here, week after week, year after year, while our window of opportunity passes.

"So my proposal is simply this — that we help bring relevant articles and books to publication, and widest possible distribution, by giving them the endorsement of this elite team of high-ranking military officers and prominent scientists."

No one broke the silence that followed.

"I realize we will want to take a vote on each item — each article or book — so I include that step in my proposal."

Without waiting for the physicist to go into any more detail, Heather stood. Doctor Po-selem saw the determination in her eyes and quickly sat down.

"Since the proposal includes another layer of voting, I'm not going to call for discussion today — we'll have plenty of time for that, and we've been doing little else for six weeks."

Several people chuckled deeply.

"First, the team will vote, excluding Sam, Malcolm, and me. Ben, please make sure everyone has paper and pencil, and remember that the enlisted security people are all on the team."

While Lieutenant Ta-nibon circulated with a pad of paper and extra pencils, Heather noticed that General Ko-fenral still looked a bit sore, but was making a good effort to breathe deeply and contain himself. Sam looked completely happy with the situation, and somewhat to Heather's surprise, George also.

The team members voted, folded their papers, and handed them to Ben, who returned to the records specialists' couch.

"Sam and Malcolm get separate votes," Heather went on.

Two-star General Bo-seklin smiled at her. "I vote *yes*."

Three-star General Ko-fenral took one more slow, deep breath. "I vote . . . *yes*.

Heather looked at Ben, busy sorting his pile of votes. A pregnant silence lingered while he finished.

"I have fifteen *yes* votes, and one question mark."

"That was me," the security corporal by the stairs said.  "I just don't know enough."

"That's okay," Heather assured him.

Then she saw everyone looking at her, but only smiled.

✴  ✴  ✴

## Chapter 35: A New Team Purpose

Heather let a long moment of silence pass.

"I haven't forgotten my future memories *yet!*"

Some team members roared with laughter, led by Doctor Po-selem the physicist, and the rest cheered.

Heather grinned as they settled down. "I smell delicious aromas coming from the kitchen . . ."

Many people nodded.

"Next week is vacation for *everyone*, except a few of our faithful security people."

"Not a day too soon," General Ko-fenral mumbled.

Heather smiled. "Sam?"

"Generals and colonels, my office at twelve hundred thirty. Inner Support Team, fifteen hundred."

Heather stood in the center of the circle and took a breath to clear her mind. "We have many details about our vote to work out, many other aspects of the climate-change predicament to study, and many other bits of the future we can look at. That will all come in due time. The obvious task now is to watch for the articles and books that might need our help, and do so *without* violating top-secret-umbra or P-Seventeen program security, until we vote on each possible endorsement."

She noticed both George and Lisa nodding.

"Everyone, have a wonderful week off. Sergeant, please close the session."

*

"How does she *always* know what to do or say," General Ko-fenral wondered aloud from a plush chair in General Bo-seklin's office, "even when *we* don't?"

"Ninety-two years of life experience," Colonel Ma-soran suggested, "all packaged in a young, healthy mind that can think circles around us."

General Ba-kerga chuckled softly and nodded.  "She realized the team needed a new sense of purpose, and the postponing of discussion, because of the second round of voting, was absolutely brilliant.  If she ever decides to run for president, the other candidates better watch out!"

General Bo-seklin, behind his desk, laughed, but looked thoughtful. "We've all come to accept the occasions when she steps on our toes, because . . . on reflection, she always turns out to be right.  To me, that's worth almost as much as her track record."

Everyone nodded.

After a long silence, Colonel Bo-torin, the newest member of the team, took a deep breath.  "This new . . . team purpose . . . could be tricky.  You two," he said, looking at Generals Ko-fenral and Bo-seklin, "have the stars to make endorsements without asking anyone, but if higher-ups become displeased . . ."  He raised his eyebrows and let his thought linger.

General Bo-seklin nodded slowly.  "We'll do what we need to do under the radar as much as possible, as long as possible.  I want a draft endorsement, with blanks for names and titles, from each of you.  Especially you, John. Sarah, get Heather's thoughts, too.  We'll pull together the best ideas from each."

The room fell silent.

"What's Heather doing next week?" Sarah asked.

"Wants to stay close, I think," Lisa reported, "see her boyfriend a few times, maybe a couple of short trips."

At that moment, the telephone rang.

"You can grab it here, Sarah," Sam said.

She scooted close to the general's desk, picked up, and took notes as she listened to the caller.  "Yes . . . Yes, we can handle a group of that size at this location . . . There's a meeting in progress, but they'll be out by fourteen hundred . . . Okay . . . We'll be ready."

She set down the telephone.  "Safe-house guests, high-profile, high-security, family of seven with children, fifteen hundred today, seven or eight days."

General Bo-seklin's mind went into high gear.  "John, you're about to see the *other* thing we do here.  I'll have you coordinate getting the professors out by fourteen hundred, except Doctor Bo-kamla — she always stays late on Fridays, and will help us spot any special needs in the safe-house guests.

"Lisa, move up the Inner Support Team meeting, switch off the security lamp once the professors are out, and double the guard schedule for the next eight days.

"Sarah, get out your checklists and the orientation kit.  See if Maria wants extra hours, get a cook from the air base if not, and schedule the medic."

Colonel Ma-soran nodded while making notes.  "First time we've had children at this facility since Heather's been here.  I wonder if she'd enjoy doing some babysitting . . ."

*  *  *

## Part 3: Ko-tera Three, 3669

### Chapter 36: Recognition

The lithe and supple fourteen-year-old danced to the throbbing music with all her heart.

Teens of all ages, and a few tweens, looked on with open mouths, the soft drinks in their hands forgotten. Three young celebrities sat at the judges' table, pencils poised over score sheets.

For five precious minutes, the main dance floor of the teen club belonged to the dancer. The flashing, spinning lights glowed just for her. She had chosen the music, paid the entry fee with her own money, and practiced for weeks.

A handsome sixteen-year-old boy watched also, filled with pride that the girl everyone was watching belonged to *him*, much more than to any of them.

The music faded, the dancer held her final pose, and the room exploded with applause. She stretched up to her full height, only an inch shorter than the handsome boy, and bowed to the judges and the audience.

The cheering and clapping made the dancer glow with happiness.

"That was Priscilla Ka-mentha! Chelsea Ko-renlo is up next," the D.J. announced.

A minute later, the dancer slipped into the seat beside the sixteen-year-old boy. He wasted no time grabbing her and kissing her so deeply that she went completely limp and began wishing they were alone.

"You were awesome," he whispered when they finally parted.

"Mmmmmm. Even if I don't win the contest, that kiss was the best prize any girl could get. Can I have another?"

He didn't answer, just delivered.

Finally they parted again. "I don't see your body guard anywhere. We could slip out into the night . . ."

She chuckled. "Two tables to your left, blond hair."

He looked. "Darn."

Just then, a server stopped by the table. "Another mango-whatever juice?"

"Mangosteen. Crushed ice, lemon twist."

When the server was gone, the boy raised his eyebrows. "How come you get free drinks, and I don't?"

"Because I *bring* them the mangosteen juice. They can't get it from their regular suppliers. They sell a few to other people who see mine and get curious, so that makes up for the ice and lemon twists. It's really good with rum . . ."

He laughed. "Not here!"

"Okay, everyone," the D.J. boomed. "That's it for this month's dance competition. They were all so great, I'm glad someone *else* has to choose the winners. You all know our judges — film star Pipi Bo-kelem . . ."

Most of the boys in the room cheered and called her name.

". . . singer and heart-throb Brad Ta-doric . . ."

He grinned and waved from the judges' table, and most of the girls screamed with excitement.

". . . and world-class dancer Kristine Ka-sarta."

She received a more modest cheer from both sexes.

"It looks like the judges have completed their tallying," the D.J. continued. "I can see them putting the results into *The Envelope*, sealing it, handing it to the owner of this fantastic club, and he's coming up the stairs. He's walking along the balcony now, approaching the D.J. booth, and laughing his head off at me as he comes. He's handing me *The Envelope*."

The room was tense with excitement.

"I am opening *The Envelope*."

The room fell almost completely silent, as silent as a teen dance club could ever be.

"Oh my God! You won't believe this, boys and girls. Best musical interpretation, Priscilla Ka-mentha!"

The room erupted with cheers and whistles. Priscilla stood and waved.

"Best technical dance, Priscilla Ka-mentha!"

The cheering continued, people started crowding around the winner's table, and the blond security sergeant made sure she was one of them.

"Sexiest dance, Priscilla Ka-mentha!"

Boys, and a few girls, started pawing at her from every direction. Priscilla bounced up and down with excitement.

The security sergeant watched everyone like a hawk.

"Best all-around dancer, Priscilla Ka-mentha!"

The cheering and screaming continued, and the owner shoved a microphone into Priscilla's hand.

A minute passed before the winner could be heard, even with amplification. Another half-minute passed before she quit giggling with happiness.

"I promise not to enter the contest again!"

The entire room filled with laughter, and a glimmer of hope entered the hearts of the other six dance contestants.

* * *

## Chapter 37: Slow Progress

"Department of Defense program P-Seventeen, Session Seven Sixty-Seven, twenty-one April 3669, zero-nine hundred hours, four minutes. Alpha Team is present.  Beta team is present except Doctor Ko-rensis, on a scheduled vacation."

"Thank you, Sergeant Ma-tirol," Heather said to the young blond woman behind the tape recorder.  "I hear that Beta Team has some exciting news.  Who's presenting?"

Doctor Bo-leden the philosopher poked his hand up.

"You have the floor, Larry."

"First of all, I've been asked to announce that there are *four* ribbons temporarily on display in the dance studio, as *someone* we know did a clean sweep at the monthly dance competition of the city's most popular teen dance club last Saturday."

Everyone clapped and Heather turned red.

The philosopher cleared his throat.  "And, of course, I've also been asked to remind you that it is a violation of top-secret-umbra security to associate, in *any* way, that dancer with our Heather, outside of this room with that green light on."

They all promised with mummers and nods.

"Okay, down to business."  He looked at a sheet he held.  "Of the seventeen articles we have endorsed so far, nine have been published, and five more have been accepted for publication.  That's eighty-two percent, *much* better than their fate in Heather's timeline."

A rumble of approval ran through the room.

"But the good news is that one of the first, the one about the exponential increase in pollution by a chemist at Southeastern University, published in a scientific journal almost a year ago, has now been re-written and accepted for publication by a popular magazine."

He stood smiling while the cheering passed.

"There is a dark side to this news, of course.  The magazine also plans to publish the opposing view, and the person they've hired to do that is not a scientist, could not *be* a scientist and honorably refute the well-established facts of the matter, and is known for his blatant use of the four main tactics of debunking.  Richard, you remember those better than I do.  Would you do the honors, please?"

The philosopher took his seat, and the historian stood.  "I've heard them so often, I've got them memorized."

Several people chuckled.

"One.  What the people don't know, I'm not going to tell them."

Heather frowned.

"Two.  Don't bother me with the facts, my mind is made up."

Remembering it from other sessions, General Ko-fenral nodded.

"Three.  If I can't attack the data, I'll attack the people."

"Ad hominem fallacy," General Bo-seklin mumbled, and the philosopher, seated near, verified with a nod.

"Four.  I do my research by proclamation because actual investigation is too much trouble."

Doctor Ko-silma the chemist shivered with distaste.

The historian sat back down and Heather stood.  "Thanks, Larry and Richard.  Although I feel the temptation to add the team's voice to the debate, just as I sense many of you do, this article is probably not important enough for that.  Our endorsements of a few scientific articles don't go beyond the publishers.  That ethical system works to our advantage, and hopefully we can continue in stealth-mode until something really important comes along."

The team looked frustrated, but seemed to understand.

"You'll get us copies of both articles, pro and con, as soon as possible, Larry?"

He nodded.

"Next, I believe we have a new candidate.  You had that, right Tanya?"

Doctor Po-morna the biologist stood and held up a thin manuscript.  "This just circulated in our department for comment.  The author is not well known, but the work is sound.  He gathered a number of estimates of bio-diversity, both pre-historic and recent, did some curve fitting, and concluded that we might be headed for an epoch in which human activity will become the dominant evolutionary force.  He even went so far as to propose the term *anthropocene*.  The idea is a bit radical, so it will probably need our help to get published.  He does *not* see the danger we do — greenhouses gasses and climate heating — but then no one else does, at this point, either."

Discussion took the rest of the session, and by the time Doctor Po-morna sat down, a security corporal was back from the air base with copies of the manuscript.

Heather stood.  "Please remember that this article may not be classified, but where you got it, and why you have it, is.  We'll vote on Wednesday.  Let me see ..." She looked down at her note pad. "Alpha Team is having breakfast with Doctor Po-selem on Wednesday to review the Time Traveler's Paradox, and Beta Team meets on Friday afternoon." She looked around. "Sam?"

"No command meeting today, as several of us have to go places, and no issues are pending. Enjoy your lunch."

Heather looked around the room one more time, then nodded to the blond security sergeant. "Rachael, please close the session."

✳ ✳ ✳

## Chapter 38: Danger Zone

On Wednesday morning, Heather knew that Alpha Team would be more comfortable discussing the Time Traveler's Paradox without her present, so she loaded her breakfast tray and went to find Susan.

"Good morning, therapist mine," she said, taking the comfy seat across from Doctor Bo-kamla in the safe-house corridor.

"How are you this pretty spring morning?"

"Still unwinding from the dance competition. I felt guilty, you know."

Susan cocked her head slightly.

"It's a zero-sum game. For me to win, others have to lose."

"And your prize money . . ."

Heather scrunched her face. "Was from *their* entry fees."

"What are you going to do about that guilt?"

"Give each of them a nice gift certificate to the club. They're just kids, at best with some little part-time, minimum-wage job. I make five grand a month."

"So you wanted the ribbons, but not the prize money?"

"Yeah. And I only wanted the ribbons once, just to prove to myself that I could do it."

"What else do you need to prove to yourself that you can do?"

"Nothing much. Just . . . you know . . . save the world."

✳

On Wednesday, since everyone had read the bio-diversity article, the final discussion took less than half an hour, and the vote was unanimous. A top-secret research team of the Department of Defense would endorse the article's publication. They could clearly imagine the grin on the author's face.

Heather was just about to announce a new topic, a low-priority look at a less-important corner of the future, when she noticed Doctor Ko-silma the chemist standing at her chair holding a think stack of papers.

"Betty, do you have something to share?"

The chemist nodded.

"You have the floor."

"Don't sit down, Heather."

"Um . . . okay."

"Corporal?" the chemist prompted.

Heather watched as the security corporal picked up one of the small tables no one was using, carried it into the circle, and placed it in the exact center of the space. Doctor Ko-silma then reverently placed the thick stack of type-written papers onto the little table.

Heather looked down. It appeared to be a manuscript. But not an article manuscript. Rather, a book manuscript.

"Although I've been very careful about security," the chemist began as she ambled back to her seat, "word does get around when a scientist takes an interest in a certain topic. This manuscript comes from an international group of four scientists who collaborated on a computer model that runs from 3600 to 3800. I do not know if this is *the* book — you will have to make that determination, Heather — but it appears to fit the description you gave us, and has surfaced about when you predicted."

Heather dropped to her knees in front of the little table, and for a moment seemed afraid to touch the manuscript. She spoke, almost to herself, not looking up from the sacred object before her. "There are so many things — books . . . music . . . movies — that I can easily see or hear in my mind, but don't even bother to try to find, because they haven't been *written* yet. This, of all those things, if it's what I think it is, is the most important. The title doesn't match, but titles are often changed during publication."

She didn't start at the beginning, as most of the team expected, but went directly to a point deep in the manuscript, and began to search forward from there. Only a few pages later, she stopped and stared with wide eyes.

As if in a dream, she stood and clipped that page to the top of the blackboard. During the next ten minutes, the room remained completely silent, save for the scraping of the chalk, as Heather copied the illustration for all to see. As the drawing took shape, it reminded them of her own graphs of the future, but not completely.

Eventually she turned back to the team, replacing the page she had borrowed from the manuscript. "I think this is the book. I'll read it this afternoon and know for sure. Anyone who can stay is welcome to read with me."

She pointed at the blackboard. "I know this graph, like I know the streets in that neighborhood where I . . . died. *Everyone*, after about 3715, will know this graph because it will tell them the truth, far more than their political, social, or religious leaders ever do, with rare exceptions.

"As you can see, this is not the same as the graph I drew for you about this point in the future. The authors modeled resources, food, industry, and pollution, but not simple temperature. Climate change was not on their radar. They thought the population would crash much later in the next century than I experienced. Considering they weren't even *attempting* to model what actually got us, they did a very, very good job. It will match reality quite well for almost fifty years, until . . . reality goes into high gear.

"Although it will not ultimately be accurate — and no model can be — it gives a very clear message. The next century will not be pretty. *That's* the message that needs to come out *now*."

✳

The experience of finding the book made Heather ravenous and talkative. After feasting and chatting for the entire lunch hour, she and Lisa, last of all, stepped out of the dining room.

Heather was surprised to find most of the team back in their seats. The manuscript still waited on the little table, but the surrounding chairs and couches had been rearranged slightly so that pages could be handed from person to person, snaking around the room and eventually ending at Doctor Ko-silma's seat.

Tears threatened to come to the fourteen-year-old. "You guys are so sweet for waiting!"

General Bo-seklin smiled. "We know how important this moment is."

Sarah nodded agreement. "Chris had to jump in a transport and go teach a class, but promised to read it in Betty's office tomorrow."

Heather blinked like an owl to keep her feelings under control as she rolled her chair up to the little table and its precious manuscript. She picked up the title page, gazed at it for a moment, and handed it to Colonel Ma-soran.

✳

Just as it took half an hour for the first page to get to the last reader, Heather found herself with half an hour to kill while the rest of the team read the last few pages. She thought of chatting with Maria, putting on some music, or visiting the garage-level security guard, but instead just stayed in her seat, closed her eyes, and let her mind drift away into the future.

✳   ✳   ✳

## Chapter 39: The Book

By Friday morning, everyone on the team had read the book manuscript. Several professors had arranged with Doctor Ko-silma for an extra read on Thursday. The chemist herself was on her third read.

At a few minutes after nine o'clock, Heather stood with a strange expression on her face. Some thought they saw tears glistening in her eyes. Others perceived strength and determination they could hardly describe.

"Yes, the book we read on Wednesday is the book I remember. In the future I know, it will have no equal until it is updated in about 3705. That will spawn many new books, some of them perhaps a little better, but all of them indebted to this book."

She paused for a deep breath and noticed several professors anxiously looking at the empty table in the middle of the circle. "Fear not — Rachael's at the air base making a copy so we'll have one here and one in Betty's office."

Everyone relaxed.

"The team must decide what it should do about this book. I open the floor to discussion."

Every member of the team had questions about the book publishing process. Luckily, most of the professors had titles of their own in print, and could answer.

By eleven o'clock, the new copy of the manuscript was in its place of honor. Hands immediately shot into the air with questions about the contents of the book. Heather let the professors answer most of those questions, especially about the underlying science. She sat at the manuscript and looked up passages or illustrations whenever they wanted, and made sure everyone got a chance to speak, but sensed it was time to step out of the process as much as possible.

At half past noon, Maria stood in the dining room doorway with hands on her hips. "I can't keep it hot forever!"

⁂

Time started to move faster and faster for Heather. She kept her body and mind in good condition out of habit, and ran the P-Seventeen sessions as well as ever, but they seemed to come and go almost before she realized it.

An entire week was consumed by questions and discussions related to the book manuscript that remained in the center of the circle. During that week, a Contact Team of three professors was formed, with Doctor Ko-silma as their leader. By the end of the week, she had a response from the authors — they would be thrilled to receive the comments and endorsements of such well-known professors. They were surprised, but wanted to know more about a possible endorsement by the Department of Defense.

Heather felt a growing sense of unreality, as if somehow the world was leaving her behind. She talked about it with Susan, but they couldn't identify the cause. Heather's knowledge of the future was as good as ever. Her ability to lead the team was unaffected. Dancing and skating, and the sweet kisses of a certain boy, continued to bring her comfort almost daily.

⁂

The following Monday, the Contact Team had good news. The authors of the book had found a publisher on their own, an academic printing house that sold mostly to university libraries from a catalog they put out once a year.

"Absolutely useless!" Heather blurted out, standing up and interrupting Doctor Ko-silma. "That will get a few hundred copies gathering dust on deep, dark shelves in gloomy library sub-basements. This book had *that* the first time . . . the time I lived through . . . the time the world ended."

Seeing her passion on the issue, and her point, the team silently forgave Heather's outburst. After an hour of discussion, the Contact Team was entrusted with the task of convincing the authors to *not* sign a contract with that publisher.

When the generals and colonels emerged from General Bo-seklin's office after lunch, Betty and her fellow professors received a carrot they could dangle — an invitation for the authors to meet with the full team that Friday, with travel expenses covered by the Department and all the arrangements handled by Colonel Ma-soran.

Heather could almost feel the world spinning around her, knew with certainty that she could not lead Friday's session, and sensed that her role as voyant — or something like that — was coming to an end.

A part of her wished she wasn't aware of so many other things she still needed to do.

⁂

Wednesday was primarily a planning meeting for the upcoming visit. Colonel Ma-soran reported that all travel arrangements had been completed, and the authors would arrive at the airport between zero-five and zero-seven hundred on Friday morning.  A member of the Contact Team would meet each flight, and blind transports would whisk them to the facility.  Maria was planning an international breakfast.

Heather hardly had to say a word during that entire meeting.

*　*　*

## Chapter 40: Authors

Susan was so worried about Heather that she cancelled some regular clients on Wednesday and Thursday to spend extra time at the facility. Between that, lots of dancing, and outings with Ginny and Rachael, the fourteen-year-old managed to keep her feet on the ground and her head on her shoulders — just barely.

On Friday morning, after a few dances between four and five o'clock, then a hot bath, Heather put on her *someone's daughter or granddaughter helping out for the day* clothes. By seven, she was in an apron, puttering around the kitchen with Maria, keeping the dishes washed and the counters clean.

The security lamp was off. As team members came up the stairs, Lisa made sure they noticed.

The authors arrived when expected, two in one blind transport, the other two separately. Three of them had thick foreign accents. General Ko-fenral showed them the sleeping rooms where they could leave their luggage. He gave them tours of the facility, then escorted them to breakfast. They were delighted by the international assortment of foods and drinks.

The military people and Heather knew why General Bo-seklin was in his office with the door closed. Most of the other team members guessed.

A few minutes before the session was supposed to start, Heather took off her apron and planted herself on a chair in the very back row between Susan and Betty.

The rest of the team, and the four authors, filtered out of the dining room. The authors graciously accepted front-row seats with General Ko-fenral.

General Bo-seklin emerged from his office and stepped into the middle of the circle. For a moment, he looked at Heather's empty plush chair — today, his seat — and felt a twinge of foreboding.  He hid it with a deep breath and turned to the assembled team and guests with a smile.

"Good morning.  I must apologize for keeping to myself earlier this morning.  Normally, this team operates at a level of security *above* top secret.  Today we cannot, and yet we must skirt that line to talk to you about your research and your book.  I had to review some rules and get clear in my mind what was important today.

"Let us begin with introductions.  I am Two-star General Samuel Bo-seklin, commander of this facility and the programs housed here.  Only one of those programs is relevant to this meeting . . ."

Heather experienced a deep contentment listening to someone else talk about the team she had brought to life over the previous seven years.  Somehow, that made it more real.

Eventually, the four authors were invited to introduce themselves, and General Bo-seklin sat down.

"I am Professor Dennis Ma-zolen, and I am honored to be here.  My specialty is agriculture and the global food supply . . ."

Heather remembered little of his fifteen-minute introduction, but had the impression he was sincere, if long-winded.

"Good morning, I am Doctor Jargen Bo-tora, and my contribution to this project is my knowledge of non-renewable resource depletion . . ."

Several people in the room, including Heather, noticed his frown any time he glanced at anyone in the military.

"My name is Doctor Donella Po-tirel, and my expertise is pollution of all kinds — air, water, and land . . ."

Heather felt a moment of frustration, almost anger, that someone would call herself an expert on pollution, but miss the kind that would bring civilization to its knees.  She breathed slowly, and reminded herself that Doctor Po-tirel had lots of company on that issue.

"I am William Ko-poran, industrial output specialist.  I'm very curious as to why the military has an interest in our little book . . ."

Heather smiled slightly, feeling an immediate liking for the man, even though she had little interest in the study of industrial output.

General Bo-seklin stood back up.  "Thank you, and welcome.  I have a short presentation, and then we will open the floor to questions while the entire team is here.  We will continue less formally this afternoon, with some team members needing to return to the University.  Tomorrow, only the military staff will be present, and Sunday will be completely free, with transports available at any time.  Monday morning the entire team will be back, and you all have return flights that afternoon.

"Everyone on this team has read your manuscript — most of them several times — and all of us would give you a glowing endorsement.  As you know, there are some big names here, not to mention three generals and four colonels, for what that's worth."

Most of the authors smiled.

"The situation is . . . this highly-classified team, for the past seven years, has been studying almost exactly the same scenario that you modeled, and came to very similar conclusions. We cannot share with you our research methods, but we assure you that they are strongly cross-checked and verified, and include modeling with the University's super-computer."

General Bo-seklin noticed several team members smiling, and was glad the guests, in the front row, couldn't see them.

"However, for many reasons, it is not our intention to publish our own findings, nor to compete with your research in any way. Rather, we wish to do what we can to increase the chances of *your* work being effectively published."

The four authors looked relieved. Even Doctor Bo-tora, with his dislike of the military, appeared to relax a little.

"As our Doctor Ko-silma has already expressed to you, we want to talk you out of signing with a small, academic publisher. Instead, with our help, we want you to find a publisher who will get this excellent book into bookstores all over the world . . ."

✳

Heather felt very proud of Sam's talk. She, and other team members, had succeeded in teaching him a great deal, and he remembered more of it than she expected. Even with her broad knowledge of history, she could think of very few generals, of any nation, who had ever presided over moments as important as this.

General Bo-seklin soon finished his presentation, they took a break, and then he opened the meeting to questions.

"Professor Ma-zolen?"

"Exactly *why* is the military concerned with our book sales? Are you intending to get a cut, or a kickback, in exchange for your endorsements?"

Heather could see that Sam was flustered for a moment, but he hid it well.

"Well . . . um . . . neither. This program has no interest in making money. But let us be blunt — your model predicts a possible collapse of civilization sometime in the next century. Our research tells us that your model, if anything, is too conservative, and the danger is closer in time, and greater in magnitude . . ."

The resulting rumble seemed to fill the room, even though it only came from the four authors.

"Our *results*," Doctor Bo-tora began defensively, "are merely *indicators* of the system's behavioral *tendencies*."

The entire team began grumbling, but General Bo-seklin raised his hands for silence, then took a deep breath. "In any model that begins with real-world data, those *behavioral tendencies* constitute a prediction. The only question is — how accurate? Your model happens to roughly match our research for about the next fifty years.

"The Department of Defense is charged with the protection of this country," the general continued, "and that task would not be possible if civilization was collapsing all around us.  This team believes that the publication and *wide* distribution of your book would be a positive step in any effort to avoid that collapse.  If you want your work to just become a few hundred copies sitting on dusty library shelves, you have that right.  Colonel Ma-soran can probably get you flights home this afternoon.

"But if you'd rather be part of the solution at this critical moment in history, then you're welcome to stay, eat with us, talk with us, and see what we can accomplish . . . together."

Heather had tears of joy and pride dripping down her cheeks.  Susan grabbed her hand on one side, and Betty on the other.  They could all see that Sam was exhausted.

"Even though it's a little early," General Bo-seklin went on more softly at about eleven thirty, "I'm going to declare a long lunch break.  The team will meet again at thirteen . . . I mean, one o'clock . . . *if* our guests would like it to."

Heather squeezed the hands of the two ladies surrounding her, then dashed into the kitchen to get drinks ready so Maria could concentrate on the gourmet dishes she was preparing.

✳   ✳   ✳

## Chapter 41: National Security

Although the team wandered toward the dining room, the four authors quickly disappeared into the large safe-house sleeping room.  No one attempted to eavesdrop, but the walls were not thick enough to hide the fact that an argument, sometimes hushed and sometimes heated, was in progress.

Maria got lunch onto the serving line five minutes early, and Heather placed a *Reserved* sign on one of the dining tables.

Sam smiled and nodded from the line of people filling their trays.

Half an hour later, as most team members were getting desserts, the four authors emerged to discover, to their surprise, that plenty of food remained. They glanced at the reserved table, looked at each other sheepishly, and lined up at the serving counter.

With both Heather and General Bo-seklin setting the example, no one bothered the authors for a decision.  The team members savored desserts, looked over their notes, or called the University to arrange for teaching substitutes.

Heather slipped out a few minutes before one o'clock to change clothes.

*

When the authors emerged from the dining room, everyone else was milling about.  The four guests found General Bo-seklin.

"We would like to speak to your team," Doctor Po-tirel said.

Sam nodded to Sarah and Lisa, they whispered to others, and within a minute, everyone was seated.

The woman author stood.  "It is challenging to collaborate on such a complex project with language and cultural differences sometimes making communication difficult.  But . . . we have *tentatively* agreed to pursue your idea of seeking publication by a more . . . public . . . publisher."

The entire team burst into applause.  No one but Susan and Betty, in the back row, noticed who started it.

Doctor Donella Po-tirel almost blushed.  "The truth is, our manuscript sits, probably forgotten, at several large publishers, including one in this city. We just have no idea how to motivate them to look at it."

"That's where we come in," General Bo-seklin said from Heather's chair. "If you will permit us to grease some wheels, I believe we can work a little magic."

The woman sighed.  "We would be honored, as long as nothing is actually . . . cast in concrete . . . until all four of us sign a publishing contract."

General Bo-seklin stood.  "Of course.  If you will go with Colonel Ma-soran to her desk, she will get a little information from you and make a few phone calls.  While you're doing that, the team will be signing some endorsements we've put together . . ."

✳

The facility was abuzz with chatter and activity for the next half hour as endorsements were signed, phone calls made, and feelings of anticipation shared.

The authors, seated around Colonel Ma-soran's desk, tried to contain their nervousness as they listened to one side of several telephone calls.  After the last call, Sarah put down the telephone and looked at them.  "We have an appointment with the chief editor at three o'clock today."

"But how did you . . ." one of the men started to ask.

"It's amazing what can be done when national security is involved."

Colonel Ma-soran stood, announced the situation, and began making arrangements for a blind transport and a car to depart at fourteen hundred. The three generals all indicated they were going.  Sarah glanced at Heather, who nodded.

The authors dashed to their sleeping rooms to freshen up.

The professors huddled, and decided to not crowd the chief editor too much, so they asked Doctor Bo-leden the philosopher to present their endorsements.

Drivers and security people were quickly selected, and as two o'clock approached, a corporal held the steel door to the garage as the large group filed down the stairs and into the awaiting vehicles.

Doctor Bo-leden and Heather winked at each other as he followed the authors toward the blind transport, and she went with the generals in the car.

Back upstairs, Colonel Ka-markla switched on the security lamp so those who remained could share their hopes and fears.  Maria had all the help she needed cleaning up from lunch and starting dinner.

✳   ✳   ✳

## Chapter 42: Publishing

Harold To-kamra, chief editor of Po Publications, was not about to be bullied just because three generals, an international team of respected scientists, and a well-known professor with a stack of endorsements, filled his office.

He looked slowly through the manuscript. "I have been asked before to NOT publish things on national security grounds, but I have never been asked TO publish. When the government wants something published, they usually just do it themselves." He glanced up at his visitors through tri-focal glasses.

"The research methods we use are highly classified," General Bo-seklin explained, "so we prefer to endorse parallel work by civilians, whenever possible. We have been endorsing academic publication of appropriate articles for years, but as you can see, this book is for general readers. It needs a publisher who knows how to get it to the people."

The editor looked at the manuscript a bit more. "Well, I can certainly get it into print, as long as the authors are available to validate any editorial changes . . ."

All four of them nodded.

". . . but this just *isn't* something that's going to generate much interest. It's still basically academic. It's about reality. That doesn't sell well."

"But does not the publication of a book come with a publicity budget?" William Ko-poran asked.

"Yes, but only in proportion to the interest we think the title will generate. For something like this, I can't imagine the publishing board putting more than . . . five or ten thousand into publicity — just enough to bring it to the attention of libraries and a few specialized bookstores."

A tense moment of silence lingered.

"I think I can shed some light on that issue," a female voice came from the back of the room.

Generals Bo-seklin and Ba-kerga scooted their chairs farther apart so she could be seen.

"And you are?" the chief editor asked.

"My name and most of my credentials are classified," the slender young lady in business clothes said, "but among other things, I represent a consortium of private donors who have earmarked a substantial fund for publicity efforts for this book."

The generals and Doctor Bo-leden knew Heather well enough to not be surprised.  The authors had seen the young lady at the team meeting and in the dining room, and had thought nothing of it.  Now, they were open-mouthed but speechless.

"How substantial?" the chief editor asked, adjusting his glasses.

"I have not looked at the fund balance *today*, but it's something north of seven figures," she replied, "and climbing."

Harold To-kamra's eyes snapped open wide.  "With a publicity fund like *that*, everyone on the *planet* will know about this book!"

"Something along those lines is our goal," she said calmly.

"And what does this . . . consortium . . . want in exchange?"

"Only two things.  First, that you work with the authors to get the vocabulary to the twelve-year reading level . . ."

"That's ridiculous!" Doctor Bo-tora burst out.  "We will NOT allow our book to be put into baby-talk!"

The chief editor looked at the irate author, and could see that the other three had similar feelings.  "You have not written for general readers before, have you?"

"No," Doctor Bo-tora nearly spat out.

"The twelve-year level IS the general public's reading level.  Let me give you an example."  He opened the manuscript randomly.  "*Logging operations, if not done carefully, often exacerbate water pollution.*  All we need to do is change *exacerbate* to *worsen*.  See how easy?"

The four authors tried to collect themselves.

"It will be a challenge for us, but I believe we can do it," Donella Po-tirel said, looking at her colleagues.

"And your other condition, young lady?" the chief editor asked, looking toward the back of the room again.

"That the book be *in bookstores* by the end of this year."

The chief editor whistled.  "I'll have to shuffle some priorities, re-assign some people.  When, and how much, can we expect up-front?"

"When all contracts are signed, one hundred thousand, with similar amounts periodically after I see what you're doing with that much."

"In that case," Harold To-kamra said, "I believe we are going to publish a book!"

⁕

Back in the car, General Bo-seklin looked at Heather.  "Consortium?"

"Sounded impressive, didn't it?"

"I can't deny *that*.  I know you've done some very profitable investing, but isn't that amount going to drain you?"

"Yes, but as long as I can grab a sandwich in the kitchen, crash on a bunk in the bomb shelter . . . and maybe save the world . . . what more could a girl want?"

General Ko-fenral chuckled.  "As long as there's food in that kitchen, and a bunk in that bomb shelter, you'll be welcome to them!"

General Ba-kerga smiled but didn't say anything.

"The facility, direct?" Rachael inquired from the driver's seat.

"After a brief stop at my bank," Heather asserted.

General Bo-seklin verified with a nod.

✳   ✳   ✳

## Chapter 43: Courage

Sam came in for a leisurely breakfast on Saturday morning with the four authors.  Heather was back in jeans and a t-shirt, puttering around the kitchen to help Maria.  The authors glanced at the teenage girl repeatedly, and when they sat down with the general to eat, she joined them.

"You wear many hats, young lady," Doctor Po-tirel commented, smiling. "Are you *really* going to pay the publisher a hundred thousand for publicity as soon as we sign a contract?"

Heather swallowed a bite of scrambled eggs.  "Already got a cashier's check, as I have a hunch your editor is going to get things moving very quickly."

"It is so strange not even knowing your name."

"You can call me *Heather*.  It's just a handle for use around here."

"Well, thank you, Heather.  Our dream of publication is coming true almost faster than we can . . . run along behind!"

The other three authors laughed and continued enjoying their breakfast.

By mid-morning, the four guests were in General Bo-seklin's office with the door closed.

"I don't believe it!" Doctor Bo-tora spat out.  "It's just *not* how things are done!"

Sam considered his response.  "I agree.  Does that mean you are going to turn down the offer of publication and the publicity fund of a million plus?"

The scientist was suddenly silent.

"Perhaps . . ." Professor Ma-zolen began thoughtfully, ". . . if there was some way to reassure us that this . . . fund . . . actually exists . . ."

The general sighed.  "Heather already anticipated that you would be skeptical . . . *and* she told me which of you."

The two men looked slightly ashamed, but still defiant.

General Bo-seklin opened an envelope and placed the cashier's check face-up for them to see.

"And how do we know this is real?" Doctor Bo-tora questioned.

The general looked up sharply. "I was with her at the bank when she got it, yesterday afternoon, after the meeting with the chief editor."

"We apologize," Donella Po-tirel said with warning glances at her colleagues. "This is just all so . . . unusual."

"Your book is unusual," Sam pointed out as he slipped the check back into its envelope. "This moment in history is unusual. The collapse your models predict . . . and that our research verifies, will only threaten the human race once, God willing. There is nothing routine about this entire situation. If you wanted a routine publishing experience, you should have written a different book."

The authors took deep breaths to settle themselves.

"So," General Bo-seklin began, changing the subject, "why don't we go over to the air base, switch to a comfortable van with windows, and go see some of the sights of this fair city of ours? It's springtime, and some of the public gardens are gorgeous this time of year . . ."

✳

Heather spent most of Saturday and Sunday skating, hiking, kissing Brian, and talking with Susan about all her recent frustrations. She admitted, sometime Sunday afternoon, that as passionate as she was about the publication of this book, she was really looking forward to the authors getting on their planes and going home.

It was a very good thing she was relaxed and refreshed by Monday morning, because Generals Bo-seklin and Ko-fenral both needed her.

"You were right, Heather," Sam said from behind his desk as he continued scanning the type-written sheets of paper. "That chief editor must have jumped right on this and worked all day Saturday. The envelope arrived at the air base yesterday by courier, and came in the mail pouch with the first transport this morning."

The two generals finished with the parts they were reading, then swapped.

"I'm not surprised," she said softly. "They're going to make lots of money."

Sam pressed his intercom button. "Sarah, please get a lawyer from the base, someone who knows publishing contracts. Eleven hundred today."

"Yes, Sir," her voice said.

"I don't see anything else to worry about, Malcolm," Sam said. "Do you?"

"No. It's actually a very nice contract, from the authors' point of view."

Sam lowered the papers he was holding and took a slow breath. "We asked you in here, Heather, to share some of your seemingly-unlimited courage with us."

She smiled, but was still in the dark about their concern.

"The publisher wants at least six professors from the team who are willing to give glowing endorsements of the book — for print, radio, and television."

She nodded.  "I'm sure we'll have plenty of volunteers.  They all know what they can and can't say."

"I'm not worried about that," Sam assured.  "They also want at least two generals willing to do unscripted, spontaneous, televised interviews.  It's not an option.  No generals, no publishing contract."

"Oh," she breathed.

"Now you see why we need some of your courage?" Malcolm asked.

Heather nodded.  "That would scare anyone."

"So," Sam began, "please tell us how you found the nerve to give *all* your money to this one little book."

She took a deep breath and closed her eyes for a long moment.  "From the life memories of our nameless future psychologist, I seemed to have gained a sense of how history works.  Ideas that change the world form around seeds.  Those seeds are often speeches, but in modern times, books can also do the trick.

"There are still pieces of the puzzle I can't imagine — steps that must be taken to get knowledge of the approaching danger from our team, to the world.  But the seed is still necessary, even if we can't see *how* it will grow.  My intuition tells me this book is that seed.  It certainly *would* have been, in the future I know, but was discovered by the world too late.  It needed thirty more years, the thirty years we can give it.

"My courage comes, I guess, from knowing what will happen if I don't do . . . what I must do.  Nothing else matters.  I have a purpose, and when you have a purpose, you don't get a life.  You don't get all the other things most people think they're entitled to — school, career, marriage, family.  If you're lucky, maybe you can grab a little bit along the way, like I do with Brian.  But you're always on history's sacrificial altar, ready for the ceremonial knife to come down.

"But running away is for little people.  God doesn't choose little people for purposes like this.  Neither of you are little people, either, or you wouldn't have put your reputations on the line for this team, and learned all the things I taught you, and the professors taught you, over the last seven years."

She fell silent.

The two generals just breathed for a minute.

"Also, a good, hearty breakfast can really help with courage," she added with a grin.

Sam looked at her, smiled, and rose from his desk.  "But you're leading the meeting."

She squinted for a moment, then smiled and nodded.

✳

"Good morning, everyone.  Now that our guests know me a bit, the generals and I decided it was safe to lead my team again."  She smiled at the four authors in the front row.

Three of them smiled back.

"But I must say, Sam did a very good job last Friday."

Most of the team professors clapped, and several military people and Donella Po-tirel joined in.

Heather could see General Bo-seklin blushing.

She looked at the authors again. "Today, I believe, is a very important day in the history of human civilization. Today, after a short and easy meeting, we will hand the authors of this great book the publishing contract that was received in the mail this morning. A lawyer will be here at eleven to help them spot anything shady in the wording, and Sam and Malcolm have agreed to do their part for the book's publicity. The contract also calls for a few professors from the team to endorse the book in writing, audio, and video . . ."

More than a dozen hands shot into the air.

"I didn't think we'd have any trouble with that. Have you got those, Sarah?"

Colonel Ma-soran was frantically scribbling names. "Almost . . . there."

"Thank you, everyone. Someone once said, *Stick with the truth, and you will have help beyond your imagination.* Sorry, I can't remember who. You four authors did that, even knowing it would probably make you enemies. All important truths have that same burden.

"Now you have help, because *now* is the time for this book to be placed in the hands of millions of people all over the world. And, yes, a few of them will hate you for it. If things get too ugly, you can always come and hide here."

The entire team chuckled or smiled.

Doctor Po-tirel raised her hand. "We were wondering why security was so tight here. I think we understand now."

Heather smiled. "There are several reasons for that, but doing what needs to be done, without interruption, is certainly one of them."

She paused, glanced at the clock, and looked at the authors again. "It's almost ten o'clock. That gives you an hour to study the contract before the lawyer arrives, and another hour to hear his opinions, before lunch. Your transport leaves for the airport at two o'clock."

She looked around the room. "Alpha Team, Beta Team, and everyone else, thank you for coming in today. Sometimes history-making events must cut into vacation time a little."

Her team grinned back at her.

"Everyone is welcome to stay and chat, have lunch, and see our guests off. Sam?"

General Bo-seklin stood. "Generals and colonels at fourteen hundred. The full team meets again next Monday at the usual time, and if all goes well today, we'll begin talking about our relationship with the publisher."

Heather nodded.

Finally, Sam took the large envelope from his chair and approached the four authors. They rose, and he placed the envelope in William Ko-poran's hands.

All four bowed slightly, then retreated to the privacy of the large safe-house sleeping room.

✳

None of the team members left.

Some lounged in the meeting area, or sipped tea in the dining room, while discussing light topics or ideas for endorsing and promoting the book.

With Lisa's permission, a few crept into the bomb shelter so they could speak freely on any topic.

Heather floated from place to place, and noticed Susan listening to General Ko-fenral's fears and frustrations in a corner of the dining room.

The lawyer from the air base arrived and was shown to the sleeping room where the authors continued to study the publishing contract.

At noon, Maria provided a hearty spread of sandwich makings and homemade soups that everyone enjoyed.

Finally, after spending another half hour in privacy, the four authors emerged from their rooms with their bags packed and the contract signed.

In the middle of the large meeting room, with the entire team standing around them as witnesses, General Bo-seklin received the precious envelope and promised its delivery, along with the cashier's check, to the chief editor of Po Publications, in person, that very afternoon.

Many handshakes and some embraces were shared, security people carried the authors' luggage downstairs, and with some reluctance, the four authors followed.

Heather sighed deeply and melted into Susan's embrace.

Knowing the book publishing contract was signed and in good hands, the team members finally felt free to return to the air base, the University, or their homes.

✳   ✳   ✳

## Part 4: Ko-tera Three, 3670

## Chapter 44: Publicity

Harold To-kamra, chief editor of Po Publications, was not overjoyed with the idea of spending half a day away from the office.  His inbox was a foot thick, and his to-do list was threatening to become a book in itself.

And yet, he was already making money, and expected to make lots more, from this silly book that *someone* wanted in bookstores so badly they'd put up a huge pile of cash, and risk the reputations of several respected generals and scientists in the process.

As he waited, briefcase in hand, just inside the ornate beveled glass doors of Po Publications, he smiled to himself.  He'd get it into bookstores, easy. He'd make sure every man, woman, child, and pet hamster in the world knew about it.  But he was quite sure no one would actually *buy* it.  It was bad news, the end of the world as they knew it, a downer if anything was.

The military van pulled into the loading zone exactly when it was due.  An armed sergeant hopped out of the front passenger seat, slid open the side door part way, then stood with his hands behind his back.

Harold To-kamra took a deep breath and pushed through the ornate doors.  As he approached the van, he recognized the young lady who controlled the money.

"Identity verified," the young lady said.

The sergeant slid the door open wide.

"Um . . . thank you," the chief editor said.  "Is tipping customary?"

"No, Sir."

"Come on in, Harold!" the young lady invited.

With some uneasiness, he stepped into the van and took the nearest seat.

A female officer smiled and extended her hand as the door was slid closed. "Good morning, Mister To-kamra.  I'm Colonel Lisa Ka-markla, chief of security at the facility we're heading toward."

He smiled and shook hands, then looked at the young lady.  "I really need something I can call you.  Gertrude, Brunhilde, something."

The younger female laughed.  "Everyone on the research team calls me *Heather*."

"Happy to meet you again, Heather."  He looked around as he felt the vehicle move along the street.  "It's a bit strange not being able to see where we're going."

"Most of our scientists have been going through the same process for years," Lisa explained.  "They park at the air base, then chat about anything and everything, in one of these transports, on the drive to the facility."

"I did a little research.  Top secret *umbra*, right?"

"That's just the general clearance to get you in the building.  To actually be on the team, a specific program clearance is also necessary."

"I don't have either . . ."

Lisa smiled.  "We won't be operating in that mode today.  Same thing happened when the authors were here, and when we have to bring in scientists or other specialists for a day."

Harold nodded.  "I see.  Isn't this weather we're having quite beautiful for February?"

※

When the door was slid open and Harold To-kamra was finally able to see outside the vehicle, he beheld a concrete block wall and a steel door. Stepping out and standing up, he noticed that the geometry of the parking garage did not allow him to be seen from the vehicle entrance, behind them, nor the exit, ahead.  Thick red lines on the floor appeared to mark the safe area.  No one was making sure he stayed inside the red lines, but he imagined that more important guests might be handled differently.

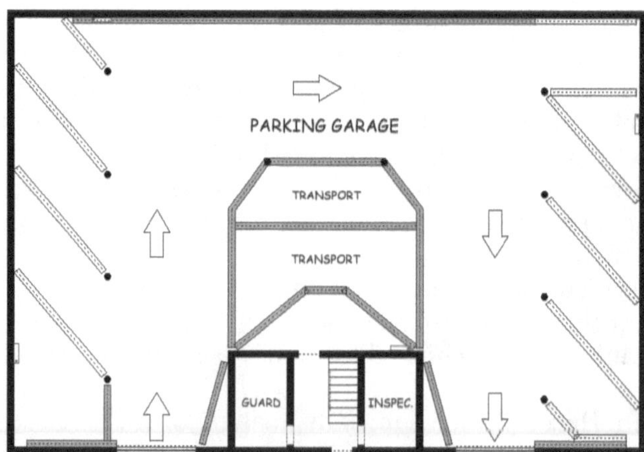


The sergeant spoke into an intercom on the wall, and a corporal unlocked the door from the inside and held it open for the new arrivals.

Harold To-kamra followed Heather into the building, past a staircase, and into a small room.

The sergeant stood behind a desk and grabbed a small lock-box from a cabinet.

Heather placed her pistol into the lock-box, and left her shoulder purse open on the table. The sergeant tapped it and smiled, but didn't look inside.

"Mister To-kamra," the sergeant began, "please take a look at the chart on the wall. If you have any of the items on this chart, such as guns, knives, or explosives, I must keep them locked up for you while you're in the facility."

"No, nothing. Do you wish to search me?"

"No, you're already on our list of trusted visitors."

"Thank you."

Heather collected her purse and led the way upstairs.

✳

Harold To-kamra was enchanted by the pleasant atmosphere, the hospitality, and the tasty breakfast. Colonel Sarah Ma-soran, about his age and quite attractive, introduced him to the scientists and other professors who arrived in a constant stream. He had met the philosopher, but was familiar with the rest only by reputations, and their signatures on endorsements for the book he had so recently published.

The chief editor asked a few open-ended questions to see if he could discover any more about the top-secret programs that met in the building, but didn't learn anything new.

✳

"Program name and session number deleted for security, twenty-three February 3670, zero-nine hundred hours, thirteen minutes."

"Good morning, everyone," Heather said, rising from her seat. "The security lamp is off, as we have a special guest. Please tell us about yourself, Mister To-kamra."

He had it all planned. For several days, he had worked out what he was going to say to these people. He intended to put everything in glowing terms, tell them exactly what they wanted to hear, and utter not a single word that would tarnish their hopes and dreams. Those checks for a hundred thousand were what mattered. He'd be able to skim quite a bit, since an impressive publicity campaign wouldn't cost anywhere near what these unsuspecting fools thought it would.

He stood, looked at the team of generals, colonels, majors, enlisted personnel, professors from the University, and one mysterious young lady, and his mind went completely blank.

Heather didn't immediately notice, but she saw a concerned look on Susan's face.

"I . . ."

The entire team waited, and tried to remain calm and respectful.

"I . . . I'm sorry . . . I seem to have . . . I don't know . . . I seem to have forgotten . . . maybe I should sit down . . ."

A rumble began until Heather stood and raised a hand. "While Mister

To-kamra takes a break, I'll summarize what I know.  Most of you heard the radio endorsements that Chris, Larry, Betty, and Tanya put together.  A couple of you were absent when we played those, Sarah has the tapes.  Last week, while we were on vacation, Chris and Betty did their first video endorsement, and we'll get a copy of that as soon as the editing is done.  Sam is scheduled to do his first . . ."

"Oh my God," Harold To-kamra said from his seat, staring into space and paying no attention to Heather.

Heather nodded to Susan, and the two of them converged on the chief editor's chair and knelt down.

"I just realized . . ."

Sarah knelt down with them and whispered, "Medic?"

Susan shook her head.

"Oh my God, my grandchildren!" the stricken chief editor lamented. "What's going to happen to my grandchildren?"

On a hunch, Sarah touched the man's trembling hand.  After a moment of hesitation, he grabbed it and held on tightly, all the while gazing into space. "But . . . even if it's true . . . it shouldn't affect them!"

Heather struggled to make a decision, and glanced around at the concerned faces of generals, colonels, and professors, but realized the situation didn't allow the luxury of a conference.  "Our research tells us . . . the collapse may come sooner than the authors predict . . . by twenty or thirty years."

Harold To-kamra looked at Heather with wild, frightened eyes.  "I saw fires, scorching heat and withered crops, and my grandchildren starving in their prime.  Please tell me that's not going to happen . . ."

Heather looked into his eyes and saw the pain of suddenly understanding that the message in the book he had published was not about something that would happen in the distant future, or to strange people in some far-away land, but to his own flesh and blood, right here in their homeland.

✳

After a long break, a slice of apple pie, and a glass of cold milk, Harold To-kamra managed to regain his composure.  He asked to speak to the team again.

"I came here to tell you . . . a bunch of bullshit.  You deserve better.  And I'm going to give you better.  I just . . . don't have anything prepared yet, so you'll have to bear with me."

Many members of the team nodded with sympathy.  No one looked angry.

"I saw my grandchildren in a scorched land unable to produce any food. It was *this* land.  I just need to ask you, to your faces, if you truly know this is coming."

"No one can *know* the future," Doctor Bo-leden the philosopher answered from his seat, "in the same way we *know* the past or the present.  But we study the forces at work in the present that will shape the future.  We take into account the track record of every technique we use.  We especially look for those tendencies that several different forecasting methods all predict. We analyze everything from multiple points of view, which is why this team is highly inter-disciplinary. We do not *know*, but we do *believe* that a future WE DO NOT WANT is right around the corner, and yes, it probably includes extreme droughts and other unusual weather that will cause a collapse of commercial agriculture and massive starvation."

Harold To-kamra stared at the philosopher for a long moment, then looked around the room and saw well-known scientists and high-ranking military officers agreeing with nods. He swallowed before trying to speak again. "And . . . this book . . . will help change that?"

"We do not *know* that either," Doctor Ko-silma the chemist answered, "but it's the best thing we've found, so far, and was researched and written independently of this team. That counts for a lot in the world of science."

The chief editor looked around again, and saw the same verification from everyone.

"I need some time to think," he eventually said, "and I need to make some changes . . . some improvements . . . to the publicity that was planned for the book. Can I come back in . . . a week?"

Heather stood. "What's on our schedule, Sarah?"

She opened a binder. "Yes, a week from today would be fine."

The chief editor looked around like a lost puppy for another moment, then whispered, "Thank you."

✳

Harold To-kamra was so anxious to work on his publicity plans that he declined their offer of lunch, and was back in a blind transport by eleven o'clock. After a break to see him off, the security lamp was switched on and the team reconvened.

With a wrinkled brow, General Bo-seklin stood. "Anyone care to speculate on what happened today?"

Doctor Po-selem the physicist raised his hand. "When I joined this team, seven and a half years ago, you wouldn't have caught me *dead* saying what I'm about to say."

Most of the team chuckled or smiled.

"I think that today we witnessed a little bit of divine intervention."

✳ ✳ ✳

## Chapter 45: Success

For the next few months, the P-Seventeen program began a new routine. Every Monday, Harold To-kamra, chief editor of Po Publications, arrived at eleven thirty, at which time the security lamp was switched off.  He shared the publicity ads that had recently appeared in newspapers and magazines, and on radio and television.  Most team members had already seen or heard each one, but they knew he took great comfort in making his report.

He also shared the latest sales figures.  At first he could only claim, with a cringe, that a few hundred copies had sold.  In March, when the print and radio ads began to appear, the numbers quickly climbed into the thousands. April brought General Bo-seklin's first televised interview, and the sales shot into the tens of thousands.

Harold was honored to accept their invitation, every Monday, to stay for lunch and talk to the military and academic people who were attempting to keep his grandchildren from starving in the not-too-distant future.  Although he had no hopes of getting the security clearances needed to actually be on the team, for the first time in his life he was filled with a sense of purpose, a warm feeling that no job or business deal, however profitable, had ever given him.

✳

One or two days a week, Heather went back to revealing and analyzing minor events later that century or early the following century.  The entire team, both professors and officers, listened respectfully and asked appropriate questions, but just couldn't find much excitement in the topics, considering the much-larger issue that was never far from their thoughts.

The rest of the sessions were devoted to the scientific-journal and popular-magazine articles the team continued to endorse.  With the publication of previous articles, and the book itself, the number of manuscripts was increasing rapidly.  Some were finding publication on their own, and others were poorly-written, but a few good ones still needed the team's help to get into print.

＊

Generals Bo-seklin and Ko-fenral arrived at Po Publication's small video studio, in full dress uniforms, a little unsure of themselves. For the first time, the chief editor wanted them to do a televised endorsement together, without a host putting questions to them. It was an experiment, he admitted, but he had high hopes that it would speak well to the common people.

"Good morning, Sam."

"How are you, Malcolm?"

"Nervous, but I guess the television cameras might have something to do with that."

General Bo-seklin smiled. "How did we get into this awkward situation?"

"As I remember, it started almost eight years ago when I handed you the task of looking as far into the future as available methods would allow."

"You, as my superior, let me run with it, as neither of us had much hope for the project."

"That changed quickly, when our research about the *future* started having a better track record than some newspapers reporting on the *past!*"

"That was an eye-opener. So when we discovered, three years ago, that we were staring at a future no one wanted . . ."

"And a team of respected professors was checking us at every step . . ."

"And then we discovered that an international group of scientists had arrived at a similar conclusion without *any* knowledge of our work . . ."

＊

The two generals might have been a little embarrassed, but the rest of the team glowed with pride as the video was played on a small television, placed in front of the blackboard, on a Friday morning in early May.

Heather, in the back row with Susan, knew her name could never be mentioned in any of the endorsements. She was quite happy only stepping into the spotlight at the skating rink and the teen dance club, and here in this top-secret facility — all places she was known and respected.

But as the video ended and she returned to the front to lead her team, she had the nagging feeling that she would not always be able to avoid that larger spotlight, the one where people were watching who didn't know her, nor respect her.

＊

In late May, the team returned from vacation and voted to endorse two scholarly articles and one popular magazine piece, but rejected another in which the author had slipped in his own political agenda.

"The security lamp is off," Heather began after a short break when the blind transport arrived, "and our favorite chief editor appears, by the look on his face, to have just won the jackpot. Harold, you have the floor."

"Okay, I'll admit that I've gotten some very nice bonuses recently . . ."

The entire team chuckled.

"But I'm *most* happy to announce that the tenth printing of our beloved book has just been shipped, and it includes the *millionth* copy!"

The room broke into cheers and clapping, so Harold To-kamra opened a large envelope and pulled out one of the books.  Eventually the joyful noise tapered off and allowed him to speak.

"There's no way to know exactly *which* book is the millionth, of course, but I wrote the number *one million* inside six copies — four for the authors, one for you, and one for me.  Perhaps you could get the authors to sign yours — *and* mine — next time they visit."

Nods assured him they would do that.

"I have no doubt we will sell out the tenth printing this summer, and there will be an eleventh printing . . ."

Cheers again greeted his announcement.

"There's more!"

They chuckled or grinned with expectant faces.

"We have arranged translations into five other languages, three of which the authors can check for accuracy themselves."

More clapping greeted his announcement.

"Also, we are starting to receive derivative manuscripts.  Some are just copy-cats, and some are poorly-written, but I've picked the best five, and would appreciate opinions, even if the team doesn't want to actually endorse them."

Several of the professors waved their hands, eager to read them, and Colonel Ma-soran jotted down those names.

Harold took that moment to bask in the privilege of standing before such an elite group.  "In publicity, it's always difficult to know which of your efforts are paying off.  I want to give you my analysis that *all* of our methods are working and should be continued, but the most valuable are the no-host video ads by the two generals, which were clearly responsible for pushing book sales into the hundreds of thousands."

The cheering and clapping caused Sam and Malcolm to squirm, and Heather used that moment to stand and present the chief editor with another cashier's check.

It was Harold's turn to be embarrassed, and he shuffled his feet like a bashful schoolboy as Heather stood near, clapping and grinning at him.

Eventually the applause died down, Harold took his seat, and Maria looked out to see if they were *ever* going to get hungry.

* * *

## Chapter 46: Observations and Questions

Heather's outing facilitators — usually Lisa, Ginny, or Rachael — had always enjoyed taking her places, even if they could do nothing but sit and watch.

Now they all started to hate the task, and did everything possible to get out of it.  The colonel often passed it to the lieutenant, and the lieutenant to the sergeant.  Unfortunately, Sergeant Ma-tirol hated it the most.

Heather had taken to spending several hours in a bookstore, two or three times a week.  First, she would locate the shelf or display of the book her team was endorsing.  Depending on the bookstore, it consisted of ten, twenty, sometimes as much as a hundred copies ready for people to grab.  Then she would move three or four feet away, plant herself on the floor, and pretend to very slowly look at other books.

And while thus pretending, she listened.

✳

"Here it is, Honey!  We have *got* to find out what's ahead for our grandkids.  That general on T.V. has grandkids, too."

"Oh, poppycock!  If you think bad things are coming, you'll just make them more likely."

"Well, you don't have to read it."

"But I suppose I have to pay for it . . ."

"Yes, Honey, you do."

✳

"Mom, look!  It's that book about the future that *everyone's* reading!"

"Do you just read things because everyone else does?"

"I brought my own money!"

"Which you have to save for your brother's birthday present."

"Oh . . . okay . . ."

"I'll be next door in the beauty parlor for an hour."

"I'll look at magazines, I guess."

Five minutes later, Heather noticed the boy creep back to the book display, grab a copy, and slither toward the cashier while keeping an eagle-eye on the front door of the bookstore.

*

"Here they are, the abominations," a man in a black suit declared.

"Only God can know the future!" his female companion in a long dress asserted.

"They have eighteen, and we only have enough from the special collection last Sunday for ten."

"That will still make a nice bonfire," she said to encourage him.

The man grabbed ten, the woman slipped religious pamphlets into the other eight, and they made their way proudly to the cashier.

While no one was around, Heather scooted over and took one of the pamphlets. She had a hunch Harold might be interested.

*

Four older teens gathered around the display. They wore leather, torn denim, and patches with skulls and daggers. The odors of sweat and motor oil mingled, causing Heather to shrivel her nose.

"Here's what we've been looking for — proof that grown-ups are gonna wreck the planet and leave us with *shit*."

"This could be the seed of the next revolution!" the only girl in the group declared.

"We've *got* to have one of these at the hideout, even though it'll set us back a box of ammo."

"Let's do it. We need more than ammo. We need *intel*."

They all searched pockets, then huddled on the floor and made a pile of crumpled and wadded money. The girl smoothed the bills and declared it enough, as long as they split something cheap for lunch.

*

Sergeant Ma-tirol was *so* glad Heather wanted to go skating. In the car, Heather sensed Rachael's joy. "I hate it too."

"What?"

"Sitting in the bookstores. It's an emotional roller coaster. One minute I'm happy that someone is going to learn about what's coming, and I know there's a thousand more like them all over the world buying the book and reading it with open minds and open hearts. A minute later, I have to listen to someone who hates it, hates us, hates me. And there's a thousand more like *them*, too."

"So why do you do it?"

Heather had to think for a long moment. "I'm pretty sure there will come a day when I'll have to somehow make them happy. All of them."

"How in the world could you possibly do *that?*"

"I don't know. Probably just . . . dance."

*

Priscilla and Brian shared a tender reunion, skated hand-in-hand to a slow, romantic song, then found a free bench in the game room.

"School year's almost over," she commented.

"Yeah. I used to hate school. Now . . . it's not such a big deal. And I'll be eighteen next year." He stopped, suddenly at a loss for words.

She looked at him with loving eyes.

"Would you ever . . ." he tried to continue, but didn't get far.

She took his hand.

". . . you know, want to spend your life . . ."

"Yes?" she coaxed.

". . . with a guy like me?"

She suddenly laughed deeply.

"What's so funny?"

"I'm sorry, I'm not laughing at you. It's just . . . I can't imagine spending my life with any *other* boy! And it's been that way ever since I met you when I was ten."

He breathed a sigh of relief.

"So . . . are you asking?" she prodded.

He looked at her. "Yeah, I guess I am . . . if you don't mind my little . . . criminal record . . ."

She snickered. "That's nothing. How many people in the world actually hate you?"

"Um . . . actually, personally hate me, not just doing their jobs . . . two — the prosecutor and the judge."

"Is *that* all? I've actually sat and listened to *fourteen* people who hate me and would kill me if they could, so that means there are . . . maybe . . . fourteen thousand of them somewhere."

"Wow . . . because of the work you do that you can't tell me about."

She nodded, smiled, and began kissing him, causing some young teens nearby to snicker and giggle.

"So . . ." she began after they finally parted, ". . . you and me get married, you'll have a job, I'll keep house, maybe work a little, maybe have a baby or two . . ."

He nodded. "What do you think? I already have a job lined up for this summer, I think, and it might be full-time after I graduate."

She snuggled close to him, enjoyed his warmth and sexy male scent, and let herself dream of having a normal life, with a little house and some beautiful children.

He didn't notice the tears that slowly trickled down her cheeks.

✳

On Monday, the fifteenth of June, 3670, Harold To-kamra arrived at eleven thirty to give his weekly report. Confirmed sales were rapidly climbing toward a million, two of the foreign-language translations were almost done, and the book was now required reading for about half the majors at several universities. One of the derivative works was in print, with two more close behind.  More of the scientists on the team were now doing television ads, and the public reaction was good, but those by the two generals were still their greatest assets.

When Harold took his seat, Heather stood, and since noon was at hand, everyone thought she was about to adjourn the meeting.  Then they noticed that she held a pamphlet in one hand and an envelope in the other, and was looking at the chief editor.

"Harold, how would you like to send someone with a camera to a book burning?"

His eyes lit up.  "That's worth a hundred thousand copies, right there!  Those things always backfire on the religious people because it's a sign to everyone *else* that the book contains lots of important stuff."

"My condition is that you do nothing to disrupt the event," she said sternly.

"No problem.  We'll just fit right in, only take pictures with permission — which they'll gladly give because they *crave* publicity — and they won't know what hit them until they see it on T.V.  But they will, at that point, be royally pissed off . . ."

"No way to avoid that," Heather acknowledged.  "You might want some extra security at Po Publications . . ."

"Police station's just down the street."

"Good.  Any other concerns from the team before I give Harold the info?"

After a long moment for everyone to ponder the question, General Ko-fenral's hand came up.  "Keep to the issue.  Don't identify the church or its people in your ads."

Harold and Heather both nodded.

"Finally," Heather began even as she glimpsed Maria in the dining room doorway with hands on her hips, "I have another publicity check for Po Publications . . ."

"I don't need it yet," Harold To-kamra admitted, although he was a little surprised to hear himself saying those words.

"I know," Heather said, "but this one's for something special.  Young people, my age and even younger, are taking an interest in the book.  I want this check to be dedicated to bringing it to their attention, and even giving them free copies when they can't afford it."

"Fascinating angle!  I'll hire students on summer break to hang out at the teen spots with brochures and coupons."

Heather smiled.  "Thank you.  I figured you'd know what to do."  She looked around, and could almost hear tummies growling as everyone breathed in the aromas from the kitchen.  "Sam?"

"Generals and colonels, the usual time and place . . ."

✳   ✳   ✳

## Chapter 47: Difference of Opinion

"What the HELL is going on in that little fringy program of yours?" the president roared.

The five-star general, among several others at the long, polished mahogany-wood conference table, looked flustered.  "I . . . um . . . was unaware of it until recently, Sir."

"Unaware of it!  They've got the whole country stirred up — people writing letters, signing petitions, preachers burning books.  The military is NOT supposed to be sponsoring controversial social movements!"

"I just got a preliminary report on the matter this morning, Sir, and it appears that the program is doing exactly what Congress mandated fifteen years ago.  If you remember, Sir, it became known that the Beklans were far ahead of us at remote viewing, pre-cognition, and other psychic abilities that gave them . . ."

"I *know* what Congress mandated, as I was a senator at the time, remember?  But *no one* in Congress actually thought it would *work*.  We mandated the military look at that . . . psychy stuff . . . to appease the Far Right who jump up and down every time they discover the Beklans can tie their *shoes* better than we can.  The mandate wasn't intended to actually be *followed*."

"Well, Sir, I don't know what to say, other than it *was* followed, by military chiefs at that time and ever since, but for several years it had no results.  Then, in 3662, they began to report some success, but needed a few years to develop a track record.  The budget for the program was so small — it shares staff and an old building with an essential safe-house program — that no one had any reason to complain . . ."

"Well, I'm complaining now!  I'm getting flack from every direction, people are panicking, and I want it stopped, shut down, cancelled, and its records sealed!  And I want the publication of that damn book stopped!  By God, my wife has a copy, and my *grandson* wants one!"

The five-star general sighed. "Yes, Sir."

An hour later, on that pleasant Monday in early July, the five-star general sat at his desk with a troubled expression as his aides — all lesser generals — gathered.

"Report, Percy."

"The program has never actually *published* anything, Sir, they're just endorsing things written by respected scientists.  None of it's political, and none of it reveals any of the top-secret aspects of the program.  The operative is never mentioned, nor any of his or her predictions.  The publisher is highly respected, and is apparently spending huge amounts of money on publicity, but that money is not coming from any military budget."

"How do you stop *that?*"

A three-star general raised his hand.  "National security.  Most businessmen will back down at the mention of it."

"Okay, write up something for me to sign.  What about the program itself, Harvey?"

"I immediately spotted it's weakness, Sir.  Ko-fenral and Bo-seklin are both past retirement age.  The executive too, Colonel Ma-soran, a woman. You can force them into retirement with the stroke of a pen, then cancel the program because it's . . . um . . . lack of useful results . . . do not justify scarce leadership resources."

"I hate doing that, but I guess it's the best way."

"I'm troubled, Sir.  They're doing exactly what Congress mandated . . ."

"I know, Marcus.  This is political.  I have to take the president's orders, and this . . . what's name? . . . Bo-seklin . . . has to take mine.  Congress can deal with the president, if they want to.  Write up the retirement and program cancellation orders, both effective this Friday at midnight, and I'll sign them."

His aides filtered out the door to do their work, but the five-star general called to the last one.  "And Percy, get me a copy of that book!"

"Yes, Sir."

On Wednesday morning, Harold To-kamra was at his desk when the military courier arrived with the order to cease publication of one of his books on national security grounds.  He had to sign once that he had received it, again that he had read it, and a third time that he understood it.

After the courier was gone, the company's lawyer came in and they read it together, then discussed it for an hour.

Harold To-kamra went to lunch and thought about the order as he slowly worked his way through a sandwich and salad.  His mind revisited all the events of the situation, from first meeting the authors more than a year before, to watching another book burning two weeks ago.

Returning to his office, he took care of a couple of small but urgent tasks, then leaned back in his plush chair. His eyes were drawn to the pictures on the corner of his desk, one of them his grandchildren. A minute later, he punched the intercom button on his telephone.

"Sir?" a female voice responded.

"Helen, please bring in your tape recorder for dictation."

The secretary arrived a minute later.

"From me, blah, blah. To Five-star General Ko-doran, any other military officers involved, and the president himself."

Helen raised her eyebrows, but didn't interrupt.

The chief editor smiled at her as he continued the dictation. "You have got to be *kidding*, exclamation point. You obviously need a dictionary if you think that, quote, *national security*, unquote, is violated when respected scientists analyze data that has been in the public domain for years, if not decades. Paragraph.

"You are also out of bounds because the research and writing were not even done in this country, nor do the authors live in this country. Paragraph.

"I recognize that you have the authority to stop publication temporarily pending court review, period. Are you sure you want to use that authority, question mark. More than one million copies have already been sold, and the publicity created by a court review, which you would obviously lose, would probably cause another million copies to fly out the door. Paragraph.

"Under law, I have three days to implement your order, period. If I hear from you by five o'clock this Friday, you can avoid the embarrassing court review and resulting *increase*, underline previous word, in sales. Paragraph.

"Sincerely, blah blah. I'll sign it as soon as you type it. Delivery by express courier to the general, with signature required."

✳

The chief editor immersed himself in his work and had nearly forgotten about the issue until the telephone call came through at four thirty that Friday.

"Hello Mister To-kamra, this is Lieutenant Mo-pora," a female voice said. "I'm calling from General Ko-doran's office, and he wanted me to assure you that the national security order you received was sent in error, and he apologizes for any inconvenience."

Harold smiled, and felt sympathy for the poor lieutenant who had to make the call.

After hanging up, he buzzed his secretary again. "Our letter to that general worked, Helen."

"It sure sounded like they were over-stepping."

"Let's take some precautions anyway. Make copies of the book-printing masters, and all the publicity sheets and tapes, and send the whole works to our overseas office."

"I could do that this evening and take it right to the airport if you authorized overtime."

Harold thought for a moment about the elite team tirelessly endorsing the book, the cashier's checks for a hundred thousand, and his grandchildren. "Overtime authorized."

* * *

## Chapter 48: The Last Command

That same Friday evening, about when the secretary at Po Publications was addressing the airmail box to their overseas office, Colonel Sarah Ma-soran arrived at the top-secret facility where she had worked for most of her adult life.

"Leave the gate open, Corporal. A truck from the air base is right behind me, and they'll be loading all those old P-Seventeen file boxes. When they're done with those, I'll have a few more from upstairs."

"Should I help them, Ma'am?"

"No. With the gate open, you're strictly security."

"Yes, Ma'am."

Colonel Ma-soran entered the building and climbed the stairs for what would probably be, she realized, the last time.

She found General Bo-seklin in his office putting files into a cardboard box. "Good evening, Sam. How is Malcolm taking it?"

"Not well. When I left, he was cleaning out his desk and grumbling about this new president who's trying to please everyone. And, like us, he's worried about Heather. I'm glad she's on vacation right now."

At that moment, General Ba-kerga came up the stairs.

"George!" Sam greeted. "What punishment did *you* get for being in the only successful P-series program?"

He collapse onto the couch by the office door. "They recognized that I haven't been in a leadership position in the program for years, but I could tell they weren't happy until I offered to step down as base security chief."

"I'm sorry," Sarah said. "Everyone knows you were doing a great job."

"Any idea what you're gonna do?" Sam asked as he closed the cardboard file box and labeled it *P-17 COMMAND*.

"I already offered and they jumped on it. You are looking at the new head of the safe-house program."

Sam cringed slightly. "That's ten steps down."

George nodded as he gazed across the room. "It's okay. I'm not that far from retirement myself. The first thing I have to do is get rid of two buildings and keep only one. Guess which one I'm keeping."

Both Sam and Sarah smiled.

"Truck's all loaded, Ma'am," the corporal said from the doorway.

"Truck and garage all locked and secure?"

"Yes, Ma'am."

"Okay, you and the other men take a break, get whatever you'd like from the kitchen while I pack my files."

"Yes, Ma'am."

✳

An hour later, all the remaining P-Seventeen files and records had been packed into boxes and loaded onto the truck. The sound of its engine, as it faded away into the hills surrounding the top-secret facility, caused a feeling of deep sorrow in all three officers.

When the evening twilight had become silent and still again, the three went back upstairs and the corporal returned to the guard room to read a magazine.

The officers gathered in General Bo-seklin's office once more.

"Something feels . . . unfinished," Sam mused from behind his desk.

Sarah nodded. "We aren't sure we've . . . done what's necessary to avoid the future Heather warned us about."

"If Doctor Po-selem is right," George began, "and she'd lose her memories if we *had*, then we haven't."

Sam covered his face with his hands. "What can we do in . . ." He uncovered his face enough to see the clock. ". . . two hours, with no team, no records, and no Heather?"

After a long silence, George spoke in a soft, distant voice. "You could . . . release them."

Sam's eyes snapped open wide. "From secrecy?"

Sarah looked at George with equally-wide eyes.

George nodded. "What does the program cancellation order say?"

Sam searched his open briefcase. "Let me see . . . blah blah blah . . . here it is . . . *since the program has produced no useful results for the Department of Defense, it is hereby* . . . blah blah blah."

"*No useful results,*" George echoed. "What could be wrong with releasing civilian contractors . . . including one Priscilla Ka-mentha . . . from secrecy oaths for a program that supposedly accomplished nothing and no longer exists."

"You'd be on thin ice," Sarah mumbled.

"You *are* retiring," George pointed out. "I'd share the risk with you if I could, but only you, Sam, have the authority. And you only have it for two more hours."

General Bo-seklin leaned back and closed his eyes.  "Doctor Bo-kamla once suggested we just . . . hand the whole mess to the world, let them work it out.  I guess this is sort of like that."

"By canceling the program, that's what's happening," Sarah said.  "The only question is, will they — Heather and the professors — be afraid to talk and act."

Sam took a slow breath.  "I might be spending my retirement in federal prison, but if Heather taught us anything, it was how to find our courage.  Sarah, how long will it take you to type up a letter to each of the civilians?"

"With that new memory typewriter of mine, an hour at the most!"

"As long as you sign and date them today," George began, "I'll get them delivered.  Heather won't be back until tomorrow afternoon or evening."

"Okay, gather around my desk.  Let's word this thing as carefully as we can . . ."

*  *  *

## Chapter 49: Cancelled

When Heather and Ginny arrived at the facility on Saturday afternoon, laughing and chatting about the many exciting moments on their recent river-rafting trip, they found Susan talking with George in the general's office.

Heather wondered why George was sitting behind Sam's desk, but didn't say anything.

Hearing them arrive, Lisa emerged from the dining room with a cup of herb tea.

"Come on in, everyone," George said.

Heather sensed something was wrong, and was sure of it when Lisa pulled the door closed.

✳

"General Bo-seklin would do this himself if he could, but he cannot," George began.  For the next quarter hour, he went over the facts of the situation, and handed Heather her letter of dismissal as an independent contractor for the Department of Defense, which also released her from her P-Seventeen secrecy oath.

Both he and Susan watched closely to see how their young friend was taking it.  Her eyes were not dry, but she was holding herself together.

"You still retain your top-secret-umbra clearance," he explained, "and that might be useful.  It means, among other things, that you must keep the location of this facility to yourself."

Heather nodded.

"I am now in command of the entire safe-house program for this area, and in another week or two, this will be the only facility in that program.  I am able to keep this building because it was recently remodeled, and because it has three sleeping rooms."

A tear rolled down Heather's cheek.  "I can move in with Susan."

"I know," he assured.  "I also know that this has been your home for a very long time."

"More than half my life."

George nodded.  "So I have an offer that might interest you."

Heather frowned, unable to guess what he could be talking about.

"I need an on-call cook.  I could always get someone from the air base, and still can if there's ever a scheduling conflict, but I know from experience that safe-house people hate military cooking."

"What about Maria?"

"Maria wants full-time work, and can easily get it, especially with the glowing recommendation Sam wrote her.  Safe-house usage is, as you know, very unpredictable.  But you'd always get a day's pay each week to keep the kitchen stocked and the plants watered, and you have the clearance to come in any time you want, putter around the kitchen, dance in the studio, sleep in the bomb shelter, whatever."

Heather smiled slightly.  "That would . . . be nice.  I think I'll get a bicycle."

*

George spent another hour getting familiar with the safe-house files, then said good-night and went home.

Susan, Lisa, and Ginny stayed with their friend as she slowly packed her things.

"Grieving process," Susan said with a gleam in her eyes.

Heather laughed.  "I think I'm grown-up enough to skip the *denial* step!"

"Your *heart* may not be as grown-up as your *head*."

"Good point," the girl admitted as she continued to pack books into a box. "What does all this mean for you, Lisa?"

"I'll be security *and* executive for the safe house, so we'll see each other often."

"It'll be strange not having a body guard."

"You still have a thirty-eight and a concealed carry permit."

Heather smiled weakly.  "Yeah, I guess I'll be safer than your average teenage girl on a bicycle."

"I pity the poor guy who tries to mess with *you!*" Ginny declared.

Heather chuckled as she started pulling clothes out of her wardrobe, and trying to get her head around the new circumstances of her life.

*

By the time the sun neared the horizon on that warm summer evening, Heather had removed all the personal belongings from her room, including her precious old vinyl records and master reel-to-reel tapes.  She left some tapes in the dance studio that were just copies, as she always did, for safe-house people.

With her friends tagging along, she checked her bathroom, the laundry room, her mail drawer, and the bomb shelter for anything of hers, then wandered into the kitchen.

"Help me out, guys.  It needs sandwich makings all the time . . ."

"Milk, juice, coffee, and tea," Susan said.

"Bacon and eggs," Ginny added.

"Stuff to make hearty meals quickly, like noodles and sauce," Lisa suggested.

Heather searched pantry cabinets and refrigerators as they spoke, and found most things well-stocked.  The only missing items were already on a shopping list Maria had started.

"My sadness over what just ended will pass, right, Susan?"

"You know the answer as well as I do."

"Yeah, I know.  I just feel about seven years old again, normal seven, and want my mommy to tell me everything's gonna be okay."

Ginny wrapped her arms around the forlorn fifteen-year-old.  "Welcome to life, kid."

"I hope I get to see *you* often, too."

"Since I already have safe-house experience, I'm sure Lisa will be asking for me, especially when women and children are here."

Lisa nodded.

✳

Heather's boxes filled a blind transport.  Last of all, she went with the corporal to the inspection room for her gun.

As they returned to the parking garage and all four lingered near the transport, Heather took on a serious expression, reminding her friends of the many times she had stood before the team and led the session.

"The P-Seventeen program is no more.  The name *Heather* has no further purpose.  I am now *Priscilla Ka-mentha* at all times and places.  I have top-secret-umbra clearance, I have passed a Doctoral Entrance Exam, I am legally an adult, and I carry a concealed weapon.  And besides all that, I'm now a safe-house cook!"

They laughed, climbed into Susan's car and the blind transport, and waved to the corporal who stood at attention beside the open exit gate.

✳ ✳ ✳

### Chapter 50: "It begins."

On Sunday morning, while Priscilla, still in pajamas, yawned and unpacked a few boxes in the spare bedroom at Susan's house, Po Publications was burned to the ground.

Sunday afternoon, as Susan and Priscilla worked their way up and down the grocery store aisles, twenty-seven bookstores across the country were broken into. Although Priscilla didn't know why — and Susan wouldn't say — their grocery cart contained a large number of sweet rolls, sliced cheeses and meats, individual cans of juice, and paper plates and cups. None of the bookstores had their cash registers broken open, and only one thing was missing or set afire, the same thing in each bookstore.

In the evening, while Priscilla alternated between dancing on the hardwood floor in Susan's living room and unpacking more boxes, Susan made or received more than a dozen telephone calls, all of them in her bedroom with the door closed.

Priscilla blinked like an owl when she awoke on Monday morning to the sounds of Susan working in the kitchen. She glanced at the clock and frowned. Susan had clearly said she only had clients in the afternoon. *Why* was she loudly making breakfast at seven in the morning?

The fifteen-year-old tried to ignore the noise, but when she started hearing furniture being rearranged at about seven thirty, she could stand it no longer. She hopped out of bed, yawned, and opened her door.

"You'd better get dressed!" Susan said firmly as she carried platters back and forth from the kitchen to the dining room.

"Why?"

"Because it's Monday morning!"

Priscilla shrugged and staggered into the bathroom. She had been *thinking* of sleeping until nine, warming up slowly, then taking the bus that afternoon to the bank and a bicycle shop.  She was, after all, still grieving the loss of the P-Seventeen team and her entire life's purpose.  Now ... she wasn't sure *what* her day would look like.

When she emerged from the bathroom, she immediately spotted Doctor Bo-leden the philosopher, Colonel Bo-torin the political scientist, and Lisa, all lounging in the living room.  Priscilla, only half-dressed, slipped into her bedroom before they spotted her.

With her heart pounding from a mixture of happiness and confusion, she quickly dressed and brushed her hair.

When she finally stepped into the living room to see what was going on, more than a dozen team members were circling the dining table, loading sweet rolls and other goodies onto paper plates, doctoring cups of coffee, or opening cans of juice.

"Good morning, Heather!" several said.

"Priscilla," she said softly, but they didn't seem to notice.

More team members came through the front door, including Doctor Tu-feltin the blind historian, led by a man she didn't immediately recognize.  Then she laughed aloud at herself, realizing it was General Bo-seklin — *retired* General Bo-seklin — out of uniform.

"Good morning, Sam and Richard!" she called.

"Good morning, Heather!"

"Priscilla," she mumbled.

✳

By eight thirty, the entire team had crowded into Susan's little house, with only the enlisted military people missing.  Some team members had brought folding chairs, and the eldest were given priority on the two couches.  A few even made themselves comfortable on the floor.

"Well, girl," retired Colonel Ma-soran began, juggling a plate and cup of coffee, "are you going to get some breakfast, or just stand there with your face hanging out?"

Priscilla tried to master the grin she had been wearing for the last few minutes, without much success, as she got a plate.

While she was at the serving table, someone put a comfortable chair in front of the unlit fireplace in the living room, but didn't sit in it.

When the youngest person in the room turned to see where there might be a space for her, everyone set down their plates and cups and started clapping.

Priscilla blushed.

Retired Three-star General Ko-fenral pointed to the free chair.

She was embarrassed to take the chair of honor, especially with some people on the floor, but he *was*, after all, a three-star general.

"I ... don't know what to say ..."

"Don't say anything," General Ba-kerga, her new boss, ordered.  "It's not nine o'clock yet.  Just eat your breakfast."

She smiled.  "Okay."

✳

As the traditional starting time of the old P-Seventeen team approached, everyone took a break from eating and chatting to get rid of plates, refill cups, or accept offers of pillows from Susan.

Eventually they all got settled and the room fell silent.  One by one they looked at the girl.

"I . . . um . . . thought the program was . . . cancelled . . ."

"You have *no* idea what you created, do you, Heather?" Sam asked.

"Priscilla.  My name is Priscilla Ka-mentha."

"Okay, Priscilla," he responded with a smile.  "Over a period of almost eight years, you created a team that is dedicated to walking with you down the road you are destined to walk.  You can't get rid of us, any more than you can get rid of — what you know is coming."

Suddenly he frowned.  "You *do* remember what is coming, don't you?"

She sighed.  "You mean the end of human civilization because of anthropogenic climate change, and all that?  Yes, I remember, although I often — three, four, five times a day — wish I could forget."

Sympathetic chuckles coursed through the room.

"Maybe you will forget someday," Doctor Po-selem the wild-haired physicist said, "and we have reason to believe that will be a day of celebration, as you know.  But today, we beg you to accept our apologies for the . . . um . . . unwise actions of persons with power who are hiding in their ivory towers.  And we beg you to lead us, as you have done for eight years, although we will share with you the actual work whenever we can."

In the silence that followed, Priscilla breathed, at first unsure she could do it anymore.  Then she felt her mind kick in, and her emotions take back seat, a transition she had gone through countless times before.

"Okay . . . we don't have a tape recorder, so we need someone to take notes."

Retired Colonel Ma-soran raised her hand, note pad and pencil already in her lap.

"Thanks, Sarah.  Let's start by sharing recent events that some team members may not know."

"We can skip Po Publications events because Harold will be here at eleven hundred thirty," Sam said.  "I propose that we continue to NOT share with him the exact nature of our . . . um . . . research methods."

"That would be best," Doctor Po-morna the biologist asserted.

Heads nodded all around the room, Priscilla added hers, and Sarah recorded the decision.

Retired General Ko-fenral took the next hour to go over everything that was known about the process that led to the cancellation of the P-Seventeen program, and the forced retirement of its commanding and executive officers.

Doctor Ko-silma the chemist reported recent news about scholarly articles the team had endorsed, and shared her belief that future endorsements would be almost as effective if the publishers received a large number of letters from individual scientists and retired military officers.

Finally, with a few minutes remaining before Harold To-kamra was expected, Priscilla talked about her new job as the on-call cook for the safe-house program at the top-secret facility they once shared.

✻

The entire team sat wide-eyed and open-mouthed as the chief editor described the national security order to stop publication, his response, the back-pedal, and the fire that had destroyed their building.

He went on to tell about the bookstore break-ins and fires that were sweeping the country.  Some of the perpetrators left religious pamphlets, which were allowing police to make some arrests.

When Harold concluded his presentation, Priscilla took a deep breath.  "It begins."

✻  ✻  ✻

## Chapter 51: New Realities

At noon, a stack of pizzas arrived.  While eating, the team decided to meet at the same time and place each week, and the professors planned a meeting of their own at the University later in the week to work on article endorsements.  The three active military officers promised to come on Mondays whenever they could, but would not always be able to slip away from other duties.  General Ba-kerga asserted that he would get a cook from the air base whenever he had safe-house people on Mondays.

*

"This meeting of the National School Board is in session," the chairman said.

The twenty men and two women seated around the table shuffled papers in and out of their briefcases, or sipped on coffee.

"The biggest issue today is this . . . *book* about the future that everyone's up in arms about.  We're getting buried in letters from parents and special interest groups.  The religious say it's trying to do what only God should do.  The atheists say it undermines the foundational beliefs of our modern democracy.  *Everyone* is saying it shouldn't be in the public schools.  You all have the wording of the proposed decision."

"I wasn't aware this book was *in* our classrooms," a gray-haired man said.

"Well, it's not," the chairman admitted, "but they want us to ban it anyway."

"How can we ban something we aren't using?"

"Most of the letters say they want it removed from school libraries, and the majority want students suspended for even *talking* about it."

"Did I accidentally come to the wrong building?" another man questioned. "Is this the *Beklan Empire* School Board?"

The chairman sighed.  "As an elected school board, we have to do what the people want."

"How is that different from supporting a specific religious point of view, which we are forbidden by law to do?" a woman asked.

The chairman had to think. "Neither the book, nor our draft decision, mentions any religion, religious person, or deity."

"I am familiar with our constitution, as I'm sure you all are," the gray-haired man stated, "which is certainly where one would find the *foundational beliefs of our modern democracy*. This book does not conflict with anything in our constitution. The belief this book challenges is that tomorrow holds no major problems that need to be addressed today. That belief is an article of faith, which makes it a religious belief."

"Be that as it may," the chairman began with an irritated expression, "the wording of the draft decision does not technically support any religious point of view. All in favor?"

He counted hands.

"All opposed?"

Three hands came up.

"The decision is now National School Board policy."

*

Priscilla selected a sturdy five-speed touring bicycle with a luggage rack over the rear tire, saddle bags on both sides, and a basket in front. After strapping a milk crate onto the luggage rack, she was ready to go shopping for the few items the safe-house kitchen needed.

Less than an hour after leaving the grocery store, she coasted down the last hill into the little hollow where the top-secret facility nestled, once the home of her beloved P-Seventeen team. Her heart beat faster, even though she was not at all tired.

After parking her bike in front of the entrance gate, she stepped to the intercom by the rarely-used outside door and pressed the call button.

"Um . . . hello?" came a timid male voice she didn't recognize.

"Priscilla Ka-mentha, the cook," she said.

"Um . . . okay . . . I just started here about an hour ago, and no one's trained me yet."

"And no one else is there?"

"No. General Ba-kerga grabbed the other security guard and ran off to deal with some emergency at another safe house."

Priscilla blinked a few times. "I'll talk you through the entrance procedure, if you want."

"Well . . . okay . . . but how do I know I'm supposed to let you in?"

"There's a green binder beside the intercom. The third tab is *Civilians*, I should be listed, and I have I.D."

"Um . . . here it is . . . yep, you're listed, all days, all hours, all areas. Okay, what do I do first?"

"Come down to the inside of the entrance gate."

*

He looked barely eighteen, had no stripes on his shoulders, and still possessed some of the clumsiness of adolescence.

"You *should* be wearing a side arm," Priscilla said through the bars, holding out her I.D. for him to see.

"They haven't given me one yet."

"Okay, the first step is to look around, see if anyone or anything looks suspicious."

"Girl . . . bicycle . . . green hills."

"If you're comfortable with the scene, there's a key-switch on the wall to your left. Big silver key, turn it clockwise to open the gate."

He did and the gate began to slide open. Priscilla walked her bike through and parked it in the corner with the lawn mower and trash cans. He turned his key the other direction and the gate closed while she got her bag of groceries, change of clothes, and purse.

"Now direct me into the inspection room."

"Which one is that?"

She suppressed a smile. "The one on the left past the stairs."

"You know this place better than I do!" he admitted as he held the steel door for her.

"Yeah. I've been here a time or two."

*

She placed her thirty-eight on the table.

He stared with wide eyes. "What do I do with *that?*"

"Since I'm not a military security person, I can't take it upstairs. Behind you, steel cabinet, small lock-box."

He fumbled in the cabinet, almost dropping the lock-box. When he started to reach for the gun, Priscilla blocked his hand.

"Never touch someone else's weapon. Let them put it in the box."

"Okay," he said with a broken voice.

"Next, you have to determine, to your satisfaction, that none of the no-no's on the chart are in my purse or bags."

He gazed at the chart. "That's a lot of stuff!"

Priscilla smiled. "Normally, since I work here, you'd just trust me, but since this is your first time, you should go through the motions."

He was soon convinced that none of her bags contained nuclear, chemical, or biological weapons.

"Now you log me in, printing neatly."

He filled out a line in the log book slowly and carefully.

"All done! See how easy?"

The young man looked exhausted.

*

Two thousand miles away, at the National Stock Exchange, decisions were made behind closed doors by men in very expensive suits.

Not much later, shares of Po Publications stock crashed to a small fraction of their earlier value. A rumor began to circulate that the recent fire had been set by employees of the company, and as a result, the damage would not be covered by insurance.

The city fire chief smelled a rat, and didn't think it would be good for his career to sleep with that rat. He quickly called a press conference and informed the world that the rumor was completely false.

Also, Po Publication's overseas office was busy putting out press releases saying there would be no interruption in the delivery of books, *especially* one certain controversial book.

As a result, the value of Po Publications stock on the *World* Stock Exchange was rising.

Back at the National Stock Exchange, a computer programmer's conscience got the better of him, and during his lunch break, he stepped into a telephone booth.

Within an hour, federal investigators swarmed into the building, began questioning everyone, and whisked the computer programmer to a safe house.

Twenty floors up, in a plush corner office, the chairman of the board of the National Stock Exchange used the pistol in his desk drawer to take his own life.

Since no one, except a few preachers and their small congregations, had actually sold their Po Publications stock, once the truth was out for everyone to see, the value of Po Publications quickly rose to record highs on both the National and World Stock Exchanges.

✳

As General Ba-kerga drove through the entrance gate of the top-secret facility late that afternoon, he was impressed by how smoothly the untrained private handled the entry procedure. When he stepped into the building, he smelled a delicious aroma and immediately understood how the young man had received some training.

"Cookies?"

"Yes, Sir. Priscilla talked me through letting her in, stowing her gun, and logging her. I hope she told me right."

"You can trust her, Private. She knows the place . . . and could do *my* job without breaking a sweat."

The young man looked relieved.

As General Ba-kerga climbed the stairs, he began to hear music coming from the dance studio, a quick-tempo song he had heard many times when the girl wanted a good workout. He walked in that direction, and the private followed.

Priscilla waved when the pair appeared in the doorway, but continued dancing.

The private stared with admiring eyes.

"No drooling while on duty," General Ba-kerga said quietly but firmly.

The young man mastered himself and took on a neutral expression.

The song ended and Priscilla bowed to her small audience. "Good evening, George!"

"Let's go into my office, Priscilla, and talk about . . . menus."

"I just have to take the last batch of cookies out of the oven first."

"Do I get to try one of those, too?" the private asked with adolescent excitement.

"Of course!  Chocolate chip, this time."

✳

A few minutes later, Priscilla carried two small plates bearing cookies into General Ba-kerga's office.

"You're earning your paychecks already, I see.  Sorry they won't be as large as your previous checks.  By the way . . ." He looked through a pile of mail. ". . . here's your last P-Seventeen check."

"Thanks.  I'll spend it wisely."

George laughed.  "You'll probably invest it and turn it into ten times that much!"

Priscilla grinned.

"Thanks for training the private."

"It was that, or sit on the curb waiting for you."

"I had a mess to deal with, and Lisa and Ginny are still dealing with it.  I'll be *really* glad when these people are gone and I can shut down that house." While speaking, he handed her a catalog.

"Furniture?"

"I need your former room to handle a family, and I want it coordinated with the color scheme, so who better to ask than the original interior decorator?"

Priscilla smiled.  "That brings back old memories.  It's gonna be tight . . . I'd get this solid-oak bunk bed with rails all around the top, then swap desks with the guard room — my big roll-top would protect their radio and intercom from curious fingers.  The wardrobe and bookcase can stay.  A curtain rod and full-length drapes across the end of the room would give the parents a little privacy."

He took the catalog back.  "Sounds good.  By shutting down the other houses, I have a little money to spend.  We're gonna need a new washing machine soon, as I remember.  You know, Priscilla, that private admires you, and since you don't live in a top-secret facility anymore . . ."

"But my favorite boy still lives in an orphanage."

"Oh, yes.  Well, I'm sure you'll figure out something."

"I've been thinking about it.  Thanks for the fatherly support."

"Mmmm, these cookies are delicious!"

✳

Priscilla stayed at the facility for three nights.

In that time, the kitchen took on a somewhat different atmosphere.  While Maria liked everything put away when not in use, Priscilla preferred all her tools and spices spread out on the work table where she could see them.

The young private was obviously interested in her, chatting whenever she wasn't busy.  She was tempted, but eventually decided that the five years she had waited for Brian were enough of an investment to allow her to wait a little longer.  Anyway, by the second day, the private was gone and Lisa was back, training a corporal who was already married.

When no one else was upstairs, Priscilla alternated between puttering in the kitchen, watering plants, and ambling from room to room, touching the walls, furniture, drapes, and carpets — feeling how much a part of her this old building was, or perhaps how much a part of it she was.  She felt grateful to George for allowing her to work here, and told him so the next time he came in.

✳

On the third day, she found an old suitcase in the garage that someone had forgotten years before, put her name on it, and took it down to the bomb shelter to keep her spare clothes neat and clean.

On her last day at the facility, the new bunk bed arrived, with strong men to move everything.  George put her in charge of the work, and she installed the new privacy drapes herself while the men did the rest.

By late afternoon, the workmen were gone, and only the security corporal remained, reading training manuals in the guard room.

Priscilla did a load of laundry, packed her extra clothes into the suitcase, and wandered about the facility feeling that her mental and emotional transition — her grieving process — was complete.  Her old room was no longer hers, but the kitchen and bomb shelter were very much hers.

Except on Mondays.

She smiled, realizing that this facility was now her get-away, her retreat from the real-world problems her team was trying to solve.  But she finally felt ready to go back, talk to Susan, kiss Brian, and get ready for next Monday.

With just enough daylight remaining, Priscilla Ka-mentha, the new safe-house cook, went through the exit procedure at the top-secret facility, and pedaled home.

✳   ✳   ✳

## Chapter 52: Strange Advice

The following Monday, only General Ba-kerga was missing, and Lisa conveyed his apologies, and his intention to arrive by eleven thirty for the Po Publications report and lunch.

It touched Priscilla deeply that an on-duty general would make such an effort to get to the team she had created.  Then she looked around, saw two retired generals and all the other officers and professors, and had to hold back tears.

"All last week," she began, sitting in her new place of honor in front of Susan's unlit fireplace, "I was juggling emotions and trying to get through that *damn* grieving process as quickly as possible . . ."

She and her therapist exchanged knowing smiles.

". . . and George really helped by letting me work in the facility.  Then I spent most of the weekend pouring out my hopes and fears to Susan and Brian.  Don't worry, Brian still gets an edited version — I don't wanna scare him."

Most people chuckled with sympathy.

"Okay, let's jump into news, other than Po Pub stuff."

Doctor Ko-rensis the anthropologist shared the National School Board decision, which had silenced the anti-book crowd, but now they were flooded with complaints from the pro-book people.  The chairman had resigned, and teachers were on strike at twenty-three schools over the issue.

Priscilla couldn't help but laugh deeply, tried to apologize to Doctor Ko-rensis, but couldn't collect herself enough the get her words straight.  The tears of sadness that had been close earlier, came out as tears of humor.

Eventually she settled down. "Sorry. Next?"

After grinning at Priscilla, Colonel Bo-torin the political scientist shared that bookstores owned by churches were refusing to carry the book.  However, they were finding that too many of their customers wanted the scriptures AND the controversial book, and when they couldn't get one, they went elsewhere for both.

Sam smiled. "Money *does* have a way of talking, doesn't it?"

Several more book-burnings were reported, and numerous libraries were experiencing so much demand that they no longer allowed the book to circulate, but instead set aside reading areas with copies chained to the tables.  In other places, children's librarians were reporting that seven and eight-year-olds were looking at the pictures and graphs, and struggling to sound out the words, or begging older kids to read to them.

"Amazing," Sarah breathed. "I think . . . we started something."

✳

The news reports, and the summaries of scholarly articles the professors were endorsing, took the team to about ten fifteen.

Then silence lingered, with more than an hour before Harold To-kamra was expected.

Priscilla gathered her thoughts.  "Normally, we would now explore other little topics about the future that might teach us something.  I guess . . . there's no point in doing that anymore.  Thoughts?"

"I just want everyone to understand," retired General Ko-fenral began, "that the Department of Defense did not *choose* to abandon our project.  They were *ordered* to by our civilian leadership — the president, and whatever political forces he is under."

Most people nodded understanding.

"Thanks, Malcolm. Larry?"

Doctor Bo-leden cleared his throat.  "Although that's good to remember, I think we should avoid putting much energy into finger-pointing and blame.  But I *do* think we should explore small topics, whenever there's time, that seem related to anthropogenic climate change.  It's a complex system that interacts with many other systems."

Priscilla nodded.  "I agree with both Malcolm and you.  Chris?"

The physicist took a deep breath.  "I have . . . a small but related topic, at least to me, and I beg an hour of the team's time to . . . get some feedback . . . so I will know how to proceed with . . . an opportunity I have in the near future."

Priscilla looked around.  "Any objections to giving Chris this hour?"

No one spoke.

"You have the floor . . . I mean, the seat by the fireplace."

They switched while others chuckled.

✳

"For reasons I don't fully understand, during the eight years I've been on this team — learning all the things that Priscilla, and the rest of you, and the situations themselves taught us — I got religion."

Many chuckled and a few moaned.

"Bear with me, as I assure you that my religion is not the book-burning kind, and it doesn't have an address in the telephone book.  In fact, it's probably a religion of *one*, just little ol' me."

Some of the blank faces in the room changed to smiles.

"In this very-unique religion of mine, I have discovered that communicating with my deity — what most people would call *prayer* or whatever — is not something that is easy to do. It takes a great deal of thought and preparation, and opportunities to do it are . . . very rare . . . or perhaps once in a lifetime."

A few murmurs arose, but quickly faded.

"So . . . I'm not here to convert you, or tell you any more about my personal religion. I simply beg your wisdom helping me know what to say — or not say — if I can send a message to my deity, a message that might, somehow, help us with this situation in which our civilization is about to destroy itself . . ."

✳

Doctor Po-selem's hour began with an uncomfortable silence. Susan's hand, hesitantly rising, finally broke the ice.

"I don't know if this will be useful, but I thought I'd just summarize the psychologist's understanding of prayer."

"I'd appreciate that," the physicist said.

"Prayer is natural for children, as they live in a magical world in which their needs and wants are turned into real things by asking for them. Even if a child *sees* a parent buy or make the desired item, they still believe in the magical connection between expressing their desire and it coming true.

"The child's prayers are mostly selfish, of course. They pray for birthday presents, cake and ice cream, et cetera. With adolescence, the prayers become slightly less selfish, with the recipient becoming the person and a significant peer or small group of peers — couple or tribal.

"In adulthood, the groups become larger — clan, race, nation — but the prayer requests are still basically selfish — help me and mine, not them and theirs. People who pray for strangers or enemies are very rare, and I suppose always will be."

Doctor Po-selem looked very thoughtful as Susan fell silent.

Eventually another hand came up.

"I must admit, I have not practiced my parents' religion since leaving home," retired Colonel Ma-soran began, "but something they taught me comes to mind."

Chris nodded with interest.

"They taught me that all prayers are answered, but that's not the same as *fulfilled*. In other words, God, deity, the universe, whatever you want to call them, give you what *they* think you need, not what *you* want."

"I already believe that," the physicist shared. "But thank you."

The silence lingered again.

"I've heard," Doctor Po-morna the biologist began, "that you get something good from every prayer, but only once. If you pray with others watching, you get the social rewards of *being seen* praying — acceptance, honor, punch and cookies — but that's it.  You got something out of it, now what do you want?  If you actually want something deeper, something spiritual, then you must forgo the social rewards.  In other words, pray in private, without any other kind of recognition or gain."

Doctor Po-selem's mouth was open.  "Um ... I hadn't thought of that. Thank you."

Priscilla could see Susan nodding thoughtfully.

✳

General Ba-kerga arrived, sharing that he would soon be able to wind down the other two safe houses.  Others brought him up to date on news and summarized Doctor Po-selem's discussion topic.

Harold To-kamra reported on the wild ride that Po Publications' stock prices had recently taken, and that the eleventh printing had been ordered, which would bring them to one million one hundred thousand copies.  He also shared that the overseas office, in conjunction with the authors, was working on a small condensed paperback edition, and expected it to sell like hotcakes to younger readers.

Priscilla agreed, and handed him another cashier's check.  She made the decision, on the spot, that it should be especially for promoting that paperback edition.

✳  ✳  ✳

## Chapter 53: Butterflies

Doctor Po-selem tossed and turned in bed that night.  He woke up three or four times, turned on a small lamp, and scribbled something onto the note pad he always kept by the bed.

His wife snuggled close and put her arm around him.  "A new theory, Chris?"

"Hi, Honey.  Sort of.  More like ... a way of saying something that I haven't tried before.  And every time I get it written down, it looks wrong."

"Maybe morning light will bring clarity."

"I hope so."

⁕

The next day, Doctor Po-selem gave two physics lectures, but knew his mind wasn't on them.

His students could tell too, and one of them asked if something was bothering him.

He affirmed, and apologized, but didn't elaborate.

An hour later, he was glad to get home, and immediately sat down in front of the altar he had been assembling for the past six or seven years.  It now contained twenty-three little statues of gods from around the world, seventeen religious symbols, and various other objects and tools, from an incense burner to a holy-water sprinkler, all of which he had studied in depth, but few of which meant much to him personally.

He lit a candle on the altar, then grabbed a note pad and began scribbling down phrases as they came to him.  Frowns and grimaces revealed that none were quite right.

When a sheet became too full, he lit it from the candle and placed it in a small iron pot that already contained old ashes.

"Hi, Dad!" a teenage voice interrupted from behind.

"Hi, Son.  How was school?"

"Not bad.  I think I aced the chem test."

"Great!  Need a homework buddy?"

"Naa.  Going skate-boarding with Jeremy.  Besides, I can *tell* you're communing with the gods of time-travel theories, or whatever."

"Yeah, I guess I am.  They're . . . just not being very forthcoming today."

"Hang in there!"

"Thanks, Son.  Have fun with Jeremy!"

Once the house was again quiet, Doctor Po-selem scribbled one more phrase, burned the sheet, then sat silently with a dejected expression.

On Wednesday, after his first lecture but before the grad students arrived for seminar, Doctor Po-selem closed his office door, looked up a telephone number, and dialed.

"Hi, Shawn, it's Chris Po-selem."

"Good morning, Chris!"

"You know that sentence I get to put on the plaque on the space probe next month?"

"With the deadline coming up, I've hardly been able to *think* about anything else for the last two weeks!  You wouldn't *believe* how many people are offended by the rule that their sentences can't be offensive to others."

Chris chuckled.  "My question is sort of about that."

"Shoot.  Got the rules right in front of me."

"Is it okay if my sentence is encrypted, so it will just look like gibberish?"

Shawn was silent for a long moment.  "Wow.  You got me, there.  It hasn't come up.  Everyone else WANTS the world to know what they said."

"That's what I figured.  So . . . does that break any rules?"

"Well . . . first let me say that as soon as they're published, day after launch day, every nerd in the world would set his mind to breaking your encryption . . ."

"Of course.  I don't have my final wording yet, but I'm using some strict criteria, and it won't offend anyone."

"Okay, it looks like you are slithering through the very thin gray area between Rule Seven and Rule Eight.  But I warn you, if anyone decodes it, and is offended, I'll give them your lecture schedule."

Doctor Po-selem laughed deeply.  "Fair enough!"

"Deadline is Friday at five!"

"I know.  Thanks, Shawn."

"Bye!"

Early Thursday morning at three something, Chris suddenly sat bolt-upright in bed and groped for the lamp.

"Theory properly worded," his wife mumbled, still half asleep.

"I think so," he said as he began scratching with the pencil, only to discover he was using the wrong end.

A minute later, finally able to focus his eyes, he succeeded in getting the sentence down.  Actually, he admitted to himself, it was three sentences, but by using semicolons, one of the few punctuation marks allowed, he could make it into one.

He stared at it while his wife slept.  In one sentence of less than one hundred characters, it said everything that needed to be said.  It followed all the criteria he had set for himself from his personal and professional values, and from the advice of Priscilla's team.  And it wouldn't offend a fly, even the most sensitive fly.

Now he just had to encrypt it so well, somehow, that *no one* on the planet would ever know what it said.

With a sigh, he placed his note pad on the bed-side table and fell into a deep sleep.

*

"Foreign languages?" a female voice said after Doctor Po-selem dialed a campus number.

"Hi, this is Doctor Chris Po-selem over in Physics.  Do you have anyone who knows dead languages, like maybe one of the old native languages?"

"That would be me.  Doctor Jean Bo-hilson, at your service!"

"Jean, I have an urgent situation.  Could I bring a tray from the cafeteria, with whatever you'd like, to your office sometime today, in exchange for a little help?  I need to put a sentence into the most obscure language I can find.  It could even be pre-literate, as long as I can capture the spoken words in our alphabet."

"Let me think . . . steak sandwich medium rare, chef salad, chocolate malt, lemon cheesecake . . . uh oh, the only time I can do it is one o'clock.  Other than that, I'm in and out of classes all day."

"I'll take it!"

"See you then!"

As soon as he got off the telephone, he stepped into the outer office of the Physics Department, and to his delight, spotted a grad student.

"Bill!  Can you do my one-o'clock lecture?"

Bill's eyes lit up at the opportunity.

*

Of the four languages Doctor Bo-hilson offered, Chris selected the most obscure — a pre-literate tongue that was only known through one long story-telling session, made on a very early tape recorder, by the last surviving native speaker of the language.

Although Chris could see that the letters were correct as he listened to Jean speak the words, he had great trouble pronouncing the words himself because the language placed several sounds side-by-side that no modern language dared.

Doctor Bo-hilson smiled as she took another bite of her delicious lunch.

As he walked back to his office, Chris became aware of the great value of the folded piece of paper in his pocket.

*

"Math Department?" a young female voice declared.

"Hi, this is Doctor Chris Po-selem over in Physics. I need to encrypt a ninety-eight-character sentence. I need it today, early tomorrow at the latest."

"You need my Rent-A-Nerd Service! Twenty an hour, one hour minimum. There's a student rate, but you already said too much to get that."

Chris took a deep breath, then remembered that the deadline he was rushing toward was absolute. "Okay. When can you do it?"

"I'm about to go to a class, then I'm going dancing, so it'll have to be tomorrow at nine."

"Where?"

"Where else? Computer room."

Chris was not happy getting the final step done on the last possible day, but at least he would have a *few* hours left if something went wrong with the Rent-A-Nerd Service.

✳

"I'm not sure of the right term, but I want it as encrypted as possible without requiring the recipient to have any other information."

The female grad student looked at the three sentences, in an obscure dead language, separated by semicolons. "It almost looks encrypted now."

"I know, but I want you to pretend it's not."

"Hmm. Can I assume *any* standard keys, cipher pairs, or hash tables that the recipient would try?"

"No. You must assume we have not, and cannot, communicate with the recipient."

"That rules out all the strongest methods. We can't use an old-fashioned code. It's not long enough that we can trust the recipient to figure out a cipher by letter-frequency analysis. Sure, we can re-break. That's what children do to make secret codes — I started at five."

She demonstrated by re-writing the entire thing, putting the spaces between words at different places than originally. "I left the semicolons where they were. What do you think?"

He looked. "I like that. Is there anything else we can do?"

"We could bit-shift or byte-rotate, if it's going into a computer."

"No, it'll just be printed. Engraved, actually."

She raised her eyebrows. "We could do an old-fashioned alphabet rotate, another kids' trick. A becomes B, B becomes C, Z becomes A. But the question remains, how many times we rotate. Is there *any* number the recipient might guess?"

Doctor Po-selem's mouth suddenly opened. "Seventeen!" he blurted out almost before thinking.

"Okay. That still leaves the uncertainly of whether we shift forward or backward. Can we trust the recipient to try a *few* simple variations?"

Doctor Po-selem took a slow breath, and felt like he was stepping way out onto a limb. "Yes."

She quickly scribbled down a translation key, and about five minutes later, had all the letters shifted forward seventeen places in the alphabet.

"That's about all we can do without more shared assumptions with the recipient. You can re-break it until you think it looks just right. I prefer small bills, but will take a twenty if that's all you have."

Chris smiled and dug out his wallet.

Doctor Po-selem found a grad student for his afternoon lecture. He only had a few hours to make sure his message was just right. After getting a tray full of things from the cafeteria, he marked himself *Out All Day*, went into his office, and locked the door.

His hands trembled as he went through the entire process again, thinking over the needs of the situation, his own strange religious values, the suggestions he had received, and the steps he had gone through, with the help of others, to make the message accessible to his deity, hopefully, but hidden from human eyes, hopefully.

Four o'clock was upon him when he realized that if he stared at his note pad any longer, he would just want to burn it. Instead, he dialed a telephone number.

"Hi Shawn, it's Chris Po-selem. How's that for close?"

"Hey, you've got a whole hour left!"

Chris laughed, releasing some of the nervousness he felt. He dictated the ninety-eight letters, spaces, semicolons, and one period, while the other man typed them into his computer. Then he waited for the other to print it out and read it back, letter for letter.

It was perfect.

"Am I the last?"

"Nope. There's one more, and if he doesn't call by five, I'm putting in a little poem my daughter wrote about butterflies."

Doctor Chris Po-selem, physicist, smiled. Somehow it felt right that his little message would share the plaque on the space probe with a poem about butterflies.

## Chapter 54: Forgetting

Over the next few weeks, the team settled into its new routine at Susan's house. More details about anthropogenic climate change were explored, with the team pushing Priscilla to tell them all the ways in which the book they were promoting was too optimistic.

Po Publications rented temporary office space, and architects started sketching proposals for their new ultra-modern building.

With the other two safe houses now closed, the facility in the green hills west of the city became rather busy. Colonel Ka-markla didn't call Priscilla when they had only one or two guests. She, or the guard on duty, made frozen waffles, canned soups, and sandwiches. Most of the guests were quite happy, knowing they were as safe as the Department of Defense could make them.

But when a large family came in, usually fleeing a change of government in a country that still did such things by violence, the telephone at Susan's house started ringing. If Lisa didn't find Priscilla there, she next tried the skating rink, followed by the teen dance club.

It happened for the first time on Friday, just as Doctor Po-selem was getting his message ready for the space probe. During the afternoon skate session, the owner skated out to the middle, where Priscilla was practicing figures, and informed her she had an emergency telephone call.

Since both Lisa and George were still a bit new at doing the jobs Sarah and Sam once did, and Maria was no longer in the picture, they tended to forget little things like shopping lists.

So after explaining that the family was on a ten-hour non-stop flight, and would arrive in a secure transport at about eighteen hundred and be quite hungry, Lisa had to admit, with sheepish apologies, that recent safe-house guests had left the cupboards and refrigerators almost bare.

Priscilla, sensing that Lisa had a million other things to do, promised to take care of it, and ended the call.

"Family illness?" the rink owner inquired with sympathy.

Priscilla chuckled. "Work. Can I make a call to arrange transportation?"

He nodded.

She dialed, and an air-base operator answered.

"This is Priscilla Ka-mentha, clearance T.S.U., program L-Six.  In approximately one hour, I will check out at Food Depot with about four carts full, and I need a small truck and a driver cleared for the L-Six location.  It's time-critical, as we have guests en route by air."

The skating rink owner raised his eyebrows.

"Yes . . . Colonel Ka-markla . . . yes . . ."  Priscilla responded to questions, and soon ended the call.

"That's some *special* kind of work you do!" the owner said.

"That's my *easy* job. Thanks, Simon.  See you sometime next week!"

٭

Priscilla's cooking was not as fancy as Maria's, but she made sure everyone was happy.  They were at stressful moments in their lives, she knew, and needed comfort almost as much as safety.  Between her tasty home-cooking, the cozy atmosphere of the entire facility, and the complete security provided by the military, safe-house guests could, for a few days or a week, relax and ponder their futures.

She knew that many of them, when they left, would be hunted by foreign governments or powerful corporations, and would have to go into permanent hiding, or change their identities.  Some of them deserved it, but their children did not, and yet lived under the same danger, whether newborn, child, or teenager.

With few exceptions, Priscilla didn't know enough about the adults to judge them.  She focused on making them comfortable with nourishment, treats, a friendly ear whenever she could spare it, well-tended plants throughout the facility, and music to fit the mood.

Although she wasn't paid for it, Doctor Bo-kamla often came in to help bring hope to the hearts of those who dared not step outside the building.  She realized it was a fulfillment of her dream of counseling refugees.  It also allowed her to keep an eye on the one person in the world she had vowed to always protect and support.

Priscilla, of course, was especially happy any time Susan felt like doing a few dishes.

Although it had been rarely used during the P-Seventeen years, the television often now glowed from a shelf at the back of the dance studio, sometimes for the adults to keep up with the news, sometimes to entertain the children.

Priscilla had taken down the dance posters, and arranged the extra plush chairs — once for generals and scientists studying the future — around the outside edges of the room.  She convinced General Ba-kerga to buy more large pillows, and these she spread out on the floor for the kids.

The warm days and pleasant evenings of early August floated past as a family of four, political refugees from a small country, and a middle-aged couple, corporate whistle-blowers, shared the top-secret facility.

Priscilla was strolling the hardwood floors with watering can in hand when she overheard part of a news broadcast on the television.

". . . as we try to piece together what happened here, neighbors are telling us that the parents *set* the fire in the tree house when they discovered their children, and several neighbor children, were keeping and reading books up there . . ."

Priscilla frowned, and wanted to learn more, but *had* to get a batch of cookies out of the oven first. She was back a minute later.

". . . firemen are lowering the body of the girl who was still in the tree house when the fire was set. Medics are examining her, but it appears nothing can be done. Police are keeping reporters away from the parents, but neighbors are saying the girl was eight years old . . ."

For a split second, Priscilla felt all the sensations the girl must have experienced — fear of being trapped, panic as she tried to find a way out, the choking smoke, the burning heat and flames — and tears started flowing even as she stood there, just outside the old dance studio.

". . . a fireman is coming down the ladder now with a scorched book in an evidence bag . . . can we get a camera on that bag, Terry? Yes, ladies and gentlemen, as you can see on your T.V. screens, it appears to be a copy of the same book about the future that everyone seems to either love or hate . . ."

Priscilla's heart was in her throat, and it clearly intended to stay there. She struggled to breathe, but only managed a few gasps.

". . . out on the front lawn, something else is happening. Jason, can you get out there with a camera? It appears that a preacher is talking about what happened, and people are gathering around to listen. Our cameraman is arriving on the scene. Another preacher is arguing with him. Both are saying things at the top of their lungs. Your sound isn't working, Jason — we have visual but no audio. The preachers are now taking punches at each other, ladies and gentlemen. This is unbelievable, right here on this front lawn, so near to where a tragic death just occurred, these two men of God are having a scrappy fist fight . . ."

Finally her breath came a little easier as Priscilla continued to listen and silently cry.

". . . a policeman is breaking up the fight. Over in the driveway, I can see a couple of female detectives, with a tape recorder, listening to the children who got out of the tree house in time . . ."

Priscilla hoped they would find their courage and tell the whole story.

"Okay, ladies and gentlemen, here's a new development. The parents are being led to a police car, and I believe I can see . . . yes, I can see it clearly now . . . they are definitely in handcuffs . . ."

Priscilla's face remained streaked with tears as she breathed a deep sigh and returned to the kitchen to set out the freshly-baked cookies.

✳

The following Monday, Harold To-kamra arrived with everyone else for breakfast. Before finding a place to sit, he handed Priscilla a video tape.

"Good morning, everyone," she said as they got settled at nine o'clock. "It's the tenth of August, Sarah is taking notes, George is here, and Lisa must be at work."

George nodded. "We're going to take turns whenever possible."

"Good. Harold is here today, as his staff got copies of all the news coverage of the tree-house incident. I only saw bits and pieces on one channel, and I know some of you didn't see it at all, so we'll all learn something."

For the next hour, they watched the coverage of the event on location, and some commentary in the television studios later on. The entire group was very sullen when the video ended.

Retired General Ko-fenral cleared his throat. "There are casualties during any big change. We always wish there weren't, especially innocent children, but nations, and the world itself, cannot change without them."

The team absorbed his comment in silence.

Doctor Ko-silma raised her hand. "Harold, are we in time to add a dedication to that paperback edition?"

"Certainly."

"Great idea, Betty!" Priscilla declared. "She's the first anthropogenic climate change martyr, and deserves to have her name remembered."

"That could rile up her parents."

"Our book has the whole *world* riled up."

"They might take legal action!"

"What kind?"

"Do we care?"

"We might not, but Po Publications might . . ."

Everyone fell silent and looked at Harold.

He laughed. "There's no law against dedicating a book to someone. Besides, those who fear this book already burned down our building. If Po Publications was squeamish, you'd know it by now. Fact is, every publisher *dreams* of having a banned or hated book in their catalog. I'll dig up a nice picture of the girl, find out her birth date, and put together a very respectable epitaph on the back cover. What was her name?"

Sarah looked at her notes. "Tiffany Ko-moran."

✳

Priscilla made sure everyone had a chance to express their opinions about the dedication and epitaph. Most were in favor, as long as the parents weren't mentioned. A few continued to worry about the publisher.

Colonel Bo-torin the political scientist waited until everyone else had spoken, then raised his hand.

Priscilla sensed he had something important to say as she pointed to him.

"I think this is a piece of a larger process.  The general public has heard a lot about our book recently.  Po Publications advertises it, many scientists and a few other insightful persons promote it, most of the small religions condemn it, community leaders and educators are split down the middle.  The average man and woman can only hear so much about something before getting tired of it.  I think they're near that point now, and the tree-house incident just might push them over the top.  When the general public burns out, the news media will go with them.  Next week, they'll turn their attention to the space probe launch, and I don't think they'll want to turn it back to our little book any time soon."

At that moment, the doorbell rang.

"Lunch," Susan said as she stood up.

"Thank you, John," Priscilla said while Susan paid for the pizzas.  "We can talk more while we eat, but I know several people have to leave soon.  I propose we dedicate next Monday to exploring this idea, see if we can figure out how it will affect us, and how we might want to change our plans."

Everyone nodded as they turned their attention to the serving table.

Harold To-kamra sat with a frown on his face, lost in thought.

✳

The celebrations began nearly a week before the launch.

The world was sending its first space probe to all the outer planets, and then onward to the stars.  Many nations had contributed designs, technology, experts, or money.  Leaders, scientists, and celebrities had sent in greetings to whatever aliens inhabited the universe.  All over the world, the space probe was seen as a symbol of what the human race could accomplish — no challenge was too great, no distance too far.

It was an especially important moment for those who believed that no limitation should stand in the way of progress.  The planet was so vast, and its resources so great, that they could never be exhausted.  Human ingenuity was limitless, and nature was to be tamed and controlled.

Everywhere, people partied.  Telescopes and star charts were sold out, shelves were stripped bare of snack foods and drinks, and only the very rich could get a dinner reservation within sight of the launch pad.

Even in the Beklan Empire, spirits were high.  True, their own space probe was still months away from launch, but they had eyes and ears in place, and planned to learn from anything that went wrong with *this* launch.

As Colonel Bo-torin had predicted, all news coverage ceased about a certain book that did not give the same message about human potential as the space probe launch.

While the rest of the world celebrated, Harold To-kamra outlined, for a small group meeting in a little house, his modified publicity plan.  With sighs and mixed feelings, they saw his reasoning, and agreed.

When the advertising managers at large media outlets decided to cancel the ads for a certain Po Publications book that was just *not* fashionable at the moment, they were surprised to discover that the ads had already been withdrawn.

The world rejoiced on Launch Day.  The countdown, lift-off, multi-stage separation, and trajectory into space went so perfectly that the Beklan spies had little to report.  People danced and partied everywhere.

Many children forgot dreams of being firemen or nurses, and vowed to become astronauts.

Tiffany Ko-moran, and the book that had played a part in her death, were forgotten by nearly every upstanding citizen in the world.

What the world didn't notice was the publication, a week later, of a small, plain paperback book that included a coupon for another copy, free of charge.

That paperback book didn't mean anything to those wide-eyed children who dreamed of being astronauts.

But to youth old enough to know how the world *really* worked — about ten and up, but not yet busy with the concerns of adulthood — it meant a lot. They knew in their hearts that very few people could ever be astronauts, even in a perfect world.  They also knew that perfect worlds only happened in fairy tales.

If the original hardcover book had found its way into a few tree houses, the little paperback edition spread like a virus.

But since it was so small and plain, and hardly took up any space in a daypack or shoulder bag, the upstanding citizens of the world never noticed it.

*  *  *

**Part 5: Satamia**

**Chapter 55: A New Mission**

The crew members of the deep-space response ship Manessa Kwi were excited about their next mission because of who the mission commander would be, but didn't yet know anything about the mission.

They entered the Mission Assignment Room and shared greetings with some people they knew and some they didn't, then began climbing one of the spiral ramps.  Around them, reptiles and mammals trudged up or pranced down the ramps, birds ascended with powerful wing-beats or floated down effortlessly, a few large insects buzzed in flight or moved up and down their own threads, and glowing non-material beings of many colors appeared and disappeared at will.

Slender, freckled Rini, knowing the room even better than his captain, pointed when they came to the right path, a bridge that arched across an open space and ended at a platform high in the air.

A small furry bear sat at a control console, nimbly changing scenes, view angles, or magnification when teenaged Ashley pointed, feathered Kolarrr'ka lifted a wing, or T'sss'lisss flicked her forked tongue toward the display.

Scenes from a planet of humans came and went, often showing crowded, trash-littered city streets, or wide roads filled with cars and trucks belching smoke.  The five crew members from medieval Sonmatia Three frowned.

At other times, they glimpsed elegant gardens, noble statues, or beautiful art works, and smiled.

The three members of the Education Service were snuggled so close together, with the snake's tail completely around the bird and her head on the human's shoulder, that they almost appeared to be one creature.  Only the different colors and textures of skin, feathers, and scales revealed which parts of the ensemble belonged to which person.

The response-ship crew settled onto the soft floor behind the three.

Ashley glimpsed them and started speaking without taking her eyes from the display.

"The planet we're going to, after a little training, is approaching the most critical transition of its entire history. As you may know, all mortal planets go through three huge challenges — population, power, and pollution. Most sapient races — of those that survive — tackle these one at a time, at most two. We monkey mammals have the bad habit of — what's that saying?"

"Sweeping things under the nest, bok," Kolarrr'ka answered.

"Oh, yes, thanks. When a planet does that, they wind up with all three challenges in their faces at one time, and the interactions between population, power, and pollution make the entire mess eight times more difficult than it could have been."

"Jussst another monkey-mammal tessst," T'sss'lisss commented, lifting her head from Ashley's shoulder to look at the crew. "Every type of creature hasss them."

"True," Ashley continued, swiveling around to face her friends while stroking Kolarrr'ka's feathers, "although sometimes we seem to get more than our share."

The entire crew laughed or smiled while nodding.

"The dominant species on Ko-tera Three is human, so Shemultavia made me mission commander. My partners have already had their first commands, but this'll be my first, so I want all of you to give suggestions any time you think of them."

"Shemul . . . tavia?" muscular Boro questioned.

"Head of the Education Service," green-eyed Ilika, the captain, informed.

Boro nodded, saying the name to himself.

"The mission has several phases," Ashley continued, "and the first is to contact the three other sapient races on the planet, and check the status of the six near-sapient races. To do that, we'll have several contact specialists on the mission — I'm borrowing Ss'klexna here for the ursines, and there will also be an equine, a feline, a small cetacean, and a large testudine. My dear partners T'sss'lisss and Kolarrr'ka will check on the land reptiles and the birds, of course."

Shaggy-haired Kibi's eyes grew large. "I'll need a tank for the dolphin and the sea turtle!"

Ashley nodded. "In addition to ship preparations, I want each of the contact people to have a helper from the crew who can take over in a pinch. Ilika will be the exception, staying focused on the ship."

He nodded.

"The mission actually started many years ago when Shemultavia arranged for a Temporandek Teacher to emerge within the dominant monkey-mammal race. The Teacher has enhanced memory, high intuition, and is open to direct guidance. She has now done about all she can to prepare her people, and the next step will be up to them. They will choose to get control of their exploding population, their appetite for power, and their constant pollution of the air and water, or they will not. Our role should ideally be passive, but Shemultavia anticipates some possible surprises, and wants us to remain flexible.  We'll go over everything in detail tomorrow as soon as the other contact people are assigned, then zip down to Satamia Two for training . . ."

✳

Ashley's brief description of the mission had the entire crew excited, so after leaving the Mission Assignment Room, they got some fruity snacks and found a table overlooking Blue Hall.  Several tapped at knowledge pads as they ate.

"Could be lots of surface travel," Boro pondered aloud.  "A little extra fuel wouldn't hurt."

Ilika nodded.  "We might need the water gear.  Everyone up to date on fanator training?"

They all nodded.

"Too bad Kolarrr'ka isn't big enough to ride," Rini mused.

Mati, seated close beside Rini, looked at him askanse.  "Ashley would *never* forgive you.  Those three are about as close as you and me."

Rini smiled.

"Ko-tera Three has birds that *are* big enough," stout Sata, younger than the rest, mentioned while looking at a knowledge pad, "but they're not sapient."

"That would be a *wild* ride," Boro, beside her, said with a grin.

Sata nodded and chuckled.

Kibi's mission bracelet chimed, so she looked at its tiny display.  "That was fast!  There's a team of technicians at the dock waiting for me so they can install the tank."  She kissed Ilika and hopped up.  "I'll work on my galley list while supervising."

✳

The technicians turned out to be a pair of the goofiest quanasia Kibi had ever met.  When she arrive at the little waiting room just outside the boarding tunnel, the two lanky reptiles were telling each other a constant stream of jokes *while* tumbling and wrestling on the floor.  Large cases of materials sat on a pallet nearby.

Kibi stood grinning, and was sure they saw her, but they appeared to be in no hurry to cease their play.  She, however, had a galley to stock, including food for several species she had never served on her ship before, so she used her bracelet to take control of the pallet and guide it into the boarding tunnel.

The pair of quanasia noticed, and followed, but didn't quite cease their jokes and play.

✳

Kibi smiled when she realized that the dolphin and the sea turtle could eat the same foods, mostly fish, but that the horse was strictly vegetarian.  She tapped at her knowledge pad, and tried very hard not to look at the two technicians, so busy playing and chatting that she was sure it would take them *days* to get the tank installed — real Satamia days, about five times as long as her ship days.

But when she finally felt she had everything on her list for humans, bird, snake, cat, bear, horse, dolphin, and turtle, she looked up to discover that the tank was complete, and the pair of quanasia were wrestling playfully on the floor.

The tank, to Kibi's surprise, was not a simple enclosure for water, but a complex maze of both horizontal and vertical passageways, all transparent. They began at the hatch, ascended to the ceiling, crossed the passenger area overhead, came back to floor level at the rear of the ship, and included one entire toilet room.  In addition, a section on the floor allowed the water creatures to join those at the big oval table for meals or planning.

As Kibi gazed at the gleaming construction, she became aware that it was slowly filling with water.  "But . . . won't the water just run out at the lowest point, down by the hatch?"

One quanasia made some effort to get serious.  "We have to teach her how to use it now!"

"Can't we do that tomorrow?" the other pleaded.

"I'm in mission briefings and training tomorrow," Kibi informed them with a firm voice.

They settled down, but never completely ceased poking each other.

"The gravity in the tank is local at all points," the more serious of the two explained, "so to the water, and the people in it, it's flat.  There's a new control group on your console . . ."

Kibi looked and nodded.

". . . but most of the time, your ship can take care of everything.  It's connected directly to the ship's waste-processing system, and aquatic Nebador people know how to interface with that."

"Okay, my turn!" the goofier one asserted.

Kibi smiled and continued listening.

"This case contains enough minerals for *one* emergency refill with fresh water, but as long as your passengers are air-breathers, it's usually better just to keep them wet and dash for the nearest star station."

Kibi nodded, and guessed that the briefing was over when her technicians began wrestling on the floor again.

✳   ✳   ✳

## Chapter 56: Graduation Party

The evening dance celebration on Satamia Star Station had nearly begun when the crew, less Kibi, entered the main hall.  Suddenly, a huge spider blocked their way.

"Greetings, M'palta!" Ilika said.

The others gathered around, remembering with fondness the biologist from their first deep-space mission.

"Good monkey mammals, extra claws are needed moving furniture and carrying food.  Hands will work almost as well, I suppose."

"We were just wondering how we could help," Rini said.

Boro and Sata bowed and headed off to join some ursines carrying furniture.

Mati and Rini pointed their feet toward the nearest busy kitchen.

"Do they know?" M'palta asked Ilika quietly.

"I decided to let it be a surprise," he replied.

The spider twitched her mandibles with humor.

✳

Sata immediately recognized Brora, and after the bear set down the small couch she was carrying, they embraced warmly.

"So good to see you!" Sata declared.  "How is Siminia Three Planet Station?"

"A little slow right now, as it's the rainy season, but the desert retreats are hopping.  Everyone in the *universe* wants to see the shrine in the sand dunes behind Kemlo.  Let's move this big one against that wall."

They worked together to lift the long couch.

"I'm just back for a few days of training," the ursine continued as they slowly walked with their burden, "then I'll be the traveling healer, going from retreat to retreat, and helping out at the planet station when needed."

They set that couch down and went back for another.

"I was so sad," Sata shared, "knowing they were dying, as we listened to Teina and Jimox tell their stories."

"You made them happy by listening.  Someday you and I will be old, and take joy in telling our stories."

Sata nodded thoughtfully as they picked up another couch.

Rini smiled when he recognized Silmula Sorafax as she rode a floating pallet into the kitchen.  It stopped beside the table where he and Mati were busy assembling trays of finger food, rose up to the exact height of the table, and hovered motionless.

Mati's mouth opened in surprise.  She could see the mission bracelet on the big feline's upper left arm, but the wearer hadn't touched it during the entire maneuver.  "How . . . did you do that?"

"Do what?"

"Control the pallet."

"Oh, that.  I can control the bracelet with my mind, and the bracelet controls the pallet."

"Wow," Rini breathed as he placed trays all around the seated cat.

"Monkey mammals can rarely control their bracelets mentally, but *you two* might be exceptions.  Talk to Memsala in Psychic Development."

"We're about to start a new mission," Rini said, "and I think Memsala might be on it."

"Oh . . . yes . . ." Silmula said with a sparkle in her eyes.  "Toran's on that mission, too."

Mati swallowed.  "That might be a challenge for Kibi."

The cat chuckled in a very feline way as Rini squeezed the last tray onto the pallet.

After Kibi made sure her new tank wasn't leaking, and got comfortable with all the additional controls on her console, she looked at the two lanky reptiles, still laughing and playing on the floor of her passenger area.  "Everything looks good.  You guys going to the party?"

"Of course!"

"We wouldn't miss it!"

She gestured toward the hatch.

They hopped onto their pallet, then continued poking each other and telling jokes as they floated out of sight.

"Manessa, you comfortable with this new tank?"

"Yes," the ship replied.  "All diagnostics indicate that it was properly installed."

"See you after the party.  Big mission tomorrow."

"With your help, I will be ready."

When Kibi arrived at the main hall, musicians were playing and people dancing.  She spotted Ashley, Healer Dakalio, and a fanator with white feathers dancing together, so she joined them.

"Hi, Kibi. I'm sure you know Dakalio . . ."

Kibi nodded as she exchanged smiles with the human healer while picking up the dance rhythm.

"And this is Kelatorrra."

Bird and girl bowed to each other as they danced.

✳

Boro and Sata sat by one of the pools eating fruit cups to replenish their energy before hitting the dance floor.  Suddenly, a sleek gray dolphin head emerged from the pool behind them and slipped onto the deck beside Sata. "My favorite monkey mammals!"

"Trekila!" Sata recognized.

"I'm your cetacean contact specialist for the mission that starts tomorrow."

"Wonderful!  I still remember the day we tumbled down a water ramp together."

Trekila laughed.

Another gray head appeared beside Boro.

"And this is my sweet lover," Trekila announced proudly.

Boro offered his fingers to the sharp teeth of the large and powerful male dolphin, but felt only a wet tongue.

✳

Ilika and Kibi got snacks with Sss'rol'ti the quanasia, and they laughed about the pair of brothers who had just installed the tank on the Manessa Kwi.

Glorm the ursine docking controller pranced up a storm with Boro and Sata for two songs, then had to get ready for work.

Mati spotted the family of six tiny Ti'ias making patterns in the air that somehow captured the mood of a sad, almost heart-rending song.

Rini basked in the joy and wonder he felt from the sparkling decorations, the good food and good people, and the deeply-moving music.

About half-way through the celebration, a ballad sung by Sorrano and Rossilia came to a close, and the group of avian musicians, including Sata's friend Drrrim-na, put away their instruments.  A shimmering form began to slowly spin in the middle of the hall.

Everyone found places to float, perch, or sit.

Kerloran slowly appeared as a beautiful green bird, larger even than a fanator.

"I am deeply honored to have such a happy star station under my care!"

All the assembled creatures honked, cheered, screeched, or made other joyful noises.

"A very wise insect once observed that Nebador citizenship tends to creep up on you.  You're just enjoying life, day by day, learning more and more, undertaking challenging assignments, and one day you wake up and realize that *universe service*, symbolized by the chiming of your mission devices, is as satisfying as any party, any feast, any game, even ... any sexual relationship ..."

Everyone chittered, whinnied, or laughed.

"There is, of course, still a place, in every mortal creature's life, for parties, feasts, games, and sex."

Many sounds of humor and relief filled the main hall.

"As new citizens of Nebador, please come forth and stand before your fellow citizens and friends.  Prrr-han, Trrra-hana, and Tem'rrr-han of Peliantora Two."

Everyone else hooted, flapped wings, or splashed flippers as the three reptiles came up, Kerloran embraced them, and they bowed to the assembled audience.

"Kibi, Boro, Rini, Sata, and Mati of Sonmatia Three."

The welcoming sounds continued as the five monkey mammals were embraced by the master of the star station.

"Ssssmsmsmsmmmamamaaaaa of the Inner Blue Ring Nebula."

Few of those present tried to say the name, but they made the creature of green and purple mist feel welcome.

"P'torrra and K'larrra of Havertona Four."

The two birds bowed deeply as a group of reptilian musicians, on cue, began a lively song, and the evening celebration on Satamia Star Station resumed its festivities.

* * *

## Chapter 57: Mission Briefing

After the dark hours, during which the main hall of Satamia Star Station was one huge party room, came the quiet hours of dawn and sunrise.  A few people, not yet asleep, readied the room for the day, then wandered off to their nests.  Those who had retired early began to awake, find nourishment, make sure the main hall was in good shape, then go to their assignments, classes, or free-time activities.

A small conference room near the Mission Assignment Room was designed so every type of Satamia sapient life could meet together at once.  T'sss'lisss, Ashley, and Kolarrr'ka arrived early, their minds spinning and their knowledge pads flashing with all the details of the mission that needed their attention.  Soon a giant sea turtle swam in through a shallow channel, followed by a dolphin.  Through one door came a small bear and a large cat, then through a larger door, a huge horse.

The crew of the Manessa Kwi arrived a few minutes later and seated themselves on some benches against the wall.

Kolarrr'ka stood.  "Ashley has put me in charge of the contact and evaluation phase, bok.  Taking into account each of your strengths, please prepare for the following assignments.

"Trekila Spimalo, you will contact the cetaceans, all seven species, bok, and inform them of the possibility of evacuation in about twelve planetary years if it appears to be necessary."

The dolphin, used to taking water samples, opened her mouth at the importance of the assignment, but closed it without speaking.

"Memsala, you will contact the giant testudine with the same message, bok.  We also recognize that you are probably the wisest among us, so we welcome your input at any time."

The sea turtle nodded slowly, and Kibi smiled with happiness that her Psychic Development teacher would be on the team.

"Boro, since you swim almost as well as a fish, you will be helper for both Trekila and Memsala.  Please go sit with them."

He grinned with excitement, quickly shed his outer clothes, and hopped into the shallow tank, then splashed a little water to make sure both his charges were completely wet.

"Malika-Terno, I am well aware that your species has chosen, on all the planets where they live, to suffer the cruel treatments dished out by the young dominant races in order to teach them and stand at their sides when they, eventually, grow up.  That is a noble task, bok, but the equines of Ko-tera Three may not get that chance.  Spread the word that evacuation may be necessary, and assure them that we will only follow that course if the planet is beyond hope."

The huge horse, resting with his feet tucked under him, made a throaty sound and nodded.

"Mati, as I understand it, you could ride an equine before you could walk . . ."

She smiled and nodded.

". . . and since you're so light, Malika-Terno will hardly notice you if a journey together is necessary."

Mati hopped up and settled herself beside the horse's muscular neck, stroking his golden hair.

"Ss'klexna Rrr'tak'fi, unlike you, bok, who can think circles around most of us . . ."

The small bear laughed, showing very sharp teeth.  All the crew members of the Manessa Kwi smiled at her, remembering her story from one of the first videos they had ever watched.

". . . the ursines on Ko-tera Three are not yet sapient, so your task will be much harder, bok.  Attempt to determine what problems would arise if we tried to evacuate some of them to another planet.  But keep in mind — they are not unique, so be prepared to withdraw without conclusive results."

"I understand," she said with a nod.

"Sata, if for any reason Ss'klexna cannot complete the evaluation, you must retreat to the ship or another place of safety *immediately*."

Sata nodded as she went and sat beside the legendary Ss'klexna Rrr'tak'fi.

"Rini," Kolarrr'ka continued, "you will provide general assistance to both myself and T'sss'lisss, but cannot go all the places we must go, so you may have few responsibilities outside the ship on this phase of the mission."

Rini nodded.

Kibi could feel herself trembling.  The only remaining contact specialist was a large male cat.  She recognized those stripes.  She knew the day had come that he had foretold — she was now a Nebador citizen, and they were on a mission together.

She knew she *wanted* to be completely true to Ilika.  She just wasn't sure her body was going to cooperate.

"Toran Takil," Kolarrr'ka continued, "you have the same task as Ss'klexna.

Evaluate the possibility of evacuating some of the great cats, but take no unnecessary risks."

He blinked and nodded.

"Kibi, same restrictions as Sata.  Help if you can, but above all else, come back alive and well, bok."

Kibi sat down beside Toran Takil, but had no fear that coming back alive would be her main problem.

After a short discussion about the other near-sapient species they would be evaluating, the meeting broke up so everyone could get a hearty meal. When they returned to the room, T'sss'lisss stretched up from her coils.

"Phassse Two of the misssion, which is my resssponsssibility, isss lesss well defined right now.  The monkey mammalsss of Ko-tera Three have sssent a probe to their outer planetsss.  It includesss a plaque that expresssesss a *ssslight* awarenesss of their sssituation, thanksss to the Temporandek Teacher they were given.  We are planning the misssion ssso that Phassse One will be finished about when the probe completesss itsss work and becomesss nothing more than a . . . what'sss that sssaying, Ashley?"

"A message in a bottle."

"Thanksss.  At that point, we will review everything we know, lisssten to all available wisssdom, including Manesssa'sss training ssspecccialissst Arantiloria, and decccide what to do."

T'sss'lisss descended into her coils and Ashley stood.

"Our best guess of mission duration is eight, maybe twelve days.  Food and water re-supply will be possible on several uninhabited islands of Ko-tera Three.  Please prepare yourselves and your ship, and gather at the Manessa Kwi in eight hours."

Satamia Two, their first destination, had fascinated the crew since their early days on the star station, being one of the few worlds in the region of Satamia that hosted a true mortal civilization.

A civilization, they now understood well after Ashley's mission briefing, was one that had passed the three tests of population, power, and pollution. Before that, a race of sapient people might have language, technology, and many other trappings of civilization, but if they hatched all the babies they wanted, grabbed all the power they could get, and fouled their nests, they were no different, in the eyes of the universe, than simple non-sapient creatures.  They would be watched over and guided, but would not be considered a truly irreplaceable part of Satamia in Nebador, any more than the algae in a pond, or the mice in a field.

The crew members pondered this, some silently and some in conversation, as they stocked the Manessa Kwi from the pallets that floated in with food, fuel, and other supplies.

To Rini, it made perfect sense, but he knew Mati was troubled by the limitation on having children.  She went back and forth as they worked to prepare the ship, sometimes sharing with Sata her frustration that people on a civilized planet couldn't have all the babies they could support, later admitting to Rini that even though the parents could support them, that didn't mean the planet could.

Sata listened to Mati, but was going over in her mind the many times her parents had made use of slaves, at least indirectly, because they had the money to do so. Ilika had never done that, she reminisced with Boro in the utility room. As soon as he bought the nine slaves, he freed them, promising to do nothing to stop them from leaving even before their bills of freedom were done. Kodi had tested and proven that promise.

Boro encouraged her to forgive her parents. It was nearly impossible for a single person to go against their culture, he believed. But he admitted complete ignorance of how a planet could get from constant abuses of power, like slavery, to a true civilization, and planned to ask Ilika, Ashley, or maybe Arantiloria.

As Kibi stocked the galley, she wasn't sure she wanted to have *any* children. She just didn't relate to the craving of some people to fill the world with whining brats. Her own childhood had been painful, her home without love or respect. Then slavery had shown her what people did when they got a little power, and she wanted no part of *that* game, either.

She was stacking large packets of grass in the storage room, and pondering the third test of mortal planets — pollution — when her eyes suddenly opened wide with a realization. On Satamia Star Station, there *was* no pollution at all. The great station tree and other plants took care of the air, and no one smoked or did anything else to pollute it. The water was constantly monitored and cared for by the creatures who lived in it, and a few tireless machines they lovingly tended. Even trash, every bit of it, was reused in some way. On most planets, she knew, trash was burned or just piled up, deeper and deeper.

✳

Malika-Terno needed no seat in the passenger area, just a clear space on the floor. T'sss'lisss had her own seat in the front row between Ashley and Kolarrr'ka, but seemed happier sharing a seat with one of her partners, sometimes both at once.

Kibi programmed two new seating arrangements, one for viewing the big screen, the other for gathering around the table.

Unlike the one deep-space mission Kibi remembered, the specialists could not bring family members on this trip. It was expected to be much shorter, the work more intense, and excursions outside the ship more frequent. Kibi smiled and felt very lucky to be able to curl up with her lover in their cabin, even though moments when they were both off-duty might be few on this mission.

She watched from her console as the specialists got settled, stowed their travel bags under the bench at the rear of the passenger area, adjusted their seats, and chatted about the mission.

Malika-Terno requested that Kibi test his emergency inertia net, and it worked perfectly, ready to hold the big horse in one place on the floor during unexpectedly-rough flight.

Memsala and Trekila Spimalo both poked their heads out of the open section of tank at table level, and reported that all was well with their aquatic environment.

Toran Takil was already curled up in his seat, eyes closed, napping.

Ss'klexna Rrr'tak'fi had an intuition, and she gestured for Kibi to come close so she could share it privately. "Something tells me we're going to have passengers at some point on this mission. You might want to plan an alternate seating arrangement . . ."

* * *

## Chapter 58: Training

"Deep-Space Response Ship Manessa Kwi on Satamia Two standard approach," Rini said at navigation.

"Greetings, Manessa Kwi!" a gray fanator responded from Rini's screen. "How may we serve the gods?"

Rini felt himself blush for a moment. "Um ... we'd like to do a little wilderness training in preparation for a difficult mission on another planet."

"Bok. All Nebador citizens with medical clearance?"

"Yes."

"Good. I'm sending you the current planetary status map."

It slowly formed on Rini's screen and he sent it to all stations.

"The northeast continent just closed for ecosystem adjustments," the fanator explained. "The south-central continent is available for wilderness training, but closed to any group larger than twelve."

"Our training will be done mostly in pairs, trios at the most," Rini said.

"Okay. We hope you'll stop by Satamia City to enjoy our hospitality before you depart, perhaps after you've gotten your fill of the wilds, bok!"

Rini chuckled. "We might be able to do that. Thank you, Satamia Two. Manessa Kwi closing."

✳

Ilika swiveled the commander's chair and looked at Kolarrr'ka, busy studying the planetary map from his seat in the passenger area.

"Bok," the bird began thoughtfully. "Let's put our aquatic team near a little tropical island in the central wilderness zone, and sprinkle the other teams on the south-central continent. Tropical rain forest, Toran?"

The big cat, now sitting up tall in his seat, nodded.

"Grasslands to the south, Malika?"

"Yes, please."

"Ss'klexna?"

"Boreal forest in the mountains, just below timberline."

Kolarrr'ka nodded. "I know T'sss'lisss wants to slither around that desert on the west coast."

Rini, remembering with fondness the sand dunes on his home planet, grinned with anticipation as he began to construct a flight plan that would put all the training teams in the right places.

※

With the warm tropical ocean lapping at the bottom of the little ship, Boro, wearing only shorts, adjusted his buoyancy belt to take him just under the surface swells, slipped on his breathing mask, and nodded that he was ready.

"You're *sure* you don't want a suit?" Kibi asked with a worried look. "There are things with *teeth* down there."

"*Trekila* has teeth!" Boro pointed out through the intercom in his mask.

"I meant non-sapient teeth!" Kibi clarified.

Boro laughed. "This is *wilderness* training. I feel bad enough that I have to use a breathing mask. I hope someday I won't have to."

Kibi looked out the hatch where Trekila Spimalo and Memsala were floating nearby. "I want my crew member to come back safely!" she called to them.

The dolphin promised while splashing with her tail, and the giant sea turtle nodded.

Boro jumped in, and Kibi could see him begin to kick in a steady rhythm about a meter below the surface of the blue-green water, following his two mission specialists toward the nearest little island.

※

While Mati looked for an opening in the dense tropical canopy forty meters or more above the ground, Kibi got ready in skimpy clothing, moccasins, and light gloves that would allow her to climb trees easily in the warm, humid rain forest.

Eventually the pilot found an opening, but could not get the ship all the way down to the surface because of fallen logs, branches, and creeping vines.

"This is a jungle," Toran Takil declared from the entryway, looking through the open hatch. "We may not walk on solid ground all day long."

Mati nudged the ship next to a fallen tree. "How's that?"

Kibi stepped beside the large male cat and swallowed. They would be in the wilderness together, with no one watching, and no time limit until the Manessa Kwi picked them up the following day.

Toran leapt to the fallen tree, then looked back at Kibi.

Her mind raced, trying to think of any excuse to avoid the test she was about to . . . pass or fail. None came to mind. With her heart in her throat, she jumped to the log, wobbled for a moment, then found her balance.

※

Mati transferred the helm to Ilika so she could change into the long pants, boots, full shirt, and sun hat that would allow her to survive the wiry grass and hot sun of the plains region.

Ilika brought the ship to the ground and extended the ramp. Malika-Terno clopped out, threw back his head, and whinnied loudly at the thrill of a day in open wilderness where he could run like the wind.

Mati came down next.

"I'm used to a saddle, you know," she pointed out with a grin.

"That's what today is for," the large horse replied. "You must become as much a part of me as the hair on my back. Only then will you know the joy of running across the open prairie as only an equine can."

Mati was ready. She reached around the base of his mane while launching herself with her feet, then slipped flat onto his back before attempting to center herself.

"I remember when I was a cripple, and couldn't *dream* of doing that!"

"Those days are no more," he said, and set off across the grasslands at a trot for her first lesson.

※

Sata *felt* like a bear in thick boots and insulated clothing as she stepped from the ship's ramp onto cold rocks with white snow glistening in the shady places. The sun blazed in a deep-blue sky, but the nearby mountain peak was wreathed in ominous clouds. A few twisted trees bore silent witness to the unexpected arrival.

Ss'klexna sat upright on another boulder not far away, taking the measure of the place with bright eyes and sensitive nose. Then she looked at her monkey-mammal student. "There's a stream about an hour's run from here, but I will let you find it."

"Run?" Sata questioned. "I can barely *walk* in these thick clothes!"

"That will come in time. First, quit thinking and start smelling. The fish in the stream are almost making my mouth water even at this distance . . ."

※

At the final drop-off point, T'sss'lisss was the first one down the ramp, anxious to feel the sand under her belly. Kolarrr'ka spread his wings at the hatch and glided over his partner's head, then flapped to gain a little altitude and scout the area.

Rini pranced out last, wearing light shoes, loose but long pants and shirt, and sun hat.

Ashley stood in the hatch and watched them go. "Have fun, desert rats!"

Rini chuckled as he dashed along a sandy wash behind T'sss'lisss, both of them keeping track of Kolarrr'ka by the shadow that occasionally flashed across the land.

Ashley closed the hatch and nodded to Ilika at the helm. "I envy them," she said, perching on the steps to the bridge while Ilika piloted. "We already *know* the status of the humans on Ko-tera Three, and it's nothing to be proud of . . ."

※

The tropical island had looked close from the air, but Boro soon discovered he would be swimming for a long time.  As the minutes became hours, he wondered if he would have the strength.  His teachers each pulled him a little, just so he would know where to hold, but showed no intention of making his journey easy.  And when the island finally seemed to be getting closer, they started calling to him to explore the ocean floor with them, where coral beds and colorful fish created a maze of sights and muffled sounds.  He adjusted his buoyancy belt, looked inside himself for another burst of energy, and followed them down.

Toran Takil had been right — after hours of balancing on fallen logs, climbing up slender trunks, and sometimes leaping from branch to branch, Kibi could not remember ever standing on solid ground.  Rushing streams passed by beneath them, but never did they get wet in those streams.  They were both, however, soon drenched from the damp leaves, dripping bark, and creeping mists of the jungle.  And to make it all worse, Kibi felt completely lost, and was sure she could never find the place they had been dropped off, somewhere in the vast jungle on a continent with nothing but wilderness.

At first Malika-Terno held himself to a trot as he moved across the seemingly endless grasslands, and Mati held on to his muscular neck and believed herself to be going faster than the wind.  Eventually, when he knew they were in an area of tall, soft grass, he changed his running rhythm slightly and picked up speed, and soon Mati was bouncing up and down on his back and screaming.  A moment later the horse felt his light burden vanish completely, so he slowed to a walk and circled back.  "You were *sitting* on me," he said to the sore monkey mammal in the grass trying to catch her breath.  "You must learn to become the hair on my back, at all rhythms and speeds.  Only then can we hope to catch up with the wind!"

After Ss'klexna Rrr'tak'fi yelled at Sata four times to quit thinking and use her senses, and once reinforced it with sharp teeth that didn't break the skin, much, the response ship navigator got the message and followed her nose.  With a bear right behind her, she ran.  She knew her teacher didn't mean sprint, but just a steady lope that would slowly eat up the kilometers.  Three-quarters of an hour later, the faint smell of water gave way to the clear sound of a gurgling mountain stream, and soon fish could be seen leaping from pool to pool.

Rini was filled with joy as he pranced about in the sandy desert, explored little eroded canyons with T'sss'lisss, and climbed to high points to scan the wild horizon with Kolarrr'ka.  To the west lay an ocean, and to the east, mountains, both too far to visit in one day.  But as the hours passed, his joy was tempered first by noticing secretive glances between his teachers, then by hearing faint animal sounds, like the bark or yap of a small canine.  As the sun neared the ocean, he became sure of it, and was also convinced the sounds were coming from every direction.  "Ah!  He doesss have earsss!" T'sss'lisss commented.  "Kolarrr'ka and I have decccided to let *you* figure out how we will sssurvive the night, with carnivorousss latransss all around usss.  They hunt in packsss, *love* fresh sssnake and bird meat, and even though they don't get it very often, I'm sssure they'd enjoy a tassste of monkey mammal, too."

Ilika and Ashley, after parking the Manessa Kwi on a pristine beach and collecting some tropical fruit, opened a packet of grains and vegetables from Ubalora Three and began reviewing all the mission documents.

✳ ✳ ✳

## Chapter 59: Wilderness

As the long afternoon slowly passed, Mati learned how to be the hair on Malika-Terno's back.  Her reward was catching up with the wind and eventually leaving it far behind.

Seldom was she able to sit on her willing mount.  Except at a few smooth gaits that Malika-Terno rarely used, Mati pretended she was a saddle blanket, her arms on both sides of the horse's huge neck, her face pressed close beside his mane.  After falling off four more times, she finally resisted the temptation to wrap her legs securely around his belly, and realized that the only way to stay on was to always be in imminent danger of sliding off.  Once she learned that lesson, her legs stayed high and she could feel his powerful muscles working to outpace the wind.

With Mati's profile now very low, Malika-Terno approached his top speed, came to the crest of a hill, slowed and said, "Hold on!"  As soon as he felt Mati press her arms tightly on both sides of his neck, he came to a full stop, reared up on his hind legs, and whinnied for all the world to hear.

To his surprise, his little response-ship pilot was still on his back when he landed on all fours, so he began walking to cool himself.  "Your training is complete."

"Whoopee!" Mati cheered, finally daring to sit up.

"Now let us see who comes to my Call to Council."

Mati slid off the horse's back and began to explore the top of the low hill, wondering what she might find for dinner.  Malika-Terno continued to walk to and fro, Mati heard other horses whinny far off in the distance, and sometimes Malika-Terno answered.  She found a cluster of brambles on the sunny side of the hill, and the berries were edible, so she started picking.

The first group of wild horses arrived about half an hour later, a stallion and five mares, but they looked askance at the monkey mammal and kept their distance.  Malika-Terno spoke to them in the common equine language, and they came a little closer, but still peered at Mati as they would a wasp's nest.

"Find your value," Malika-Terno said to her.

"What do you mean?"

"It is their nature to love you and hate you, to allow you to be their master but never fully trust you. Break that cycle. Be their servant for one evening. You were once a slave, so you know how."

Mati thought about it. "I didn't have much value as a slave. I pulled a few weeds, washed a few dishes . . ."

"And now?"

"I can walk, run, swim, and dance. I'm a response-ship pilot and engineer. And now I can be the hair on a horse's back and chase the wind!"

"Among all that, find your value to these wild sapient equines. Find the service you can provide them to earn their trust."

Mati frowned and looked around. She was very sure they didn't eat berries. "If only I had a brush . . ."

"You have a little knife on your belt, do you not? Perhaps, therefore, you have a brush."

"No . . ." she started to say, then stopped herself as her eyes opened wider and she began to search among the grass. It wasn't long before she found what she wanted, a wiry little bush.

"Would this work? I don't want to use something they're allergic to."

Malika-Terno came close and blew deep breaths to smell the plant, then nibbled at it. "That is a good choice."

For the next quarter hour, Mati worked with her pocket knife to fashion a brush from part of the little plant. Then she stood and looked over the situation. One of the mares was closer than the others, and slowly wandering even closer as she grazed.

"How's this look?" Mati asked Malika-Terno and stood with arms outstretched, palms up with the make-shift brush across them, and her head bowed.

"About as harmless as a monkey mammal can be!"

Mati took a deep breath and slowly walked toward the mare. When she was about half-way, she heard the stallion rumble a warning, so she stopped and knelt down, but kept her hands and her offering out in front of her.

Using only her ears, Mati determined that the stallion had relaxed. Barely daring to look, she sensed the mare continue to approach. Perhaps eight minutes later, a large black equine nose was blowing and smelling Mati's hands and the brush. At the same time, Malika-Terno was saying something in the equine language from the hill top.

Once the mare stepped back a little, Mati slowly took the brush in one hand and carefully brushed her other arm with it.

The mare, for a moment on the edge of fear, eventually snorted and went back to grazing.

Mati carefully stood and touched the brush to the mare's shoulder.

The huge animal twitched but continued ripping at the grass while keeping one eye on the little human.

Mati began her task.  Within minutes, the mare was making contented sounds, and the other mares began to wander over.

She had barely finished brushing the first mare and was starting on the second when the stallion nudged the mares out of the way and presented himself for brushing.

Mati resisted the temptation to laugh.

By mid-afternoon, Sata had learned to run like a bear — slow and steady, hour after hour if necessary, while keeping her eyes and ears open for anything of interest in her environment.

She knew what Ss'klexna Rrr'tak'fi was doing.  By running, Sata didn't have *time* to think about anything.  All her mental energy went into figuring out where to put her feet, when to crouch low to avoid branches, when to pause and listen for dangers.

Ss'klexna ran along beside, almost effortlessly at Sata's best speed, modeling for her student the rhythms and postures needed in each situation. Sometimes her nose was thrust forward, examining every molecule of the air. At other times her ears twitched to catch the slightest pebble-fall on the mountainside.

They came to a flat rock outcropping, and the bear stopped and perched on the edge, surveying the wilderness below.  Breathing deeply, Sata joined her.

"I don't think I've ever had to *sense* so much, and *think* so little!" Sata remarked.

"Good," Ss'klexna said, "but you've just been sensing the physical world. Good place to start, but you're a Nebador citizen now, so you must go deeper."

Sata swallowed.  "What . . . should I do?"

"Dance.  And while you dance, listen to the planet."

"But . . . there's no music . . ."

"Find the music.  It's all around you."

Very self-consciously, Sata shuffled to the middle of the rock outcropping. After standing for a moment, and noticing that Ss'klexna Rrr'tak'fi did not turn to watch her, Sata started to move her feet, even though she really didn't hear any music.

As the minutes passed, and the bear continued to gaze in a different direction, Sata felt herself relax into the dance and release the embarrassment she had been feeling.  Again, just like with running, the act of dancing made thinking almost impossible.  She could sense the massive rock under her, hear the rush of the crisp mountain air into and out of her lungs, feel the coolness on her skin, but could not, at the same time, think about much of anything.

Ss'klexna's posture, perching as still as a statue at the edge of the outcropping, told Sata clearly that she intended her student to dance for a long time.  Sensing this, Sata kept her rhythm slow and steady, just like her running earlier, so she could dance for hours if need be.

A quarter hour had passed — maybe half an hour, Sata couldn't be sure — when she became aware of movement around her, and none of it was Ss'klexna.

Some was very slow, like the creeping shadows as the day approached evening.

Some moved slowly at times, and at other times dashed from tree to tree. Sata smiled, for just a second, as she glimpsed something furry with bright eyes trying to get close enough to satisfy its curiosity without exposing itself to danger.

And some arrived suddenly, by air, and settled onto tree branches, cocking their heads to watch the two big mammals, one still, one moving slowly but constantly.  They were mesmerized and fascinated.

Sata saw them, but didn't stop dancing, and didn't try to think.  She trusted that if any of the creatures did anything threatening, she would sense it, and her body would respond.  With no *need* to think, Sata realized she was dancing to music, but not music heard with her ears.  Suddenly she felt completely free, and her dance became much more sensuous and expressive.

The birds noticed, and couldn't tear their eyes away.  More arrived, and more mammals crept close.

Suddenly Sata realized that Ss'klexna Rrr'tak'fi was dancing with her, weaving patterns with her on the rock slab while they both remained aware of the birds and mammals watching, the mountains and forests around them, the jungle, grassland, and desert farther away, the oceans beyond those, more continents with farms, towns, and cities of sapient peoples, and ice caps far to the north and south . . .

Without thinking, Sata followed the bear's dance rhythm as it became slower, smaller, and lower, finally settling onto the rock until nothing moved but their hearts and lungs.

And yet, somehow, their awareness of the entire planet remained.

One by one, the curious mammals crept away.

In twos or threes, the birds took wing.

Bear and monkey mammal continued to sit facing each other, looking into each other's eyes, breathing deeply.

After what seemed like an hour or more, Ss'klexna Rrr'tak'fi spoke.  "Is this a happy planet? Don't think. You *know* the answer."

Sata grinned.  "This is a *very* happy planet . . . and it has been for a long time."

"What about Siminia Three, Jimox' and Teina's planet?  Don't think. Remember."

"It *was* sad, until all the innocent ghosts were released, and now is . . . starting to become happy again.  The planet station and retreats are *very* happy, even though . . . their creators are gone.  But the ruins are looking forward to ... the day when all manner of plants and animals can live in them ... without fear."

"You are ready for this mission," Ss'klexna Rrr'tak'fi declared.

As the sun sank into the tropical ocean, Boro could barely drag himself onto the beach when his day of training finally came to an end. By that time, several small native cetaceans — dolphins, seals, and manatees — and a pair of giant sea turtles, had joined the gathering. They frolicked in the still water of the island's lagoon with Trekila Spimalo and Memsala, bringing Boro tasty fish to eat.

With shaking arms, he dragged himself to a rock by the water's edge, unfolded the little knife from his buoyancy belt, and sliced himself some dinner, quite amazed at how hungry he suddenly felt. One large and two small fish were quickly reduced to bones and guts.

After nutrition and rest, he stood on wobbling legs and gathered fruit from the edge of the forest while enough evening light remained, and offered pieces to his teachers and their new friends, but they passed.

"Everyone here is sapient, aren't they?" he asked from his little rock table at the edge of the ocean between bites of fruit.

"Yes," Trekila replied, "although our local friends do not speak the language of Nebador. However, cetaceans have a universal language, so we can speak to them. The testudine can speak with each other through their minds."

Boro nodded. "What keeps them from ... some kind of contest or ritual to decide who's dominant, whose territory this is, and all that?"

Trekila laughed, said something in the high-pitched cetacean language, and soon all the dolphins were laughing, the seals barking, and the manatees grunting.

Boro frowned. "What's so funny?"

With smiling eyes, Trekila deferred to Memsala.

"Even though we are in the middle of a vast wilderness, we are also in civilization," the giant sea turtle said slowly. "Humans, along with most avians, tend to think of civilization and wilderness as opposites. At its foundation, civilization is a state of non-aggression between sapient peoples, and requires the ability to recognize sapience in self and others. I believe you might say, *live and let live.*"

At that moment a tall, muscular, nearly-hairless monkey mammal, carrying a long spear, came walking toward them across the beach.

All the aquatic people watched him carefully.

Boro turned where he sat, realized his little pocket knife was useless, and tensed his sore muscles to jump into the lagoon if necessary.

The tall human stopped a few strides away, laid his spear down in the sand, said something in a strange language, and sat down near the water's edge.

None of the Nebador citizens or their friends had any idea what the human had said, but one of the dolphins submerged, came back up a moment later with a fish in its teeth, and tossed it to the new arrival.

Boro thought for a moment, then held out his knife, handle first, so the man could clean and eat the fish he had been given.

*

Kibi washed up from her dinner of jungle fruit at a trickle of water coursing down a tree trunk. Toran Takil just used his tongue after feasting upon a plump but slow bird.

The mottled light was beginning to fade into evening shadows as Kibi noticed Toran become tense and wary, often listening to the jungle sounds around them. They continued looking for a place to spend the night where Kibi would have little chance of falling while she slept, and if she did, wouldn't fall far.

As twilight descended around them, they discovered two horizontal logs side by side only a few meters above the tangled floor of the jungle. Kibi started to say something but was quickly silenced by the slap of Toran's paw, luckily with claws retracted.

"Show no fear," he whispered, then silently turned his head to scan with eyes and ears again.

*Of whom?* Kibi wondered, but made no sound.

After what seemed like hours of straining to sense what her teacher already knew, she faintly heard the low rumbling sound that could only be another large feline. It was some distance away, and she could still see Toran's silhouette right beside her in the twilight.

A moment later he replied with a similar rumble.

Then Kibi heard a word, or sound, spoken by another monkey mammal, a girl who sounded fairly young.

"Hello?" Kibi called softly, making sure no fear showed in her voice.

The unseen girl, now closer, spoke more sounds, but they seemed halfway between words and feline rumbles, and Kibi had no idea what they meant. Then the young voice came again, from just meters away, saying in the language of Nebador, "You from star station?"

Toran Takil intoned another deep rumble, then added, "Yes. My claws are sheathed."

"A star-station kitty!" the girl said excitedly.

In the fading twilight, Kibi made out two shapes side by side on the logs not far away, one only slightly taller than the other. The taller one pulled something from a bag or pouch at her side, shook it vigorously, and it began to glow, casting a faint green light that revealed a human girl of about eight years standing beside a large striped cat, as big or bigger than Toran Takil.

The feline growled a warning that nearly froze Kibi's blood.

"Stay standing," Toran said softly even as he got down on his belly and placed his head on the log.

The girl giggled. "Boys! Okay, Bad Kitty is boss, your kitty is smart. Wanna camp and tell stories?"

Toran remained silent, so Kibi took a deep breath. "We were going to sleep here, as there doesn't seem to be anywhere better. We'd love to share stories!"

Toran nodded his head slightly without lifting it.

"Many better places, but too late to find them. What name, your kitty?"

Toran remained silent, so Kibi spoke. "This is Toran Takil, and I'm Kibi. We're in training for a mission on which Toran is a contact specialist, and I'm his helper and the steward of the ship."

"You his mate?"

Kibi was unsure how to answer, just for a second. "No."

"Mommy and Daddy went on missions and things. Maybe I would, but now . . . diff'ent life."

Both the girl and Kibi sat down on the log, each beside their feline companion.

"How do you know the language of Nebador?" Kibi asked.

"Born on star station, Sa . . . tamia. Then I was four, me, Mommy, Daddy visit here. I love trees, go on walk. Mommy and Daddy busy. Got dark. I cried. Animals come to eat me. Bad Kitty save me, bring food, protect me."

Kibi realized the girl had been living here, with her feline companion, for three or four years. "Do you want to go home to Satamia Star Station? A ship will be picking us up tomorrow, and we could easily drop you off before going on our mission."

The girl was silent for a long time. She shook the light again to brighten it, and scratched the big feline's neck while she thought. Eventually she spoke.

"No. Me and Bad Kitty a team. Jungle my home. Kitties don't live long as monkey mams, so one day when Bad Kitty go up to stars, I come out. Then I ready for missions and things. Not ready yet."

As the twilight deepened into night, Kibi told stories from her travels and training, the girl shared many secrets about her jungle home, and the two large male felines remained wary of each other.

Eventually Kibi curled up beside Toran Takil, but lay awake for a long time pondering the circumstances that would cause a young girl to make a long-term commitment to a wild animal, even when offered a chance to return to her original home.

An intuition told Kibi that when this girl finally did step out of the jungle, she would be wise and strong far beyond her years, sort of like . . . someone who had been a slave. Kibi smiled at the thought, then fell asleep.

✳

Rini sat cross-legged on the boulder, keeping an eye on the dark desert to the east. Kolarrr'ka, close beside him, faced the fading sunset light over the ocean in the west. T'sss'lisss went back and forth, from Rini's shoulders, watching north and south, with her tail coiled tightly under Kolarrr'ka.

"The breeze isss from the north!" the snake said loudly so she could be heard. "Should be a warm night!"

"What?" Kolarrr'ka responded.  "I can't hear a thing, bok!"

All three looked down.

The number of yapping coyotes, doing their best to reach the tasty morsels on top of the boulder, had increased to five, and more could be heard in the distance.

"Do they ever sleep?" Rini asked anyone who cared to speculate.

"My guess would be *no*, bok, as long as they're hungry!"

Just then, the largest of the canines leapt with all his might, coming within half a meter of the Nebador citizens, then falling onto a smaller boulder below and yelping in pain.

"Sssorry, but we didn't *asssk* you to do that!" the snake hissed, glaring down at the coyote.

"My compliments on your choice of boulders, bok!  It looks like we will be safe!"

"I just wish we could hear ourselves think!" Rini shared with frustration. "It's always easy to find a quiet place on the star station!"

"I have a hunch about that!  More latransss are arriving.  Let'sss sssee what happensss!"

During the next few minutes, the number of coyotes around the boulder more than doubled.  At first the noise was deafening, but it soon fragmented into several fights that didn't leave the canines time to yap and howl.

The three on the boulder watched with a mixture of relief and sadness.

A quarter hour later, two coyote were dead, six or seven limped away with severe wounds, and the remaining few acted much less confident in their reduced numbers.  They continued to prowl the evening near-darkness, or tear at the ones who had fallen, but seemed to lack the will to continue the assault on the boulder fortress.

"Welcome to the wilderness, bok."

"Sad that it took a war to get them to relax.  I'm not happy about it, but glad *we* didn't start it."

"Ssso . . . now that the noissse isss much lesss, what were you sssaying about wildernesss, my dear feathered friend?"

"From what I have read, bok, this continent is where anyone can go . . . or is sent . . . who can't live in peace with others — young people who need to test themselves against nature, criminals, and anyone who wants a very simple life."

Rini chuckled.  "The young people *choose* to come here, and the criminals get *sent*, I imagine."

The bird nodded.

"I remember the approach controller sssaying no groupsss larger than twelve."

"That's so no one starts kingdoms, nations, guilds, corporations, or empires, bok.  That's when things get too complicated for some people."

"But the other continents are different, right?" Rini asked.

"Yesss.  One continent allowsss tribesss of up to a hundred, so they're huntersss and gardenersss.   Another hasss communitiesss of up to a thousand, mossstly farmersss and craftersss."

The discussion was interrupted by three or four canines fighting in the darkness below.

"But ... what if ..." Rini began thoughtfully when the desert again became quiet, "... you're on one continent, and decide you are ready for a change?  In either direction?"

"Bok, there are Consulate Offices sprinkled all over each continent where people can go to ask for a new home.  They'll talk to you, give you tests, show you videos, anything else to help you find the right level of civilization where you can be happy."

Rini smiled, glad places existed where people didn't enslave and abuse each other, like happened so often on a certain planet he knew well.

✳ ✳ ✳

## Chapter 60: Civilization

The next morning, Boro and the spear fisherman sat around a cheery blaze just above the high-tide line, turning shellfish at the edge of the fire until they were cooked just right.  They had not been able to speak a word to each other, except for their names and a few nouns for objects close at hand, but they felt like old friends.

Dolphins, seals, manatees, and giant sea turtles played in the lagoon, occasionally tossing a shell onto the beach for the monkey mammals to consider.

About mid-morning, a golden sphere settled onto the water of the lagoon, the hatch opened, and Ashley looked out.  "Ready to tear yourselves away from this paradise?"

Trekila and Memsala shared farewell touches or squeaks with the friends they had made, then slipped into the clear tunnel just inside the partly-submerged hatch.

Boro shared a strong hand-clasp with the spear fisherman.  "Good fishing to you!"

"Blor-shesh tim'ta!"

Boro nodded and smiled, then waded into the water to swim out to his deep-space response ship.

*

Mati sat proudly atop Malika-Terno, her knees bent, ready to become the hair on his back if he broke into a run.

The golden ship extended landing struts and touched down on the ridge between that hilltop and the next.

Malika-Terno called an ear-piercing farewell, and the stallion echoed.  The five mares added their own words that Mati did not understand, but she imagined they were saying *thank you for the brushing*.  She waved to them.

Without a word from the horse, or a pause in his motion, Mati slipped off

Malika-Terno's back as he approached the ship, knowing horse or rider would fit through the hatch, but not both at once.

*

Ss'klexna Rrr'tak'fi and Sata crouched side by side on a cold mountain boulder surrounded by snow, both ursine and monkey-mammal noses thrust out to catch any interesting scent on the crisp air.

Mati, back at the helm, brought the hatch right to them.  Ilika, at the steward's console, lowered the ship's air temperature so the new arrivals wouldn't faint.

*

Kibi was deeply torn.

A part of her was tempted to be very assertive, almost forceful, with eight-year-old Triss about returning with them to the star station to look for her parents.

Another part of her was ashamed of that temptation as she remembered her own slavery, and wondered why she would contemplate forcing *anyone*, to do *anything*, who was completely happy with their environment and their current companion.

Then she realized the problem.  Triss had what Kibi couldn't have.  Kibi was jealous.

Nearby, finishing his breakfast of raw snake, Toran Takil made eye contact with her.  "I sense your inner conflict."

Kibi blushed, and hoped he only sensed the part about Triss.  "I know I have to respect her choice."

"Yes, you do.  There are many planets where people are *not* allowed to choose their paths, even when they are ready.  Those peoples have not mastered the craving for power, and they play out that craving in all aspects of life.  Those are *not* civilizations.  You were born on one of those planets, I believe."

Kibi took a deep breath and nodded just as Triss and Bad Kitty returned from their own short hunting trip.  The huge tiger carried a bird in his mouth.  Triss handed Kibi a piece of ripe fruit.

Kibi was just a few bites into her delicious breakfast when the Manessa Kwi began to slowly descend from the jungle canopy high above.

"Our ship," Kibi said with a sad voice.

Triss wrapped her arms around the conflicted Nebador citizen.  "Triss remember Kibi, ask for you when I get to star station . . . someday . . . when I all grown up."

The ship arrived beside them, the hatch opened, and Ashley looked out.

Bad Kitty growled a warning.

Triss scratched him behind the ears.  "He protect me, always."

Toran Takil leapt into the ship.

With tears in her eyes, Kibi hugged Triss once more, then jumped across the meter of space that separated the jungle from her deep-space response ship.

✳

The Manessa Kwi made quick work of the journey over the mountains to the desert.

Ilika, at the watch station, wondered why the three tracer symbols were so close together on his screen, almost on top of each other, then quickly saw the reason.

As the ship approached, the sun finally rose over the mountains to illuminate the boulder where Rini, Kolarrr'ka, and T'sss'lisss snuggled close together, staying just out of reach of the three or four coyotes who still had hopes of a feast of bird, snake, and if they were very lucky, monkey mammal.

Mati smiled as she lowered the ship so they could step right into the hatch.

✳

Ilika took the helm and piloted the ship to Satamia City very slowly so his crew and passengers could get baths and clean clothes.

The capital of Satamia Two was almost impossible to see from the air, nestled under towering trees of many kinds in the planet's temperate zone — not too hot, cold, wet, or dry.

The port controller directed them to a grassy field where a small Nebador cargo ship was unloading pallets from another planet, and preparing to take on pallets of local forest products.

Most of the contact specialists dashed away to visit old friends or enjoy their favorite parts of the city. Trekila Spimalo and Memsala wished the others a good visit, but both planned to catch up on some reading, instead of braving the nearby fresh-water river that would give them rashes and chaffing for weeks.

Ashley knew this was the first opportunity for her monkey-mammal friends, other than Ilika, to see a true civilization. She thought it would be very good for them, before arriving at their mission on Ko-tera Three, to glimpse the lives of people who had successfully solved the huge challenges that all sapient races eventually faced.

A tall reptile, who knew both languages, greeted them and identified himself as their guide.

✳

The crew's first stop appeared to be a lush botanical garden. The caretaker, a fanator, showed the visitors some of the many things that arrived in wheel barrows, jugs, or tanks, from caustic chemical reagents to waste cooking oil, none of which could be returned to the environment directly.

They walked through a building where scholars dug through reference books, searched databases, or ran simulations on computers. The guide explained what each person was doing.

Finally they explored the gardens themselves where countless plants, and some simple animals, went through their life cycles, and in the process changed many pollutants into things that could eventually be returned to the natural world.

At one point on the tour, Mati commented that the fruit on a certain tree looked delicious.

The guide, translating for the fanator, informed her that the fruit was full of a poisonous metal, and it would be composted and sent through several more biological processes before it was safe.

✳

After a snack of fruits and vegetables from a regular garden, the crew visited a grove of trees where small groups of students were studying different subjects.

Several young equines and an ursine listened to an older horse.  The guide translated part of the lesson for the visitors, and they smiled, recognizing the quantitative logic they had learned in the mountains of their home planet.

In another part of the grove, avians and a pair of young monkey mammals were learning to read under the patient direction of a bright-eyed bird. Although the visitors did not know the language, they could tell the students were being sorely challenged.

"Does everyone have to learn to read?" Rini asked.

"No," their reptilian guide answered, "that's not possible.  This is a general society where we have to accommodate everyone, unlike Satamia Star Station where the citizens are highly selected.  But on *this* continent, basic reading is required because we all have to use technology.  The class you just observed is the lowest level, those who are barely going to qualify after lots of hard work.  But they are all motivated, as they've already lived in a simpler society on another continent, and know they're not happy there."

Boro used to think he was a slow reader.  Then he remembered that he had learned to read and write one language in half a year, and speak, read, and write another the following year.  Suddenly, he didn't feel so slow.

Soon all the study groups took a break and everyone lined up at a serving table laden with a variety of foods.  After taking some fish and fruit, the two young monkey mammals timidly approached the group of visitors.  The reptilian guide smiled, knowing how rare sapient monkey mammals were in the universe.

"Are you brother and sister?" Sata asked.

The guide curled his mouth with humor before translating.

The young pair burst out laughing and cringed at the same time.  The girl said something in her native language.

"She said, 'You mean extras?  No way!  Our parents weren't over-breeders! They wanted us to have a chance to learn things and apply to live on other continents.'"

Sata considered this as she ate her fish.  "What would have happened if they *were* brother and sister?"

The guide cleared his throat.  "They probably would have to take their chances on the *wilderness* continent where life is very hard.  And their over-breeding parents too, of course.  No creature, unless highly selected and trained like Nebador citizens, can resist the temptation to over-breed without strong motivations."

"So ... people here can only have one child?" Mati asked with a barely-hidden frown.

"Right. That leaves room for a few of those who survive the wilderness continent, and a few immigrants. We don't mess around with that issue. This planet can only support about two billion large animals, and the wild creatures get half of that. We will *not* go back to the times when *millions* died of starvation every year just so a few could enjoy the luxury of having all the babies they wanted."

✳

Mid-afternoon was passing when the reptilian guide led the visitors into an area of the city partly indoors and partly out. The outdoor area immediately fascinated the monkey-mammal crew as several people were pedaling what looked like small mechanical horses. Even one equine was doing it, his machine much larger.

Mati squinted, noticing that as hard as they pedaled, they didn't move a centimeter. "What are they doing?"

The guide smiled with pride. "They're helping to charge the city's electrical batteries. Night is approaching."

"Are they slaves?" Boro asked with a frown.

"No! Mostly they're folks who just finished a work shift at an easy job and want some exercise. The bird over there is in physical therapy to heal an injury, which is why she's pedaling very slowly. The equine is working out his frustrations after his mate got sent to the wilderness. He might go too, but hasn't decided yet."

Boro nodded his satisfaction over the slavery issue, and they wandered into a building. Several technicians, mostly avians but also a pair of nimble-handed monkeys, sat at work benches making or repairing solar panels.

"We don't use as many of these as some cities," the guide explained, "as we live in the forest and don't want to steal the light from our precious trees, but we stick a few in each clearing. Some cities make electricity from falling water, but we don't have any nearby."

Ashley got a gleam in her eyes. "The planet we're going to makes electricity by burning things."

"Oh my god, *what?*" the reptile asked with wide eyes.

"Coal, oil, Methane gas, wood, anything else they can get their hands on," the education specialist answered with a straight face.

"I bet they're headed for a crash!" the guide speculated. "Of course ... it's none of my business ... but I image that's why you're going ..."

Ashley just smiled as the crew of the Manessa Kwi listened with keen interest.

✳

When evening mealtime approached, Ashley and the crew were led to a large outdoor space with many long tables beneath protective tree boughs. At first, no one else was there, so they wandered around.

"I don't see any . . . food," Boro began with hesitation. "Should we . . . go find our own in the forest?"

The guide shook his head, and wore a slight smile, but said nothing.

Kibi found a mushroom on the forest floor that *resembled* an edible species on Sonmatia Three, but quickly decided that wasn't enough with mushrooms. Rini found some berries that were a bit dry, but would keep a starving person alive.

Soon people started arriving, mostly avians and equines, but also a sprinkling of most other Satamia sapient peoples. Each carried a platter, pitcher, or bowl, with the horses lugging the biggest, brimming with fresh vegetables or fruits, sometimes both.

Twenty, thirty, forty of them set their serving dishes on the long table. The five crew members, who had never before visited a civilized planet, looked on with delight at the bounty and variety.

Soon the number of other dinner guests, and serving dishes, passed a hundred, and more were coming into the outdoor banquet hall from every direction.

*What do you think?* Mati wondered for only Rini to hear. *Two hundred?*
*Yes, and heading for three!*

Their guide finally spoke. "It's not often we get to serve the gods this directly, so you would make the citizens of Satamia City most happy if you would take a tiny bit from each serving dish."

"But . . . we're not gods!" Boro asserted.

"No, of course not, but you walk and talk with them, and carry out their assignments. That makes it a great honor for us to eat with you. The crew of that little cargo ship at the port got the same treatment yesterday. Only a fraction of the citizens of the city will be here today, just a thousand I think, selected randomly."

Mati's eyes opened wide as she wondered how she could possibly eat something from a thousand different serving dishes.

*

Sata smiled to herself as she looked at the small worm on her spoon, knowing that without Drrrim-na and her other avian friends, she might have offended someone by avoiding it.

Boro stopped himself after forking *two* slices of raw fish from the same platter onto his plate, suddenly realizing how many serving dishes he still had to visit. He was happy to find several more platters of fish farther along the tables.

Mati was taken back to a tense moment in her early days on Satamia Star Station as she took a small frog's leg, dipping it in a savory sauce before putting it on her plate.

Rini delighted in all the leaves and stems in the big bowls brought by the equines, and discovered a tangy sauce that seemed to go well with all of them.

Kibi grinned when she found a fruit tray that reminded her of her meals with Toran Takil, Triss, and Bad Kitty.

Ilika managed to squeeze bits of nearly a hundred different foods onto his plate, then joined his crew wandering among those already seated until sparkling eyes invited them to eat with the most advanced citizens of the only true planetary civilization in a very large part of the local universe of Nebador.

✳ ✳ ✳

## Part 6: Ko-tera Three

## Chapter 61: Planetary Approach

Ilika knew that when he didn't say otherwise, and especially when the situation was colored by emotions, his crew always returned to their original stations.  On the flight to Ko-tera Three, he felt it too.

This was his crew's first mission observing, and possibly influencing, a world approaching a critical turning point.  On all their other missions to date, big decisions about the survival of the local people were already in the past, or far in the future.

Ko-tera Three was face to face with the knife-edge of a planetary crisis.  They had all the science necessary to understand the threat facing them.  They had enough time and resources to fix it.  They just hadn't yet decided whether or not they wanted to.

Ashley had trouble relaxing and clearing her mind for star transit, as she was painfully aware of all the situations that could get the mission team tangled up in the affairs of Ko-tera Three.  Eventually she settled into a meditative state and felt the star drive engage.

*

When they popped back into space and time, Mati sat at the helm blinking for a moment, trying to remember how she had gone from pulling a few weeds in her masters' gardens, to piloting a starship and assisting a contact specialist during the most important moment in a planet's entire history.  She shook her head slightly and reached for her display selector.

As Rini re-activated his sensors, he felt in his bones that the world they were rushing toward was going to need more from them than they realized, more than just a deep-space response ship witnessing events so that others could learn from them.

Boro, gazing at the tiny planet floating all alone in the star-studded blackness, took a deep breath to calm his stomach before warming up the engines he knew his pilot would need.  The sensation of being all alone suddenly made him shudder, and feel very glad that he, his friends, and even his backward little home planet, were being watched over by Melorania, Kerloran, and others.

Kolarrr'ka fluffed up his feathers as he gazed at the large display over the steward's station, feeling a tiny bit of the deep cold of space, even though the air temperature inside the Manessa Kwi had not changed at all.

Toran Takil smiled to himself, seeing the planet where the sacred trust he had been given would continue to play itself out, and, with a bit of luck, be completed.

As Ko-tera Three grew larger on the screen and the blue color of its oceans became visible, Trekila Spimalo let out a soft squeak of excitement from the open part of the tank.  She knew her contact assignment would be teaching her many new skills, building her confidence, and hopefully allowing her to go on other challenging missions in the future.

T'sss'lisss peered at the display, glimpsed the yellow of desert sands on two or three continents, and reminded herself that the next time she was surrounded by hungry canines, Rini might not be there to lift her up to the safety of a large boulder.

As they rushed closer and closer to the little planet, Malika-Terno began to see the shades of green that meant grasslands and temperate forests — the homes of most equines.  He swallowed, knowing well the deep fears that often caused his fellows to be stubborn and inflexible, sometimes to their deaths.

Sata found all the necessary charts with her hands, but her mind was struggling to understand how the universe could be thought of as *friendly*, even *loving*, when the survival of an entire race hinged on the decisions those monkey mammals made in the very near future.  She knew they *had* to make those decisions, or they would just continue to avoid them and never grow up, but it still felt a little unfair.  "Chart to our base of operations is on channel five, a tiny tropical island far from anything."

Ss'klexna Rrr'tak'fi glanced up when Kibi switched to the chart view.  She looked forward to breathing salty air and loping along the beach before preparing for her contact mission that she had a hunch was going to require everything she could give . . . and perhaps a little more.

"Prepare to de-orbit," Kibi heard Ilika say, and switched the large screen to the forward visual, knowing most Nebador citizens enjoyed watching the ground rush toward them.  She had learned to tolerate the falling, crashing, about-to-die sensation, but would never love it.  What she couldn't avoid, by not looking, was the mixture of excitement and dread, deep inside herself, when she imagined being alone with Toran Takil again.

After the rapid descent under ion drive, the ocean and small tropical island froze on the display screen a thousand meters beneath the ship.  The near-smile on Memsala's turtle face matched the deep calm she felt, knowing that she might live or die on this mission, and the monkey mammals of

Ko-tera Three might fix their reproductive, political, and ecological problems, or they might not, and in either case the universe would continue to unfold as it should.

*   *   *

## Chapter 62: Feline

The jungle that Toran Takil and Kibi traversed was very different from the one on Satamia Two. The plants and animals were similar enough, but it was scarred and fouled everywhere with dirt roads, rusty fences, electric wires stretched from pole to pole, and oil wells that leaked onto the ground almost as much as they pumped into barrels.

Kibi held a strand of barbed wire so Toran could belly-crawl underneath. "Do the nearly-sapient cats actually *live* near this . . . ugly stuff?"

"No, but I wanted you to see what they have to deal with. We'll be in their territory soon, but they must pass through areas like this to interact with other groups, to migrate during extreme weather, and sometimes just to find mates."

Kibi blushed, and hoped Toran didn't see.

At every fence, road, or pipeline, the large cat looked around carefully, sometimes climbing a tree, before prompting Kibi to cross. Several times she stayed hidden behind large green leaves as smelly vehicles roared by on dusty roads, with Toran Takil beside her or on a tree limb above.

Eventually they seemed to leave all the ugliness behind as they continued deeper into the jungle.

Kibi froze when she heard the first growl.

Toran responded with a throaty rumble, then said, "No need to freeze. I've taught you what that growl means."

"Yeah, you're right. There are some growls that *should* make me freeze, but that one just means *identify yourself.*" *Or be eaten*, Kibi thought silently.

"Yes, *or be eaten*, but freezing is still the worst thing you could do."

Kibi smiled, remembering the ability of all the big cats to easily read her body language, if not her mind.

"We are about to be visited," he began. "If you were alone, you should remain standing and act assertive. But in this case, you must appear to be my inferior, so go down to your knees and stay behind me."

*I AM your inferior*, Kibi thought. *You're the contact specialist. I'm just the helper.*

Toran continued to slowly move forward, first along a faint dirt path, then across a large fallen log. Kibi crawled, not wanting to be caught looking too large at the wrong moment.

The contact came unexpectedly, with Toran suddenly face to face with another huge male tiger. Kibi stayed as low and inferior-looking as she could, her two dark eyes peering forward, past Toran's shoulder, from under her shaggy black hair.

Several growls were exchanged by the two felines, and some swats, but no blood was drawn. After a long minute of exchanges that were just ritual introductions, Kibi guessed, the two tigers sat down facing each other for nearly a quarter hour of soft rumbling and snarling.

Kibi thought back to the mission briefing. The large felines on Ko-tera Three were believed to be pre-sapient, and yet she was witnessing a civilized conversation between a Nebador citizen and one of them. At a pause in the exchange, she whispered, "He seems sapient."

"He's right on the edge," Toran responded without turning to her. "Simple language often arises before sapience. But remember, it's a long way from here to ... civilization. Bad Kitty is making that journey quickly because of his relationship with Triss, and it wouldn't surprise me if they stepped together into a Consulate Office, in the near future, asking to move to a different continent."

"You mean ... she's helping him become sapient?"

The native tiger said something in the primitive feline language, so Toran continued the conversation for a few minutes.

Kibi suddenly realized that the big cat facing them was looking at *her*, almost as much as at Toran.

Eventually Toran answered Kibi's question. "A close relationship is *the* fastest way for a creature to make the mental leap into sapience. The opportunity to guide another on that path is considered a sacred task in every true civilization, a task that should never be turned down, if placed in your hands by the powers of the universe, without very good reasons. And by the way, he's a lone male, and he admires you."

Kibi swallowed. With Toran Takil, although she was sorely tempted, she knew that *he* would never break his vows with Silmula Sorafax.

This was different. The decision that had suddenly been thrust onto Kibi would be hers alone to make. She looked over Toran's shoulder, and found the native tiger looking back at her. Their eyes stayed locked for a long moment.

After a while, the lone male tiger growled something soft, almost musical, that Kibi couldn't translate, and laid down on his belly in front of Toran Takil.

"He is asking me for you," Toran revealed. "I've already told him that you are just my servant for this journey, nothing more. You can have what Triss has — the sacred task of guiding a fellow creature into sapience, not to mention the love and protection of a powerful male animal — if you really want it."

A moment later, Toran Takil made a soft rumbling sound and rolled onto his side. He was no longer in a position of authority, and no longer in between the native tiger and Kibi.

Kibi's mind raced as she continued to look into the tiger's beautiful eyes. Thoughts about possible compromises came to her, ways she could be with this powerful creature and Ilika too.

Then she stopped herself. She was a Nebador citizen on Satamia Star Station, the steward of a deep-space response ship. That was a full-time job if any job ever was.

"I can't be a part-time Nebador citizen, can I, Toran?"

"No."

"And . . . this couldn't be part-time either, could it?"

"No one can half-heartedly do anything that's important to the universe."

Kibi continued to look at the beautiful tiger before her, sometimes gazing into his mysterious eyes, sometimes admiring his sleek stripes. After a few minutes, something Toran said began to echo in her mind.

*. . . a task that should never be turned down, if placed in your hands by the powers of the universe, without very good reasons . . .*

"Toran, when I became Ilika's lover, that was a sacred task too, wasn't it? That was placed in my hands by the powers of the universe too, wasn't it?"

"Yes, to both questions. And yet, not all relationships are happy enough to continue when . . . another option comes along."

"But . . . I *am* happy with Ilika. I just . . . want them both."

Toran Takil remained silent.

The native tiger continued to look at Kibi with his intense male eyes.

After a long silence, Toran said, "If you decide to refuse his offer, it would be safest if I tell him."

Kibi suddenly knew what she had to do. "No. I have to do it. I have to tell him the truth and . . . live with what he decides to do."

"There might be blood . . ."

"I know. You'll translate for me?"

"I'll do my best, but I must put everything into very basic terms, so keep your ideas as simple as possible."

Kibi nodded and began crawling forward until she was right in front of the huge native tiger. He sat up, and Kibi did the same so their heads were at about the same height.

"I have already given myself to another," Kibi began with her heart in her throat.

Toran rumbled a translation.

Kibi could see the expression on the big cat's face change. She immediately felt the cold tingle of mortal fear throughout her body, but somehow forced herself to go on. "But I am powerfully drawn to you . . . and tempted to be yours."

Again Toran translated.

The expression on the tiger's face softened slightly.

"I will accept your decision."

Toran rumbled briefly, then fell silent.

Suddenly a powerful paw slapped Kibi so hard she fell over sideways.  The stinging sensation on her face made her want to scream, but she managed to hold it in.  Through tears of pain, she saw the native tiger turn and walk away into the jungle.

✳

Toran Takil sat up and kept his eyes on both the jungle around them, and Kibi, as she slowly picked herself up.  Eventually she was sitting again, but crying silently and cringing in pain.

"Feels like he nearly tore my face off," she muttered through tears.

"I just see four shallow cuts that won't bleed much," Toran reported.

"It would have been *nice* if he'd kept his claws retracted."

"They *were*.  That was little more than a gentle, playful, pat.  If his claws had *not* been, you would be without much of a face, and we would be back on the Manessa Kwi trying desperately to stop the bleeding."

Kibi swallowed and nodded.

Toran remained silent as he scanned the jungle around them for any dangers.

"What was my mistake?" Kibi finally asked through her shame and pain.

"You tried to walk the fence, not decide, not jump onto one path or the other with your whole heart.  You will have scars to remind you of that lesson."

Kibi sighed.

"Shall we go find some more felines to talk to?  I want to get at least five reactions to the ideas I'm presenting."

Kibi cringed, and remained silent for a long moment.  "Sure."

✳   ✳   ✳

## Chapter 63: Equine

Mati felt frustrated, but knew it was a small fraction of what Malika-Terno was feeling. Something was wrong, very wrong, but the huge horse would not yet talk about it. Mati got the impression that he hoped their next stop would have a different result.

The problem was, he had been hoping that for the last seven or eight stops. They were at the fourth location on the third continent, keeping the Manessa Kwi busy any time it wasn't transporting another contact specialist. Three times Ashley had been about to harvest some strange fruit on their uninhabited tropical island, when Ilika had called her back to the ship to pick up Malika-Terno and Mati, and take them to yet another grassland, woodland, or high-desert prairie.

All Malika-Terno would say was that the continents had been sliced up into thousands of little pieces with equine-proof fences. The native horses, both wild and captive, could still communicate across vast distances by relaying messages, but that took time. It would work for whatever Malika-Terno wanted to tell *them*, but not for getting their answers within the timeframe of the mission.

So he kept asking the Manessa Kwi to move them a thousand or so kilometers, or across a body of water that horses, on their own, could not cross, and he grew more and more frustrated.

*

Night was falling as they huddled in a ditch not far from a road with roaring, smoking machines going in both directions. Mati worked her way to the bottom of a food packet she had grabbed on their last flight, and Malika-Terno chewed on the grasses around them.

"If you're not going to let me help you, then why are you dragging me along?" Mati finally asked in the darkness after finishing her dinner.

Malika-Terno didn't say anything, but his labored breathing told Mati he was still stewing.

"I need an answer," she pressed.

He snorted, then hung his head in the darkness.  "It's because … I'm embarrassed."

"Why, Malika-Terno?  *You* are not responsible, in any way, for the equines of Ko-tera Three!  You're a Nebador citizen, more highly-trained and experienced than I will *ever* be.  You can't blame yourself if they're stuck in some rut, and too stupid to get out, even when their planet is in danger!"

Mati figured she had said enough, so she fell silent and just stroked the big horse's mane.

After a few minutes, he made a sound deep in his throat that could only be some kind of laughter.

"What?" she asked softly.

"It's … a little different than that.  I am embarrassed because … I am ashamed.  The equines of Ko-tera Three — every one of them, as far as I can tell — are proving to be far nobler than I.  They are choosing to stay with the dominant monkey mammals, even if those same monkey mammals are destroying the planet … or at least … all sapient life on it …"

✳

After Malika-Terno poured out his shame and frustration to Mati, they finally got some sleep.  When morning light crept into the sky, they made their way out of the ditch, dealt with a couple of low fences, and put some distance between themselves and the noisy road.  After finding a secluded field, he grazed while she picked apples from an abandoned orchard.  As the sun climbed above the trees and began to warm them, they settled down in the grass to eat fruit together.

"Last night," Mati began, "you said the local equines were being noble. Okay, that's one way of looking at it.  Another is that they're not as sapient as you think.  There comes a time to let go of *anything*, seems to me.  I had to let go of my home planet to get my knee fixed and become a pilot and engineer.  I could have held onto it and been a … goatherd's wife.  If those equines can't let go of something that's dying … a planet … a relationship … maybe they aren't smart enough to be *worth* saving.  I don't really know, and I don't have the wisdom — or the right — to judge.  It's just a thought."

Malika-Terno was silent, except for the crunching of the apple in his mouth.  Eventually he swallowed it.  "They think … and I agree … that the monkey mammals of Ko-tera Three will need them before … the end."

"You mean, want to use and abuse them because they won't be able to keep their machines running after the climate gets weird?"

The horse curled his lips.  "Yeah, something like that."

"Really, really poor excuse for staying in slavery when they have a way out."

Malika-Terno hung his head.  "I know."

✳

The contact specialist and his monkey-mammal assistant put many kilometers behind them that day, spoke to native equines in five captive situations, and came upon one pair of wild horses, quietly living in an undeveloped area between two small cities.

They all told Malika-Terno the same story. They would stay, and live or die with their planet.

Mati tried yelling at them once, and the horse beside her translated. She couldn't tell if the three horses on the other side of the fence were angry, or were laughing their heads off at her. Malika-Terno later told her it was a bit of both.

✳

As evening approached, Mati stated the obvious. "You have received many opinions on the question of evacuation, Malika-Terno, in about twenty places on three continents, and they've all been the same. Do you have any hope that gathering a few more opinions will change anything?"

He stood silently, scanning the horizon that included a tangled interchange of roads and fences with roaring cars and trucks going every which way. To continue their journey, without another transfer by ship, they'd have to somehow get through that mess.

"Now I think I see why — at least in my case — I was assigned a helper. Because the equines of this planet are my species, I'm too close to them to think clearly all the time. Thank you, wise monkey mammal."

"You're welcome, wise equine."

"The answer to your question is *no*. Let's rejoin our friends on the ship."

"Agreed."

The horse lifted his left front leg and touched the wide mission bracelet with his muzzle. "Manessa Kwi, we are ready for pick-up."

✳ ✳ ✳

## Chapter 64: Reptile

Rini quickly discovered what his main contribution to T'sss'lisss' assignment would be.  The desert around them was very flat, with the only tall plants too slender and spiny for even a snake to climb.  Any time the reptilian contact specialist wanted to see far, she asked Rini to stand still with his arms over his head.  She slithered up his body, wrapped her tail firmly — but not too firmly — around his neck, placed her middle in his elevated hands, and stretched herself another meter straight up into the air.  From that vantage point, nearly three meters up, she turned her head slowly, scanning the wide desert.

They slithered and walked for hours, occasionally pausing to look at animal tracks, examine a rusting piece of old mining equipment, or scan the distance.  The sun slowly passed its high point and began to creep toward the western horizon.

As the full heat of afternoon came and went, T'sss'lisss became interested in some low barren hills to the north.  Signs and traces left by large reptiles were getting more frequent as they went that way, she explained.

Rini trusted her completely.  He had no idea how to find what they were looking for.

✳

T'sss'lisss writhed with excitement when they got close enough to the hills to see, from her perch atop Rini, holes in the eroded sides of a dry wash, twenty or thirty of them, all arranged in a very regular pattern.

After the contact specialist slithered down, Rini shaded his eyes and scanned in all directions.  "No roads or other monkey-mammal signs."

"I didn't see any either.  Let's go closer."

They covered most of the distance on the upper rim of the dry wash, but as they came near the hills, boulders and spiny cactus plants forced them into the wash itself.

Rini felt a little nervous about the situation, but T'sss'lisss slithered ahead like she was going to a party, so he ignored his discomfort.  The going would have been much harder in the boulders and cacti, he admitted to himself.

"Oh, yesss.  Sssee how regular and organizzzed thossse holesss are?  Sssomeone here isss getting near sssapienccce, ssseemsss to me."

"Okay . . . but who?"

T'sss'lisss didn't seem to hear Rini's question, and was already moving forward at a good pace.

✳

A quarter hour later, the little caves high up on both sides of the dry wash — forty, fifty, maybe a hundred in all — towered over the pair of visitors.  Completely regular in their arrangement, the holes only broke the pattern when forced by a large rock imbedded in the dirt.

Rini was sweating, even though the evening had become pleasantly cool.

T'sss'lisss hissed a greeting in the most basic, universal reptilian language.

The regular caves on the sides of the wash remained silent, but a scaly head emerged from a random hole lower down.  It looked at the approaching pair for a moment, then disappeared back out of sight.

Rini caught a glimpse of wild, hungry eyes just before the scaly head vanished.

T'sss'lisss called a greeting again.

"I don't think ..." Rini began, but his thought was cut off as heads emerged from several holes near the floor of the wash.  Thick snake bodies followed and began slithering across the sand toward the two visitors.

T'sss'lisss called one more time, but was becoming worried.  She wasn't getting any response from the native reptiles, other than their rapid approach from all directions with the lust of the hunt in their eyes.

"I think we found the wrong ..." was all T'sss'lisss was able to say before the first snake struck at her, grabbing her tail in its mouth and quickly wrapping coils tightly around her lower body.

Another lunged at her middle, missed, but quickly found her neck and a second later was squeezing the life out of her.

Rini dove into the fray to help T'sss'lisss, but quickly realized his mistake as a powerful snake wrapped itself around his neck.  He tore at it, but his slender hands were no match for its wiry strength.

✳

Manessa knew the moment T'sss'lisss and Rini lost consciousness, and sounded an alarm.

Ilika wasted no time checking the landing site or waiting for engines to warm up.  Ashley, busy in the galley cutting clusters of fruit into manageable chunks, was amazed at how few seconds passed between the alarm and the ship streaking away from the island at ion three.  Although she didn't realize it until they returned, several trees were uprooted by the sudden departure.

Ilika focused his mind on covering nearly two thousand kilometers in the shortest time possible.

*

Snake blood was everywhere.

But it wasn't hers, T'sss'lisss slowly realized as she struggled to breathe. Her entire body felt bruised, maybe broken in some places, and her breath was still coming in labored gasps. Every bit of air she could suck into her lungs was a precious gift, after being without any for . . . she had no idea how long, but it must have been just a few minutes, for she felt alive, if in terrible pain.

Eventually she remembered Rini, and tried to turn her head to look for him, but her neck wouldn't go that way and screamed at her with more pain.

She relaxed and the screaming pain passed, leaving only the terrible pain in the rest of her body. After a few breaths, she tried turning her head the other direction.

That worked better, and she glimpsed Rini lying on his back. Bite marks on his arms and face still oozed blood, but his chest was rising and falling.

Then T'sss'lisss began to see something else. On the rim of the wash, or poking their heads out of the regular holes, reptile faces peered down at them. But, she slowly realized as she struggled to focus, they weren't snake faces. They were something else. Front feet began to appear beside the faces. Eyes swiveled in a way that snake eyes could not. Those eyes held a gleam of something T'sss'lisss had been looking for — sapience.

And she began to understand where all the snake blood was from.

*

Less than a minute after T'sss'lisss regained consciousness, the Manessa Kwi swooped down, the hatch flew open, and both Ilika and Ashley jumped out, mission bracelets ready to deal with anything and everything.

The lizards backed into their holes.

The new arrivals quickly took in the dead or dying snakes, sometimes in several pieces, that littered the floor of the wash. They spotted their friends, and Ilika went to Rini while Ashley knelt beside T'sss'lisss.

"Don't try to move me yet!" T'sss'lisss hissed, even though the effort caused her more pain. "Rini may alssso have broken bonesss!"

Ashley, fighting back tears, nodded and relayed the warning to Ilika.

"But our misssion was a successs, even more than I had hoped!" T'sss'lisss went on. "I believe we may have found sssapient reptilesss!"

Ashley looked around at the dead and dying snakes, and frowned.

"No, not thossse!"

*　*　*

## Chapter 65: Cetacean

Boro followed Trekila Spimalo into the warm tropical ocean not far from a fairly-large island.  From the air, they had already seen the small monkey-mammal city on one end of the island, but only occasional developments along the shore at the other end where the island thrust into the open ocean.

Trekila began calling every time she dove under the water, and within an hour, dozens of seals, several dolphins, four manatees, two small whales, and one large whale had all visited.  The contact specialist spoke to each for a few minutes, then the native cetacean departed.

Boro just floated nearby, with his buoyancy belt set to maximum, trying to look as unimportant as possible.  Even so, he knew that each visitor eyed him cautiously until Trekila spoke to them, explaining who they were and where they were from.

As the sun found the western horizon, contact specialist and engineer parted, one aiming for a small, hidden lagoon, the other for something on the shore that Ashley had called a *hotel* when she pointed it out from the air.

*

As the twilight faded on that warm tropical evening, a young man walked out of the ocean wearing nothing but shorts, a strange belt, and an unusual diving mask.  He pulled off the mask, scanned the dozen or so little buildings at the top of the beach, and walked toward the one with a flashing sign he couldn't read.

When he stepped inside, a much older man in some kind of uniform looked at him with a frown and spoke words that meant nothing to the young man from the sea.

The young man pulled a folded piece of paper from a small pouch on his belt, unfolded it, and laid it on the counter for the older man to see.

The older man, still frowning, turned it around and began to read it.

The young man then pulled a smaller piece of paper from his pouch, printed in many colors with a picture of an old bearded monkey mammal in the center, and a symbol in all four corners.  This piece of paper he also placed on the counter.

The older man smiled, rang a bell, and another man in a similar uniform came in quickly.

✳

Boro had been hoping for a cot and a bowl of stew.

Instead, he was shown to his own building with sleeping room, sitting room, kitchen, toilet room with bath, deck that overlooked the beach, and refrigerator and cupboards brimming with food.

Boro couldn't think of any use for most of the luxuries around him, especially since he wouldn't be here during the daylight hours, but he ate a hearty meal, relaxed onto the soft bed, and was instantly asleep.

✳

For the next two days, Boro slipped out of his room at dawn, waded into the warm ocean, and was not seen again on land for the rest of the day.

Trekila Spimalo continued to call, cetaceans of all sizes came, she spoke to them, and they raced off in every direction.  Boro floated near, or leisurely played in the water, accepting that he couldn't help at this point in the process, but determined to be there if he was needed.

As darkness fell each day, he walked out of the ocean to find his room with fresh towels, restocked refrigerator and cupboards, and bed carefully turned back, ready for him to crawl in.

✳

On the fourth day, Trekila and Boro lounged about in the warm water a few kilometers off shore, but the dolphin no longer called.  She explained that the earlier visitors were spreading the word to every corner of the planet, but had to swim out to the stretches of ocean not used by monkey-mammal ships, whose noisy engines made long-distance communication impossible.

For the first time, Boro succeeded in cleaning and eating a fish, caught for him by Trekila, while floating on his back.

The first cetacean to return, a large and powerful male dolphin, arrived about mid-day.  He and Trekila chattered for several minutes, then he turned and departed, giving Boro a good splash with his tail.

Boro spat out a mouthful of seawater, then smiled.

"I recorded the original conversation," the contact specialist said once the male dolphin was out of sight, "and I want you to record my translation."

Boro tapped a code onto his bracelet.

"Tzil-p'zikia Pod, part of the K'rez'krilia Nation, would be delighted to get off this . . . how did he put it? . . . noisy, polluted, monkey-mammal infested rock . . . and he is quite sure the other pods will agree, but they are farther away and will probably respond later today or tomorrow."

Boro barely held in his amusement while Trekila finished the translation, then burst out laughing.

About mid-afternoon, several seals arrived.

They all barked at once, and Trekila had trouble making sense of their excited words. After convincing them to slow down, and listening to their entire message several times, she finally felt she had the gist of it.

"The Barna-palakta Confederation, which covers the entire east coast of the south-central continent, verifies that the monkey mammals of the planet have indeed made every harbor into a dead-zone with their spilled oil and trash. Also, putrid things no one can eat or drink come down all the rivers. They beg us to take them away *now*, and promise they won't be any trouble on the voyage. They'll even bring their own fish, if they can find any worth eating. I promised to ask the mission commander."

Boro sighed. "Ashley's not going to like making *that* decision."

"No one would."

Just as evening was approaching, and Boro was starting to wish for solid ground, a single manatee appeared. As all manatees, she spoke few words, but her somber message was clear when Trekila translated.

"The Mmm-somuna Nation awaits your decision, and will be ready to depart, if any of us are still alive at the end of the twelve-year grace period you intend to give the monkey mammals of this world . . ."

After a brisk walk on the beach in the twilight to clear his head, a hearty meal, and a sound sleep, Boro awoke refreshed and slipped into the ocean once more.

Trekila meet him in barely enough water to swim. "The whales are coming! We must hurry!"

Boro adjusted his buoyancy belt, made sure his breathing mask was fitted properly, and dove under the water where he could eat up several kilometers with his strong legs, side by side with the dolphin.

He first knew whales were near when a massive surge of water suddenly lifted him to the surface, then sent him sliding down a slippery gray back.

Trekila danced on her tail while laughing her head off.

Without a breathing mask and good swimming skills, Boro knew, that would have been a brush with death. But he soon caught a glimpse of a large eye looking back at him from just under the water, so he got over his momentary fright, waved and smiled.

The large eye slowly closed and opened again.

Five more medium-size whales wanted a turn at playing toss-the-monkey-mammal, and with each surge from beneath, behind, or to the side, Boro became more and more used to the game. The fact was, he *did* have a breathing mask, was a very good swimmer, and was in no danger. And besides, he couldn't really blame them for wanting to take a jab at the species that was currently threatening their planet.

After half an hour of play, all six whales settled down to business with

Trekila Spimalo, speaking to her in their slow voices that could be as high-pitched as a shrill bird one moment, as deep as a fog horn the next.

For two hours, the whales leisurely swam around each other, occasionally taking turns speaking, and whenever possible, giving Boro a tumble with a slow swish of their flukes.

Trekila mostly listened, sometimes said something, and recorded the entire meeting.

Mid-day was passing when the whales finally filtered away, one at a time, after parting words and touches with the contact specialist and her monkey-mammal assistant.

Silence lingered on the open ocean as Trekila just floated and breathed for a few minutes.  Boro did the same, knowing she would speak when she was ready.

"Please begin recording," she eventually said.

Boro tapped his bracelet and held it above the water.

"They told many stories, most of which I will not translate at this time. But a theme ran through their stories, which I think I can put into the language of Nebador."

Boro waited patiently.

"The sea can provide food, and absorb wastes, from those who live in it. The monkey mammals of this world do not live in it, yet they take from it all the food they want, and dump their wastes into it.  When they did that just a little, in past centuries, the sea could handle it.  Now, it is too much.  The sea cannot be pantry and toilet for land creatures.  They must get their food, and handle their wastes, on land, or the sea will die."

The silence returned as Trekila relaxed into a low, effortless float, with only her blow hole above water.

After a moment of sadness, Boro touched his bracelet and settled onto his back to look up at the blue sky.

*

The following day, dolphin and human waited for hours, knowing more reports were coming, but not sure when they would arrive.  The sun came out, forcing them to spend much of that time underwater.

Afternoon was sinking toward evening when Trekila became excited. Boro thought he heard — or perhaps just felt — a very low-pitched rumble under the water, but couldn't be sure.

An hour later, the sea around them seemed to erupt as a giant black whale, thirty or forty meters long, rose from the depths below, causing Trekila almost as much fright as Boro.  They both went tumbling to the sides, feet and fluke on top, heads below.

When both managed to surface and clear their mouth or blow hole, they saw the massive whale floating with his hump above water, but heard laughter from another source.  Looking around, they beheld a small female dolphin dancing on her tail not far away.

Trekila Spimalo called a greeting.

Boro waved.

Both the whale, with his ultra-deep voice, and the little dolphin, chattering like a monkey, responded with sounds of friendship.

For the next hour, Trekila listened to the whale, and the little dolphin remained respectfully silent.  Boro at first assumed the massive creature was speaking slowly, and saying little.  About half-way through the long conversation, he changed his mind, seeing how often Trekila's eyes, mouth, and flippers twitched as she listened.

Eventually the whale fell silent, and the little dolphin said something.

To Boro's surprise, Trekila immediately asked for Boro to provide an open channel to Ashley.

"Ashley here.  Ilika is also present."

"The great whales," Trekila began, "have gathered vast amounts of information on the status of the ocean ecosystems, and because of the reduced communication range — down to less than a thousand kilometers because of noisy ships — have entrusted it all to a pod of gifted students, one of whom, a small female dolphin, is here and is willing to go with us."

Ashley was silent for a moment.  "That would save lots of time.  Is she willing to submit herself to your guidance on the ship and star station?"

Trekila and the little dolphin chatted for a moment.

"Yes," the contact specialist replied.

"Okay.  Are you ready for pick-up?"

Trekila looked at Boro, and he nodded.

"We are ready, but no hurry."

"Probably within the hour.  Manessa Kwi closing," Ashley said.

Trekila returned to speaking in the cetacean language, and a few minutes later the giant whale rumbled something, then slowly submerged.

Both dolphins immediately began laughing hysterically.

"What?" Boro begged.

"He requested, if we see them, that we thank the monkey mammals of the planet for all the fish.  They were, until recently, quite tasty."

✳   ✳   ✳

## Chapter 66: Avian

Kolarrr'ka sat at Rini's bedside as the bitten and bruised lad carefully turned himself so he could see the avian education specialist.

"Bok," the bird said with sympathy.  "If I had been squeezed by wild snakes like you were, I think my gizzard would have popped out my toes, and that would have been the end of me!"

Rini chuckled, then regretted it as his lungs felt like they were grating against his ribs.  "Ouch.  I think my gizzard was about *half-way* to my toes when those sapient reptiles came to the rescue."

Kolarrr'ka nodded.  "T'sss'lisss is in Kibi's bed, she's about as sore as you, and won't be slithering anywhere for a few days.  I'm here to tell you that you *also* are not going anywhere.  To assist me on my mission, you'd have to climb trees and perch in them for hours at a time."

Rini moaned at the thought.

"Bok.  I'm going to take Ashley on one excursion, but work alone most of the time.  Get well, my friend."

"Actually, nothing's broken, it just *feels* like everything is."

"Bok."

*

Kolarrr'ka began by listening.

Luckily, he resembled a species of large bird that was known, by all other birds on Ko-tera Three, to be very easy-tempered, vegetarian, and non-territorial.  He planned to use that fact to his advantage.

He made himself comfortable in about a hundred different trees on four continents.  Sometimes his arrival scared away flocks of little nervous birds, but they would soon return and resume their chatter after realizing what kind of bird he appeared to be.

In other trees, large birds who could defend themselves stood their ground, but soon relaxed as Kolarrr'ka found an unused branch and settled in for an hour or two of listening.

For short transits, he flew, and each time he descended, he first scouted the area, taking in the sounds of the local avians and their profiles in flight, then selecting a tree with a different sort of bird than he had listened to previously.

For the trans-oceanic flights, even though he could make some of them if he had to, he called on the Manessa Kwi to save time, and to avoid a day or two of recovery upon arrival at the far shore.

Some of the birds, especially the smaller species, were clueless about the danger that currently walked upon the land.

Others, including many medium-size birds, were not concerned, as they had figured out how to live off the trash and pick over the vast fields of crops that the monkey mammals harvested with machines.

It was the larger birds, from Kolarrr'ka's size up to nearly-fanator size, who knew what was going on, and whose eggs were becoming more and more fragile because of the chemicals the monkey mammals sprayed all over their fields.  These were the birds that Kolarrr'ka knew he had to listen to the most, and try to determine if they might be ready, able, and willing to leave.

✳

At two remote locations where hundreds of flightless birds waddled from place to place, one on a rocky coast and the other on an icy shore, Ashley slowly walked about, with Kolarrr'ka at her side, no faster than the native birds could waddle.  She watched, he listened, and when no other birds were near, they discussed what they were learning.

The large birds in such remote places did not have strong feelings about the monkey mammals of the planet, but sensed that something was wrong with the world, and chatted about which way they should go to find better conditions.

What remained unclear to Kolarrr'ka and Ashley was whether they would be willing to get in a ship, even if completely crewed by avians, to take their chances somewhere totally unknown to them.

Kolarrr'ka was of the opinion that they might, once the changes to their environment were much more obvious, such as the water heating, the ice melting, and the fish dying.

Ashley wasn't so sure.

✳

When Kolarrr'ka was beginning to think that his survey mission was almost complete, he received a scare that nearly made him call for immediate pick-up.

He had returned to working alone, and had entered the jungle-covered tropics.  After a few hours of scouting, he knew where to find the large, intelligent birds who had the best chance of being near sapience.

But he quickly realized that something was different here.  The avians gathering in trees around him to talk were not local birds, but rather had flown in from two, possibly three different continents.

And they were angry.

He perched off to the side and remained as inconspicuous as possible. When most birds were listening to someone speak, he listened too. When the speaker caused an emotional reaction in the crowd, he fluttered his wings or squawked just enough to fit in with the mood of the gathering.

They were angry that smoking monkey-mammal machines had taken to the skies. They all knew someone who had been sliced to bits by one of those machines, or choked to death by the hot smoke that was nearly invisible.

They were bitter that the wires strung from pole to pole, that used to only tingle when landed upon, were now much more dangerous, and most birds who made that mistake did not survive.

The longer the meeting went on, the angrier the birds became, and Kolarrr'ka was hard pressed to continue to fit in. Sometimes they worked themselves into a frenzy, and began tearing out feathers from their own bodies, or each others'.

That's when Kolarrr'ka slipped away, found a quiet tree, activated his mission collar, and described to Ashley what he was seeing.

The mission leader asked many questions, and Kolarrr'ka tried to answer, but eventually she asked the one question he almost wished she wouldn't ask.

"If conditions continue to get worse, and they are offered relocation to a planet where no one is polluting or using dangerous machines, would they go?"

He had to think about it for another day as he continued to observe gatherings of angry birds, usually from the safety of a nearby tree with thick leaves.

Finally, with a deep sigh, he activated his mission collar and carefully worded his answer.

"No. They are not smart enough to direct their anger in the right direction, and so are engaging in many self-destructive behaviors. The flightless birds we observed are more even-tempered, and might be an exception . . ."

✳   ✳   ✳

## Chapter 67: Ursine

Ss'klexna Rrr'tak'fi and Sata walked on frozen soil and cold boulders deep in the last remaining wilderness on Ko-tera Three.  The bear was letting her nose guide her, Sata knew, and it wasn't toward the scent of water or fish.

Every quarter hour or so, the contact specialist stopped, breathed deeply for a minute, then poured out a roar that seemed to echo off the mountainsides.

At first Sata thought it was just a roar, perhaps a simple call of some kind.  But as the hours passed, and she started recognizing complex patterns in it, Sata realized it might be more like a sentence, maybe even a paragraph.

Eventually, Ss'klexna started to look tired and hungry, until they discovered a pond hopping with countless frogs.  The bear waded right in, and when her appetite was sated, the frog population was down to about half.

Sata had never before eaten a raw frog, but rose to the task, and felt stronger for it — especially after five of them.

✳

Two days later, answers to Ss'klexna's calls started to rumble through the rocky peaks and glacial valleys.  At first Sata thought they might just be echoes, but the timing was wrong.  They had to be other bears.

The great ursines of the wilderness — brown, black, and nearly white — watched the newcomers for two more days, letting themselves be glimpsed, but no more.  Sata ate fish, frogs, and berries whenever the pair found them, then slept close beside Ss'klexna Rrr'tak'fi for warmth.

Finally the local bears ceased hiding and stood proudly and sternly, watching the small bear and human from a distance even as they replied to Ss'klexna's roars.  Many were twice Sata's height when they stood up, some three times.  Their voices nearly shook the mountains.

As the hours of that day passed, Sata noticed several changes come over Ss'klexna.  The contact specialist slowly became afraid and defiant, then resigned and a little depressed, and finally, toward evening, calm and resolute.

That night, curled up together, Sata felt the bear trembling, and even heard her whimper once or twice.

"What's wrong, Ss'klexna?"

"Just . . . fear of the unknown."

"I thought you could see and understand the spiritual realities in *any* situation."

"I guess . . . I can . . . but . . . that doesn't mean I don't feel fear when . . . things get very personal.  You see, Sata, I think . . . this might be . . . my last mission as a Nebador citizen."

After that, the bear seemed to fall asleep, and another day passed before she would explain her statement.

*

Ss'klexna Rrr'tak'fi no longer needed to gather her breath and send her message out into the wilderness.  Every ursine for a great distance around seemed to know exactly where the pair of visitors was eating berries, catching frogs, or fishing.

Sata noticed that her companion was savoring every bite, rolling each berry around in her mouth, and eating each fish slowly and thoughtfully.  As they sat on the edge of a clearing and enjoyed a few more berries, Sata tried to work up her courage and ask about Ss'klexns's statement the night before, but the bear spoke first.

"Remember, my friend, the ursines of Ko-tera Three are not fully sapient.  They are close, and have rules and customs they live by, but are still very much wild animals."

Sata nodded, but figured she didn't yet know enough to say anything.

"They want blood . . . they want a sacrifice . . . and for several reasons, I will give it to them."

Sata's throat suddenly closed so tightly, she could barely breathe.

"Most importantly, it will prove to them the sincerity of what I have told them, that they might need to go to a different world when the years have passed that can be counted on two paws.  My sacrifice will not guarantee that they will leave willingly at that time, but without it, they will certainly not."

The longer Ss'klexna Rrr'tak'fi spoke, the calmer she became, and the closer Sata was to tears.

"Secondly, my death will allow you to live.  They have sworn to me that if I give them my life, they will not touch you.  I believe them."

Sata was crying openly now, but was aware that several huge bears, and many more that were merely large, were gathering in the trees around them.

"And finally, my friend, I am very old.  I was old when I left my home planet, and even older when that video was made."

Sata smiled slightly even as she continued crying softly.

"I have been fascinated, all my life, by the spiritual adventure that lies ahead, and I am deeply honored to begin that journey after being of service to these noble creatures. I did not know I would feel fear, but I guess a few surprises are part of the process. Anyway, I seem to have mastered it now, and my heart and mind are quiet . . . and ready."

Part of Sata wanted to scream and throw rocks at the stupid bears, but another part knew that would only make things worse. Although it took every bit of her self-control, she somehow managed to remain still and almost silent.

"When I am gone, my friend, you should sit quietly and wait for the ursines to leave, in their own time, of their own accord. Any noise or defiance from you could make them take back their promise."

Sata choked back the rest of the sobbing noises she was making.

Ss'klexna Rrr'tak'fi, of Satamia in Nebador, stood and walked forward into the clearing.

The largest of the great ursines of the last wilderness of Ko-tera Three came forward and seemed to embrace the smaller bear, then thrashed his arms about quickly several times. Blood flew everywhere, and Ss'klexna Rrr'tak'fi fell to the ground and lay still.

*

At first Sata hoped with all her heart that the wild bears would leave right away so she could call Manessa, then cry for hours in Boro's arms.

The bears of the wilderness lingered just long enough to observe Sata's reaction. Within five minutes, they seemed satisfied, and she was left completely alone with the silent contact specialist.

Those five minutes allowed Sata to realize that she wasn't quite ready to cry in anyone's arms. There would be time for that, soon enough. First, there were a few other things she had to do, things Ss'klexna Rrr'tak'fi would have wanted her to do. She felt somewhat surprised by the calmness she suddenly felt.

She went to her friend's body, and was amazed how completely the small ursine had been torn to pieces. She must have died very quickly, Sata realized. Although it required getting blood all over her hands and arms, she managed to find Ss'klexna's mission bracelet, tapped the release code, and slipped it into a pocket.

Next she stepped back and looked over the scene. The clearing was completely natural and unremarkable, and would be difficult to recognize again once the body and blood were gone. Birds and carnivorous mammals were already gathering for the feast. Sata selected four large rocks, picked them up one at a time, and arranged them closely around Ss'klexna's body in a perfect square.

Finally, after a deep breath, Sata walked downhill to the stream, washed her arms and face, and sat at the edge of the rushing water, pondering all the responsibilities that came with being a citizen of Nebador.

*   *   *

## Chapter 68: Testudine

Memsala and Boro swam for hours, following a native giant sea turtle who guided them farther and farther into the open ocean.

After about two hours, Boro started to feel embarrassed — his tired leg muscles were forcing him to slow down.

As three hours approached, he felt better because Memsala was looking exhausted too.

Their guide slowed with them, but didn't offer to stop and rest, or even tell them how much longer they had to swim.

When they arrived, both Nebador citizens immediately knew what their guide wanted them to see.  The native testudine stopped a hundred meters short of the edge of a huge floating mass of trash that bobbed on the ocean waves — crushed plastic bottles, empty cups, pieces of rope, broken toys, and a thousand other things, all mixed with oily chemicals that created an iridescent film on the surface.

The turtles looked at each other and exchanged silent thoughts for a few minutes as Boro paddled closer to examine the floating mess.

"This is only a small part of what the monkey mammals dump in the sea," Memsala explained when they were all back together.  "The heavy stuff sinks to the bottom.  Many creatures die when they eat bits of it, thinking it might be food.  Many more become sick drinking the polluted water, then larger creatures eat *them*, all the way up to the monkey mammals who fish with huge nets."

The turtles conferred a bit more.

"The monkey mammals eat the fish and then have babies with missing parts, or clumps of cells in their bodies that don't know when to stop growing, and they can't figure out why."

Boro raised his eyebrows.

"Yes, my friend, there is ultimately justice in the universe," Memsala continued, "even though many innocent creatures must suffer along with the guilty ones."

*

The three swam slowly away from the floating garbage dump, all in a somber mood. The journey that had taken four hours the first time, took six on the way back.

But when they arrived at the lagoon of a small uninhabited island, Boro was amazed by the sudden change. Turtles began arriving from all directions, some huge and scarred with age, others just hatched, and every size in between.

They all immediately began playing.

Boro smiled, but absolutely *had* to find something to eat. Luckily, the island provided plenty of fruit not far from the lagoon. After devouring several pieces and drinking deeply at a little stream, he waded back into the water to join the fun.

Memsala shared with him, in the language of Nebador, things she heard with her mind, but none of the chatter was about floating trash or polluted water. As the turtles played, they spoke of hidden caves and tasty fish, secret lagoons and laughing dolphins. Boro felt like he had been transported to another planet, and the nearest problem of any kind was light-years away.

But eventually the sun found the western horizon and evening settled over the lagoon. The many testudine of all sizes slowly ceased their merry-making and took on serious moods. It wasn't long before Boro realized they were all looking at Memsala and him.

For a time, the contact specialist was silent.

Finally she spoke to share with Boro what was going on. "I have told them that we are about to give the monkey mammals of the planet a twelve-year warning. Those humans already *know*, thanks to the Temporandek Teacher, what is coming. Now it is time for them to decide to *act*, or not, as they choose. If they do not, we will return with ships for any sapient and near-sapient peoples who would like to move to a better home. I have asked the testudine if they would like a ship to come for them."

Memsala fell silent and Boro was soon dying of curiosity. "What did they say?"

"About what I thought they would say."

Boro waited anxiously.

"They will think about it, and if it seems like the right thing to do at the time, they will go with joy in their hearts."

* * *

## Chapter 69: Banana

Boro and Memsala, who had not yet heard the news about Ss'klexna Rrr'tak'fi, wondered why everyone was very quiet on the flight back to the tropical island that had been Manessa's base of operations for several Satamia days.

After Boro toweled off and slipped into a dry robe, Sata snuggled close beside him in the passenger area.  He could see that she had been crying.  He guessed she was off-duty for some serious reason, not just normal crew rotations.

"You . . . want to talk about anything?" he asked her softly.

She shook her head.  "You'll hear all about it . . . as soon as we land."

He held her close and gazed at the large screen over the steward's station as the ocean flashed by beneath the ship.

Rini hobbled out of the ship very slowly, with Mati on one side and Ilika on the other.  Ashley and Kibi carried T'sss'lisss on a large pillow.  By the time everyone had gathered on the sand in a half-circle at the water's edge, or was floating in the warm tropical water nearby, Boro was painfully aware that one of their contact specialists was missing, and the bear couldn't still be working in the field because her helper was right here.

Sata took a slow breath.  "I tried to get out of this.  I begged Ashley to do it, or Kolarrr'ka, or *someone*."

Respectful eyes met hers all around the circle.

"I finally got it through my head that no one could really do this but me.  I was there.  I know what Ss'klexna was thinking, if anyone still alive does."

Boro put the pieces together and felt a deep sense of sadness.

"She wasn't supposed to do what she did.  She wasn't supposed to knowingly walk into mortal danger.  And yet . . . she had several reasons for doing it — all of them good reasons — and I guess . . ." Sata paused to rub her eyes. "... I guess if I had that many good reasons for ... dying ... I would have done it too ..."

The crew, mission leaders, and contact specialists talked for hours, sharing memories of Ss'klexna Rrr'tak'fi, many different opinions about the reasons she had done what she did, and how the remainder of the mission was affected.

Boro noticed that the eldest two — Memsala and Malika-Terno — seemed to be most sympathetic to Ss'klexna's decision, and the younger ones felt she should have found a way to come back alive. Sata was the exception, joining the elders.

Everyone finally fell silent as the sun prepared to set over the ocean. One by one they looked at Kolarrr'ka to see if he had any more mission activities planned for that day.

He looked at Ashley.

"There is one more thing we simply *must* do today," she began, "partly in honor of Ss'klexna, who would have *loved* what we are about to share. But perhaps more importantly, it will lift our spirits."

Several people wore knowing smiles. Others looked clueless.

"I realize some of you will not enjoy these treats as much as monkey mammals, so the crew has also prepared a tasty green salad for our equine, and something fishy for our aquatic friends."

Memsala, Trekila Spimalo, and the young cetacean memory specialist, all squawked or splashed from the water's edge.

Ashley smiled. "For weeks now, I have been *trying* to serve a delicious fruit that I know from my home planet, but every time I was about to bring some down from the trees, or cut it into chunks I could carry, or stow it somewhere it would ripen, we had to dash off to move a contact specialist from somewhere to somewhere else ..."

All the contact specialists laughed, but none appeared to feel guilty over the issue.

"Well, I *finally* got it done, and the crew has been helping me make fruit salads, pies, and several other things from these long, yellow fruits." She held one up, peeled it half-way, and took a bite.

"Are you sure it isn't sapient?" Trekila Spimalo asked from the water.

"*Very* sure!" Ashley replied as everyone else howled or squawked with laughter.

# Part 7: Ko-tera Three, 3671

## Chapter 70: Pause

Priscilla Lo-saran awoke in her very favorite place in the world — Brian Lo-saran's arms.

She still used the name *Priscilla Ka-mentha* whenever dancing or skating, as everyone in those places already knew her by that name.  But she was very happy to at least symbolically submit herself to Brian's dominance by changing her legal name to his — especially since almost every other aspect of their lives was, and would probably continue to be, dominated by *her* work.

"Good morning, beautiful," he said softly.

"Mmm.  This is my favorite time of day, because you usually do to me, again, the same thing you did to me last night."

"Bad news!"

"What?"

"It's Monday, and we woke up late.  It's almost seven o'clock.  So unless you want a quickie . . ."

Priscilla chuckled.  "If we do *that*, then I *won't* let you out of bed for *at least* an hour!"

Brian pretended to pout for a second.  "But I have to cook breakfast and lunch for . . . how many are we down to?"

"Hmm.  Malcolm's still recovering from his last surgery . . . John got reassigned last month to somewhere on the other side of the world . . . and another scientist got bored and quit . . . so that makes ten, eleven if both George and Lisa can come."

"I'll make enough for twelve."

"Everyone *loves* getting home-made stuff, instead of packaged pastries and delivered pizzas."

"The least I can do.  I can't find a job, and you guys are trusting me with *the* biggest secret in the world, so secret the *president* doesn't even want to talk about it."

Priscilla laughed. "Well, we *did* publish a book about it that sold more than a million hardcovers, and I think we've passed three mil on the paperback, the book no one over twenty knows about, but everyone under twenty has."

Brian smiled, then gave her a quick kiss. "Okay, I'm up before Susan beats me into the bathroom."

✳

While savoring her scrambled eggs with cheese and crumbled bacon, Priscilla listened to the chatter among the team members — the people who used to be official members of the top-secret Department of Defense P-Seventeen team. Often she glanced up to see the love of her life working happily in Susan's kitchen.

Priscilla didn't care that Brian couldn't find a job, and knew he felt much better about himself after Susan asked him to take care of all the cooking and yard work. It allowed Susan to schedule more clients, and it kept Priscilla from feeling guilty when *she* had to disappear for days at a time to work at the safe house.

But she also knew it was a serious ego-challenge for Brian. Both his new wife, only sixteen, and the psychologist they shared a house with, made more money than either of them needed. Priscilla hoped with all her heart that he wouldn't let the situation threaten their relationship. So far, he seemed to be coping, and she planned to continue to do everything she could to keep him happy.

Brian walked through the living room collecting empty plates from everyone. Priscilla looked up and their eyes met for a moment, taking them both back to their years of dating, always with a body guard not far away and an early curfew at his orphanage. They smiled at each other and he returned to the kitchen.

"Good morning, everyone," Priscilla said from her seat in front of the fireplace. "Let me see . . . it's the fourth of October, session . . . I forget."

"Sixty-five," retired Colonel Sarah Ma-soran said, glancing up from her note pad.

Priscilla smiled. "This is the *second* time we've worked our way through the one and two-digit numbers . . ."

Everyone remembered with fondness their first year at the top-secret military facility in the green hills west of the city.

"How's Malcolm?" Priscilla asked.

"Not good," retired Two-star General Samuel Bo-seklin answered. "He hates not being able to come to our meetings, says it's the only important thing in his life, since his wife passed away."

"We share with him every detail when we visit," Sarah added, "even what Brian cooked that day, and he really appreciates it."

"The three of us are planning a visit as soon as he's out of recovery," Susan mentioned.

Sarah nodded and smiled.

"Okay," Priscilla began, sitting up straighter and getting serious. "We have a publishing report from Betty, a space probe report from Chris, and my crystal-ball routine."

Everyone chuckled.

"Betty?"

Doctor of Chemistry Betty Ko-silma cleared her throat. "Harold says the eleventh printing of the hardcover is moving very slowly, but the little paperback is still a hot item. It will never show up on the *Best Seller* list because so many copies are given away free, not sold."

"I think that's best right now," Priscilla slipped in, "as we've talked about."

Many nodded agreement.

"The translations are doing well," the chemist went on, "with all but one in their second printings."

"Thank you," Priscilla said. "I get the feeling that our little book is sort of . . . in God's hands now."

Chuckles filled the room again, and Doctor of Physics Chris Po-selem grinned at the sixteen-year-old team leader.

She grinned back. "Chris, you ready?"

He ruffled his wild hair. "I've learned a *little* patience in the last nine years!"

Several people laughed, recalling the many times he nearly bubbled over with time-travel theories.

"As all of us have been watching closely, especially Susan . . ." He made eye contact with the psychologist. ". . . most people seem to be recovering from the nation-wide depression of last summer when we learned the probe was unable to transmit back any pictures. That's another point for Priscilla, of course. What are you up to?"

"Something like a hundred and fifteen, I think."

"Hundred and seventeen," Sarah corrected with a smile.

Doctor Po-selem nodded. "Finger pointing has tapered off, and most scientists are getting down to business with the basic telemetry we're receiving. That data verifies that the probe is on course, seems to be undamaged in all other ways, and even tells us *how many* pictures are in its memory, waiting to be transmitted back — two hundred and twenty-six."

Several people moaned with sympathy for the crippled machine and the disappointed scientists.

"It's now approaching the last planet in the solar system, Ko-meriana."

"What can we expect from that fly-by?" General George Ba-kerga, commander of the safe-house program, inquired.

"Unless the image transmitter suddenly starts working, we'll just get some gravity and magnetic flux measurements, one last verification of position and course, and then that's it. All those pictures, including dozens more it will take of Ko-meriana, will just sit in the probe's memory until it completely runs out of power in ten or fifteen years, somewhere far out beyond the edge of the solar system . . ."

＊

Ten o'clock was passing as everyone took a break, then got settled for the main presentation.

"A while back," Priscilla began, "someone put on the list that I talk about the darkest, ugliest part of the collapse that I lived through. I don't remember who, it might have been John before he was reassigned."

"I think it was him," Sarah said.

Priscilla nodded. "I've been pondering it, but I guess I was also avoiding it, not because I dislike talking about bad stuff, just because it was hard to know how to approach the topic. Well, I guess I'm ready, and can't think of any more excuses . . ."

Her listeners smiled at her.

"Of course, the darkest, ugliest time for any person or family was when *their* water or food supply failed, or *their* loved ones died. You all understand that, so there's no point in approaching the question from that angle."

Nods assured her that they understood.

"And that happened to people, families, and whole communities at *so many* different times — from 3715, to who-knows-when after I was gone — that it's almost meaningless to even talk about the average. So I decided to approach the question from a completely different angle. I decided to imagine that I was on a flying saucer in orbit, looking down, completely unaffected by events below. I decided that I shouldn't be paying attention to individual suffering, as much as I might want to. I should be paying attention to the civilization as a whole. What was its darkest, ugliest moment?

"And I don't mean *darkest* as in no electricity for lights. I mean darkest *morally*, *ethically*, as God and the angels would see it and judge it."

Several people nodded.

"After I got clear in my mind what I was after, the answer was obvious. It wasn't the time period when most people were dying. It was the five or so years before then, when our so-called leaders and role models — or as John would say, the power and money people — were doing everything they could to keep the coal, oil, and gas flowing so a few of *them* could go on living the way they were used to. It became known as the Brown Years because it included repealing or ignoring all pollution laws. Also, most forms of legal, social, and medical protection for ordinary citizens disappeared when governments handed almost all their powers to private corporations . . ."

＊　＊　＊

## Chapter 71: Phase Change

Except for an occasional rain storm, the weather on the small, uninhabited tropical island remained pleasant following the return of Memsala and Boro from the last contact mission.

For the next eight days, with all Education Service people present (although one still slithered about very slowly), all contact specialists there (of those who were still alive), and all crew members back on duty (one with a new appreciation for the simple ability to walk), they began the process of telling the many stories they had heard or observed, asking questions, and coming to some tentative conclusions.

And all during those eight days, one purple-haired being — in a class by herself — sat on the sand or the galley counter and listened, but said nothing.

No one had any doubt that the whales, dolphins, seals, manatees, and other cetaceans, would be ready and willing to leap into evacuation ships in twelve years' time.  Boro thought they'd be lined up, watching the sky, in eleven.  Everyone splashed or laughed deeply.

The testudine were more of a mystery.  The sea turtles knew what was happening to their world, and Memsala thought some would leave, but couldn't be absolutely sure.

Boro had no insights to add.

Just as the meeting was about to take a break for food and play, Toran Takil noticed a funny expression on Memsala's face — a face not known for very many readable expressions — and asked everyone to stay for a few more minutes.  They all sat in silence, waiting for the respected teacher to gather her thoughts.

"I think . . . they sense that they have a part to play in the drama that approaches . . . and do not feel good about giving us a decision . . . until they figure out what purpose they might still have."

She fell silent for a long moment.  Everyone waited.

"That *might* mean," she eventually went on, "that they will not leave in twelve years, but would appreciate a ship checking on them every few years . . . until it becomes too late."

Rini thought he saw Arantiloria nod slightly.

※

Malika-Terno was clearly full of mixed feelings as he talked about his fellow equines.  Many others asked questions, and the situation became crystal clear as the day progressed.  There was no evidence that *any* horses would leave the planet of their birth, no matter what.  It was just not in their nature.

Mati remained silent, knowing she had already contributed, while hiding with Malika-Terno in various weedy places during their contact mission, everything she could.

Ashley wasn't going to let her off the hook so easily.  "Mati, what's your opinion of the equines of Ko-tera Three?"

Mati sighed, then took a moment to consider her answer.

"I was a slave once, a slave who had no hope of getting out of slavery.  I just couldn't *do* anything that would earn me a living in any other way.  Of course, back then, I didn't know about piloting starships, or any of the other things I do now."

Several people chuckled or clucked.

She smiled.  "I almost got married to the wrong person at one point in my life, but discovered that slavery can follow you *anywhere* if you're not careful and make good choices."

She paused to gather her thoughts, and noticed Rini trying not to smile.

"So . . . I guess I've come to *understand* why the equines won't leave.  But I keep thinking about a training exercise we did recently in which the simulated bunnies *could not* make good choices about the situation because it was too far outside their experience.  We had to choose for them.  I don't know if this situation is like that, and we should *force* the equines to move to a new home, or if we have to respect their wishes.  Someone with much more wisdom will have to make that decision."

"Thanks, Mati," Ashley said.

Kolarrr'ka turned his head slightly and tried to read the expression on Arantiloria's face, but could not.

※

The near-sapient races were easier to talk about.

Everyone quickly agreed that a special mission by reptiles should be sent to the lizards T'sss'lisss had found.  She just didn't have enough information, and she freely admitted it from where she lay on the warm sand trying to stretch the kinks out of her spine.

Rini had not seen the lizards at all, so could add little to the meeting.

When they turned their discussion to the native avians, Kolarrr'ka proposed a ship collect a few thousand large birds, after putting them to sleep, from the tropical gathering places.  Another transport, kept at a very low temperature, should be offered to the flightless birds near the poles.  He believed they would take it willingly.

Ashley wasn't so sure, but agreed there was no harm in giving them that option before rendering them unconscious.

※

"Bok," Kolarrr'ka began after a leisurely breakfast the next morning that included all the bananas they could eat, "I'm sorry the ursine report rests entirely on your wings, Sata ... I mean your shoulders ... but as I understand it, you would have had a hard time getting back alive without Ss'klexna Rrr'tak'fi's sacrifice."

Sata swallowed.  "Yeah, unless Manessa had arrived *very* quickly."

"When we listened to your story the first time, bok, we focused on the events.  Now we want you to give us your opinions, your evaluations, your judgments."

The navigator was silent for a long time.  Eventually her mouth began to move back and forth between a slight smile and a worried frown.

"Part of me is still angry at the bears, and is tempted to say *leave them, let them die with the planet.*"

As she took a slow breath, she could almost *feel* Arantiloria looking at her.

"But I know that's not an emotion I should act on.  That would make me ... like the stupid bears ... and only *near*-sapient."

Chuckles and splashing noises all around the circle of listeners made Sata smile.  She looked up to see Boro grinning from ear to ear at her.

"The bears have some kind of code of honor," she went on.  "Ss'klexna understood it, but I don't pretend to.  They kept their word and didn't harm me, so that's something.  I guess ... they should get a chance to relocate if the planet cannot be saved.  But I recommend they be put into a *deep* sleep first, or someone could get hurt."

Several other thoughts about the ursines of Ko-tera Three were expressed by others, but no one contradicted Sata's primary recommendation.

※

During play time that day, everyone got at least a little wet in the warm tropical waters of the lagoon.  Kolarrr'ka floated on the surface, and T'sss'lisss slithered quickly across the water, later saying it felt wonderful to her sore muscles.  Malika-Terno surprised everyone by preferring the open beach, where he walked out as far as he could, then swam another hundred meters before starting to feel a cross-current that would have taken him out to sea.  At that point, he turned back.

After shaking, toweling dry, or running in the sunshine, they gathered in a circle at the water's edge once again.  Everyone looked at Toran Takil, the only contact specialist who had not yet made his recommendations.

"You all know me.  You know I would never speak lightly on such matters, or with any intentional conflict of interest.  And I offer as proof that I have never made a recommendation like this before, even though I have been a contact specialist to felines several times."

They all sensed the gravity of his words, and remained silent.

"If the climate of Ko-tera Three can be stabilized so the hydrological cycle continues to function — in other words, so the tropical rain forests are preserved — either by the actions of the monkey mammals or our actions after they are gone — then I believe the large cats of this planet are a very good candidate to become the next dominant land animal."

※

The team discussed Toran Takil's recommendation for hours.

They agreed that even if the humans acted quickly, some climate heating had already begun, and the jungles would expand, along with the deserts. Monkey mammals could live in both, but not thrive in either.

It was also explained that the humans had already raised their population far beyond what the planet could support in the long run.  By whatever means their dominance came to an end — voluntary or forced by a changing climate — they would experience a huge die-back, and their culture would be greatly simplified in the process.

Toran Takil was quick to point out that if the planet lost its hydrological cycle, no rain would fall anywhere, vast deserts would span the globe, and nothing, no matter how sapient, could preserve anything beyond simple, tribal culture.

Arantiloria seldom revealed what she was thinking, but to the big cat's last comment, she nodded.

※

After another day of playing, relaxing, gathering tropical fruit, and discussing the recommendations that had been made, T'sss'lisss rose up from her coils as the sun found the western horizon.

"Ashley has informed me that I am now in charge.  I guess I healed my poor broken body — and learned some hard lessons about wild snakes — just in time."

Everyone smiled, laughed, or whinnied.  Rini's ribs were still too sore to laugh, so he just grinned.

"The monkey mammals' space probe is approaching its final assignment, the last major planet in the system, Ko-tera Eleven.  It will take pictures, make some measurements, then continue on into the blackness of inter-stellar space.  Let us go witness this historic event, and consider the next step in *our* mission."

Everyone went into action, bringing in beach balls, towels, pieces of clothing, or one last bunch of fruit, before beginning pre-flight preparations or settling into passenger seats.

※　※　※

## Chapter 72: An Historic Event

From the near-darkness at the edge of the Ko-tera solar system, three Education Service personnel, four contact specialists, one other dolphin, six monkey-mammal crew members, and a deep-space response ship watched as the flimsy space probe — bristling with antennae, solar panels, and cameras — made its closest approach to Ko-tera Eleven.

Behind the gangly little machine, the misty deep-blue surface of the planet's atmosphere appeared still, but Sata knew that the rotational velocity of even a small gas giant was thousands of kilometers per hour. Storms — like the three purple spots she could see on her screen — could be moving many times as fast, and mixing several layers into a chaotic soup of hydrogen and whatever else was at hand.

"Pleassse magnify the plaque on the ssspaccce probe," T'sss'lisss requested from the passenger seat she currently shared with Kolarrr'ka, her coils under his feathers, their heads side by side.

Rini adjusted his visual sensors until the golden message, covered with fine engraved lettering, filled the screen.

"Bok," Kolarrr'ka began thoughtfully. "Would you translate the relevant part again, Ashley?"

She opened a shoulder bag hooked over the back of her seat. "Got it right here in the mission documents, as it's in some weird language I can't read. It's the next to last line on the plaque. It says, *Heating; please save the innocent others; hints appreciated how we can save our own most innocent.*"

"And the last line?" Toran Takil requested.

"*Lepidopterae are so bright, their touch so light, they flutter through my dreams at night.*"

"Butterflies," Kibi said softly in her native language for the benefit of her fellow crew members with less Nebador vocabulary.

*"Please save the innocent others,"* Kolarrr'ka repeated.  "We're doing *that."*

Just then, Sata announced that the space probe was firing its navigation thrusters, so Kibi switched back to the wide view.

Everyone saw the probe change course, and the smaller of the two antennae swivel slowly to again point at its home, a barely-visible speck in the blackness of space, not far from the brightest star in the sky.

The larger antenna tried to turn, but then jerked a few times and stopped.

Sata frowned, drew some lines on her console screen, made some calculations, then frowned even more deeply.  "I think . . . it's broken."

"Pleassse explain," T'sss'lisss said, stretching up taller and looking intently at the display.

"The little antenna is pointed right at Ko-tera Three.  The big one stopped more than two degrees off.  Do they have any off-planet tracking stations?"

After a long moment of silence, the snake spoke in a thoughtful voice while still gazing at the screen.  "No . . ."

✳

Gathered around the table in the passenger area, from seats, the tank, or the floor, they discussed the situation.

"Our mission is to observe, contact other species, and tentatively evaluate the situation," Ashley said firmly.

"Yes, bok," Kolarrr'ka agreed.  "We're not supposed to interfere with the native monkey-mammal culture."

"If they don't feel the pain of having their technology fail," Trekila Spimalo said from the tank, "they will never be motivated to make their machines good enough to survive the harsh environments of inter-planetary space."

After a long silence, Malika-Terno's deep voice asked, "Were you able to analyze the data stream from the small antenna, Sata?"

"Yes, but Manessa gets the credit.  There are four hundred and twelve photographs that the large antenna has been trying to transmit, but the probe has never received confirmation that any were received, so it continues to re-transmit them, over and over.  The rest of the small antenna's data stream is just position and a few simple measurements.  Manessa now has all the pictures from the large antenna, many very beautiful."

Kibi sighed from the steward's station.  "Makes me sad that they'll never see them, especially since this might be their only space probe."

Toran Takil made respectful eye contact with Kibi and nodded.  "Many sapient races make the same mistake, using up the mineral wealth of their planet in one big burst of high, easy living that lasts only a century or two, then having little to work with in the long millennia that lie ahead . . . *if* they avoid ruining their climate and ecosystem."

After several more Nebador citizens had spoken, and the consensus appeared to be universal, T'sss'lisss declared a long break for a meal and whatever else needed to be done.  Most of the specialists and crew members filtered away toward the lower deck, the galley, or the bridge.

T'sss'lisss remained in her seat after Kolarrr'ka got up, gazing at the space probe on the big display screen as it slowly put more distance between itself and the last planet, with nothing left to do but try, again and again, to transmit its pictures back to Ko-tera Three with its broken antenna.

She wondered about the nervous feeling that remained throughout her slender body, the nagging sensation that they were missing something ... and then realized that Memsala had not said a word at the meeting, and Arantiloria had not even shown herself.

Over the next hour, everyone noticed T'sss'lisss' thoughtful expression where she remained coiled in a seat at the table, so after dishes were done and the on-duty crew members rotated, they all returned to the passenger area.

T'sss'lisss turned her head.  "Wise Memsala, I feel in my bones that we are missing something, and I beg your thoughts on the matter."

Memsala let the silence linger for a moment before speaking.  "Any time you find yourself working hard to brush aside an event as if it was merely a so-called *accident*, you can be sure you are missing something.  There are no pure *accidents*.  All levels of space, time, and eternity are inter-woven with the manifestations of physical, mental, and spiritual realities, even when the gods do not actively intervene in the affairs of mortals ... which ... is not the case on this mission."

Everyone sat in complete silence pondering the sea turtle's words, and wondering how badly they would have screwed up the mission without her.

Memsala eventually spoke again.  "A very good reason to interact with the monkey mammals of the planet was just presented to us.  No, I take that back.  It was just shoved into our *faces*.  Will we take the hint, or do we need Kerloran himself to come to the ship and spell it out for us?"

Another long silence lingered.

"You work for Kerloran, Shemultavia, and Melorania," Memsala added.  "Do not be afraid to fill their shells in the small ways that are entrusted to you ... to us ... on these missions."

The testudine fell silent and settled lower into the water.

Ilika noticed Boro and Mati frowning slightly, Kibi and Sata looking very thoughtful, and Rini smiling.

"And remember the last part of the message on the plaque," Malika-Terno rumbled.  "*Hints appreciated how we can save our own most innocent.*"

Several heads around the table nodded.

T'sss'lisss let out a deep sigh and descended into her coils.

## Chapter 73: Delicate Cargo

After a quiet time of several hours during which most people got some sleep but T'sss'lisss could not, she found Ashley in a seat at the back of the passenger area, so she coiled herself into the monkey mammal's lap and looked at her with mesmerizing eyes. "Perhapsss . . . thisss isss a good time for you to take charge of your part of the misssion. I feel . . . ssstretched thinner than I'm sssupposssed to be."

Ashley smiled while shaking her head. "Not until we get to Ko-tera Three, my friend. At that time, I'm sure I will have my hands full, *especially* after Memsala got us back on track."

The snake sighed, rested her head on Ashley's shoulder, and closed her eyes for an hour of sleep.

*

"Captain," T'sss'lisss began after everyone had eaten and otherwise refreshed themselves, "please prepare to transport that space probe back to its home planet."

His crew, sensing the critical nature of the next flight leg, were all at their original stations, looking at their commander.

"Mati, match the probe's speed and course, and bring us to eight meters ahead of it. Sata, prepare a low-acceleration flight plan to Ko-tera Three, no ion drive, probably limited to about three gravities on the external cargo, but we'll know more after some tests. Rini, low-frequency images for the stress tests."

They all went to work, and Kibi made sure her passengers had the best view of the space probe.

"Twelve . . . eleven . . . eight meters and locked," the pilot announced a few minutes later.

"Boro, all maneuvering thrusters under ship's control. Manessa, see what stresses this thing can take, *without* breaking it worse than it already is."

The ship slowly nudged herself closer to the spidery craft, then reached out with four grappling arms.

Kibi switched her large display to the low-frequency image, the ship shook the probe slightly, and most of the specialists in the passenger area moaned or hissed as they observed stresses and strains rippling through the flimsy metal framework.

"That was two gravities," Manessa reported, "and I can now calculate a better grappling pattern."

Sata worked at her console for a moment.  "The trip would take twenty-seven Satamia days at two gravities."

Most everyone moaned.  T'sss'lisss hid her head in Kolarrr'ka feathers.

"Yes, please try a different grapple, Manessa," Ilika said to his ship.  "We don't want to die of old age on this mission."

"Actually, we don't have enough fuel for that flight plan," Boro added from his station, "so it's not an option."

Several sighs of relief were heard, and everyone watched as the ship moved three of her grappling arms, then added four more.

"Manessa, you are now an honorary arachnid!" Ashley said with a smile.

The ship didn't respond, but proceeded to shake the gangly craft again. "Two point five."  She moved two grappling arms, then shook again.  "Three point two."  Finally, only one arm was moved a little.  "Three point six, and I calculate that is its limit."

"Thank you," Ilika said.  "Sata?"

She worked in silence for another long moment.  "About two days, and there's a planetary freeloading opportunity at Ko-tera Seven to save fuel."

Everyone clapped, honked, or splashed with appreciation for both ship and navigator.

Then Ilika looked at Boro, and everyone fell silent again.

"The biggest problem's gonna be atmospheric entry at Ko-tera Three without melting the space probe."

He worked in silence for another minute.

"Whew, that's close!  With the freeloading, we can do it, but just.  I'm sure glad I grabbed some extra fuel!"

Everyone cheered again.

Ashley was especially happy.  She knew she needed *at least* two days to figure out what she was going to do and say on Ko-tera Three.

✳

Colonel John Bo-torin, political scientist for the Department of Defense, was quite bored at his new assignment five thousand miles away from Priscilla's team.  He called once or twice a month, talked to Priscilla, Susan, or even Brian if no one else was home, to keep in touch with events of some actual importance to the human race.

On a Saturday in late October, Colonel Bo-torin was in his quarters when he heard something in a news broadcast that made him reach for the radio dials.  It wasn't so much what was *said* in the routine report about the space probe's progress, it was the *way* it was said.  As a political scientist, he knew that phrasing and tone of voice — something was being covered up.

After increasing the volume and tuning better, he listened intently to the rest of the news broadcast.  When the station switched to sports, he quickly cranked the tuning knob to the far end of the short-wave radio band, a station in another country and another language.

Since other countries were not so motivated to keep everything about the space probe looking rosy, he soon started to hear bits and pieces of rumors.  Two hours and five foreign radio stations later, he felt he knew the gist of the situation.

He reached for the telephone and dialed a military-base number.  "This is Colonel John Bo-torin.  I have an emergency back home, and need to get on a flight today if possible, tomorrow at the latest . . . .Eighteen hundred?  I'll be there.  Thank you."

*

Priscilla smiled at Brian as he took her plate.  "Good morning, everyone.  It's the twenty-fifth of October, Session Sixty-Eight, and today will be a relaxed meeting with a short presentation . . ."

At that moment, a knock was heard upon the door.

Priscilla looked around the room, but didn't see anyone missing who was expected.

Susan stood and looked through the beveled glass.  "It's John!"

Colonel Bo-torin, in uniform, was smiling as he entered the room.  Everyone rose to shake hands and welcome him.

Another pillow was located and Brian made him a breakfast plate as he got settled.  "Sorry I'm a little late.  I was on the other side of the world less than two days ago, and some of my flight connections . . . didn't."

Everyone chuckled in sympathy as they found their seats.

"I have some news you're not going to get anywhere else for a while.  If the telemetry is accurate, the space probe recently experienced some very weird gravitational forces acting upon it, and now it appears to be . . . coming back . . . fast!"

*   *   *

## Chapter 74: Nexus

Colonel John Bo-torin inhaled his breakfast, then took the next hour to share everything he had learned about the space probe. Too many scientists, with their values of honesty and public disclosure, he explained, were involved in the space program to keep significant events hidden for long. At its current speed, the little machine would be home in about ten days, on a journey that had taken more than fourteen months the first time.

Retired General Samuel Bo-seklin quickly voiced what everyone was wondering, and while speaking, he looked at the person he hoped could answer. "What would cause a space probe to come *back?*"

Doctor of Physics Chris Po-selem ruffled his hair to give himself time to think. "Er ... um ... a solution to anthropogenic climate change might be easier to imagine ..."

Nervous chuckles came from several places in the room.

"Seriously ..." Chris went on, "... the probe would have to encounter an unknown, fast-moving planetary body, such as a comet, in *just* the right place so that it swung around the body, was greatly accelerated, and then broke free of the body's gravity at *precisely* the right moment to be pointed back home."

"What are the chances?" Doctor of Philosophy Larry Bo-leden asked with a frown.

Chris just shook his head. "Especially since we've never detected *anything* that could do that."

"That's what I thought," Larry said, leaning back and gazing up at the ceiling.

After a moment of silence, Colonel Lisa Ka-markla looked at Priscilla. "Do you know anything about this?"

"No, and that makes sense, because our source person doesn't have access to a short-wave radio, and isn't fluent in any foreign languages at this point in her life."

The silence lingered again.  Brian, starting to work on lunch in the kitchen, tried to be very quiet.

"What will it do when it gets here?" Doctor of History Richard Tu-feltin asked.

"Hmm ..." Chris considered.  "It doesn't have much mass ... if it's *perfectly* on course and actually *does* get back here, it will just burn up in the atmosphere.  At that speed, nothing of a craft that small would make it to the ground, and *we* have nothing that could go out and meet it to slow it down.  But of course, if it *was* following the laws of physics, it wouldn't be *coming* back."

The thoughtful silence stretched for nearly a minute.

"I think ..." Doctor of Biology Tanya Po-morna finally began, "... this might be your *divine intervention*, Chris."

The physicist sighed.  "I was hoping for the solution to our climate predicament, not a melted space probe!"

Several people chuckled.

"I know I'm not a commanding officer anymore," Sam admitted, "but I want everyone to tap into any news sources you have, and make a note of *any* information or speculation that comes to you, no matter how strange.  And we're going back to our old schedule — Monday, Wednesday, and Friday — until this thing plays itself out, to whatever end."

Susan and Priscilla nodded.

"I think we should visit Malcolm in the nursing home after lunch," Sarah proposed, "as many of us as can go, and bring him up to date.  He's one of us, and deserves to know what we know."

Most everyone agreed with waving hands.

✳

At the local diner on Tuesday afternoon, a top-forty song started playing from the juke box.  Priscilla wiggled in her seat, and almost wished the place had a dance floor.

"Can you tell me ..." Brian began after enjoying the first bite of his deluxe cheeseburger, "... in words a nineteen-year-old boy can understand ... what's going on?"

Priscilla finished sucking on her chocolate milkshake and stirred it with the straw while she thought about his question.  "I wish it was that easy.  Our space probe is coming back home and no one knows how, or why.  We're trying to figure out if it's something important, or if it'll just burn up when it gets here and everyone'll sweep it under the rug as another embarrassment to add to the embarrassment of not getting any pictures out of it."  She sank her teeth into her fish sandwich.

"So ..." he said, contemplating the curly fry in his hand, "... you don't know any more than anyone else?  That's not like you!"

"I know!  That tells us it's probably nothing . . . at least nothing we'll ever know any more about.  But the scientists are making phone calls today with every free minute of their time, so we might find out something tomorrow."

He took a long pull of his soda.  "That means I have to cook again tomorrow.  We need to hit the grocery store on the way home!"

*

The situation changed long before Wednesday arrived.

Somewhere in the echoey halls of government, someone realized that if the entire *rest* of the world found out the truth while *this* country was still in the dark, the embarrassment of a cover-up, added to the embarrassments already created by the pictureless probe and its mysterious return, could push the people over the edge.  They could call for new leadership.  They could demand blood.

The president sighed but agreed, a new story was invented to cover up the cover-up, telephone calls were made, and by the evening news on Tuesday, the truth about the space probe was finally told to the people of the country who launched it.

*

Priscilla didn't sleep that night.

Brian watched her dance in the living room, sat in the kitchen to sip chamomile tea with her, and dragged her off to bed to make love to her.

But he could not figure out how to help her relax.

*

The team members looked at Priscilla with narrowed eyes, almost hostility, as they arrived to find her sitting on the living room floor eating banana pancakes.  They got food and drink, whispered among themselves, and found places to sit.

"Good morning," she said from the floor.

"Were you lying to us?  Did you know?" General Ba-kerga asked pointedly.

From the kitchen door, Brian bristled, and was a moment away from teaching the general a little respect for his wife, with fists if necessary.  Then he saw the tears in Priscilla's eyes and heard the calmness in her voice.

"No.  The timeline has changed.  Our source person could have missed the short-wave broadcasts in other languages, but not what is all over the newspapers, radio, and television today."  She picked up the morning paper from beside her and unfolded it in the middle of the floor for all to see.  The headline, and several stories on page one, were all about the space probe and its mysterious and rapid journey homeward.

Seeing that Priscilla was taking the situation with humility, the others relaxed.

"Are you . . ." Tanya began hesitantly, ". . . absolutely sure that you . . . I mean our source person . . . didn't just happen to miss reading the newspaper that day . . . I mean today?"

"Yeah, I'm sure.  At sixteen, she followed the space program with a passion, was even thinking of being an astronaut. I remember it all with crystal clarity — the disappointment over the lack of images transmitted back, and the final planetary fly-by of Ko-meriana, known only through basic telemetry. She even followed the telemetry reports from the probe for years to come, after everyone but a handful of scientists had forgotten about it. The probe stayed on course, and exited the solar system in the direction and at the speed it was supposed to. It faithfully measured gravity and magnetic flux, and transmitted those numbers back. There were no weird gravitational forces, and certainly nothing to fling it back toward home."

"So . . ." Sam pondered.

"The timeline has changed," Priscilla repeated. "And to the best of my knowledge, this is the first time. That other point I missed, about eight years ago, was just me mixing up the details of several very similar events . . ."

"And us taking the opportunity to see how you would handle a humbling situation," Sarah admitted.

The sixteen-year-old almost smiled at the retired executive officer.

*

For a few minutes, some people ate in silence, and others, who had not yet had the opportunity, gathered around the newspaper. John verified that it matched what he got from the foreign radio stations, except the lame excuse for the cover-up.

"Doctor Po-selem," General Bo-seklin began, "I feel the urgent need for us to gain a much better understanding of what she means when Priscilla says *the timeline has changed*, and I sense that she'd like a break from leadership today . . ."

Priscilla, still on the floor, nodded.

". . . so would you do the honors?"

"Sure," Chris replied, "but I'll do it from this folding chair, and leave Priscilla's seat at the fireplace for her, whenever she feels ready for it."

Most people nodded agreement.

"There now appear to be two universes, two timelines," the physicist began with his heart in his throat, "and I don't say this lightly or with any jest. Priscilla has the clear memories of a girl who lived in a universe whose space probe did what it was supposed to do, as far as flight path goes. We are now in a different universe. They might have been the same until very recently — perhaps until the probe's fly-by of Ko-meriana — or they might have diverged earlier and we just had no way of knowing it. Let me think — Priscilla's most recent verified prediction was . . ."

After a moment of silence, Sarah said, "No pictures from the space probe, admitted by the government, after lots of hedging, about five months ago."

"So it's probably safe to assume that the two timelines were one at that point. We may never know exactly when they diverged . . ."

"But what does that *mean?*" George demanded.

Chris took a moment to breathe as he looked at the ceiling. "It means, I believe, that any predictions Priscilla has made, or will make, about the future from this point forward, may no longer be valid.  In other words, her track record has just been reset to zero."

The rumble lasted several minutes, and Chris let it run its course.  He noticed that Priscilla had her eyes closed.  Eventually he raised his hands for silence.

"But," he continued his earlier thought, "her predictions CAN still be accurate.  The two timelines CAN have things in common.  In fact, it's possible that the space probe's course is the ONLY difference."

Doctor Bo-leden the philosopher raised his hand.

"Larry?" Chris called.

"I think we should approach this question with a little logical perspective.  All our speculations about Priscilla's predictions notwithstanding, the important question is whether or not our civilization is going to collapse not far into the next century."

Most people nodded.

"And that collapse will be caused by climate change, which is the result of the slow accumulation of certain gasses in the air.  The course of a space probe, however interesting, does not, *cannot*, have any logical effect on those gasses.  In other words, please, let us not confuse purely human concerns, like Priscilla's track record, with much larger, physical things that care nothing for our human issues . . ."

Priscilla was *so* glad when they all finally left.

She crawled in bed and slept deeply for the next five hours.  Susan and Brian used that time to get groceries in Susan's car.

As the coolness and quiet of evening approached, Priscilla moped around the house in pajamas, looking and acting like a lost puppy.  Brian tried to cheer her up, but as evening darkened into night, he admitted defeat and retreated to the kitchen.

Susan waited.

Priscilla poked at her dinner, ate a little but didn't seem to taste it, then stared at the blank television screen in the living room.

Susan picked up a book, but didn't get far.

"Do you . . . have a little . . . free time?" Priscilla asked.

The therapist smiled and nodded.

When Priscilla finally emerged from the counseling room two hours later, her eyes were red but she appeared ready to rejoin the human race.  She washed her face and brushed her teeth, then crawled into bed with Brian.

"Now I know what a fish would feel like without water, or a bird without wings.  My entire life has been based on *knowing* what's coming.  Chris thought I might someday lose my memories of the future.  This is worse.  I still have them, but don't know if they're *right* anymore."

Brian let some time pass to make sure she had said all she wanted.

"Maybe . . . you could just enjoy being a girl for a while — a very smart and talented girl, but still, you know, a girl."

She snuggled closer.  "Yeah.  With Susan's help, that's what I decided to do."

✴   ✴   ✴

## Chapter 75: Reaction

The denial and finger-pointing started on Thursday.

Priscilla, doing her best to be a happy sixteen-year-old girl with a cute boy at her side, spent the day at the park, the shopping center, and the local diner, so she didn't personally witness any of it.

The rest of the team members, even Susan, were kept busy with audio tapes, video recorders, or note pads. By evening, the voices were getting quite loud, and no one could find a radio or television channel without hearing *something* about the space probe every few minutes.

✳

*". . . and I KNOW, my fellow God-fearing people, with ever fiber of my being, that the DEVIL himself, and all his minions, have taken control of that infernal machine that I TOLD you, before it was launched, was going to somehow be used AGAINST everything that is descent and holy . . ."*

Doctor Po-selem stopped his little tape player. "Now, it's true that over the last nine years I've developed some interest in religion . . ."

"Not what you had in mind, Chris?" Betty inquired with a big grin.

He shook his head.

"Something tells me," Priscilla said from her seat by the fireplace, "that today is going to be very interesting from a sociological point of view, but we'll learn nothing new about the space probe itself."

"That's correct," Chris verified with a nod.

"Who wants to go next. Sarah?"

Her video player was already hooked up to Susan's television. After a few seconds of static, the recording began. A congressman stepped up to the venerable podium in the capitol building.

*"It's time to take the gloves off. The liberal MINORITY, only ramming its agenda down our throats with the help of a couple of disloyal DEFECTORS, after wasting MILLIONS on this useless piece of junk that has succeeded at*

*NOTHING but lining the pockets of a few liberal SCIENTISTS, is now trying to use this CHARADE, obviously a liberal CONSPIRACY, to move us closer to losing our SOVEREIGNTY to a world government, run by bureaucrats who aren't even CITIZENS of this great nation . . ."*

Sarah stopped the video when everyone started rolling their eyes.

"Nothing unexpected there," Doctor Po-morna said.

Priscilla smiled at the biologist.  "Let's give equal time to the opposing view, shall we?"

Both Sarah and Tanya laughed.

"I've got that one," Colonel Bo-torin said with a smile and a hand in the air.  "Sorry I didn't have any recording equipment — I'm still living out of a suitcase."  He paged through his note pad, then started reading.

"MTQP Radio, Six O'clock News and Commentary, twenty-eight October 3671.  *Research has turned up new evidence that we can blame the ENTIRE failure of the space probe on conservatives who cut the program's budget last year, probably resulting in sub-standard parts being used for the image transmitting antenna.  This continues their anti-science, anti-media stance that was CLEARLY responsible for the cover-up last week . . .* That's the gist of it."

"Thanks, John."

"The only problem is," Betty began, "the cover-up obviously came from the president's office, who's a liberal!"

John smiled.  "Accurate information is seldom a concern in politics."

Betty sighed.

"I've got one that *transcends* politics," retired General Bo-seklin announced with a slightly-wicked grin.

Priscilla nodded at him.

He started his portable tape player.  "*. . . but if you think the space probe is ACTUALLY coming back, you have been duped, ladies and gentlemen, you have been fooled by special effects, like in the movies.  The fact is, not only is the space probe NOT coming back, it never even LEFT in the first place!*"

Once the laughter started to die down, Sarah slipped in, "At least he didn't make it a religious issue!"

The laughter resumed until everyone noticed Brian carrying lunch platters to the serving table.

✳

Priscilla was giddy with happiness when Lisa called, late that afternoon, announcing that a family of four was on its way to the safe house, and wondering if Priscilla could cook for the weekend.

She assured Brian, with deep kisses, that it wasn't *him* she needed to get away from, and was on her bicycle a quarter hour later.

Something about the silent green hills and the thick concrete walls allowed Priscilla to relax in a way she couldn't anywhere else.  She and Ginny shared a warm hug before Priscilla went upstairs to see her old friends — the strong wooden trusses, the potted plants throughout the building, and the birdhouse, feeder, and birdbath on her old patio.

Eventually, she poked her head into General Ba-kerga's office.  "Hi, George."

"Hi, Priscilla.  They're expected about nineteen hundred, and will probably be quite hungry."

"One feast, coming up!"

"Anything interesting at the meeting today?  I haven't had a chance to catch up with Lisa."

"Denial ... dissociation ... cognitive dissonance ... the usual stuff coming over the air waves, just more of it, and all using the space probe as a substitute for the regular targets of their frustrations."

George nodded, then turned his attention back to the paperwork on his desk.

✳

Lisa arrived in the blind transport with the family of four, all with jet-black hair and facial features that clearly revealed their origin on the other side of the planet.  They were more nervous than Priscilla had ever seen safe-house guests, as if they were stepping into a gas chamber.

Instead, they smelled aromas that might have come from their own kitchen back home, and followed their noses to the dining room where a round table held four place settings and several serving dishes.

Lisa didn't interfere.  She already knew, because of the honesty of the boy, about twelve, and the girl, about eight, that they hadn't eaten all day.  She had checklists to go through, but those could wait an hour.

Although it was not the usual routine, Priscilla brought everything right to their table.  Breakfast tomorrow was soon enough to get them used to the serving line.

The parents and the boy immediately began treating Priscilla as hired help, demanding seconds, or more sauces, or refills of their drinks.

The eight-year-old girl looked at Priscilla with dark, penetrating eyes, and didn't ask for anything, but Priscilla could tell she was smiling without letting her parents see.

✳

By Saturday morning, Priscilla had an assistant cook.  The eight-year-old girl said little, but clearly intended to help with everything, unless ordered by her parents to be elsewhere.

The first two times the girl's work came to a halt, she was in the dining room, or on the outside of the serving line.  The lecture she received from her mother was in a language Priscilla did not know, but the meaning was clear.  Her daughter was nobility, and only servants did kitchen work.

The third time, her father discovered his daughter in the kitchen itself, happily slicing vegetables.

Again Priscilla could not understand the language, but he pointed at the red lines on the floor while he ranted, so Priscilla quickly responded.  She knew they all understood her language, even if they didn't speak it perfectly.

She held up her hand for silence in a way that no servant, in his experience, had ever done, and made solid eye contact. "The red lines may be crossed with permission. The girl has my permission. Someone to talk to is very important when dealing with any stressful situation, and being forced to leave your home is one of the worst. A little work to do helps with stress, also."

The father suddenly felt like a little boy sitting at the feet of a wise priest, and he bowed and departed.

The girl smiled and went back to slowly and carefully slicing vegetables.

✳

By the next day, the girl began talking as she buttered bread or chopped celery.

"We had a big house. There were nine or ten servants to keep it clean all the time. Me and my brother each had a servant of our own. Now we have . . . almost nothing. My father grabbed a few gold coins before we left, and he found out they'll buy us a little tiny house here, but no servants. My mother took our sacred chalice, but that's all she could carry. We had to leave quickly, before the rebels got there."

Priscilla blinked a few times while sautéing vegetables. "I used to live in a big house, and I had guards to protect me everywhere I went. I had more money than I knew what to do with. It was fun, but it couldn't last forever. Now I live in a little house with my husband and my best friend, and we have much less money, but I get to work in this beautiful place, so I'm very happy."

"What happened to all your money?"

"Something very important came along that needed it. I'd do it again in a heartbeat. That's like you leaving your country — you lost many things, but you had to do it."

"Yeah. I just wish . . ."

Priscilla quietly chopped garlic while listening.

"I wish we could have brought all our sacred things, and the temple room of our house. All we got was the chalice. Now mother says we can't have the Family Blessing Ceremony because we don't have all the things we need — the sacred knife, the blessed wine, and the special bread. And it has to be done in a circle on the floor. We had a beautiful rug with a circle just the right size woven into it. We don't have any of that anymore, just the chalice."

Priscilla pondered the girls words as she added the garlic to the sauté pan. "I guess . . . you'll have to make do with what you have."

"My brother thinks that, but mother doesn't want to. She's . . . sad, so sad I don't know if she'll ever be happy again. And she has to lead the Ceremony."

Priscilla started slicing mushrooms. "Maybe . . . your mother is too sad to lead the Ceremony right now, so *you'll* have to."

"But . . . it's *mother's* job."

"So you have to make a choice — lead the Ceremony until your mother is strong enough to do it again . . . or forget it."

The girl continued slicing celery, but her cheeks were wet. "That would mean . . ."

Priscilla waited.

"That would mean our family would be *dead* in the eyes of the gods."

Priscilla breathed a few times. "Your choice."

*

Colonel Ka-markla had never seen a more depressed little group of safe-house residents. They said hardly a word to each other at dinner on Saturday, a dinner Lisa knew was absolutely delicious. Then they just moped around all evening, finding no interest in music, television, magazines, or books.

They dragged themselves to breakfast late on Sunday. Lisa whispered to Priscilla that she was thinking of calling Doctor Bo-kamla. Priscilla asked Lisa to wait a little while longer.

*

Sunday afternoon was about to give way to evening, and Priscilla was getting ready to boil noodles, when a stealthy figure slipped into the kitchen with something hidden under her coat, even though the entire facility was pleasantly warm.

Almost gasping for air, the girl revealed the family's sacred chalice and held it out with trembling hands. "What do I do?"

Priscilla's mind went into high gear, and she quickly located a fancy round serving tray. "Put it in the middle, and I'll do the rest. But *you* have to create the circle and lead the Ceremony."

"I'll . . . try. What should I use?"

Priscilla hunted through drawers until she found a ball of string. "You know how big the circle needs to be. Create your circle in the middle of the big room, and by the time you're done, I'll have your tray ready."

With her heart in her throat and tears threatening to come, the girl walked to the middle of the largest open space in the safe house. She could almost see a circle there already, where furniture had once worn the carpet more than everywhere else. She paced off the distance from the center, then started laying down the string.

Her brother, sprawled on a couch, took notice and sat up. "But you don't have the chalice or the knife or . . ."

"Oh, yes I do!"

The circle was soon complete, so the girl dashed back to the kitchen. She beheld the sacred chalice half-full of grape juice, surrounded by strawberries and fancy crackers. A small, gleaming kitchen knife completed the ceremonial tray.

She smiled up at Priscilla with grateful eyes, picked up the tray, and took tiny steps from the kitchen to the middle of the circle, being very careful not to let the grape juice slosh out.

*

Priscilla had to turn her attention back to dinner, but Lisa nonchalantly observed from the outer office.

The boy waited until his sister called the family to Ceremony by clinking the knife against the rim of the chalice. He made the sacred signs with his hands, then stepped into the circle and seated himself across from her, as had always been his place.

The girl made the call again.

Her father was the next to appear, and pride filled his eyes with tears. He dashed back to the large sleeping room, spoke a few words to his wife, then returned and reverently entered the circle and seated himself.

The girl tapped the knife on the chalice one last time.

The mother entered the room but appeared to be torn, as if she would have run away in shame if she could, but her husband was already seated and was looking up at her. She forced herself to approach the make-shift circle, formed the sacred signs, and sat down.

Lisa smiled, and had a hunch the psychologist would not be needed.

✳   ✳   ✳

## Chapter 76: Alien Invasion

"Session Seventy-One, first of November 3671.  Hi, George.  Didn't we just spend the entire weekend together, trying to keep smiles on some very glum faces?"

General Ba-kerga chuckled.  "I think you and Lisa did most of the work in that department.  We were actually reaching for the phone to call you, Susan, two or three times."

The psychologist smiled, and several others laughed.

"So," Priscilla began once everyone was quiet, "what do we have today?"

Colonel Bo-torin raised his hand.  "I found a tape recorder this time, some more religious craziness . . ."

Before he could begin his presentation, the telephone rang, so Susan slipped into her bedroom to answer.  Not many seconds later, she called out to the group, "It's Malcolm!  He says to turn on the T.V."

Colonel Ma-soran, beside it, punched the *on* button.

". . . just confirmed by the last station of the Deep-Space Telemetry Network.  There's no doubt about it, Ladies and Gentlemen, and there's no cover-up this time.  Scientists are scratching their heads all over the world, and conspiracy theorists are coming out of the woodwork.  But the telemetry can no longer be denied.  The space probe is definitely decelerating, in a manner that would bring its speed from more than six thousand miles per second, to zero, about when it reaches home . . ."

✳

A lanky adolescent girl burst through the rooftop door of the old tenement building, thick newspaper under her arm, and ran to one side of the roof. Without pause, she leapt over the edge and landed on her feet on the next roof, just a few feet away and slightly lower, her bent knees absorbing the shock easily.

Only seconds passed as she crossed that roof and climbed a rickety steel ladder up to the catwalk behind a billboard.  After dodging all the places where boards were missing, she grabbed a pole with one arm and slid down into a jumble of old crates, barrels, and trash.

"Password?" came a young male voice.

"Benny, you *know* I can never remember your stupid passwords!"

"It's Corky," a deeper male voice declared.  "No one could imitate *her* voice."

An old tent flap, barely visible among the trash and junk, was suddenly pulled open.  Benny, about ten, looked out.  "Did you get it?"

"Of *course* I got it!" Corky replied, crawling in.  "Do I *ever* go shopping without getting what I went for?"

"Just wondering, 'cause you said you didn't have any money . . ."

"I *usually* don't have any money.  When did that stop me?"

The older boy, sixteen or seventeen, hunching over something in another part of the large tent, laughed.  "What'd you have to promise him?" he asked without looking up.

Corky spread out the newspaper in the middle of the tent floor.  "I just gave him a kiss, which is probably more than he got from his wife today, or yesterday.  What he *thinks* he's getting later is not my problem.  Here it is. *Space Probe Coming Home For A Soft Landing.*  Any luck with the radio, Alex?"

"I think so," the older boy replied, still concentrating on his work.  "I cleaned the battery contacts, and the batteries Benny borrowed from his mom's flashlight look like they have plenty of juice.  There."

The battered old radio, showing multiple signs of its recent origin — the dumpster behind the tenement building — burst to life with cracking static noise.  Alex adjusted the volume, then the tuning.  Several music stations came and went.  Finally he stopped at a news station.

*. . . are reporting that police are completely overwhelmed by the sudden rioting and looting in several cities, including the capital, and military units are rushing to help keep the peace.  Much of the unrest seems to be coming directly from the pulpits at fundamentalist churches, who are particularly angered by the obvious implication of the most recent news about the space probe . . .*

Alex switched the radio off.  "We'll listen again when everyone's here.  I think I hear Stephy now."

A crashing sound outside the tent revealed that something large and heavy had just descended from the catwalk above.

"That you, Stephy?" Benny challenged, opening the tent flap.

"Why can't I *ever* land gracefully, like Corky does?" the voice of an over-weight girl asked as she appeared among the junk and trash.  She handed a pastry box to Benny, then crawled into the tent.

"That pole is hard when carrying something," Corky said, trying to show sympathy.

No one said anything as they all selected a doughnut from the box that had obviously once contained three more than it did upon arrival.

"Got a report for us?" Alex asked between bites.

"Holy shit, you wouldn't *believe* what uptown's like!"

"Sure we would," Corky said while chewing, "if it's anything like midtown."

"Caught off guard!" a girl even younger than Benny declared as she opened the tent flap, grinning. "News from the waterfront, and cold pizza from my dad's office yesterday."

"You are so cool, Mouse!" Benny said, receiving the pizza box.

Alex cleared his throat. "Stephy was just about to tell us about uptown."

The large girl started to reach for another doughnut, but stopped herself. "Um ... it's crazy. Preachers are out on the streets, cops are trying to shut them up, and people are running around like chickens. Streets are clogged up with cars, some trying to get to the airport, some out to the highway. There's not *much* looting in uptown yet, but that's not true a few blocks north of there! I had to *run*. You know how much I hate running ..."

Her four friends laughed for a moment, then all five looked at each other in silence.

"Mouse?" the leader eventually prompted.

"Oh boy," she began thoughtfully, "first they said school would be open, then they changed their minds when the cops told everybody to stay indoors. The dock workers all took it as a holiday, so my dad got the day off. Maybe all week, who knows? Some stores got looted, but the diners are open, with big guys at the doors almost like a nightclub. Not much traffic, but the streets down there don't go anywhere. Some preacher tried to stir up people on a street corner, but someone shot him. The cops picked up the body."

The group heard similar stories from Corky, Benny, and Alex about both poorer and richer parts of town. Then the radio confirmed that the same thing was happening in other cities.

After nibbling cold pizza for a few minutes and discussing what they had learned, Alex pointed to the newspaper. "Corky got a paper, so I'd like ... Stephy ... to read ..."

"Awww. I *hate* reading."

"I know, that's why it's so hard for you. But remember, the one who's reading gets to sit close beside me so I can help you with words, and I'll put my arm around you, and after we read the news, we'll read a chapter in *The Book* ..."

Both adolescent Corky and little Mouse immediately volunteered with big smiles and hands waving in the air.

Stephy quickly reconsidered, snuggled close beside their handsome leader, and closed her eyes for a moment of wishful thinking when he put his arm around her.

*　*　*

## Chapter 77: Session Seventy-Two

On Wednesday morning between eight and nine o'clock, when the remnant of the P-Seventeen team arrived at Susan's house, Priscilla was nowhere in sight. Since Brian was serving breakfast as usual, and Susan was greeting people nonchalantly, they all relaxed and assumed their leader would appear soon.

At nine o'clock, Susan cleared her throat. "You'll have to forgive our . . ."

Just then, the spare bedroom door opened.

Priscilla had dressed nicely and brushed her hair, as always, but everyone could see that she wasn't well. Several people were thinking *death's doorstep*, but they kept their opinions to themselves. She was visibly shaking as she put a few things onto a plate.

"She didn't sleep at all last night, so be nice to her!" Brian asserted from the kitchen.

Priscilla flashed him a dirty look, but as she sat down in her usual seat by the fireplace, her expression softened. "I guess I should've expected you guys to notice . . ."

Sarah, Lisa, and Tanya all nodded.

"I'm not actually sick. I just . . . can't relax, can't think, and my whole body is vibrating all the time. The only thing that brings me any relief is, you know, dancing. That's what I was doing in the bedroom until just a minute ago, so I don't know how long I'll be able to sit with you."

Retired Colonel Ma-soran made solid eye contact with the girl. "You just do what you need to do, and listen as much was you want. We've got reports from just about everyone today, on the book, new endorsements, climate-change research, the probe, everything, so we'll just work our way through them, and you can jump in any time you want."

Priscilla smiled weakly. "Thanks. I don't know if I'll do much jumping-in, but I'll try to listen, even if I need to get up and move around . . ."

✳

At the meeting, all the usual topics were discussed, with Priscilla most often in the dining room dancing slowly to music only she could hear.  Doctor Po-selem speculated further on the implications of the timeline change.  Colonel Bo-torin reported that the space probe was still decelerating and on course for the planet.  Po Publications had sold or given away four million copies of a certain inconspicuous paperback book, and was preparing to print another million.

All morning long, and especially at lunch, Brian made Priscilla eat and drink.

After prolonged conversation, the officers and professors departed reluctantly, worry for their beloved leader clearly showing on their faces.

Once they were gone, Priscilla searched the television channels, then left it on a news station, with the volume low, as she continued trying to comfort her shaking body, mind, and soul.

By mid-afternoon, she, and almost everyone else on the planet, knew that something very strange was about to happen.  Whether it was wonderful or terrible was a matter of opinion.

✳

"What do you MEAN it's going to land in Capital Park?" the five-star general barked.

"It's now close enough to calculate exactly when and where it will reach the planet, Sir, and several scientists around the world have already done so.  Their findings closely match.  It's trajectory and deceleration are perfect to bring it to a soft landing in the middle of Capital Park tomorrow morning at zero-nine hundred hours, fourteen minutes, twenty-five seconds, local time, plus or minus a few feet and a few seconds."

The general looked ready to explode.  "And I *suppose* these *findings* are all over the radio and television?"

"Um . . . yes, Sir.  That's how we found out."

"Damn!"

✳

In the living room of Susan's house, Priscilla pondered the situation for another hour while nibbling on snacks, stretching, slowly dancing, or listening to news broadcasts.

As late afternoon was passing, she finally knew what she needed to do.  She turned, saw Susan at her little desk in the corner of the dining room, and spoke.  "I don't know *how* this probe business is connected to what our team is doing, but every nerve in my body is screaming at me that it somehow *is*.  We need to get to Capital Park."

"I'm a step ahead of you, just made a list of the airlines that can get us there."  As the psychologist finished speaking, she reached for the telephone.

Priscilla smiled for possibly the first time that day.

Brian set a chocolate milkshake on Susan's desk, then carried two more to the living room.  "Sit and snuggle with me.  Susan can handle that."

Priscilla tried to lose herself in the closeness with her favorite boy and the delicious flavor of her favorite drink, but she couldn't stop herself from noticing that Susan was making call after call, without announcing any success. After a while, they started hearing sighs, and then faint growls. Eventually the telephone was hung up with a slight *bang*, and no more sounds came from the dining room.

A minute later, Susan lowered herself into a stuffed chair in the living room. "Sorry, kids. The rest of the world beat us to it."

The five-star general didn't go home for dinner. He got a tray from the building's cafeteria, then sat in his office, fuming.

A quarter hour later, he finally turned to the shelf behind his desk and grabbed a telephone directory labeled, *Department of Defense Emergency Use Only*. Finding the number he wanted, he tapped it in and waited.

"This is General Ko-doran at the Department of Defense. If the mayor is not in his office, then I need you to connect me to him *wherever* he . . . he is? Good. I need to speak to him *now*."

The general waited, sometimes hearing hushed conversations in the background.

"Mayor Do-salan! General Ko-doran at Defense. Looks like you are sitting on Ground Zero, so I'm sending a tactical strike force to completely surround Capital Park so that *whoever* or *whatever* lands there tomorrow morning . . . what do you mean, *NO?*"

"*NO* is exactly what I mean, General. This is a scientific and cultural event, and there is no evidence of any threat of any kind. So unless Congress has declared *war* on our space probe, or some evidence of a genuine *threat* comes to light, I'm instructing all departments to handle the situation carefully and without any presumption of hostility . . . No, sorry, that's not happening either, but it may set your mind at ease that I'm establishing a circle two hundred yards wide in the middle of the park where no people will be allowed . . ."

General Ba-kerga had never felt so frustrated.

His two adult safe-house guests were more trouble than *any* children had ever been. They made demands, quarreled, or created security problems every five or ten minutes, it seemed. Lisa was tirelessly going back and forth from the kitchen, to the T.V. room, to the laundry room, leaving George to handle the offices and the guard rooms.

Then the telephone rang.

"What! . . . Sorry, Priscilla, we're just a bit stressed out right now, but our guests are only here for a few more hours, so don't even *think* about coming in . . ."

He listened for a minute.

"Absolutely and completely not possible. The entire military is on alert because of the probe, nothing but high-priority flights going anywhere.  Just as an example of how tight things are, I can't even get a security guard."

He listened to Priscilla say a few reassuring things, then ended the call. The moment he looked up, he saw his next problem.  "Hey!  Can you not SEE the red line on the floor across the stairway?"

*

Five-star General Ko-doran discussed a number of possible tactics, none of which looked promising, with the few aides he could find in the building. The mayor of the city appeared to be on solid ground, legally speaking.

"He may have the upper hand legally," one aide said, a two-star general with a reputation for getting things done, "but you will always have superior power physically.  You just have to use it."

General Ko-doran eventually dismissed the aides and took a deep breath. As twenty-one hundred was approaching, he picked up the telephone and punched in another number.

"Colonel Bo-hefra, General Ko-doran.  How many tanks do you have that could get to Capital Park by morning, using only minor roads and streets that won't draw attention?"

He listened.

"That's less than I was hoping, but I guess it'll have to do.  I want them around the park by zero-eight hundred, with their gun barrels pointed at the middle . . ."

*

Priscilla cried like a baby in Susan's arms.  "I feel completely *useless* . . . like I'm supposed to *do* something . . . the most *important* thing I've ever done . . . but I can't do *anything* . . ."  Her words faded away into deep sobs.

Susan continued to hold her friend, saying just enough to let Priscilla know she was still listening, but feeling equally powerless.

Brian sat near, ready to get anything they needed, but knowing this was a moment best handled by women.

As ten o'clock was passing, Susan needed to take a break, so Priscilla snuggled close to Brian.

"I bet you won't be sleeping again tonight," he said, just for something to say.

"Don't think I could, even if I was *dead*."

He laughed, then got serious again.  "Me and Susan won't sleep either."

She looked up at him.  "Thanks.  Even though I feel very small and useless right now, I know I'm the luckiest girl in the world in lots of ways."

He pulled her close.  "You know, if we're gonna be awake all night, waiting for . . . whatever's gonna happen in Capital Park . . . we don't have to sit here the whole time.  There's an all-night diner at the truck stop, and that old cinema plays movies and serves pizza all night.  Some of the movies they play in the wee hours are pretty bad . . ."

Priscilla chuckled for the first time that evening.  "Sounds like fun, even the bad-movie part.  Let's see what Susan thinks . . ."

✳

As Susan drove, they quickly discovered that no one else, in the entire city of several million people, was planning to get any sleep that night, either.

Streets were jammed with cars, sidewalks crowded with people. Some business had boarded up their windows. Others were open and had two or three big guys at the door — sometimes real security guards, other times just hired thugs.

The most popular places were taverns and diners with a television, and every one was tuned to coverage of the drama two thousand miles away in Capital Park.

Not long after midnight, the trio managed to find a pizza parlor that had one table left, and only a small cover charge. They soon realized why — the place had no television or radio, just a little canned country music.

They looked at each other and all nodded.

As they got settled in the little booth by the kitchen door, Priscilla took a deep breath and found her second wind. "There may have been very few people awake *last* night, but tonight I've got *lots* of company!"

✳   ✳   ✳

## Chapter 78: People

On Thursday, the fourth of November 3671, the sun was just beginning to rise over the capital city when the armored tanks rolled in.

At first no one noticed.  With the looting and other chaos going on in parts of the city, sparked by the imminent return of the space probe and all the deep-seated hopes and fears that event triggered, a few tanks rolling through the industrial outskirts hardly raised an eyebrow.  In fact, on this particular Thursday, few people were at work in those industrial areas.

But when the tanks reached the residential neighborhoods, people noticed.

No one saw more than one tank, as each was approaching from a different direction, along a different set of carefully-chosen roads and streets.  But since tanks travel slowly, news of their approach traveled faster — by telephone, citizen-band radio, or youth on fast legs.  By seven o'clock, everyone knew, and most of them didn't much like it.

If the city had been populated only by well-to-do adults and submissive kids with plenty of spending money to keep them occupied, the tanks might have reached their destination without challenge.

Alas, most of the people were not very well-to-do, and most of the young people had little spending money and dim prospects for good jobs in the future.

The tanks, slowly rolling toward Capital Park, immediately took on symbolic meaning.  They brought guns, very big guns, to the only open space in the city where people could go to relax and be in nature for an hour or two.  They clearly intended to point those guns at the space probe, the same space probe that most people had cheered on as it began its journey just the year before.  It was *their* space probe, and the fact that it was imperfect, a little broken, almost crippled, made many people identify with it even more.  It had done it's job as best it could, and now it was coming home, landing in *their* park, and it might even have pictures of the universe to show.

Still, adults are cautious and conservative by their nature, most of them having families to support, rent to pay, and jobs to keep.  The generals and colonels who sent the tanks, and chose the streets down which they would roll, were counting on this.

Teenagers, however, didn't feel quite so inhibited.  They had recently discovered, with the help of a certain book, that forces were moving their planet toward big problems.  In secret rooms in boarded-up buildings, hollowed-out places behind bushes, and old tents disguised with trash and junk, they met, shared news, and made plans.

✳

The tank, the one that would have arrived at Capital Park first, was making its way through a middle-class neighborhood when it turned a corner to discover a group of seven teenagers having a picnic in the middle of the narrow street.

Adults and other youth were watching from the sidewalks.  Others leaned out of second and third-story windows.  Some felt fear for the brave teenagers.  Others cheered them on.

The tank rolled to a stop, but had no other response for a minute.

People started coming out of the buildings.  More teenagers joined those sitting in the street, bringing more food and drink to share.

Finally a hatch opened on top of the tank.  A soldier emerged holding a machine gun.

The people started grumbling.

The soldier yelled at the youth in the street to move out of the way.

They didn't.

He yelled again and pointed his machine gun at them, but suddenly heard, all around him, the unmistakable sound of many other guns being loaded and cocked.  He carefully looked around, and saw rifles, shot guns, and hand guns of all sizes, pointed at *him*.

After taking a few slow breaths, he carefully handed his machine gun down through the hatch and said something to the men below.

A few seconds later, the tank's motor fell silent.

Then he carefully seated himself on top of the tank, pulled cigarettes from a pocket, and lit one.

The other two soldiers climbed out and did the same.

The men of the neighborhood lowered their guns, and the women and children started clapping.

One of the teenagers handed three cans of soda pop up to the soldiers on the tank.

✳

Three more tanks encountered a similar situation.  At two of them, the soldiers came out and talked to the people.  At the third, fear or duty kept them inside. The people didn't care, and soon had so much junk piled around the big machine that the teenagers who had stopped it could run off to do other things.

But one tank didn't stop.

The screams reverberated through the working-class neighborhood of tenement houses and small businesses.

Guns were already handy, and many bullets pinged off the thick steel armor, each one expressing the anger and rage of the local people, whether or not they knew the teenagers who had just died.

Other people, with slightly cooler heads, dashed away, quickly returning with more potent weapons. Lengths of iron pipe caused the tank tracks to jerk and screech, while bricks and broken concrete blocks quickly brought it to a halt.

Gasoline cans came out of every building, with jars of kerosene and small propane canisters not far behind. Soon the entire tank was a blazing inferno, and no one who watched could decide who had the kinder death — the soldier who burst through the hatch, or the ones who stayed inside.

✳

The last tank came upon five youth sitting in its path, two of them not yet teenagers.

With Colonel Bo-hefra himself commanding the vehicle, the driver didn't dare stop.

Alex realized it wasn't going to stop with mere seconds to spare, shoved Stephy with all his might and saw her grab Benny as she rolled, kicked Mouse until she scrambled away, then grabbed Corky and tumbled to the side just as the tracks of the huge vehicle rumbled by.

After catching their breath, the five friends gathered in the street as the tank slowly moved away from them.

"I've never been so scared!" Stephy gasped out.

"Thanks," Corky said, looking up at Alex with admiring eyes.

"We need a different weapon ..." As he spoke, he looked around, and soon spotted a man he knew standing beside the open door of a small carpet and drapery shop. "Mister Ta-daren! We could stop that thing if we had paint, glue, and stuff. We'll pay you back, I swear ..."

The shop owner was already in motion, quickly grabbing cans of bright colors that didn't sell well, a cheap brand of floor cement, and stacks of carpet and drapery samples he'd gotten for free. "My contribution to the cause!"

The shopkeeper and five youth quickly had armloads, several neighbors dashed in to help, more young people joined the excitement, and Missus Ta-daren came downstairs to watch the shop.

More than twenty people dashed up the street with weapons that no tank crew had ever been trained to defend against.

✳

So it was that only one armored tank arrived at Capital Park, just moments before its last view port was covered. The crew was then unable to steer or aim the big gun, and they soon discovered they could not even open the hatch.

What they didn't know was that they looked, for all the world to see, like something out of a back-street carnival.

＊　＊　＊

## Chapter 79: Approach Vector

During the last hour of the approach to Ko-tera Three with three point six gravities of deceleration acting upon the external cargo, the members of the Education Service team and all the contact specialists were quiet and thoughtful.  After Kibi finished checking on her passengers, Ilika decided it was time to see how his crew members were doing.

"Any passenger problems?" he asked his steward.

"They're tense, pondering all the unknowns in the next part of the mission.  We have plenty of packaged food, but they'll really appreciate fresh grass and fish as soon as possible."

Ilika squeezed her shoulder and moved on.

"How do things look, Boro?"

"We're gonna be scraping the bottom, but I still have that little emergency tank.  I keep reminding myself that we can do everything with anti-mass and ion as soon as we put that probe thing down somewhere.  If Melorania asks for any engine or fuel restrictions for training purposes, say *no*."

Ilika chuckled and stepped beside Mati.  "How does it look, Pilot?"

"Course and deceleration are perfect.  What worries me is that we're landing in a public park.  It brings up memories of a certain training simulation where I had to crush sapient bunnies.  I *really* don't want to do that here, Ilika, especially since they're *real*, and they're *humans*."

"We'll do everything possible to avoid that situation."

"Thanks.  I'm piloting the final thousand meters myself, just in case."

Ilika nodded and stepped beside Sata.  "Any flight-plan issues?"

"I've been reading about this city, and they sometimes have wires stretched through the air . . ."

"Another reason for a manual approach," Mati tossed in.

Sata chuckled.  ". . . and they change them too often to be on the charts. Other than that, I'm just nervous because this is the biggest, most important mission we've ever been on, even though it's not the longest."

"Everyone's feeling that.  Anything of concern, Rini?"

"Air pollution.  Moderate over the capital city where we're going, nothing that'll give Mati a problem, but it's much worse over some other cities.  Are they *trying* to be another Sonmatia Two?"

"That's what this mission is all about."

Rini nodded.  "I can *feel* the timelines branching out into the future, but I can't see where any of them go."

"Maybe we'll find out."

"Atmosphere in eight minutes," the navigator announced.

Ilika wandered up to the passenger area to see if Ashley had any last-minute instructions.

✳

"I've already told Manessa the configuration I want when we . . ." Ashley was saying when both she and Ilika became aware that Arantiloria had just materialized on the galley counter.  They, and everyone else, turned to look at the training specialist.

"You are a welcome sssight!" T'sss'lisss admitted from a passenger seat.

"There is no need to feel unsure of your decisions, my reptilian friend.  Your instincts and intuitions are right in line with the needs of the mission and the concerns of the universe."

The half-meter of T'sss'lisss that was out of her coils waved back and forth as she basked in the compliment.

"However, I'm wondering where you're going," Arantiloria continued.

"I thought it best," Ashley began, "to place the malfunctioning space probe in the park of the capital city of the country that launched it."

"Very good idea," the spirit began, "but one of you is missing."

Sata, listening from her station, stood up.  "Isn't Ss'klexna Rrr'tak'fi already on Keru . . ."

"She's right here with you, and wouldn't miss this event for all the frogs in Nebador . . . even though she can't eat them anymore."

Ilika smiled slightly.

"But there is still someone missing, someone who has given nearly every minute of her life to this mission, from birth to this very moment.  She's been awake for more than two days, but has no way to get herself and her team to Capital Park."

"The Temporandek Teacher, bok!" Kolarrr'ka guessed.

Ilika looked at Ashley.

"Then . . . I think . . . we should fix that problem," the mission leader said, noticed Arantiloria smile, and looked toward the navigator.

"Can you give us a hint?" Sata begged, sitting back down at her console.  "We have no idea where she is."

A set of planetary coordinates flashed onto Sata's display.  She quickly had a chart up.  "The other side of the continent from the capital city."

"But there are many, many people waiting for you in Capital Park," the training specialist reminded them, "and they know *exactly* when you are supposed to arrive."

"Perhapsss," T'sss'lisss began, "we should ssset the probe down in the park firssst."

"Absolutely!" Boro suddenly agreed.  "Then we can use engines that don't drink fuel like it was pinkfruit juice!"

Everyone chuckled or honked.

"Even so," Arantiloria added, "the Teacher needs an hour, after you leave the park, to get herself and her team to the pick-up coordinates."  She looked at Kibi with mesmerizing eyes.  "Expect twelve to fifteen monkey mammals."

Kibi frowned and her mind raced as she started looking around the passenger area, wondering where she was going to put them.

"Quiet on the bridge for final approach to Capital Park," Mati commanded.

✳   ✳   ✳

## Chapter 80: Homecoming

At six fourteen, their time, on that unusual Thursday morning, Susan, Priscilla, and Brian all sat close together on the living room couch, popcorn bowl in Priscilla's lap so they could all reach it, eyes glued to the television.

The mysterious golden sphere lowered itself, and the handicapped space probe it carried, to the ground on the edge of the two-hundred foot circle of low barricades. The city police were supposed to be patrolling that circle, but at that moment they were as awe-struck as the thousands of other people standing in the cool morning air.

Observatories and people with telescopes had only learned that the space probe was not alone less than an hour before. That knowledge had not reached the city officials until just ten minutes ago. The police and people on the ground, and the television cameras, were just now finding out.

The probe was placed on the ground very gently, almost like a sacred offering, right in front of a tent on the edge of the circle from which the mayor and city council watched with open mouths. The eight grappling arms retracted and disappeared, and the golden sphere floated upward.

A minute later it disappeared among the clouds, and everyone let out a collective sigh.

"I guess I was wrong," Priscilla said, "and this doesn't have anything to do with us."

✳

After staring at the broadcast for a few more minutes, the trio of housemates filtered away, but no one bothered to turn off the television.

Priscilla was brushing her teeth, feeling her mind shutting down for a long sleep, when she happened to hear something from the on-going news broadcast.

"*. . . and we've just received a report from our affiliate station in River City, that the golden ball was spotted high over the shopping center,* *heading west . . ."*

Priscilla quickly landed on her knees on the living-room carpet and turned up the volume, but the station had already switched back to events in Capital Park, where space-agency technicians were beginning to examine the probe.

"Map of the country!" Priscilla nearly screamed. "I need a map of the country!  Please tell me you have one, Susan."

"Of course I have one.  Slow down, Priscilla.  Breathe.  Here it is . . ."

"Brian, yard stick!" the excited sixteen-year-old commanded.

He smiled and opened the broom closet.

Within a minute, Priscilla had a straight line from the capital, through River City, all the way to the coast.  The three stared with wide eyes.

"Goes right through the Appala Hills, just west of here.  Isn't that about where . . ."  Brian's voice trailed off, seeing the two females staring at each other.

After a long moment of silence that seemed to last forever, but only allowed their hearts to beat once or twice, Priscilla spoke.  "We have to call everyone and tell them to meet at the facility!"

"*I'll* do that," Susan declared.  "You, wash your face and make yourself presentable.  Brian, pack some juice and snacks.  Everyone meet in the driveway in five minutes."

"But I don't have clear . . ." he began.

"Forget that crap," Susan asserted.  "Let's move!"

✳

As soon as they were in the car, Brian had questions.  "Susan, *how* did you call all those people in just *five* minutes?"

She smiled into the rear-view mirror.  "I didn't.  I just called Lisa at the facility.  The place is empty and she's bored stiff, so she volunteered to call everyone else while we drive."

He nodded.  "Why did you bring your dance bag?" he asked his young wife beside him.

"I have a hunch that's what I'll be doing today.  I'm not a space-probe technician.  I'm not a diplomat who can represent Ko-tera to visiting aliens.  I'm just a dancer."

Susan chuckled from the front seat.  "You and I both know it's not the aliens who will be the problem."

Priscilla grinned toward the rear-view mirror for a moment, grabbed a can of juice and drained it, then snuggled against Brian to try to get her racing heart to relax.

✳

"I'm thinking we should just park in the grass on the other side of the road," Susan said as they approached the facility.  "Getting everyone into the parking garage would take forever."

Priscilla opened her eyes.  "Yeah.  And that way maybe no one will notice Brian."  She looked at him.  "Act like you've been here a hundred times and this is perfectly routine."

He swallowed. "Okay."

"I think I see Sam right behind us," Susan said, beginning to slow down, "and there's another car behind him."

Priscilla turned and looked. "I think that's Betty."

Susan pulled the car onto the grass, and Lisa emerged from the rarely-used sidewalk door of the facility, then pointed for the following cars to park beside Susan. George stood in the open doorway observing.

Priscilla said quietly to Brian, "Stay with Susan," just before she climbed out and crossed the road. "Hi, George!"

"What's happening, Priscilla?"

"Your guess is as good as mine, but if I *had* to guess, I'd say we're about to get a ride to Capital Park so I can dance for the people there."

"You mean, in a . . ."

"I think so."

"I'll . . . have to report it, you know."

"Yeah, I know."

"But . . . I don't suppose anyone will notice if I happen to wait until after it's gone . . . with your non-cleared husband, of course, whom I . . . didn't see."

"But George, you're part of the team! You should come, too!"

"No. Someone has to run the safe house. The television will keep me informed."

Priscilla nodded. "Thank you. For everything. For being a very reliable father figure to me for the last nine years."

He shooed her away, just as another car pulled in.

"John!" she greeted as he hopped out of his rented car and took a moment to finish buttoning the coat of his uniform.

⁕

Doctor Chris Po-selem, physicist, arrived about two minutes later, then Doctor Larry Bo-leden, philosopher.

Less than a minute after that, the golden sphere descended from the sky, hovered silently for a moment, then sprouted landing struts and settled onto the grass not far from the parked cars. A hatch opened and a short, wiry teenage girl with faint scars on her face stood in the opening and spoke in a loud, clear voice, but was obviously not a native speaker of the language. "I have understand there be Teacher here that need ride to Capital Park, with her team also."

Most mouths were open and throats too dry to speak even if they knew what to say.

Priscilla immediately liked the alien. She appeared young, but already deeply experienced, especially with the facial scars. Priscilla stepped forward and smiled, hoping the alien couldn't see the trembling all throughout her body. "I'm . . . I'm Priscilla . . . Priscilla Ka-mentha."

"What number of team?" the alien asked.

Priscilla looked around. "Nine so far, but I hope a few more arrive in time."

Just then a car appeared at the crest of the near-by hill, raced the remaining quarter mile, and came to a sudden stop on the grass, sliding the last few feet. Retired Colonel Sarah Ma-soran stepped out of the driver's seat, went around to the other side, and helped retired Three-star General Malcolm Ko-fenral out of the car as he fumbled with the coat of his uniform.

"Doctor Tu-feltin couldn't get a ride, and I got no answer at Doctor Po-morna's home or office," Lisa revealed.

"Eleven," Priscilla said, with finality, to the alien.

"It be little crowded in here," the alien girl responded, "but we find seat for each you. The flight only last some three minutes."

George's eyes snapped open, and he realized he should make a note of that last statement for later analysis.

*

Even at the leisurely speed the Manessa Kwi had traveled from Capital Park to the Appala Hills, they had out-paced every military aircraft that attempted to intercept or follow, which were many as they crossed the country.

But in the quarter hour the little response ship was on the ground to load her passengers, the location was quickly pin-pointed by spotter planes, and fighter jets were scrambled from the nearest air base.

*

The interior of the golden ship was dimly lit, and the entering guests could see a view of the top-secret facility on a large screen at the front of the passenger area. Beyond that, at a lower level, several aliens quietly went about their business at consoles with glowing controls and displays.

Colonel John Bo-torin was guided to the back row of seats by a girl with shaggy black hair who spoke no words but was able to put him at ease with gestures and smiles. He found himself seated beside a tank of water, and thought little of it until a gray dolphin head emerged and looked at him, followed closely by a dark-green sea turtle head. He fumbled to straighten his tie.

Retired General Bo-seklin was seated at the far end of the third row, but he soon realized there was one more passenger on that row who did not have a seat — a very large stripped tiger, or something similar, its head level with the general's. "N . . . nice kitty," he babbled.

The cat turned its head slowly to look at the human, but did not show any facial expressions.

Doctor Betty Ko-silma, chemist, was guided to a comfortable seat, at the end of the second row, that seemed to adjust itself to her size and shape. Soon she noticed a slight aroma she hadn't smelled since she was young, visiting her uncle's farm. Her gaze was drawn to the huge horse beside her on the floor who seemed to be looking thoughtfully at the large display screen. She smiled to herself.

As Susan, Priscilla, and Brian were seated in the front row, they noticed a large bird sitting on what appeared to be a kitchen counter, and glimpsed a thick snake raise its head over the counter for a moment, then lower itself back out of sight. Susan shuddered, but breathed deeply to settle her nerves.

The roar of a fighter jet, flying low, was heard by all just a moment before the hatch was closed.

*

"Greetings," the short wiry girl said from beside the console at the front of the passenger area. "My name Ashley Riddle. We here not to interfere your society. The flight to Capital Park lasts three minutes about."

"I need to be the first one out," Priscilla asserted, "and I want you to play Side A of this record while I dance, repeating it as necessary." She handed Ashley a vinyl disc.

Ashley handled it by the edges, as Priscilla had done, but didn't know what to do with it. In the language of Nebador, she said, "Manessa, can you read this disc?"

"Please place it on the steward's console display."

Some of the guests looked around for the source of the new voice.

"I can read it, but need to know the speed and direction," Manessa said.

Ashley translated the query.

"Fifty R.P.M., clockwise, outside in," Priscilla answered.

Ashley translated for Manessa, and a few seconds later, the music began.

"Wow!" Priscilla breathed. "I've never heard it so good! You even took out the pops and clicks!"

Ashley smiled, and heard Kibi whisper something from her station. "Everyone, prepare to landing, please."

Priscilla hopped out of her seat. "I need to change clothes somewhere!"

Ashley lead her to the toilet room as the golden ship slowly descended into the middle of Capital Park, where thousands of people still waited, talking about what they had seen, curious about the probe and its memory full of pictures, and wondering what else they might see that day.

* * *

## Chapter 81: Dancer

Alex and Corky sat proudly atop the turret of their captured military tank on the edge of Capital Park.  Stephy, Benny, Mouse, and about a dozen other youth covered the lower portion of the huge war machine.

By that time, plenty of broken concrete blocks in the tracks had rendered it immobile.  After trying several times, the men inside finally gave up and shut down the engine.  They still occasionally turned the turret and big gun, causing the kids on the lower level to stand up and step over the gun barrel, but eventually swung it to the rear of the tank, pointed away from the park, and left it there.

Every few minutes, the men banged on the inside of the hatch, but the carpet samples and floor glue continued to do their jobs well.

The mood in the park had changed from the tense expectation of the original landing, to a relaxed picnic atmosphere as the people awaited news from the space-probe technicians.  Most people knew they wouldn't be able to see any pictures on that occasion, but they still wanted to be among the first to hear the good news.  Many picnic baskets, ice chests, and pizza boxes arrived, and the bounty was shared with friends and strangers alike.  The police moved some of the barricades to protect a small area around the probe, but relaxed their vigilance elsewhere.  The rest of the original barricades were quickly opened by the people to make more space for the community picnic.

Alex and Corky watched with open mouths as the golden ball returned and settled onto the ground, in the exact center of the park, so silently that very few people were frightened, and only those closest to the middle bothered to get up and move.

The ball immediately changed shape, becoming a circular platform about three feet high.  From an unseen ramp at the center, a teenage girl in a dance outfit appeared just as every pair of eyes in the park turned to look, and every pair of ears heard the opening notes of a popular song.

Alex, and many others, perceived a dancing angel, with white wings flowing from her arms as she slowly began to move to the pulsing music while spiraling outward on the platform.

Corky, and many other youth, saw a delicate fairy, arms playing in the air, wings fluttering, and slender body prancing as she neared the edge, then leapt to the grass below.

A few people, mostly much older, saw a devil or demon, sent to ensnare good people with a false image of beauty in preparation for an alien invasion.

The men in the military tank heard the music and wished they could have seen anything.

As the music coming from the golden platform grew stronger, the dancer moved among the people, sometimes touching a child or youth, often gesturing for them to join her, and many of the young and young-at-heart did.  The area around the platform was quickly vacated by those who wanted to just sit and watch, and was soon filled with dancers of all ages.  Corky grinned at Alex, then jumped down from the tank turret to join in the fun.  Benny and Mouse followed.  Stephy saw an opportunity and climbed onto the turret beside Alex.

Alex observed the entire park with part of his mind, but quickly noticed when a short, wiry girl appeared on the platform wearing a flowing purple robe.

She strolled around the platform watching the dancers for a moment, then stopped just opposite the mayor's tent and touched something on her arm.  Part of the platform rose until it was a slender box about three feet high.

She touched her arm again and the music became very soft.  She spoke and her voice was amplified so that everyone in the park could hear her clearly.

"Good morning.  We not here to interfere your society any way.  We brought probe back for you see the beautiful pictures it was taken."

"Thought so," Alex muttered.  "She's not from here."

A man and a woman in military uniforms emerged from the middle of the platform and walked slowly to the podium, the woman supporting the older man.  "Um . . . hello.  I am Three-star General . . ." He paused to cough.  ". . . Three-star General Malcolm Ko-fenral, retired.  It is a great honor to be here."

"I am Colonel Sarah Ma-soran, retired."

"*Those* two are from here," Alex commented to Stephy.

Benches appeared near the center of the platform, and the pair of retired officers made their way toward them slowly.  The short girl continued to stand beside the podium, and the dancer and many people continued to dance on the grass below.

A young man emerged.  "Hi, I'm Brian.  I'm just a very lucky boy.  The dancer down there's my wife."

Alex smiled.  "Him too."

A middle-aged man with wild hair stepped to the podium.  "Doctor Chris Po-selem, physicist, at your service!"

Stephy chuckled.

Another uniformed man appeared.  "Good morning.  I'm Two-star General Samuel Bo-seklin, retired."

He joined the other officers on the benches.

"Doctor Betty Ko-silma, chemist," a short woman introduced herself.

Alex noticed that the many people watching, including the mayor, city council, and police, were starting to relax, seeing that the supposed-alien space ship appeared to contain mostly their own people.

Two more uniformed officers came forth, then a philosopher and a psychologist.

"They're ours too," Alex whispered.

Stephy nodded agreement.

✳

"Priscilla?" Ashley called from the podium.

The dancer, without ever quite ceasing to dance, worked her way through the crowd and climbed onto the platform.

Ashley smiled and pointed at the podium.

Priscilla stood breathing for a moment, then stepped up.  "Hi everyone! I'm Priscilla Ka-mentha.  I'm a cook . . . and a dancer!"

Ashley stepped to the podium as Priscilla jumped back down.  "And she also one of greatest Teachers your world ever known."

Brian's eyes snapped open wide.  Malcolm, Sam, Sarah, and the other team members' minds were spinning as they absorbed Ashley's words, but they weren't, upon reflection, surprised.

✳

No one had time to contemplate Ashley's words for very long.  Part of the platform became recessed, quickly filled with water, and two gray dolphin heads popped up and looked over the edge at the dancing and picnicking people.  A moment later, a large green turtle joined them.

A huge, muscular horse emerged from the unseen ramp, walked forward and lowered himself onto his belly near the podium.

A large tiger appeared and sat on his haunches on the other side of the podium.

A big bird and a thick snake came last.  The bird flapped up to the podium, and the snake slithered around it until it was completely coiled on top.

"I bet *they're* not from here," Alex declared for only Stephy to hear.

Ashley laughed at the other two mission leaders as she returned to the crowded podium.  "My friends not speak your language, but they bring greetings you."

Finally, six more people came up the hidden ramp, all wearing loose robes of different colors, and stood at the very back, behind the seated military officers and scientists.

"Them either," Stephy guessed.

* * *

## Chapter 82: A Little Question

Ashley had thought long and hard, during the two Satamia days needed to get the space probe home, about what she would do and say at this moment. She had asked for, and received opinions from everyone on the ship.

A number of possibilities came up for speeches she could give, lectures to the people of Ko-tera Three about what they were doing wrong, and what the consequences would be if they continued.  Several of her advisors were in favor of that approach.

Others pointed out that the people of Ko-tera Three already *knew* all that stuff, and if they had any desire to act upon it, they would, of their own accord.

Ashley, of course, listened most closely to Memsala and Arantiloria.  She would have liked to know Shemultavia's thoughts on the matter, or even Kerloran's, and would have interpreted either as inviolable commands, but neither showed themselves.

In the end, with less than an hour remaining to their destination, Ashley had made the decision to do little, say little, but be open to hints and guidance that might come from just about any source, including an unexpected one.

*

The dancer continued to move gracefully among the young people, smiling at all, touching some like a visiting butterfly.  The people and animals on the alien ship-platform, most of whom weren't aliens at all, chatted and laughed, but didn't seem inclined to blast anyone with ray guns.  Catered food arrived for the mayor, city council, and space-probe technicians.  For many reasons, the relaxed picnic atmosphere returned to Capital Park.

Nearly every teenager had joined the dance, as well as many older children and a few adults.  Younger children played in groups on the grass not far from their parents, like at any picnic.

One mother was chatting with another and didn't notice her five-year-old boy toddle away.

Ashley and Brian were on the platform swaying to the music, Toran Takil had curled up for a nap in the sunshine, Kolarrr'ka had taken wing for some exercise, and T'sss'lisss was still on the podium, stretching this way and that, just for fun.

"Mister Snake, can I see inside your space ship?" the little boy asked from the grass just a few feet away.

T'sss'lisss didn't have time to get a translation from Ashley, as the worried mother was quickly on the scene, scooping up her son and scolding him as she began to walk away and he started to cry.

Suddenly Ashley knew what she had to say, and stepped to the podium. A code tapped into her bracelet caused the music to fall completely silent.

"There's . . . your . . . hint," the mission leader said loudly and clearly.

Priscilla ceased her graceful movements and turned to look.

Toran Takil awoke and sat up to listen.

The mother, still holding her son, froze and turned around.

The mayor set down his lunch and stepped out of the tent.

Nearly everyone else in the park fell silent in their conversations or play so they could hear the alien.

T'sss'lisss slithered down off the podium so Ashley could be seen.

"On message plaque on space probe," the mission leader continued, "you asked what could do to save own innocent ones from the climate change as will soon destroy civilization yours. I not come here to lecture you or solve problems for, but little boy and mother just gave better clue than could I *ever*."

Doctor Chris Po-selem was on the edge of his bench.

"It very simple. You not learned to listen your children. Only *they* know way forward during times of change great. Only *their* minds enough fresh and flexible for avoid fears that keep in old ways."

Priscilla was nodding and grinning from ear to ear where she stood on the grass.

"A ship arrives from you call Heaven," Ashley went on, "sent by you call God, and reaction is *fear*. Child's mind open to new experiences, new information, exactly what needed right now. You learn from them, or you perish. Either way, with or without, universe will go on."

Ashley touched her bracelet, the music started again, and the dancer resumed her graceful angelic or fairy-like movements among the young and young-at-heart.

✳

The mother struggled with herself for a long moment. Her son, still in her arms, looked at her with pleading eyes. Eventually, with tortured steps, she carefully approached the platform and looked up at the alien girl in a purple robe. "Every nerve in my body is screaming at me to protect my boy from anything strange."

Ashley sat down on the edge of the platform.  "Those same instincts tell hold onto all old habits, even when planet cannot tolerate another mouth to feed, cannot absorb another day pollution, cannot give more any coal, oil, and gas."

The mother stood with tears in her eyes, looking back and forth from her hopeful son, to the alien girl, horse, and tiger, to the military officers and scientists behind them.  She did not consciously understand, but she somehow felt the weight and importance of the moment.

"Please mom," the boy begged.  "I promise not to touch anything."

Ashley suppressed her temptation to smile.

"Well . . . okay . . . but just for a few minutes."

The boy smiled.

Ashley stood at the podium again.  "One brave mother find courage to listen to child, grant him freedom to learn as his heart.  More any children with brave parents there?  I give tour of little ship eight children, easily as one."

All over Capital Park, children from three years, to ten or eleven, began begging their parents for permission to see the inside of the alien ship.  Some, of all different ages, just headed toward the platform as fast as their legs could go, daring their parents to stop them.

Ashley, standing at the edge of the platform, witnessed many little discussions between parents and children, some quiet and rational, others heated.  She remained silent, except to gesture to Kibi, then explain in whispers what was about to happen.

Kibi slipped into the ship to get it ready.

❋

About ten minutes after making the offer, thirty-seven children stood on the grass near the platform, parents at their sides.

Ashley looked at them and swallowed.  "I give tour in groups eight.  All have parents decided to let your children have experience?"

Some more quickly than others, all the adults affirmed with nods or words.

Suddenly, even though the dancer had not been paying attention to the gathering of children and parents at the edge of the platform, she stumbled and nearly fell, barely managing to keep her feet under her.  *Where am I? What am I doing here? Why are all these people . . . dancing?*

She looked around, and couldn't remember anything about the situation. She was in a park she didn't recognize.  Thousands of people, mostly adults, were seated on the grass with picnic baskets or ice chests, laughing and talking, or watching events in the middle of the park.  Around her, hundreds of youth and older children were dancing to a piece of music that sounded nice, but wasn't familiar.  In the very center of the park, a low platform held a number of important-looking people and some tame animals.  A bunch of children were just now climbing onto the platform with the help of their parents.

Then the dancer noticed what she was wearing, and remembered that when she stumbled, her entire body had been in motion. *I must be a dancer. But I'm not like all the other people, who are just in street clothes moving to the music as best they can. I'm wearing a fancy dance outfit, so I must be a professional dancer — I must be the one leading the dance!*

She noticed that some people were ceasing to dance, and giving her strange looks, as if wondering if something was wrong. Even though it was unfamiliar, she began to let herself move to the music. Her body seemed to remember the music, even if her mind didn't. The people around her appeared comforted that she was dancing again, and resumed their smiling, laughing, and simple movements.

*That's it*, the dancer thought to herself, *I'm the leader of this dance! This must be a very special occasion, judging by all those important people on the platform. I should dance with all my skill and all my heart. I think my name is Jan, but I'm not really sure. Anyway, dance now, figure things out later . . .*

* * *

## Chapter 83: Alien Space Ship

Never had groups of children been so quiet.

With Ashley leading and Kibi bringing up the rear, the little ones sat proudly in the bridge-station seats and gazed with wonder at the glowing displays and control symbols.  Kibi had locked all the controls, but the children were so spellbound that it was hardly necessary.

Some jumped into the lift with both feet after Ashley explained it, others refused to go near until the tour was threatening to leave them behind.

As they wandered through the engineering ring, several decided, on the spot, to be engineers when they grew up.

A few, upon returning to the passenger area, looked with keen interest at the clear tank and wanted to learn all about sea creatures.  Two or three were touched by the little galley and declared that *they* would be chefs who could make fancy food in space.

After Ashley got them all seated in the passenger area, the children stared with big, round eyes at the display as Kibi showed them their own planet from space, their moon, and all the other planets of the Ko-tera system in much clearer pictures than they would see, a few weeks later, on television from those stored in the space probe.

✳

On the last tour, of only five children, the oldest girl seemed to be lost in a dream.  The nine-year-old lagged behind the others at every stop, and Kibi sensed she wanted the experience to last forever.

When the other four finally left through the hatch, she lingered near the steward's console, gazing at it with an intense expression.

Ashley looked at Kibi, and Kibi nodded.

"Would like you sit in steward's chair?" Ashley asked.

"Yes, please."

Kibi swiveled the chair for the girl.

She got comfortable in the seat and closed her eyes.

Both Ashley and Kibi remained silent.

When the girl opened her eyes, she slowly reached out toward the console with one hand.

Kibi wasn't worried.

The girl didn't touch any control symbols, just moved her open hand above the console. To Kibi's surprise, several symbols changed color, starting diagnostics and status checks. The results flashed onto the console display.

Both Kibi and Ashley stared in wonder.

With her hand still hovering over the console, the girl struggled to form a word. "Man . . . Manessa."

"Daphne," the ship replied.

The girl smiled.

All three became aware that another presence had just entered the room. They turned toward the passenger area to see a timeless lady in shimmering blue robes.

"Greetings, Melorania!" Kibi said in the language of Nebador.

"Hello, Kibi my dear."

With wide eyes, Daphne turned and looked. "I think . . . I'm supposed to be a steward or navigator or something," she said to the new arrival without fear or hesitation."

Melorania spoke in the language of Ko-tera Three. "Yes, you are, and a captain too."

Daphne grinned.

"You have many years of learning ahead of you," Melorania continued. "That should start now, and is not possible on your planet."

"I know," Daphne admitted with a hint of sadness.

"But do you have the wisdom to know what would happen if you stayed inside the ship right now, and did not go back out to your grandmother, who is waiting at the edge of the platform?"

Daphne scrunched her face for a moment. "Um . . . it would look bad, and make it hard for the people who came in this ship to finish what they're here to do."

"That's right. So what are you going to do about that?"

The girl took a deep breath. "I'm going to go talk to my grandmother and get her to give me *permission* to go with you!"

"Good thinking. That is your first mission, and if you accomplish it, I will be well pleased." Before even finishing her sentence, the shimmering lady faded from sight.

"Her name Melorania, head of Transport Service," Ashley explained.

Daphne just sat breathing for a long moment. Ashley and Kibi waited silently.

"I have something I have to go do," Daphne declared as she hopped out of the steward's chair and dashed for the hatch.

Both Ashley and Kibi noticed the deep determination in Daphne's voice, bearing, and movements.

*

The mission leader and steward returned to the outdoor platform where everyone was chatting and enjoying the festive mood.  Someone had delivered several boxes of pizza to those on the platform, and most of the military officers, scientists, and crew members were having some.  Kibi slipped back into the ship to get fish, grass, and seed cakes for the contact specialists.

Ashley did what she could to overhear the conversation between Daphne and her grandmother at the edge of the platform, without being caught eavesdropping.  She gathered that Daphne's mother liked having babies, but only enjoyed taking care of them for three or four years.  When they started growing up and having minds of their own, she lost interest.

Further, it seemed that Daphne and her grandmother would soon be moving in with Daphne's Uncle Bob, whose house wasn't very big.  Daphne was making each of her argument points clearly and firmly.

Eventually, the deciding factor appeared to be that Daphne wasn't really *asking* for permission to leave on an alien space ship.  She was *telling* her grandmother what she intended to do, and daring the woman to figure out a way to stop her, pointing out that she would have opportunities almost daily to disappear on her own if the requested permission was not given.

Ashley wasn't sure this was what Melorania had in mind, but decided that the head of the Transport Service was quite capable of expressing herself if not pleased with Daphne's arrangements.

*  *  *

## Chapter 84: The Snake

In the early afternoon of that very unusual Thursday in Capital Park, a squad of unarmed soldiers arrived on foot to shoo the kids off the military tank and free the men within.  They were under orders to keep an eye on the perimeter of the park, but not clash with the people or the city police.

Alex decided it was time to learn to dance, and soon joined Corky, Benny, and Mouse.  Stephy tried to move to the music, but it didn't come easily.  Alex shared with Corky that the military had finally wised up and realized this was not an occasion for guns.

Even so, there were still a number of guns in Capital Park.

Those who had brought firearms spanned all the social classes, and included both men and women, but when it became obvious that the park was going to be full of youth and children, most of those guns were quickly hidden away at the bottom of picnic baskets, purses, or day packs.

*

One gun stayed out.

Normally, all the bushes on the edges of Capital Park were kept well-trimmed so they could be easily patrolled and no one could hide in them for any purpose.

On that particular day, with everyone focused on events at the center of the park, a newspaper van had parked very close to the outside edge of a row of bushes, creating a dark space just large enough for one person to hide.

The shadowy figure looked through the telescopic sight at possible targets.

The teenage girl in a purple robe was tempting, as she was almost certainly an alien.  But after following her around the platform for a minute, and noticing the facial scars that revealed some sort of hard life, the crosshairs seen through the gun sight moved on.

The military officers, and the scientists and other academic types, certainly looked like ours.  Perhaps they were just pretending.  Impossible to be sure.  The crosshairs moved on.

The horse just looked like a horse.  Horses were good critters, once helped us with many things, and might again someday.  The telescopic image looked elsewhere.

The three bobbing heads in the water were barely visible.  Good eating, maybe, but hard to get a clear shot.  The crosshairs continued their search for a target.

The weird tiger was *very* tempting.  It's teeth were way too large to be from here.  Probably some kind of alien pet.

Then the gun spotted what it wanted.  The snake was half-coiled, half-stretching itself upward, and appeared to be *talking* to the girl in a purple robe.

"God, I hate snakes!" the shadowy figure muttered and squeezed the trigger.

✳

The dancer, although she had used every possible technique of dancing slowly to conserve energy, was getting tired.  She knew she had no money on her, and had no idea where her purse or dance bag might be.  She couldn't remember who she worked for, but guessed it was one of the important people on the platform.  If not, maybe they could point her in the right direction.

As she danced near the platform, she glimpsed pizza boxes and cans of juice, and hoped someone would offer her something.  She knew she was the main inspiration for all the young people dancing around her, so she kept her arms and legs moving to the music.

Just as she was passing the podium, the climax of the song played.  Since she had gotten used to adding a leap to her dance at that point, she did so once again, with her last burst of energy, knowing she would have to rest, eat, and drink when this pass through the song ended.

Just as she leapt, she noticed the big snake talking to the girl in a purple robe.  Suddenly something hit her and she felt herself falling.  As she saw the grass rushing toward her, she thought, *Oh, no, I can't dance anymore!*

*Yes you can,* a soft voice said as the ground ceased its approach and the dancer felt herself floating upward.  *You are a great Temporandek Teacher, and you will always be able to dance to your heart's content.  But right now, you can rest.*

*NOW I remember who I am!*

✳

"Oh, shit," muttered the shadow in the bushes.

In less than a minute, the gun was disassembled, packed into an inconspicuous shoulder bag, and the figure slipped out of its hiding place and into the streets of the city.

✳

The dancer's body slammed against the side of the golden platform, then came to rest a few feet away in the grass.  Frightened youth scattered, screaming.

Ashley looked, tried to swallow but couldn't, and touched her bracelet to silence the music.

Brian was the first one off the platform, roaring his anger and despair to the universe even as tears filled his eyes. "Priscilla! No! No! No! . . ."

Toran Takil came next, leaping over the fallen dancer and the grieving young man, then facing away while guarding them and scanning for the weapon, or any other dangers, with the keen eyes of a hunter.

Susan was quickly beside Brian, taking in the mortal wound that had torn a hole in Priscilla's chest so large that no help was possible.

As he cried, Brian tried to gather Priscilla into his arms, but she was completely limp and covered with slippery blood.

As tears filled Susan's eyes, she glimpsed all the military officers and scientists of Priscilla's team climbing down off the platform and gathering around their fallen leader, even Three-star General Malcolm Ko-fenral, with the help of others.

✳

Eventually everything and everyone slowed down.

Ashley resisted the temptation, just barely, to join those around Priscilla's body. Kolarrr'ka and T'sss'lisss guessed that the presence of a bird and a snake would only add to the confusion. Malika-Terno just closed his eyes.

Ilika asked all his crew members to remain on the platform and stay alert for any other problems or dangers.

A police medic came by to examine the victim, but quickly shook his head.

The mayor came close, and mumbled that he was very sorry and that the police were doing everything possible to locate the shooter.

Alex, Corky, and Stephy knelt on the grass not far away, wishing they could pay their respects, but not knowing how.

Daphne, who had been talking with her grandmother, stood back and watched. She had to swallow many times and struggle to control her shaking legs as she realized that this was *real life*, and it might not always be *safe*.

But after seeing how the ship's crew members were taking it, she willed her body to relax. After some deep breaths, she reached inside herself for courage and walked forward.

Toran Takil looked at her. They shared a moment of eye contact. Satisfied, he looked away.

Daphne knelt down beside Doctor Betty Ko-silma, who was silently crying a little apart from the others. After a moment of thought, the girl put her arm around the short woman.

✳

As the timeless minutes passed, Ashley became aware that some people in the park were starting to gather up their picnic baskets, ice chests, and children, to make ready to depart. Suddenly she felt, in her heart, the words she had to say. She stepped to the podium one last time.

"It *not* a gun that killed your Teacher great. It was *fear*, the fear same that is root of all *hatred*, which causes you abuse each other and planet."

She noticed most people sit back down to listen.

"The truth, we came here for arrange evacuation of all other sapient creatures from planet, ten years from now, if you not change suicidal course your civilization." She paused and listened to the little voice inside her for another moment. "If want you to play with powers of God, must learn you wisdom of God, or you will destroy selves. Your children can you teach that wisdom."

✳

After running out of words and breathing for a long moment, Ashley knew it was time. She jumped down off the platform and stepped to the circle of grieving people on the ground. "I believe should we take Teacher home now."

Brian looked up with his tear and blood-stained face, nodded weakly, then began gathering his beloved's body into his arms.

The military officers and scientists, psychologist and philosopher, all began picking themselves up and helping each other to climb back onto the platform, or helping Brian with his burden.

Ashley, still on the grass, looked at Daphne. "Need you a seat?"

The nine-year-old nodded.

Suddenly the mission leader closed her eyes for a moment. When she opened them, she looked around. Her eyes stopped at a young man, sixteen or seventeen. "Alexander Po-nortan?"

"Um . . . yeah . . . that's me . . ."

"You will be important leader during most critical time planet's history. We like you offer a year advanced training. If you wish this to do, must come now."

A hundred thoughts visited the young man's face during the next few moments.

"But Alex!" Stephy burst out. "Who will lead *us?*"

After a few more breaths, he found his voice. "Corky will be the leader while I'm gone. Then, when I get back, I'll teach her, and all of you, everything I've learned."

Corky looked proud and sad at the same time, and just nodded.

Alex kissed both girls on the cheek. "Take care of Mouse and Benny for me, and let more kids onto the team when you find them."

"We will," Corky promised.

Alex turned and climbed onto the platform with Ashley.

Toran Takil looked around one more time, then leapt up and followed Ashley toward the ship, keeping one eye on the situation behind him.

✳  ✳  ✳

## Chapter 85: Farewell

The sun was still high in the sky on the other side of the continent as the golden ball settled onto its struts in the grass across the road from the top-secret safe house.

General George Ba-kerga came out and stood on the edge of the road as the hatch opened and ramp appeared.  Considering the recent events in Capital Park, which he had followed closely on television, he guessed there would be no more fly-overs by military jets.

Brian emerged slowly, Priscilla's bloody, torn body in his arms.

George thought he would take this moment like a soldier, but instead he felt the world start to wobble under his feet.

*

During the next hour, Priscilla's body rested in the grass not far from the ship.  Those who had once come to this place three times a week to learn from her, and the orphaned boy she had married, all stood or sat in a circle around her silent form.  Words of farewell were muttered, with long stretches of silence between.  George came and went, dealing with his own feelings, and his responsibilities, as best he could.

Ashley decided this was a time to give the people of Ko-tera Three their space, so she asked the crew, specialists, Daphne, and Alex, to stay in the ship.  Two or three at a time stood in the open hatch to pay their respects.

Eventually, the full heat of afternoon arrived and flies began to find all the blood and sweat.  George noticed.  "Brian, you can bring Priscilla inside.  I've called the base for a refrigerated unit, and it should be here soon."

The young man sat in silence a little while longer, then gathered Priscilla's lifeless form into his arms again.  The team was slowly crossing the road when Ashley dashed up behind them.  "Susan Bo-kamla?"

The psychologist turned around.  "Yes?"

"I realize this time of grieving, but I informed that your work be very important to world years to come, and so we offer you a year advanced training.  If you wish this to do, must come with us this time."

Susan stood pondering the situation.  Lisa, having overheard, stepped to her side to silently offer what support she could.

"I guess . . ." Susan began tentatively, ". . . I'm the best person to . . . carry on Priscilla's work . . . in some ways."

Ashley remained attentive, but neutral.

After another minute of thought, the psychologist dug into her shoulder purse.  "Lisa, here's my keys.  My appointment book is on my desk at home, and about a dozen clients need to be cancelled.  Brian will be able to take care of everything with Priscilla's money, but help him out a little.  He might forget to pay the water bill, or . . . who knows what."

Lisa nodded.  "The team will continue to meet, and I'll make sure he's okay."

The two women embraced in the middle of the rarely-used back road, in front of the top-secret safe house.  Colonel Lisa Ka-markla followed the others into the facility where she worked, and Doctor Susan Bo-kamla walked beside Ashley back to the ship.

Those in the facility were too focused on their own concerns to notice, a few minutes later, the golden sphere silently float upward into the sky.

✳

At zero-seven hundred the following morning, Lisa managed to wake Brian where he slept on some floor pillows beside Priscilla's temporary refrigerated coffin.  She got him into a shower and clean clothes, then dragged him out to Susan's car, the only one still parked in the grass on the far side of the road.

Doctor Richard Tu-feltin, the blind historian, and Doctor Tanya Po-morna, biologist, were already waiting on Susan's porch, anxious to learn whatever they hadn't been able to glean from the radio or television.  Sam arrived a few minutes later, followed closely by Sarah and Malcolm, then Larry.  John soon pulled up in his rented car, Chris and Betty carpooled, and lastly George came in his own car, declaring he had found a sergeant with enough intelligence to answer the telephone.

With Brian not yet ready to think, much less cook, the others scrounged in the kitchen until they found enough packaged pastries, bread, butter, instant coffee, and cans of juice to get them started.

✳

"Session Seventy-Three," Sarah said, note pad in her lap.

They all looked at each other.

Eventually Betty spoke.  "This is very uncomfortable.  Our leader . . . our heart . . . is missing."

Sam nodded.  "We might be tempted to quit meeting, or meet very seldom, but Priscilla set events in motion that could go into high gear at any time."

Malcolm coughed.  "Yes, and the supreme irony is that the alien girl, or whatever you want to call her, would probably not have revealed their *real* purpose — preparing to evacuate other creatures — without Priscilla's death."

Sarah was taking notes furiously, trying to catch every word. "What did she say? *Sentient* creatures?"

"*Sentient* just means *aware of the environment*," Tanya informed. "A worm is fairly sentient. She used the word *sapient*, which means *self-aware* or *wise*."

After a moment of silence, George said, "I'd love to know who's on *that* list."

Larry cleared his throat. "There was a horse, a tiger, a large bird, a big snake, two dolphins, and a sea turtle on that platform with us."

George nodded thoughtfully. "By the way, I have cleared Brian for the L-Six facility. I had to put down a reason, so he now has a job as a safe-house cook . . . if he wants one."

"Thanks," the young man said weakly from a pillow in the corner where he huddled with his arms around his knees.

A long silence indicated that the topic had run its course.

"I've been summoned to the capital to brief the president and Congress," Sam revealed. "The courier came by the house just before I left."

"Me too," Sarah said.

"Yep, here too," Doctor Chris Po-selem added.

"Malcolm, Lisa, John, Larry, Betty," Sam began, "you'll probably get summoned also. Couriers are probably at your houses waiting for you. There's a bright side to missing yesterday's event, George, Richard, Tanya."

The historian chuckled and the biologist smiled.

"We'll be representing Priscilla, and everything she taught us," Sam went on. "Some preparation time might be a good idea. The president will most likely have a different attitude after . . . yesterday."

Everyone agreed with nods or words.

"After that, I'll have to return to my assignment in the middle of nowhere," John announced with a tone of regret. "I'll keep in touch by telephone."

"Good," Sarah said while rapidly taking notes. "We should also spend time just talking about what happened at Capital Park, for Richard, Tanya, and George's sake, and just because there was so *much* that I'm sure no one caught all of it."

"I'll call for pizza about . . . eleven o'clock?" Brian proposed timidly from his corner.

Lisa looked at him, smiled, and nodded.

✳   ✳   ✳

## Part 8: Satamia Star Station

### Chapter 86: New Arrivals

The situation on Thursday, the fourth of November, had not allowed nine-year-old Daphne, seventeen-year-old Alex, or Doctor Susan Bo-kamla, to get any of their things before stepping into the alien space ship. They had the clothes they were wearing, and whatever was in their pockets. Susan also had her shoulder purse, and Daphne wore a tiny belt pouch.

The flight had gone quickly. One moment they were chatting with each other in the front row of passenger seats, sharing names and a few details about their lives, then they all suddenly felt sleepy. Before they knew it, they were waking and their eyes were drawn to the big view screen where a huge sparkling crystal sphere floated in space, with a giant purple planet not far away.

After the ship navigated a maze of dark tunnels, the comfortable quarantine room welcomed them with a tasty spread of food and drink, and each new arrival had their own little sleeping room. The next two days, however, were frustrating because the leader — the short girl who spoke their language fairly well — asked everyone who knew it to quit speaking it.

They lost count, but during the next two days, while people and animals told stories and played games, the three new arrivals must have learned several hundred words in the language of Nebador.

*

Doctor Susan Bo-kamla was not enjoying herself.

Learning languages had never been easy for her, and her so-so grades in the required foreign language in college had almost kept her out of graduate school.

Next, she had always assumed that animals had fleas and ticks, not to mention dirty, smelly fur. These animals seemed to be clean and bug-free, but she couldn't stop herself from scratching and sneezing.

Finally, the girl in charge might have been mid-teens, but since she was short, Susan kept thinking ten or eleven.  The psychologist couldn't imagine someone so young leading a mission so . . .

Suddenly, on the last evening in quarantine, Susan caught herself thinking these thoughts, and realized she had just spent nine years of her life on a team led by someone she had come to respect more than anyone else in the world, and that person had started her leadership responsibilities at age seven.

She burst out crying, and Kibi came over to see if she could help.

Susan couldn't find enough words in the new language to explain her distress, so Kibi just sat with the psychologist until she relaxed.

When the quarantine room doors were flung open on the third morning, Doctor Susan Bo-kamla stepped through with a much lighter heart, even though a large bird was waddling in front of her, a teenage mission leader walked beside, and a horse clopped along not far behind.

*

Alexander Po-nortan had grown up with a very different concept of what was *out there* than he was now seeing.

Actually, there were two concepts.  He was, as most other young people, torn between the messages of *science*, and the stories of *religion*.  But whichever one he picked, it didn't match what he was seeing.

Science wanted him to think that *nothing* was out there, except the physical universe of stars, planets, and inter-stellar gases.  Okay, maybe they'd throw in a little primitive life here and there, if you caught them in a good mood, but it could *never* get to Ko-tera, *never* make a crop circle, *never* . . . land in Capital Park!

Religion insisted that everything was *old*, or at least old-fashioned.  Old buildings, old language, old clothes, old people.  Even the churches that tried to look and act modern, never quite succeeded.  They took away the old decorations, but didn't know how to get rid of the old attitudes.

Alex fussed and fumed for two days, trying to see how all the messages and stories from science and religion could *fit* with the reality around him. He thought about the golden ship still visible at dock, the star station he was now deep inside, and the people who might have hooves, paws, or flukes, as easily as hands and feet.

He *wanted* it to somehow fit.  He craved for at least one of the stories to be right — science or religion, he didn't care.

During his last night in quarantine, he lay awake, toying with the idea of asking to go home, back to the comfort of believing *something* that wasn't proven wrong everywhere he looked.

Then, as morning light crept into the room, he remembered a simple fact that he had forgotten.  With the arrival of the golden ship at Capital Park, *everyone* back home was going through the same thing.  Everyone on Ko-tera was struggling to understand why the old stories didn't fit with the reality that had come knocking.

He couldn't go back.

Here, he could learn what was *really* going on in the universe. He already knew from his rapidly-growing vocabulary that they did lots and lots of science here, and also that gods and angels were in charge. They didn't call them that, but he knew.

And he was one of only *two* people who were getting to see what was *really out here*, and then return home to tell others. He'd tell Corky, Stephy, Benny, Mouse, and probably a million more people.

Suddenly he smiled, hopped out of bed, and got ready to go out and meet the universe.

On that same morning, Daphne was the last to awaken because she had been up late the night before laughing and talking with four people, a bird, a snake, and a tiger, all playing a board game. Also, she never heard anyone announce the breakfast cart, which had been her wake-up cue the first two mornings.

She lay blinking for a minute, then reached to the side table and grabbed her little belt pouch. Inside were a few coins, two coupons for free ice cream cones, and a worn and faded photograph of her family, taken at a two-hour visitation supervised by social workers the last time they had all been together.

The coins and coupons, she figured, wouldn't be any good in her new home. Only the picture mattered.

She yawned and stretched, hopped up and pulled on her clothes, then opened the curtain of her little bedroom.

The big double doors to the quarantine room were open, and everyone from the ship was gone. But on one couch sat a lanky, furry mammal — almost but not quite a monkey — with a knowledge pad in his lap.

"Good morning," he said slowly in the language of Nebador. "I am the steward of the life-monitor ship Porensa Timala. The crew is gathering for breakfast in Violet Hall in a little while, and then we'll be departing on a short mission. Upon Melorania's recommendation, we would like to invite you to join us."

Daphne figured out enough of his words to get the meaning, and smiled.

## Chapter 87: The Crew of the Manessa Kwi

The day following their release from quarantine, Kibi awoke early, kissed Ilika, and wiggled out of his arms. Something in a dream had warned her that not all was well in her galley.

As soon as she arrived on the upper deck, both her nose and her ship confirmed. "I am detecting an unusual level of certain gasses in the atmosphere," the deep-space response ship began, "those usually associated with decomposition."

"Thanks, Manessa. I can smell it too. Something ... sweet. Fruit, I think."

Kibi only had to open three cupboards before discovering the problem. Thousands of tiny flies flew out into her face. "Yuk!" After waving away the flies, she quickly discovered the forgotten cluster of bananas in the very back of the cupboard. "From now on, I'm inspecting the galley *myself* before going into quarantine. How did the cleaning crew miss these?"

"Judging by my atmospheric records, the fruit did not start to decompose until after the cleaning crew had come and gone. I will send them a message so they will improve their practices."

"A gentle message. If I get the bananas out, can you deal with the fruit flies?"

"Yes, I can purge the ship of drosophilae."

"Thanks, Manessa."

"And thank you, Kibi."

An hour later, Mati and Rini conspired to make a hearty breakfast, knowing it would be a busy day of de-briefing with the Education Service team and tending their ship.

Boro could barely sit still as he inhaled his cereal and pinkfruit juice.

Sata looked at him. "I *think* we left all the ants back on Ko-tera Three, but it sure looks like you have some in your pants.”

Boro blushed. “Sorry. It’s just . . . there’s about five drops of thruster fuel on the ship right now, maybe just four, and I can feel in my bones that Melorania is *aching* to send us on another mission, especially since the last one wasn’t very hard.”

Sata’s face darkened. “Don’t forget the sacrifices Ss’klexna Rrr’tak’fi made for the ursines of Ko-tera Three, and that Temporandek Teacher made for the whole planet.”

Boro finally managed to sit still. “Yeah. I know.”

The pallet of supplies arrived two hours later, and everyone could see that Boro was relieved.

“The de-briefing is about to start,” the ship reminded them.

Sata looked at Boro with her head cocked.

“I’m okay now,” he assured her with a smile. “Just knowing the stuff’s on the ship makes me happy. We could stow it en route if we had to.”

Most in quiet moods, the crew members walked up ramps and along wide corridors toward the Mission Assignment Room. At one point, Toran Takil joined them, and a little later, Malika-Terno.

The tiger fell in beside Kibi. “I feel you are my equal now, and it will be an honor to serve with you on missions in the future. You are a feline-friend, have our respect and protection at all times and places, and that began long before you were marked by one of us on Ko-tera Three. I compliment you on all your decisions during the recent mission, especially the decision to respect Triss and her companion.”

Kibi reached up and touched the four scratches on her cheek, not yet completely healed, then put an arm around Toran Takil on one side, and Ilika on the other.

Her lover slipped an arm around her back as they walked, and the tiger on the other side rumbled with contentment.

Malika-Terno clopped over beside Mati. “Do you remember how to be the hair on an equine’s back?”

Mati smiled, reached and sprang up, and a second later centered herself on the huge horse, but didn’t try sitting up or wrapping her legs around his belly. “How could I forget!”

“It is a good skill for any relationship between sapient creatures. Touch lightly, only when invited, and don’t try to *own* the other.”

“That was true with the wild equines, too.”

“They are no less sapient for being wild.”

After a moment, Mati nodded thoughtfully as they passed through a doorway that would have knocked her to the floor if she had been sitting up.

“Good morning, everyone,” Ashley began from the middle of the conference room. “I see I’m not the only scar-face in the room. Isn’t it nice knowing that signs of experience are actually *valued* here, unlike on most planets?"

Kibi grinned and nodded.

Trekila Spimalo squawked and lifted her fluke out of the water to show an old scar, and Toran Takil turned his head so the ragged tear on one ear could be seen.

Ashley smiled. "My dear Kolarrr'ka has a report from Ko-tera Three."

"The planet is in chaos, bok, the good kind of chaos. Everyone is asking questions, especially young people. Those who would cling to the old ways, even if it destroyed the climate, are preparing to dig in their claws ... or heels. But those who don't like the idea of handing their children a dying world are rising up. Many seeds were planted by the Temporandek Teacher, and many more will be sown by others like Susan and Alexander when they return in a year to help with leadership. After Daphne learns the basics on some easy missions, her life-monitor ship will be assigned to the planet for the duration of the crisis. The captain is very happy to have her on his crew, bok."

Seeing that her dear avian friend was finished, T'sss'lisss stretched up from her coils. "Wasss the one who killed the Teacher ever found?"

"Bok. I don't think ..."

Suddenly, a glowing orange ball formed near the ceiling and floated downward, becoming an elderly reptile with wise old eyes as she settled to the floor, but still loomed over the mortals present.

"Greetingsss, Shemultavia!" the snake declared.

All three Education Service members, snake, bird, and monkey mammal, gathered at the reptile's feet.

"Hello, my skillful ones. I'm sorry I was not here to speak with you as soon as you returned from your recent mission. I was on Kerusemia talking with Ss'klexna Rrr'tak'fi and Priscilla Ka-mentha, whom you know as the Temporandek Teacher. I think those two are going to be fast friends. Both are highly advanced in their spiritual growth, and will be progressing through the required studies and experiences very quickly."

Sata smiled.

"Ss'klexna sends a message, which I endorse. Worry not about the ursine who killed her, nor the human who killed the Teacher. Neither are relevant to the unfolding of the universe. Fear and hate always think they are in control, but never really are."

Just then, a blue glow descended and became Melorania in human form. The crew of the Manessa Kwi smiled and gathered close.

"What a precious monkey-mammal crew I have! Both Arantiloria and I are very pleased, almost *amazed*, at how well you operated your fine little ship and supported the Education Service on this mission."

The six humans took a moment to bask in the warmth of the compliment.

"Want another one like it?"

"I knew it!" Boro burst out.

Melorania laughed deeply.  "But Boro, you still have that little stash of thruster fuel on supply line fifteen!"

"*And* four canisters on a pallet!" he bragged with a grin.

"Hmm.  I *could* tell Manessa to not use . . ."

Boro knitted his brow and looked daggers at the head of the transport service, causing her to laugh even more deeply.

After a moment, since everyone else in the room was howling with laughter, he softened his gaze.  "I guess . . . you would never give us a challenge we couldn't handle."

"That's right," Shemultavia answered for both service heads.  "There are enough dangers that arise unforeseen, like the deaths of your ursine friend and the Temporandek Teacher."

Boro looked into the wise old eyes of both Shemultavia and Melorania, and nodded.

✳

Once all the news about Ko-tera Three had been shared, the two service heads bowed and faded from sight to attend to the many other education and transport needs of Nebador.

Trekila Spimalo then announced that she was joining a mission to a world with water-quality problems *everywhere*, from tropics to poles, mountains to seas.  Not long ago, the task would have seemed overwhelming, but now, she felt ready for it.

T'sss'lisss nodded with understanding.

Memsala the giant sea turtle also shared her new challenge — traveling between star stations, planet stations, and the local universe capital itself, to teach the teachers and make sure the Psychic Development programs didn't get into any . . . psychic ruts.

Everyone laughed, and they could have sworn there was a smile on Memsala's turtle face.

Eventually everyone shared parting words and touches, and the crew of the Manessa Kwi wandered back to their ship.

✳

Arantiloria greeted them from the middle of the big table, her penetrating gaze nearly making them dizzy, as usual.

"Hi, Purple," Kibi said before prancing into the galley for snacks.  "I was wondering why you weren't at the de-briefing."

"I wish I could have been, but Melorania had me making arrangements for the next phase of your training."

"Uh . . . oh . . ." Boro intoned softly.

The training specialist smiled.  "As you know, in Nebador, teams that work well together and develop strong bonds, can stay together for as long as they want . . ."

"Like Ashley, Kolarrr'ka, and T'sss'lisss," Rini guessed, taking a handful of gotaka nuts from the bowl Kibi slid onto the table.

"Very good example," Arantiloria continued as the other crew members got comfortable in seats around her.  "Cross-species relationships like that are rare, and very powerful because of their multiple points-of-view. Well-bonded crews like yours have the advantages of collective intelligence and supportive affection."

All six humans wore contented expressions as they pondered the deep comfort they experienced daily with each other and their beloved little ship.

"But . . ." Arantiloria added as her voice became firmer, ". . . it is time for all of you to experience life on other ships, working side-by-side with different creatures who are your fellow crew members, not just mission specialists.  Since you are the only human response-ship crew in Satamia, we need to keep Manessa operational, so I will re-assign only one of you at a time, and only for a few days.  Sata, you are first."

The youngest crew member swallowed.

"The navigator of the passenger transport Palantia Lisa is taking some time off for surgery and recovery, and you will be his replacement."

Sata felt a little fear and much excitement.  "That's one of those huge ships, with hundreds of passengers, isn't it?"

"Yes.  You will have an assistant, a trainee, but you will be in charge and *responsible* for navigation and communications at all times.  You start tomorrow morning, right after the party."

Sata reached over to the next seat and took Boro's hand.  "I'll miss my family on the Manessa Kwi . . . but I see how it'll be good for me.  I've always had a little fear of . . . you know . . . leaving home.  I guess it's time to prove to everyone . . . and myself . . . that I can do it whenever I want to or need to . . . then come back!"

The mysterious training specialist smiled.

✳

Within a few hours, every inch of the ship had been stocked for their next mission, whatever it might be.  Boro was especially happy to see his racks of fuel canisters, all seven kinds, completely full.  Kibi was prepared to feed just about anyone who might walk, fly, swim, or slither aboard.  Only the very longest missions to the remotest corners of Nebador would require extra provisions at the last minute.

Kibi and Ilika agreed that the ship was completely ready for service, and the ship communicated the fact to the Mission Assignment Room.

In their cabin, as Sata packed a bag, Boro hovered near.  He wanted to say a number of things, but didn't find the words, so he waited until she was all packed, wrapped his arms around her, and just whispered, "I'll be here."

She kissed him deeply, then whispered, "You'd better be!"

When they finally parted and looked at each other, Boro found his words. "Um . . . who you gonna be sharing a cabin with?"

Sata grinned.  "A bird."

They both laughed.

"Shall we . . . go help with party set-up?"

"Yeah!"

✳

The six went different ways when they got to Satamia Star Station's main hall, with Mati and Rini prancing away to help with decorations, Boro and Sata heading for one of the kitchens that always needed help, and Ilika and Kibi assisting some reptile musicians with drums and other instruments.

Not much later, Mati was on fanator-back hanging lights that were actually little glowing creatures, when she spotted Daphne below helping a furry mammal with trays of drinks.

After Ilika set down a small drum beside the huge ones that only the reptiles could lift, he noticed Alexander moving furniture with an ursine in another part of the hall.

Boro and Sata, working to assemble tasty finger foods, both smiled and offered simple words of greeting when Doctor Susan Bo-kamla appeared with a cart to collect the trays.  She smiled shyly, and seemed a bit overwhelmed until Healer Dakalio showed up with another cart.  Together, they returned to the hall to set out the goodies.

✳

The evening dance party on Satamia Star Station began with a lively mood.  Many missions to troubled planets had recently returned with good results, and most of the Services, from Education to Laboratory, Medical to Transport, Culinary to Psychic Development, were well-staffed with bright and creative Nebador citizens.

At a pause after a relaxing song, Kerloran became a green glow near the ceiling that changed into an olive-skinned man wearing simple robes as he slowly descended to the floor.  Everyone found places to perch or float.

"It is my happy honor to welcome the visiting students from the local universe of Risador . . ."

A group of strange creatures, about halfway between animal and plant, waved their tentacles and made humming sounds from where they clung to a branch of the great station tree.  The Nebador citizens welcomed them with many joyful noises and gestures.

"And a special circumstance has been granted," Kerloran continued, "for two teachers from Ko-tera Three to gain all the wisdom they can before returning, a year from now, to tackle *the* most difficult transition their planet will ever face."

Alex stood and waved willingly, but Susan had to be prodded by Dakalio before finding her courage.  They received just as hearty a welcome.

"Now we have some business that is much darker and less hopeful . . ."

A rumble coursed through the huge room, as Kerloran rarely brought serious topics to the evening party.

"It has been rumored that my patience is infinite," he continued in a somber tone.

Nervous laughs escaped a few of the listeners.

"Unfortunately, it is not."

Silence prevailed.

"Twice before in the long stretches of eternity, I have exhausted all hope of guiding a planet of sapient beings from the darkness of self-destruction, toward the light of sustainable balance in all things. The first was insect, the second mammal. It has happened again, this time on a world of avians. I say this so you know it can happen to any type of creature."

A few murmurs began, but quickly faded away.

"Those of you involved with missions to this world know how hard we tried."

Many heads throughout the room, mostly avian, nodded.

"When the gods give up on a world, as the wisest of you know, we declare it an Isolated Experimental Planet. A council of mortals is formed to ... attempt whatever comes to mind, and, if nothing else, learn all they can in the process."

The murmur that followed sounded slightly more hopeful than earlier.

Mati, snuggling on a couch with her beloved, didn't pay much attention to the list of thirty names that Kerloran announced ... until the last three.

"... Memsala, Drrrim-na, and Rini. These councilors will continue all their regular activities, but meet at least yearly to share any insights they have had ..."

Mati turned and looked at Rini.

He shrugged. "I've heard of that planet, but don't know much about it. Kinda sounds like fun."

She kissed him. "You get to try where Kerloran, and everyone else, failed!"

"It'll probably take the rest of my life just to *think* of something that hasn't been tried."

Mati laughed and hopped up as a lively dance tune began.

Rini shuddered for a moment at the thought of having god-like powers and responsibilities for an entire planet, then put it out of mind and followed Mati to the dance floor.

Two pleasant days passed on Satamia Star Station before the Manessa Kwi's next mission. Boro missed Sata, but knew she was learning many new things, and that his turn would come soon enough. All five were able to get back to their Psychic Development classes, or spend serious study time with ship cross-training materials.

When Arantiloria explained their next assignment, they noticed some ways it was like the mission to Ko-tera Three, but were also glad of its relaxed pace. A scouting phase came first, with just the crew poking around on the planet, at a late-medieval stage in its history.

The most critical task was contact with a secret society that had kept science and philosophy alive all during a long dark age. Since the dominant monkey-mammal population still believed that only adult male citizens, twenty years and older, could take part in business and politics, Ilika was clearly the scout on this occasion.

✳

Just before dawn light crept into the sky, the Manessa Kwi, with Kibi at the helm, descended slowly and quietly down through the trees into a small clearing in the forest, as close as it could get to the meeting coordinates.

In a dark cloak with hood up, Ilika stepped through the hatch onto soggy wet grass, and his ship silently departed.

As he tried to take a step, his boot made a sucking sound as it pulled free of the sticky mud, and he quickly realized why no trees grew in the clearing.

With a little dawn light gathering in the sky, he set his sights on slightly higher ground, then labored to take each step through the watery black ooze. To his relief, he was soon able to pull himself onto solid ground with the help of a small tree.

Not far away, two equines lifted their heads and looked at him while still chewing grass. A little apart from them, another horse looked up, a stallion. The larger horse began advancing toward the newcomer.

Ilika touched his mission bracelet. "This is starting to look — and feel — very familiar. Are you *sure* this isn't Sonmatia Three, the swamp near the capital city of your former kingdom?"

Rini, at navigation, chuckled. "No, Ilika. By my charts, Sonmatia is about forty light-years from here."

"Your good weather looks like it will hold," Boro said from the watch station.

"Remember," Mati said from engineering, "you're not alone anymore. We'll just kick back at the top of a mountain, or the bottom of a lake, and wait for your call."

Kibi, the acting captain, spoke from the helm. "Is there a problem? Do you need us to come get you?"

The stallion stepped up to Ilika, knelt and lowered his haunches to the ground, then spoke. "We are honored to have your guidance at this critical time for the monkey-mammal culture that fancies itself intelligent and wise. If it pleases you, I will convey you to our secret meeting hall."

Ilika let out the breath he had been holding, then spoke into his bracelet again. "No, I'm okay, and it appears this planet has some very good things going for it . . ."

✳  ✳  ✳

## Part 9: Ko-tera Three, 3683

## Chapter 88: An Old Facility on a Forgotten Back Road

The bleating of goats echoed in the concrete parking garage as Brian, sporting an untrimmed beard and the slight wrinkles of middle age, finished milking the last nanny. "Okay, Pipi, go play."

The leggy goat pranced away as soon as her collar was unhooked.

Brian stood and poured the contents of the milking bucket into a filter cone perched atop a glass jar.

Just then, Susan appeared in the doorway from upstairs, still brushing her hair that included several streaks of gray. "Almost a half-gallon!" she remarked. "The children will love some when they get here."

"It's the rain we've been getting. I want to let the goats out into the pasture right away. Which group of children is coming today?"

Susan took over the filtering process and capped the jar. "Lisa's group. She's become *such* a good caregiver since leaving the military and opening her house to strays who are determined to survive the Change, even if their parents aren't."

"The *government* certainly isn't much help."

The older lady nodded, then carefully carried the jar of precious warm milk upstairs.

Brian stepped to a make-shift hand crank on the wall, and the old security gate creaked as it slid open a few feet. "Come on, goaties, let's go see what's sprouting in the pasture . . ."

*

The road, now covered with dirt, goat droppings, and weeds, quickly became a walking path toward town, and completely faded into the green hills in the other direction.

Brian strolled the entire perimeter of the goat pasture as he scanned for predators and picked wild flowers. Only one coyote required a stone from his slingshot. It yapped and limped away.

Brian turned his attention to the two memorials beside the old road.

A circle of stones marked the place where a golden ship had landed on three occasions, twice on one fateful day in the fall of 3671, and a third time a year later. No one knew if that golden ship would ever return, but the circle was now a sacred place, just as was another, two thousand miles away, in Capital Park.

A few yards outside the stone circle, Brian knelt before the concrete and brass grave marker and arranged the wild flowers at its base. "Good morning, Priscilla. The goats are happy today, and Lisa is expected with her little troop of children. We got last month's newspaper yesterday, and it said they *think* we've dropped another part per million of $CO_2$, but aren't sure yet. Sam and Sarah are on the list to get a ride up here in a bicycle carriage, but the list is long, so they sent another letter up with George last week, and Susan and I are working on a letter back to them."

He blinked several times to clear his eyes. "I'd better go check the garden for rabbits."

After lingering another moment and lovingly touching the cool concrete, he rose and strode toward the fenced area beside the old building, glancing up at the bars of the open-air patio where a girl once fed birds and watered plants.

*

The seven children arrived mid-morning, excitedly dashing in through the open front door and bounding up the stairs. Lisa arrived about a minute later and climbed to the upper level more slowly, then stood breathing deeply while the children began chattering.

"What's for lunch?"

"Me and Gina are learning how to multiply!"

"We brought five potatoes!"

"Any new goat kids born?"

"What're we gonna learn today?"

Although the parking garage was now a barn for animals and garden supplies, the upper level of the old facility was arranged just as it had been during the eight years that Priscilla led the P-Seventeen team. Twenty-one years of intense use had left carpets soiled, hardwood floors scuffed, furniture badly worn, and paint peeling, but the place was as lovingly cared for as the remaining technology allowed. An old broom leaned against the office counter, and hearing the children, Susan emerged from the kitchen carrying a wash bucket and rag.

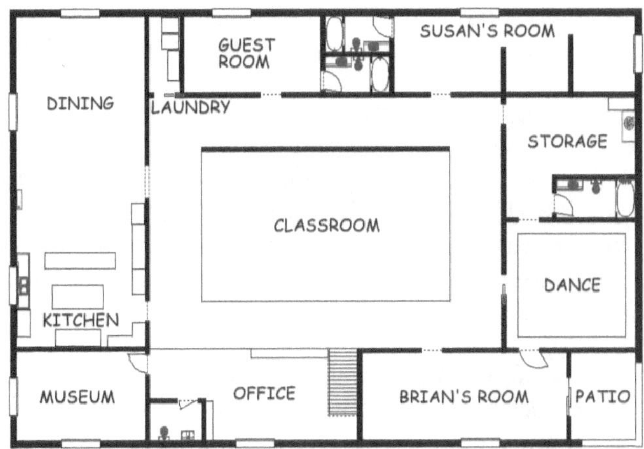


"Hello, young ones!  Hi, Lisa!  Did you guys have a fun hike?"

"We started *early*," a boy about nine revealed, rolling his eyes.

"We picked berries on the way," a ten or eleven-year-old girl explained, "so we're not as hungry as last time."

"How does fresh goat milk sound?" Susan asked with a smile.

"Yum!" they all declared and followed her into the dining room.

When the facility was a high-security safe house and classified meeting location, the kitchen had been stocked from the supermarket.  Now, it more closely resembled a homestead kitchen of a century earlier, with herbs hanging from hooks in the ceiling, thinly-sliced fruits and vegetables spread out on screens to dry, and jars of canned or dried food stacked everywhere. The big, shiny refrigerators were just storage cabinets, and the stove, once powered by bottled Methane gas, now held an old barbeque base, with a box of broken sticks on the floor beside.

Gina, about twelve, carefully brought the five small potatoes out of her daypack.  "This is all we could spare."  She glanced at Susan with a worried look.

"That's okay.  While I'm teaching, Brian's gonna make a soup, and he can use these to thicken it into a hearty stew!"

Gina relaxed.

Just then, the bearded man entered the room dangling the limp form of a small wild rabbit.  "It'll be even better, considering what I just caught trying to eat up our garden!"

All the children clapped and cheered at the thought of rabbit stew.

"You keep saying the Change was the best thing that ever happened to us," eleven-year-old Jason challenged with a broken voice from one of the old plush chairs in the meeting circle, "but that's so hard to believe when we look at pictures of the cars people used to zoom around in, the shopping malls where kids hung out, and the *food* they used to eat, almost like a *feast* every meal!"

"And that telephone in the museum," Gina added, pointing to the old general's office, "that used to let you talk to anyone in the *world!*"

Another hand, attached to eight-year-old Penny, shot into the air. "And that 'lectric typewriter that could write a whole sentence all by itself!"

"You have to step way back," Susan began from another plush chair, "and look at it from the outside — something Priscilla taught us well. Only then can you see that the fancy things we had were leading us down a dead-end road. It takes *energy* to make all that fancy stuff, and grow all that food, for billions and billions of people. Releasing energy makes pollution, and on every planet, that comes back to bite you . . ."

"Please tell us about other planets!" a nine-year-old boy begged.

"I can't. I've never seen any, except one purple gas giant from a distance. But what I *do* know is that *every* planet is the same in one way. The people on them, when they get smart enough to make cars, shopping malls, and all that other fun stuff, either keep it in balance with the ecosystem of the planet, or they kill themselves."

A long moment of tense silence lingered.

"It's been twelve years since the ship came and the Tempor . . . something . . . Teacher died," Gina remembered. "I was born that year. Now we're seven years into the Change. Are we back in balance?"

"The Plague a few years ago helped a lot . . ." Susan began, but stopped when she saw several of the children close their eyes tightly.

"That's what got my parents," Penny said with pouting lips and wet eyes.

"My father and my grandmother," Jason added.

Gina sniffled. "My mom and my best friend."

Susan waited until they had recovered, then continued very softly. "Priscilla used to show us a little matrix that explained our options . . ."

"Half a billion cave people or peasants . . ." Jason said from memory.

Gina brightened. "Or *maybe* a little high-efficiency modern stuff."

Susan nodded. "The Plague got us about half-way down to the number of people this planet can support, now *we* have to do the rest."

Then she took on a stern expression, one she had seen on Priscilla's face many times, but didn't know she, Doctor Susan Bo-kamla, was capable of until her year on Satamia Star Station. "So any of you dreaming of having lots of *babies*, or fancy *stuff*, or feasts more than about four times a *year*, had better keep all that in your *dreams*, or you will become the worst enemies of the human race . . ."

✳

Soup would have been a fancy meal. With the potatoes added, the resulting stew was nearly a feast. When they came to the small bits of rabbit meat, the children thought they had somehow become kings and queens.

Retired General George Ba-kerga arrived, walking stick in hand, half-way through the meal. Brian scraped the stew pot for him.

"So, young ones," the general began with a stern voice but smiling eyes, "report your recent productive activities."

Several of the children giggled.

Gina got serious. "I read to the others for an hour almost every morning, then work in the garden for a couple of hours. In the afternoon I have a job at the trading post, and I get paid in food to take home to everyone, usually dried fish."

"Good, good. And you, young man?"

Jason cleared his throat. "After chores and lessons, I fix things — or try. People bring me things that don't work and I see what I can do. Electronic stuff — forget it unless I have another one and can swap parts. I have the most luck with simple machines."

The retired general nodded and his wrinkled old eyes gleamed with pride.

✳

While Lisa and her troop studied ecology with Susan, Brian and George sat on old wooden boxes watching the goats graze.

"That part-per-million of $CO_2$ we thought we lost turned out to be a mistake," the older man revealed. "Just a seasonal variation."

"Damn."

"Don't lose hope. At least it didn't go *up*."

"Yeah. I just want so badly for Priscilla's death to be worth something."

"Me too," George said with a sigh.

Brian chewed on a blade of grass for a minute. "Lisa's children are strong."

"She doesn't let them think for a second they'll have easy lives. One boy thought he was entitled to special treatment. Lisa sent him packing."

Brian chuckled. "An unexpected advantage of Priscilla hooking up with the military."

"It's a good thing we can contribute *something* to the Change. All our guns and bombs certainly weren't much use when the *real* problem came knocking..."

✳

At a mid-afternoon break, the children dashed into the ravine behind the building to look for berries and lizards, and the adults gathered in the garden to pull weeds and pick off leaf-eating bugs.

"Are they learning their lessons well?" George asked with his firm tone of voice.

Susan smiled. "Some of them. The youngest two will have to hear it many more times..."

"Heck," Lisa slipped in, "*I'll* have to hear it many more times!"

Susan laughed. "And so did I at ... that beautiful place they took me and

Alex."

"Alex . . ." Brian repeated thoughtfully. "The Change wouldn't have been possible without him, would it?"

George snorted. "We'd still be forming committees to study the issue, and mostly denying the whole thing, if President Alexander Po-nortan hadn't framed it like he did."

"*A living world for your children, or a barren desert. Your choice. I'm just the president,*" Lisa quoted from memory.

George nodded. "He was the first president to step back and make Congress actually *represent* the people."

"Do you think he knew someone would assassinate him?" Brian asked anyone who cared to speculate.

Susan scrunched her face for a moment. "I think he knew it was a strong possibility."

"I know this sounds terrible," George added, "but the Change may not have been possible without his death, just as Priscilla's warning may not have been possible without another president's death many years earlier . . ."

Afternoon climatology lessons were winding down in the classroom circle when the aroma of pan biscuits started coming from the dining room. Eventually, twelve-year-old Gina asked the toughest question of the day.

"Okay, so if we can't be sure about $CO_2$ yet, and we're still maybe twenty-five years from the Methane tipping point and hope to *never* see *it*, is there *anything* we can look at that will give us hope that the world won't burn up in our lifetimes?"

Susan took a slow, deep breath, and was painfully aware that everyone was looking at her, including Lisa and George. "Yeah, there is, but it's not exactly a scientific measurement, and we . . . sort of . . . learned about it by accident."

Everyone continued to look at her.

"After Priscilla was killed, the Star Girl said they were there to arrange for the evacuation of other sapient creatures ten years later if we didn't quit harming Mother Ko-tera. We don't know exactly what species she was talking about, but we do remember who was on that ship with us . . ."

"Horse, tiger, dolphin, sea turtle, snake, and bird," Jason said, remembering an earlier lesson.

Susan nodded. "Twelve years have now passed, and even though we can't be sure what it means, at least *some* of each of those animals are still here . . ."

As the sun was nearing the western horizon, George said good-night after a dinner of soup and biscuits. Several of the children wouldn't let him get away without giving him hugs, and he fussed and grumbled, but the other adults could tell he loved it. He got his walking stick, and after a moment alone at the concrete and brass memorial on the other side of the road, set his feet on the trail to town.

The children were still full of energy, so Susan looked at Brian, busy cleaning up the kitchen. "Do we have enough electricity for the kids to dance a few songs?"

After wiping his hands, he wandered out to the office. Two adults and seven youth followed. He frowned as he gazed at the meters and switches on a home-made electrical panel beside a shelf of big batteries, the kind that once ran the lights in trailers and boats, but now were almost impossible to get.

"With the cloudy weather we've had for several days — the answer is *no* for Priscilla's big old sound system . . ."

Several young faces fell.

". . . but *yes* for the small tape player."

"Whoopee!" they cheered and began prancing and spinning long before they got to the dance studio and Susan started the music.

*

Hours later, the full darkness of night cloaked the green hills, coyotes yapped as they searched for something to eat, and the goats were glad of the steel bars that protected the old parking garage.

The children lounged around the big classroom, three reading books under the single working floor lamp, two playing a card game on the floor nearby, and the youngest two just yawning on the old, worn couches.

The adults sat around a table in the dining room with mugs of tea, but didn't have any sugar or honey to sweeten it.

"I'm so glad you guys decided to buy this place when the military started selling things off," Lisa commented.

"We couldn't have done it without Priscilla's money," Brian admitted.

"We got a *little* for my house," Susan added, "but the economy was in such bad shape that hardly anyone was buying houses."

Lisa smiled. "That's what allowed *me* to get a house with that gold I bought on a tip from Priscilla!"

The other two chuckled.

After a minute, Lisa became serious again. "Malcolm would have loved this place — memorial, museum, and learning center — still doing something important even after most of the old federal government shut down. Too bad he didn't live long enough to see it."

Susan nodded. Brian remained silent.

"He was the first one to realize Priscilla was something special," Lisa continued, "and not just a spy because she knew some lousy rocket was gonna blow up."

Brian chuckled, imagining his beloved at age seven speaking very assertively to General Malcolm Ko-fenral.

The silence lingered as they sipped their tea.

"Go fish!" a girl blurted out in the classroom.

After another sip of tea, Lisa found her courage. "Do you think we'll make it?  Will we get through the Change alive?  Do my kids have any future?"

Susan looked over the rim of her mug while taking a sip, hoping that Lisa had directed the question to Brian.  No such luck.  She swallowed and took a deep breath.

"I know we *can* do it.  It's been done many times before.  Remember, this is something that *every* intelligent, sapient race goes through."

Lisa nodded.

"The Plague," Susan went on, "got most of the elderly, the obese, and those in poor health.  I think malnutrition will whittle down the rest, especially those in places where not much food grows, and who can't migrate."

Brian blinked several times.

"The danger, of course, is that a generation or two from now people will forget the reasons we aren't using coal, oil, and gas, and decide they're tired of hard living.  They'll open the valves, and a few decades later, we'll hit that Methane tipping point, and then . . ."

"Alex's *barren desert* option," Brian finished for her.

Susan nodded.  "Your children, Lisa, are in the *best* possible situation to survive and be happy.  They don't remember the easy living, you're teaching them self-discipline all the time, and they're learning the *reasons* the planet can't support a global, urban, industrial civilization."

"I'm doing my best," Lisa offered.  "If I learned anything from Priscilla during all those years, it's that you do the job you're handed, whether the end is sweet or bitter."

Susan and Brian both nodded.

After another sip of tea, Susan spoke again.  "The ultimate answer to your question, Lisa, is not mine to know.  Only time will tell . . ."

✳

Not much later, the oldest children wandered into the dining room while yawning and rubbing their eyes.  The younger ones were already curled up on couches.

"We're sleepy.  Can we go down to the bomb shelter now?" Gina asked.

"I don't know, can you?" Lisa asked back.  "You know where it is."

"But me and Jason can't carry the others — they're too heavy."

"Then I guess you'll have to wake them up and help them down those steep stairs, one at a time."

Gina sighed, then smiled.

✳

Lisa, after discreetly watching to make sure her charges got downstairs safely, made herself comfortable in the small sleeping room.  Susan retired to her room that had once been the large safe-house sleeping room.

Brian wandered around the building, made sure the fire in the kitchen was out, and checked on the goats in the old parking garage.

Eventually, back upstairs, he took a long look at the old meeting circle where a girl had given the world a warning and a chance to survive.

In his room, he couldn't suppress a huge yawn, but took a moment to step onto the open-air patio.  Several plants needed watering almost daily, some of which had been potted twenty-one years before.  He felt a moment of regret that he didn't have any seed to put in the bird feeder.

Finally, he crawled into the large bed, the place in the world where he could feel closest to his beloved.  "Good night, Priscilla," he mumbled as he wrapped his arms around a pillow and drifted into sleep.

*Good night, my love.  The timeline has changed, and I will watch over you, always.*

✳ ✳ ✳ ✳ ✳

## Afterthoughts

The planet Ko-tera Three may be a mirror into which we are invited to look, but it will probably appear, to most people, dark and smoky. If the smoke in that mirror ever clears, which could happen very quickly, we will wish for a child with a lifetime of memories, and a golden deep-space response ship, but may very well discover that they are all busy elsewhere.

Ultimately, I'm glad that the long-term future of Ko-tera Three was not mine to know and write about. The future of our own similar predicament is also not mine to know.

We may have sealed our fate by using up the 40 years since we got *our* warning (back in the 1970's). During that time, we succeeded in giving a fair fraction of the human race the lifestyles that only kings and queens of old enjoyed. Perhaps that is natural for any intelligent species. I speculate in the NEBADOR stories that *some* sapient creatures heed the warnings and do what is necessary to get their societies into balance with the climates and ecosystems of their planets, but I don't really know.

There is no shame in belonging to a species that cannot "rule the Earth" forever. We have lots of company. Every type of creature has its limitations, and every species tends to get out-of-balance with its environment when life, for any reason, becomes too easy.

Individuals, like you and me, are always free to transcend what the "average" person thinks and does, and what society, corporations, and the governments "say" we should think and do. That's called spiritual growth. In the end, all that matters is what each of us takes with us in our hearts, minds, and souls. Societies, civilizations, empires, and entire species come and go, always have, and probably always will. NEBADOR, or whatever you would like to call it, watches over them and guides them, but is most interested in that rare, special person who never quits learning.

If even one young person, like maybe you, gains a good understanding from the NEBADOR stories of the differences between good and evil, balance and imbalance, true sapience and mere sentience, then I will have succeeded in my mission.

Farewell!

J. Z. Colby
2015

## About the Author

Born in the Mojave Desert, J. Z. Colby now lives and writes deep in a forest of the Pacific Northwest.

He has studied many subjects, formally and informally, including psychology, philosophy, education, and performing arts, but remains a generalist.  His primary profession as a mental health counselor, specializing with families and young adults, gives him many stories of personal growth, and the motivation to develop his team of young critiquers and readers.

All his life, he has been drawn toward a broad understanding of human nature, especially those physical, emotional, mental, and spiritual situations in which our capacity to function seems to reach its limits.  He finds fascinating those few individuals who can transcend the limits of our common human nature and the dictates of our cultures.

In his spare time, he flies helicopters and airplanes.

He may be contacted at the email address listed on the internet site www.nebador.com.